THAT JAZZ

THAT JAZZ

Joan Liburd

Order this book online at www.trafford.com
or email orders@trafford.com

Most Trafford titles are also available at major online book retailers.

This is a work of fiction. All of the characters, names, incidents, organizations, and dialogue
in this novel are either the products of the author's imagination or are used fictitiously.

Printed in the United States of America.

ISBN: 978-1-4269-5622-5 (sc)
ISBN: 978-1-4269-5623-2 (hc)
ISBN: 978-1-4269-5624-9 (e)

Library of Congress Control Number: 2011902026

Trafford rev. 02/07/2011

 www.trafford.com

North America & international
toll-free: 1 888 232 4444 (USA & Canada)
phone: 250 383 6864 • fax: 812 355 4082

INTRODUCTION

Jazz is a young woman whose life is dramatically impacted by the sudden death of her beloved father. Her mother, devastated by the event, is distant and uncommunicative and Jazz has difficulty coalescing their relationship. A fight between the two women is totally misinterpreted by Jazz and she flees her home in the night and is forced to forge a life for herself.

Struggling against loneliness and feelings of abandonment, a combination of good luck, good instincts, and capitalization on a good talent she had barely been aware of, sees her through, until she is betrayed by the man she had come to trust. In a fit of anger and despair, she rushes home to those she had deserted and finds, though things have changed, they are willing to forgive and forget. However, the sweetheart of her youth is about to be married and she wants him back.

The life she has created for herself is well suited to her mother, and she begins to think of switching places with her mother to be near him, if she could prevent youth's love from marrying someone else. She does succeed and proceeds to give her love a life that keeps him trotting to keep up with her.

Jazz rose with the memory of her own screams ringing in her ears. She had been dumped. She was devastated. She screamed. She had thrown a tantrum and ran screaming down a beach, and the whole island heard. Perhaps they didn't hear the actual screams, but they heard quickly enough that the missing girl was back home, and 'pul crazy'. She expected that. She was a small island girl herself. This was her home. She had grown up on the island and understood the islanders' way of thinking, but she had been unable to restrain herself; there was a lot inside her she had to get out. The exercise exhausted her and she had fallen asleep. Now, half awake, she moaned. The entire twin island federation would know by now that she was back and think she was as crazy as a loon.

She looked around as she got up from the old sofa. She possibly owned the cute little house. She remembered coming here as a child with her father to visit an old lady. She didn't remember the old lady's name but she was pretty sure the house belonged to her father then. Perhaps that is why Pim had sent her here while he figured out what to do with her.

The house was cute, the bright living room the largest room, with a wrap around veranda, windows on three sides flooding it with sunlight. A small kitchen and dining room divided off it by a low partition, and a hallway led to the back where there was a bedroom and bathroom. There was a nice backyard with fruit trees and wild flowers. There was also a neglected flower garden at the front. The house did not face the beach, which was just a three-minute walk away, but the windows on one side looked directly out to the sea.

Jazz was crying again. What was she to do now? She had disappeared from her home ten years ago without a word to her friends or her mother. She had fled the island feeling broken hearted and betrayed. Now here she was, home again, again broken hearted and betrayed. She wondered how she would face the people she had left. She would not have long to wait.

Not much time had passed when she heard the rusty squeak of the front garden gate being opened. She had not heard a car. Crystal, her childhood friend walked in with what looked like a bag of groceries. She plopped it onto the table. Crystal had not changed much. She was still strikingly pretty, a few years older but she still looked younger than her actual age.

"You might as well tell me about it now, Crystal declared, typically getting straight to the point. You look like hell, by the way, but we should get the hugs out of the way first." Jazz stepped into her friend's arms like she had last seen her only yesterday, and broke down.

I hope you drink wine, Crystal said after Jazz had calmed down a bit. I brought a couple of bottles. I figured this would take some time. Jazz took a glass of wine and sat down, silent.

"How long have we been friends?" Crystal challenged. *"I would have kept your secret, whatever it was, you know. Were you pregnant or something?"*

Jazz smiled weakly then she said: *No. I wasn't. Nothing like that.*

Everyone thought you were. Jason insisted you weren't, but it was one of the theories.

He knew I wasn't

How could he for sure?

He deflowered me two nights before I left. OK?

Oh my God!

Jazz and Crystal Vanderpool had always been friends. They met in junior kindergarten. Crystal was then an avid thumb sucker and drove her parents nuts. They had tried everything, including painting her thumb with aloe vera, hoping the bitter taste would be a deterrent. Crystal had just grimaced and sucked anyway. When they bandaged her thumb she switched thumbs. When Crystal's parents bandaged both thumbs, Jazz offered her own thumb to Crystal which somehow, seemed to be the cure. Sucking someone else's thumb was apparently not appealing.

One day Jakey Fletcher, one of their kinderclassmates, announced that he had a new sister. When Jakey explained that his new sister was older than he, and that three of his parents five kids had been adopted, both little girls found this so fascinating they each went home and asked her parents to adopt the other so they could be sisters. Their closeness and fondness for each other triggered a friendship between their parents.

How did you know I was here? Jazz asked Crystal, *not that I'm not supremely grateful that you came.*

Everybody knows you are here, but Jason told me you were coming.

He answered the phone when I called. You get along with him now? As teens, Jazz adored Jason but Crystal did not like him.

We grew close when we were grieving for you. You do know that the police and everyone were scouring the island looking for you. Jason was in-consolable! He told me that his father knew where you were all along. Is that true? You cannot imagine how mad he is. So what's up with that? Were you having an affair with his father?

Don't be silly, Jazz answered. *Pim is my godfather. I was in bigger trouble than you or Jase and I could handle so I went to Pim. He took care of it on condition that I promise not to tell anyone, not even Jase. He got me out. I send him a sketch maybe once a year. I use a different name and he never responds so I never know if he actually sees it or throws it into the garbage, or if he has forgotten me.*

Jazzie, you may as well know. Jason is getting married soon.

Jazz swallowed hard and was about to comment but Crystal waved it away as if to say that was just FYI.

He was totally torn up when we realized that nothing had happened to you and you had just opted to leave without telling anyone. We spent a lot of time back then, trying to figure out what had happened to spook you and he felt like crap that you couldn't at least discuss it with him. I did too, by the way. Anyway, Jason is back to square one now. Ple-ease let me tell him that he wasn't trumped by his own father. I think they almost got into a fist fight about it. So what was it all about, Jazzie?

"*Daddy died, and I went to hell*"

Jazz had a good life growing up. She was born Jasmine Hyacinth LaPierre, only child of Brett and Celine LaPierre. As long as she remembered she had been her daddy's little princess. He had taken her everywhere, and taught her everything. He spoke to her like an equal and by age twelve she knew enough about his business, to have been an executive. He called her Jazzie. They were very close and Jazz never felt that she needed to 'give him his space' as her mother often suggested or that he wished she was a son. She was happy in her father's company. He was happy in hers.

Brett ran an import and distribution business as well as Hey Bro, a men clothing and accessories and Sister Chic, a women's clothing and accessories store. By the time Jazz was a teen, she knew practically everything about the running of his enterprises.

Every evening when her daddy came home from work and he, Celine and Jazz ate supper together, Jazz would ask him and he would tell her about his day. She sometimes felt guilty about being closer to him and had tried to include her Mommy, but Celine appeared to have no interest and would change the topic to things Jazz was not particularly interested in and, although her Daddy did not show it, she was sure he was bored rigid.

After supper, Brett would go to his den to catch up on whatever paperwork he had not completed at the office and Jazz would follow, sitting on the other side of his desk to do her homework. He would help her if she needed. Celine would go to the living room and thumb through magazines and catalogs.

Saturdays, Brett would lime with his friends. Sometimes they came to his home and sometimes he went to theirs. The most popular place was Mont Yves Estate, the home of the Coolidges: his buddy Pim and his wife Pammy and their son Jason, and Pim's nephews, Gareth and

Ian Hollis. Brett was a cricketer. He had captained the island team for a while, and among his friends, Mont Yves was the only place with enough space for cricket. He usually took Jazz with him, which she totally enjoyed. She had a massive crush on Jason Coolidge, and had followed him around since she was a little girl. Jason was her idol, and never seemed to mind having her following him about. She shared her feelings about Jason, or Jase as she always called him, with only Crystal, and imagined that nobody but they two knew. Of course Brett noticed as well as both Coolidge parents.

Jazz loved those Saturdays she spent at Mont Yves, and wished her Mommy would join them, but Celine always declined. She didn't like farms, she said, and when Jazz protested, Celine pointed out that 'estate' and 'plantation' were the island name for farms whose main crop was sugar cane. Wasn't her wonderful Pammy always riding around on horses or donkeys or whatever? Mommy would know, Jazz was sure, she grew up one plantation over, at Stone Haven Estate.

There were indeed horses at Mont Yves. Pammy liked riding and so did Jason. It was said that Pammy used to be very good and had won several ribbons in the races. Jason had taken Jazz for a ride once, but he only allowed the horse to walk slowly while she was on. None of the others seemed to be interested in the riding, or in horses, for that matter.

Jason Coolidge was two years older than Jazz. He was a natural athlete. Pim and Pammy had also raised Pim's nephews, Gareth and Ian, the sons of Pim's twin sister, Catherine, known as Cat. The boys were all born the same year, Cat having accomplished the unusual feat of having two children in the same year. Gareth was born in January, and Ian in November. Jason was born in June of the same year. The boys grew up together, as close as triplets. There was an obvious family resemblance but Jason and Ian's physical resemblance was so close that they could easily be mistaken for twins. They were all athletes, Jason a particularly graceful high jumper and pole-vaulter, he won award after award, and with his two brother/cousins, and their friend, Ty Watner, owned the relay track.

Jazz loved Pammy Coolidge, Jason's mother. Pammy was warm and chatty, loved to cook and was always nice to her. It was actually Pammy who helped her when she got her first period. On arrival at Mont Yves one Saturday, she'd jumped out of the car to go looking for Jason when Brett noticed the stain and called her back. He summoned Pammy and she helped Jazz. She took away Jazz' clothes to wash and, not having any girls clothes, loaned her one of Jason's shirts and a pair of his shorts. They were too big, of course, and Jazz was embarrassed. Pammy told her that there were some things she should know now, but that it should be her own mother telling her. She did say, however, that Jazz might not want to hang around Jason so much anymore.

In the end, it was Brett who had given her the birds and the bees speech on the way home. He also mentioned curtailing her activities with Jason. He said that now that she was almost grown, hiking and running around with the boys might not be appropriate activities for a young lady. She was pleased to inform him that it was okay, Jason always took good care of her, and when Brett inquired how, she gave him examples.

When they were hiking up the mountain and the others were going too fast for her, Jason stayed back with her and made the other two slow down. When they practiced their racing, she couldn't run with them so Jason made her the timer, but she got so excited when he was winning that she forgot to stop the clock, and that ugly Ian yanked her hair and said she was useless. She had told him straight out that she was rooting for Jason, and he told her that officials weren't supposed to root for anybody, and Jason made him to leave her alone, and had made her the cheerleader, because he said she looked like a cheerleader when they were running and he liked to see cheerleading. Brett asked her why she thought Ian was ugly and she said he just was. He asked about Jason. She said Jason was lovely.

Back at home, Celine had just given her an odd look that seemed to combine pride and regret, and hugged her closely, which really pleased Jazz. Her mother was not normally given to emotional demonstrations.

Everywhere they went Jazz ate stacks of delicious food, and Brett bought fruit and vegetables to take home. Weekdays, Mummy cooked meals for nourishment. She prepared healthy recipes from magazines and allowed them to eat enough to keep them fit. She was successful. None of them had ever been sick in Jazz memory. But on their weekend jaunts, Brett allowed her to eat whatever she wanted. He once joked that if Mommy saw an ounce of fat on any of them, or her scales showed a half pound weight gain, she would go into spasms. Whenever they had guests over, Celine would make lovely hors d'ouvres and she would have Mrs Greaux, the lady who helped her with housework sometimes, make the meal. Jazz surmised that she knew guests would not like her type of cooking, but Mommy would have nothing to do with grease and starches. Brett had never told her directly not to mention the food on their little trips, but Jazz interpreted the joke as that it was to be their own little secret.

Those lovely weekends, Brett played cricket, cards, dominos, and drank and had discussions with his friends. Sometimes they worked on the project to convert an old sugar mill to a residence. They didn't know for whom, but they thought it was a nice idea. They teased each other and commented on how smart Jazz was and how well she was growing. They tried to tease Brett about not having a son to help with the building, but he always told them that she was worth at least three boys and two girls, and Pim would say he would have had three boys and two girls had it not been for his wife's unfortunate calamity. She enjoyed all this, and thought her father was something a little higher than an archangel.

Jason, the other archangel in Jazz' world, in addition to track and field, also played football, and could play any position on the football field, and was the most valuable player on his team, The Hermitage Rocket. The weekend after Jazz' 15th birthday, the Rocket were scheduled to play a tournament in Saba, a neighbouring island. There was also to be a school celebration rally which would end with a dance. Jazz was terribly excited about the rally. She had hoped to go with Jason if The Rocket did not make it to the tournament, but she knew they were almost a shoo-in.

On the morning of the Rally, Brett dropped Jazz off at the school and she waved him gaily off on his usual weekend jaunt. Brett was in a great mood. She would remember his smile as she got out of the car, and him driving off whistling.

The rally was fun. The day was perfect. All the energy and excitement of youth palpable in the tropical sunlight. Brett also had a good day, enjoying the company of his friends, and at home Celine was relaxing and having a facial and massage by her friend, Frances Vanderpool, Crystal's mother. Once she was done, she would return the favour to Frances. Each one of their little family was content in his/her own activity.

After the rally, as the day came to an end with a fittingly spectacular sunset, a day which was perfect in every way, Crystal's father, Ed, dropped Jazz off to get prepared for the evening's section of the festivities, and picked up his wife from the LaPierres, where she had been hanging out with Jazz' mother. They would come back again to take her to the dance and Brett would pick her up after the dance and bring her home. This has been such a beautiful day, Jazz thought. The only thing missing is Jase.

Out at the estate, Brett also thought it had been a perfect day. At the time his wife was fussing over his daughter's outfit for her first school dance and his daughter was flitting around in a heat of excitement, he was taking his leave of his group of friends. It was only a one hour drive home and he had driven those winding, not particularly well lit roads for years. All buckled in, Brett was one of the few people on the island who used his seatbelt while driving. He always did. He had a good selection of music to keep him company in Jazz' absence and he was feeling mellow.

One of the most spectacular scenes on the island, already famous for its scenery, was a stretch of road which Brett always took on his way home. Having wound its way through quaint villages, the road suddenly curves around a mountain, passes Greenhill, a sloping park, then opens up, a straight stretch of road for perhaps three quarters of a mile, open water far below on one side with neighbouring islands rising majestically on the horizon. At the bottom of the cliff randomly scattered, hundreds of sharp volcanic rocks protruded from shallow water. On the other side of the narrow road was the steep side of a mountain. From time to time, particularly after heavy rains, small stones would come loose from the mountain and fall to the road below. Not so distant ahead and to the right, the main town could be seen and in the evening the lights glowed, winked and glistened like a perpetual Christmas tree. The entire vista is seen at its best from Greenhill, and people would park there, some to take in the scenery, others for varying other reasons.

Nightime comes most suddenly in the tropics and it seems one minute you are looking at a blazing sunset and the next, a sky full of stars. Fifteen minutes after he left Brett was coming around this section of the road, admiring the view of the lights of the town across a bay, hardly noticing the half hearted guardrail between him and the sea far below. He heard the sound before he saw anything. Suddenly there was a massive boulder hurtling down the side of the mountain. He had a split second to determine whether to swerve over the edge into the water or risk being hit. Either way, he was sure he would be dead. Taking a chance he could possibly get out of the car, he swerved sharply, easily taking out the guardrail, as the car went over the edge into the water, trailed by the boulder, which bounced on the ground just at the spot where the car would have been had Brett taken the other option, and followed the car like a locked on cruise missile. The car bounced onto the rocks below, followed a heartbeat later by the massive boulder. It landed, crushing the car, with Brett in it. He did not have a ghost of a chance.

Seymour Queeley was a young man who had bucked the odds. Nobody knew who his parents were, as he was found on a beach one bright and sunny morning, a robust, squalling baby, in a makeshift car seat. He was pretty much adopted by the village and was determined to live up to everybody's expectations of their adopted son. Tiring job that was. He was fed and clothed by everyone and did chores for everyone, ever careful not to disappoint anyone. He had to make sure he was good at everything because, while other children involved in mischief, knowing, if caught, they would be punished, could avoid their parents. Seymour could be punished by anybody and therefore avoided mischief as much as possible. This had worked for most of his life but now, a teenage boy interested in girls, he was not sure how to go about things. He found himself very much attracted to Cassandra Delaney, the Methodist minister's daughter, and from time to time they would sneak up to Green Hill and get into mischief they would definitely have been punished for, if discovered.

Tonight, Seymour and Cassandra, necking in an abandoned car on Greenhill, were interrupted by the sound of the falling rock. They were the only witnesses to the entire ten, maybe fifteen seconds or so of this dramatic end to the life of Brett LaPierre.

Galvanized into action, Seymour sent Cassandra home using a back route and took off. Within a few minutes he had alerted the village and called the police. It was obvious when they got there that there was nothing they could do but try to confirm who the victim was. Three policemen were carefully lowered down the cliff, duly harnessed and secured like mountain climbers.

Seymour was pretty sure he recognized the car, and his information was very soon confirmed. The license plate had popped off and was the only thing found by the police. They searched with the hope that any passengers might have been thrown out. Poor Brett might not have had time to get both the seatbelt off and the door opened. There was no one. There was also no way they knew of to move that boulder off that car. No humans could do it and even if they were able to find equipment on any of the neighbouring islands, because there certainly wasn't any on this one, getting it to that spot would be a scientific feat. They crossed themselves and tugged the ropes to be hauled back up.

Jazz was dressed now and had to acknowledge that Mommy was indeed a fashion expert and that she looked 'rockin', even though Celine made her take off some of her makeup. Crystal and her parents were here. She heard the car pull up and the light toot of the horn. The phone rang at the same time, and Celine answered it just as Jazz pulled the front door open. Celine's shriek brought Jazz and the three Vanderpools hurtling into the room.

Celine was on the floor, the phone had fallen and she was crying and babbling unintelligibly. Frances Vanderpool picked up the phone, spoke into it. She stumbled, and groped for a seat. Jazz grabbed the phone from her. She heard the words. Her mind locked on the information but couldn't process it. Daddy was dead. She didn't scream. Like a young general, she phoned the Coolidges. She settled Mommy and gave Frances Vanderpool a glass of water. She asked Crystal to take care of

Mommy and Mrs Vanderpool . She asked Edwin Vanderpool to drive her to the scene.

Since she first saw the scene of her father's demise, actually just the huge crater the boulder had left in the road was all she could see, Jazz had nursed a secret guilt that the first thought that flashed through her mind, was of the Roadrunner cartoons she watched as a child. She knew immediately that there would be no grave with flowers for her to visit and tend and no tasteful headstone to mark his final resting place. She thought her daddy was the biggest man she knew, with the biggest heart and now his watery grave had the biggest headstone ever.

Night falls suddenly and completely on a tropical island, and even with the makeshift floodlights in place, the dangerous angle of the cliff made further search impossible, and Jazz along with the helpless crowd which had gathered, were forced to leave for the night. Jazz accepted Pim's offer and spent the night with his family. It would be easier to get to the site in the morning.

Jazz could not tell how many cups of sweet coffee she drank that night as the group, Pim and his family and some of his and her father's friends gathered in his house, a solemn group, huddled together, drawing comfort each from the other. Some time during the night she must have dozed because she opened her eyes to bright sunshine. The sun on a tropical island also rises suddenly, cheerfully, optimistically bright.

As Jazz became aware of the beauty of the morning, she wept. How dare the sun shine so happily brilliant. It would be so much easier to take had there been threatening dark clouds, a day to match her shattered heart. What was to become of Mommy? What was to become of her? She felt as broken as a two-legged dog. Daddy was more than just the backbone of the family. Without him they would be like paper in the wind. Jazzie knew then, that barely 15 years old she had inherited the responsibility of taking care of the family.

She went to the phone and called her mother. Celine was still incoherent. She had obviously had a really bad night. The Vanderpools had stayed with her and would bring her to the site. The police had said they would restart the search at sunrise. They were trying to locate any equipment capable of removing the rock. She knew it was useless. They all knew it was useless but they had to at least give it a try.

Jazz decided to walk the few miles to the site rather than wake the family who had been so kind to her. She wrote a note and stepped out into the sweet, fresh morning air. Any other day, this would be a glorious experience. Today, she dragged her feet. The thought swirling around in her head: Daddy is dead. There is nothing to bury. How awful. What were his last thoughts, did he know he had no chance? She prayed he did get out of the car and the men who went down had missed him between the rocks. He might be badly injured but alive. Could that be possible? Dared she hope? She wondered if they would let her go down, suspended on ropes, to help search for her father. She knew if he was there she would find him. She knew the rocks down there were black volcanic rocks. Daddy was wearing white. She would see him. She would want to be the one to bring him back up. Fantasies of rescue occupying her thoughts, Jazz had not heard the sound of running footsteps until Jason Coolidge caught up to her.

'Aren't you in Saba playing football?" Jazz asked.

'Daddy told me when I phoned last night so I came home. You don't have a lot of family." In fact, Brett and Celine were all the family she had, and now he was gone.

Jason did not tease her about the silliness of her question, and Jazz was grateful and impressed by his sensitivity. They walked silently together. Jason took her hand and despite the occasion, Jazz' heart gave a flutter. This was Jason Coolidge! She would remember this moment.

The spot where Brett's car went over had always been thought to have been formed by some sort of volcanic activity perhaps thousands of years before. It was a small secluded cove which, because of the generous but random scattering of sharp, glittery black rocks in shallow water twenty feet below a sheer cliff, was unapproachable by boat, and inaccessible by land.

Jazz and Jason arrived at the same time as the police team. They watched as the police set up, Jazz crying while Jason hugged and tried to console her. The police closed the road and set up some complicated and obviously makeshift, contraptions. Ten persons were lowered. Jazz begged to be lowered with them but was refused. Once the searchers went over the side, they disappeared from view, and no one dared to go close enough to the edge to look over. The best, and probably the only, place to see them was from Greenhill, and a crowd had gathered there. There were also some boats far out in the sea observing the procedure, but they couldn't come too close because of the rocks. Jazz wanted to be nearby if they brought her Daddy up and stayed at the command post.

All day, in the blazing sun, every inch of the glittering rock was searched. Those rocks were probably the cleanest place on the island. Everyone stayed away from the edge of the road. Nothing and no one ever went over. There was no previous debris. Brett LaPierre, it was decided, was squashed in his car under the boulder. The police expressed their regrets and condolences, and everyone went home.

There was nothing to bury. Nothing to burn. Brett was hale, hearty and very much alive one minute and his life completely squashed the next. The coroner declared it a death by misadventure and his family and friends were left in a stunned stupor, uncertain what to do. Everybody went home.

Brett LaPierre was well known and well liked. It was unseemly that he could be left unceremoniously at the bottom of a cliff, probably squished flat as a pancake. The idea elicited such conflicting emotions. Jazz' thoughts kept returning to the roadrunner. She wouldn't want to see her father flat like the roadrunner, then she would be ashamed of the association and regret the thought, but it kept coming back. How would Daddy look in a coffin, flat as the roadrunner. How thin would the coffin be?

It was during one of these musings that Father John showed up at the door. The only thing Brett did not do with his family was go to church. He was as devout a Catholic as Celine was an Anglican. Father John was the Catholic priest. Celine was resting in bed, Jazz informed him as she let him in. Father John had come to show respect and support, and suggested that, even though there could be no burial, funeral services still needed to be held. He wondered if they had considered whether they would like to hold the services at the church or at the site of the accident.

Jazz jumped at the suggestion. The road, closed after the accident, could not yet be reopened because of the crater where the rock had bounced. She would request permission to have the service there tomorrow afternoon. Father John confirmed that his calendar was free the next day and as soon as he left Jazz phoned the police with the suggestion. Permission was given and arrangements put in place long before Mommy woke up, and she was given the details only moments before the announcement was made after the evening news on the local radio station.

The next day was a holiday. Jazz was unsure what the attendance would be, as people usually planned picnics and parties to mark the day. However, when Jazz and Celine arrived with the Vanderpools, there already was a crowd gathering on the road near the fenced off crater where the boulder had bounced, and nearby Greenhill was also filling up

By the time the service started there were hundreds of people spread across Greenhill and the now closed stretch of road. Speakers had been set up at both locations. Jazz was still surprised at the turnout. She was aware that many had come out of curiosity, but she was grateful, nevertheless. She knew that many had come out of respect, love and concern for her father as well. Father John gave a touching homily and the gathered crowd sang 'It is Well with My Soul' and 'Abide with Me', and Frances Vanderpool sang 'How Great Thou Art.' Somehow, the sound of hundreds of voices singing those songs in the open air was able to penetrate her deep, deep sorrow. Celine was crying and Jazz felt so helpless, like she was nailed to the spot. She wanted to reach out but couldn't move – not her arms nor her feet. She sat rigid, trying to recall her last moments with her father. She remembered going to Sunday school as a child and kept trying to recall if there was any policy on going to heaven if you died in a good mood. Brett had definitely been in a good mood when he left her at the school. How could he be dead! So horribly, horribly dead.

They had reached the point in the service where the coffin would have been lowered into the grave. Someone approached her and put a harness on her attached to a strong cord. OMG! Were they going to lower her! They were patting and consoling her and someone was saying something. A bunch of flowers was put into her hands. Jazz did not understand. Jason came over and hugged her. He was telling her something. There were so many thoughts swirling in her head. It finally registered that the flowers were to be thrown on the 'grave' but she was to be tethered as a security measure so that she wouldn't fall over. Jazz walked towards the edge. It seemed to her to take a thousand steps, then she felt the tether tighten. She could go no further. She couldn't see anything but the rocks out in the water. *Poor Daddy. He had been so vibrant. How could he have deserved to be crushed under a big stone? Please, God, may he not have suffered. Goodbye Daddy.* She tossed the flowers and felt her knees buckle and she panicked. Would she end up smashed against the rocks as well? The tether held her and then there were hands helping her. Jason was there, a police officer and the funeral staff. Jason. Dear, dear Jason. He led her back and Mommy was tethered next and the process repeated. When Celine came back they clung to each other in their shared misery and despair, and cried their hearts out as each person who wished was tethered and led to the edge of the road to toss flowers on the wreck below.

How would she be able to help Mommy when she was such a wreck herself? Jazz was desolate, the depth of her despair she could never before have imagined possible. When things went wrong Daddy was always there to deal with them and make them right again. Now that he was gone, what was she to do? Somebody had to look after Mommy and for now, Jazz knew she was most decidedly unequal to the task.

The people were singing hymns as person after person was tethered and flowers tossed over the edge. Everyone wanted to take part. Jazz first heard a murmur from Greenhill where most of the crowd was, and looked up. There were so many flowers and the current was taking them out to the open water. Jazz noticed one or two at first and then a host of flowers floating in the water. It was as though Daddy was waving goodbye and saying it is going to be alright. All the flowers floating in the water gave Jazz' spirit a very slight lift, and she smiled and waved. *Goodbye Daddy. I will always love you. We will always remember you.*

This unique funeral ceremony finally drew to a close and Jazz and Celine accepted condolences, had their hands shaken and were hugged and treated to comforting words by so many, many people. It all seemed a blur, a segment of a particularly bad nightmare they could not wake up from. The one clear thing in her mind was that Jason was always nearby. Lovely, lovely Jason. She must remember to thank him. A little embarrassed by the thought, Jazz was aware that there were others who had been close and supportive: All of Daddy's friends, The Vanderpools, including her best friend Crystal, and Payne Smith, her father's right hand man. She must remember to thank them all.

Pim Coolidge cleared a path for them and took them back to his home on the estate from which Brett had just left when he met with the accident. He felt it was his responsibility to see everything went well for Brett's family. His wife, Pammy's cooking was hard to beat and she loved to feed a crowd so it was no big deal when he had told her he would ask some people back after the service. They were grateful to postpone the moment when they would be left on their own to deal with their great loss, and although they could hardly be great company right now, they were sure people would understand.

A hundred people were gathered at the Coolidges. They talked and they toasted, they reminisced, rehashed, flattered, and fed their faces. It was a not unpleasant distraction but it had to come to an end, and the hour when they must face the emptiness was closing in. Ed Vanderpool rose to indicate he was ready to leave. He would drive Jazz and Celine home. Jazz felt fear and dread creeping up around her like quicksand. Jason noticed her expression and quickly came to her side. Pammy offered them a bed for the night, which Celine quickly refused. They had to go. They had to face the swirling emptiness. Brett had taken up such a large space in their lives. Celine rose, and as Jazz tried to rise, Jason offered a hand to help her up. He hugged her and walked with them to the car. *"I'm here at any time you may need me"*, he said and gave her a quick kiss as he handed her into the car and waved them off to start a new chapter of their lives.

Adjusting to Brett's absence was by no means easy. Celine was a changed person. She spent a lot of time in Brett's robe. Her hair was growing out and the new growth was showing. In another person this would be minor but Jazz had never known Celine to let anything about her appearance go. Every morning when she saw them off, Brett to work and her to school, she was dressed well enough to be going with them. She was always in Brett's robe. She never went out anymore now, not even to shop. She had also become silent. No fashion tips, no frustration at people's lack of fashion sense, no comments on anything. Jazz tried to keep up some patter to get Celine animated again, but without success. She never cried, so far as Jazz knew, but she was obviously ravaged by grief. Jazz could not understand her reluctance to even hear Daddy's name mentioned. She missed him so very much herself, and would sometimes like to talk about him but any mention of Daddy and Celine would go to her room and would not be seen again for hours.

Jazz felt so lost. She missed him so, and longed to talk about her Daddy. Jason was now closer to her than anyone else. Crystal had always thought she was a wishy washy daddy's girl and she didn't want Jase to think the same thing. She didn't want to turn him off. She was so proud to be seen around with him, so she cried alone in her bed at night, mourning her father in secret.

Jason was having a birthday. There was to be a big party for him at Mont Yves's great house. Access to the estate was not easy so parents would have to drop off the invited kids, and a secondary party would be held for the parents. Celine had refused the invitation. She never drove anyway, and Jason had suggested Jazz come down in the morning with the overseer, on his return from business in town. Celine had not commented when she put the suggestion to her so Jazz had considered it approved.

It was six months since Brett had been killed, and this was Jazz's first occasion for dressing up and going out. The day before she asked for Celine's advice on what to wear, which swiftly sent her fleeing to her room. Jazz felt torn to pieces. Jase had asked if she would cut the birthday cake with him. There was no higher honour, and she was floating on a cloud. She could stay at home with Mommy but what if Mommy stayed in her room, what would be the point? Anyway, Jase might be so upset he would never ask her out again and Mommy would probably be out of her room by morning.

When Jason's birthday finally arrived, Jazz was up at dawn. Another beautiful day on the island! At eight o'clock Celine had not yet come out of her room. Jazz was to be picked up at ten. She decided to make breakfast. She was sure that the smell of bacon and coffee would lure Celine from her room. She wouldn't mind some herself. She sat down to eat breakfast, sure that Celine would come out at any moment. When she had eaten and there was still no sign of her mother, Jazz went to knock on her door. No answer. Mommy, mommy, knock, knock. No answer. Jazz opened the door carefully. Celine was sitting at the side of her bed, just staring. Could she not have heard? She called again and Celine didn't answer. Jazz walked toward the bed.

Mommy, are you ok? I've been knocking and calling.

Celine didn't answer. Jazz put her hand on her shoulder and bent down and kissed her. *Mommy, today is Jase's birthday party. I'm to be picked up in a short while. Are you ok? Do you want me not to go?*

Go Jasmine, Celine said.

Jazz took a quick look behind her to be sure there was no one else in the room. Her name was Jasmine but she could not remember anyone ever calling her that. Daddy and Jason and Crystal and a few friends at school called her Jazzie, Mommy and everyone else called her Jazz.

Mommy you could come too, Jazz said. *All the other parents are coming.* Celine just gave her an inscrutable look and said *'No'*.

Jazz left the room to put her evening's outfit into a bag and sat down to wait. The knock on the door came as the clock in the hall struck ten o'clock. She opened the door to John, the overseer. He said he'd wait in the pick-up, and Jazz went to tell Celine she was leaving. Again there was no answer, and when Jazz turned the handle the door was locked. She took a few minutes to write a note to Celine to let her know that she loved her and that she missed Daddy too and that she wished they could do things together to ease the pain of losing him. She pushed it under the door, told her she was leaving, phoned Frances Vanderpool to suggest she give mommy a casual call, and left.

The party was glorious. John had thoughtfully taken a detour, despite the extra travel time in order to avoid driving her past Brett's watery grave and spoiling her mood. The Coolidges home was always warm and comforting and was somehow more so today. Jason was particularly attentive, and when everyone gathered around to watch Jase cut the birthday cake with her, she believed she was in heaven. There were so many pretty girls at the party and Jason had chosen her. She fantasized that he loved her as much as she loved him, even though he had never said so. From now on everyone would think of them as a couple.

After the party, Jazz and Jason settled into a loose understanding. She attended his games, he asked her out from time to time. She never visited him because she would have to take a bus, which would drive past Brett's grave and she could not not take that. He visited from time to time but Celine was always cold to him so he didn't come often. He had kissed her a few times but he had kissed her like she was his little sister. It was a puzzle and she could not talk about it with Crystal. Crystal did not like Jason. She did not care for athletes. Jazz was also worried because Yola Ross was always flirting with Jason and although he did not seem to be especially interested in her, he didn't appear to hate it either. Yola was pretty, a year older and more sophisticated than Jazz.

It was almost a year after her father's death and Jason had taken Jazz to a movie. She wasn't following the plot. She wondered what Daddy would have thought, had he been around. Jason had kept close to her since then but he treated her with kid gloves. She wasn't sure what would happen to the relationship. He would soon be off to university. When Jason walked her home from the movies, he came in to make a call to let his family know he was taking the bus, so someone would be there to drive him up from the bus stop. They were both surprised to see Jordan Little seated in the living room drinking whiskey while mommy fussed with the magazines and catalogs, the way she always did when Brett was alive. When Jason left Jazz excused herself and went to her own room. She was not particularly concerned. Except for the fact that Daddy detested Jordan, there was no reason he shouldn't visit. He was in some complicated way distantly related to Mommy.

From what Jazz could remember from conversations over the years, Jordan and Mommy grew up on the same sugar plantation estate. Daddy was also a neighbor but his family was not as well recognized as theirs, and Jordan made sure to remind him of it. Jordan felt Celine had married beneath her and Brett had felt Jordan was beneath just about everybody and everything, even crawling insects. When their parents had died he had allegedly cheated his sisters out of their inheritance, but had quickly run through everything and ended up broke. He had tried to rejuvenate the family business but, according to Brett, Jordan's head was a wasteland that couldn't sustain even a weak idea. He had married a fairly wealthy cousin of Mommy's but she had secured her money so that he couldn't get to it. When Jordan divorced her and tried to get alimony from her, his bid was unsuccessful due to allegations that he had fathered the housekeeper's two children during the marriage.

What's the deal with Chewbacca? Jason asked when she met him after school.

What do you mean? Jazz responded.

Chewbacca. Jordan Little.

Oh, he does look a little like him, Jazz laughed. I don't know. I went in to bed.

You think he might be er, 'courting' your mother? He's looking for somebody to support him.

Don't be silly, his wife was Mommy's cousin.

Well, he's up to something, I can tell you that.

Jazz laughed and went home. Jordan showed up again that evening and Jazz wondered if he was in fact interested in Celine, but she didn't say anything.

After that Jordan became a regular visitor to their home. About a month later Jazz skipped a class for no particular reason. She felt like going home and she did, slipping into the house quietly to avoid being heard and having to explain to Celine why she was out of school. Hearing a sound, she opened the door to Brett's den where Jordan was trying to open Brett's desk.

Do you know where he kept the key?, Celine asked.

In his pocket, Jazz said. What *does he want in there?*

Mr. Little wants to go through Brett's papers so he can advise me.

Jazz was revolted! *With Mr. Little's record,* she said, *he couldn't advise a cat to lick itself.*

She was not prepared for the stinging slap from her mother. Celine had never hit her before.

Well, if he could roll away the stone he will find the key, she said and walked away fuming, to her room.

Jazz was restless. She knew that she had to do something tonight. She had no doubt that they would break the desk if they had to. She also knew that Brett had some papers in the desk, although she had never considered their importance. She had the spare key which she had taken from his office at work shortly after the death. There did not seem to be a need to say anything at the time. Celine wasn't talking, and she was never interested in business anyway. There was a safe in the office. Celine knew about the safe but so far as Jazz knew, she had never been interested enough to know the combination. Jazz did. However, it was a small safe and she was sure she could not fit all the papers into it. She hoped Jordan wouldn't take the desk away or break into it tonight. What advice could Mommy seek from Jordan? Jordan's reputation as an idiot aside, Mommy and daddy had always had everything set up so that if either of them was in any way incapacitated, they would be taken care of, and as far as finances went, there had been no noticeable difference. Was Jordan Little angling to take her father's place? He was still living with his housekeeper and their children. Was mommy prepared to accept that? There would be no chance of sleep any time soon that night for Jazz. She knew that.

Jazz emptied her knapsack, put away the contents and hid the knapsack under her bed, then she went to the kitchen to find something to eat. Jordan was still there but they had moved out of daddy's den and were watching TV. Jazz had never been able to get close to Celine, especially since Brett's death, but she did love her, and she was worried for her. What advice was Jordan going to give? They didn't talk much to each other. Mommy and Daddy talked and laughed and giggled incessantly, particularly in their room. She hoped Jordan was not going into her father's room. He already sat in Brett's chair and drank his booze and watched TV, while Celine sat on the sofa and thumbed through magazines, like she would have done if Brett was here. Jazz resented that and wondered what was going on between them.

Eventually, Jordan went home and Celine went to her room. Jazz went into Brett's den. This was not unusual. She pretended to be writing an essay, just in case mommy looked in. In fact she wrote SOS notes to Pim Coolidge and Payne Smith, the two men her father trusted most, enough to make them trustees of his estate. She had a test first period. She didn't want to put much on paper but she wanted them in the loop as quickly as possible and there was not much time to wait for them at their offices before she went to school.

Jazz finished the notes and put them away. She had just opened her biology textbook when mommy looked into the den. '*You should go to bed Jasmine, it's getting late*'.

There it was again. What's with the Jasmine thing, Jazz thought. '

'Just about to', she said. *'I just want to get this set into my head. I have a test tomorrow.'*

Celine left, closing the door behind her. What on earth was Mommy up to! A few minutes later Jazz went to her own room, calling goodnight to her mother. She had left the empty knapsack in the den. She settled down to wait. Celine snored. Brett had too, and between them the racket they had made nightly would scare away the bravest of burglars. This is what she was waiting for now. She would know when her mother had fallen asleep.

After Celine had been snoring for half an hour, Jazz went to Brett's den, slipped out the key. She took out anything of importance and stuffed them into the knapsack, replaced them with some of her old essays and newspapers, locked the desk and went back to her room.

When Jazz left for school the next day Celine had not yet come out of her room. She figured that if everything went as planned, she would just be able to make it to school on time. She walked a couple of blocks then took a taxi to her father's office. As she expected, Payne Smith had not yet arrived. She stuck the letter under his blotter leaving just enough sticking out to be sure he would notice. Hanna, the secretary was missing from her desk but she was accustomed to Jazz coming in and out and would think nothing of it if she met her there. As she was leaving she saw Hanna coming out of the bathroom. She hugged her and told her that she had hoped to scrounge a few dollars for a school project from Payne but that she would come back after school. She ran the three blocks to Pim's office. Pim's secretary, Joyce, was a much different, more nosy person than Hanna and could not be snowed as easily. Pim was not there. Anything she could do for her?

No, well come back when he's here. Jazz hoped that Payne would communicate with Pim. Perhaps Jason had told his father what he saw and his suspicions, anyway. She would find him and ask him after the test. She took a taxi to school. She hoped no one would see her and tell Celine. She had left with ample time to get to school. She didn't want to arouse any suspicions, not before she was quite sure what she was dealing with.

By the time Jazz was able to go look for Jason, he had left the school. The team was playing against a school on the other side of the island. Jazz tried to call Pim. He was out of the office, was there a message? No. Thank you for calling. She tried to call Payne. Payne was out also. She chatted a bit with Hanna and hung up. She made her way home in a cloud of disappointment.

Celine was in the living room thumbing through a magazine when Jazz arrived home. She didn't respond to Jazz' greeting, and Jazz went to the den to do her homework. It hit her with a sting harder than her mother's slap the day before. Daddy's chair was there looking forlorn, and the chair she normally used on the other side, just where it always was, but the desk was gone. Jazz' head was spinning. She had to get the knapsack out of the house now!

'Mommy, what have you done with daddy's desk? Where am I to do my homework?

You can do your homework at the kitchen table, or in your room.

There is no desk in my room, Mommy and the kitchen table is for eating.

She went to her room and changed out of her school uniform. A few minutes later, dressed in jeans and a tank top, she came back out and announced that she was going to the library.

You cannot go to the library, Celine said. *Jordan Little is coming over.*

Jazz saw red. *Jordan Little is always coming over,* she said. *The leach might as well live here. Anyway, you two will have the place to yourselves while I'm gone.*

She strode to the door, ducking just in time to avoid the book Celine flung at her. Whatever had come over Mommy? What's with this new violence? She walked to the bus stop and took the bus down to Pim's. She'd phone for a ride when she got to the bus stop.

Pim picked her up at the bus stop himself, and when he had heard the story he took Jazz into his own den and put the documents in his own safe. Jazz was relieved. Damn Jordan. He wasn't getting anything of her father's if she could prevent it.

It was about two weekends after the desk incident when Jason took Jazz to a moonlight beach party at Black Rocks. The party was fun. All of their friends were there and as the evening progressed the kids started wandering away in couples. Crystal left with Jared Scott, a new boy from one of the Windward Islands. He had just moved there with his parents. His father was the island's new Chief of Police. Crystal had a huge crush on him.

Jason and Jazz wandered over to sit on one of the huge black volcanic rocks which glistened in the moonlight. Jazz was sure she was walking on a cloud. She sat on Jason's lap and he played in her hair. She felt so cozy, so warm, so loved. When Jason said he loved her and asked if she loved him, it seemed only natural. Jason said she was beautiful and he loved her, and that he would even had she not been so physically beautiful because she was so lovely inside, and then he suggested they get engaged and they would be married when he returned home from university. He said he would come home with her to talk to her mother, but Jazz suggested he allow her to talk to Celine first. *You know,* she had said, *give her a chance to make it into an event. She can show off her style. You know Mommy. She'll love that.*

When Jason took her home, she had kissed him. *Goodnight my darling, darling, darling husband to be Jase,* punctuating each darling with a kiss. She was so happy. She had not had a chance to see Crystal before they left, and thought it was too late to call, just in case she had not made it home yet. They would chat in the morning and Jazz would share her good news. Surprisingly, Celine was still up and Jazz couldn't wait and blurted out her the good news.

Nothing could have prepared her for Celine's reaction. She flew into a rage. Jazz had never seen her so upset before. She railed, and even blamed the Coolidge family for Brett's death. How odd! She said she did not want to see Jason or any of the Coolidges darken her doorstep ever, and she certainly did not want to be related to them in any possible way. She ordered Jazz to break off any relationship with Jason and not to even think of anything so ludicrous as becoming engaged to him. After a while Jazz went to her room, slamming the door, hoping to rescue some vestige of the good feelings of the earlier evening. Why did Mommy hate the Coolidges? Daddy liked them.

The quarrel continued the next day, Sunday, and Celine warned Jazz not to bring Jason back to her home again. Celine said she would rather see Jazz under the stone in the car with her father than married into that family, but the bombshell was when she added that she had already given her consent for Jazz to marry Jordan, anyway.

J-Jordan!! Your boyfriend?

Jordan is not my boyfriend, declared Celine.

Mommy, what planet are you on?

Jazz could not believe she had said that. Actually, she could not believe any of it was happening. This raging harridan was not her mother. Mommy was calm, poised, dignified. She never behaved like that; and Jordan! He was her father's age, for goodness sake! Jazz had even thought he was interested in her mother. Something was wrong, but as the day wore on the quarrel got worse and the vitriol spewed against the Coolidges intensified. Jazz could take no more. She left, but as she was walking out the door Celine spat out *You **will** marry Jordan.* Jazz had no idea where she was going or what she was going to do. She decided to phone Pim

When Pim heard the desperation in Jazz's voice he left immediately to pick her up. Not much was said on the phone but it was obvious the child was in trouble. Pim drove Jazz home and instructed her to come to his office at lunch the next day. He said he should have things figured out by then.

Pim did not go directly home after dropping Jazz off.

The next day, when Jazz showed up at Pim's office, he gave her a file. It contained some cash and a passport almost exactly like her own passport, except her name was Jazinthe LaPlace and she was a year older. There were several papers, including reference letters, high school diploma in her new name and instructions. Pim listed for her the contents of the file and told her that she need not use the file, if she had any misgivings, but if she chose not to, she was to return it to him complete, and he would destroy it. He asked her to destroy the instructions once she had read them and made her promise not to tell any of it to anyone, including Jason, his son and, unknown to him, her almost fiancé. He hugged her and said goodbye. He told her he was doing this only because of his love for her father, and again told her that she was not obliged to go through with it.

Jazz sneaked back home carrying the file in her knapsack. Celine was out, and she went to her room to examine the contents. If she chose to go through with it, she was to meet a boat at 11:30 p.m. on the other side of the island and it would take her to St. Barts. She was to take very little so as not to draw attention to anyone she met on the way. There was enough cash to buy clothes. She could stay in St. Barts as long as it was safe but one of the reference letters was to a friend of Pim's and her late father's, who would help her get into Canada or the United States.

Jazz had about 10 hours to make up her mind. She was mad at her mother, and disappointed, but she was disconsolate about leaving her best friend and her boyfriend without a word. However, she was almost seventeen and her mother could consent to her marriage to Jordan, but she couldn't marry Jason until she was twenty one without her mother's consent. The thought of being married to Jordan made her rush to the bathroom and empty her stomach. She made up her mind to escape.

Jazz did not speak during dinner with Mommy and Jordan, but knowing how she felt about the new development, neither saw it as anything more than a snit. After dinner she got her knapsack and left for the library. If her mother noticed the knapsack looked bigger than usual, she did not say. Jazz did go to the library for a little while then left and, heart thumping, she took a bus, getting off half a mile from where her instructions said she would meet the boat. She walked down a dark pathway to the beach. There was not even a moon to light her way and she was terrified. She still had an hour to wait and she imagined all the things that could happen to her while she waited. She sat beneath a tree and waited. The boat was early but the signal matched. The boat stopped barely long enough for her to get on and they were off. She was shown to a little berth down below and she lay down and surprisingly, immediately fell asleep. When she awoke it was morning and they were landing in St. Barts. She showed her passport and Jazinthe Laplace started a new life.

At about the time Jazz was presenting her first reference letter in St. Barts, at home, Celine was discovering that her daughter had not come home the night before. When she saw the bed had not been slept in, her first thought was of Jason. She phoned the Coolidges but Jason had left for an out of town football tournament and nobody at the Coolidges had seen Jazz. She called Crystal. None of the Vanderpools had seen or heard from Jazz either. Jazz did not turn up at school. She did not come home for dinner either. Celine called the police. There were search parties and radio ads. Nobody had seen Jazz after the library. Nobody reported seeing her board a bus or get off a bus or ride a bus. Noone had seen her walk the path to the beach. It was as though she had become invisible.

Poor Celine was bereft. She knew why Jazz had run away but she could never tell, and Jordan had claimed that there were no papers in Brett's desk and she couldn't understand it. She was relieved, but she knew the papers should have been there. Where else could they be? Brett had expected to come home. He had no reason to move the papers. She regretted letting him take the desk, but what could she do?

Three weeks had passed since Jazz left. Mr. Mottron, Pim and Brett's friend, ran an inn and had given her a private little room with its own bathroom and a little balcony. He had also given her a job as a Receptionist/Girl Friday. Mr. Mottron said that Brett LaPierre had done him a huge favour and he was happy to help Brett's daughter in any way he could. He had asked no questions.

Jazz' new life was not as bad as it could be. She missed Jason and Crystal terribly. She even missed Celine, although she was still so angry with her, she could scream. She did not miss Jordan Little and she hoped to never set eyes on the toad again.

Jazz had purchased a few items of clothing but felt she needed more and decided to use her next day off to do some shopping. She liked poking around the boutiques and had begun to enjoy stargazing. St. Barts had become a haunt of the rich and famous. She had just lifted a hanger to get a better look at a lovely little top when she heard

Oh my God Jazzie!! Girl, do you know they are looking for you back home? Police, people, parents, pho-eee!!

Jazz had always hated Justine's tendency towards alliteration. Justine was a classmate and what she was doing in St. Barts was a mystery.

"Wanna go for a snack and tell me about it? Justine asked. Jazz agreed, and spent most of the time listening to Justine relate how she had won a trip and the last thing she expected was to solve the mystery of the missing missy.

When do you go home, Jazz asked and Justine said she was due to leave in about four hours. Jazz asked if she would consider not telling anyone she had seen her and Justine promised she wouldn't.

Jazz left Justine with a warm hug and a frantic heart. She dashed back to the inn and told Mr. Mottron what had happened and how sorry she was she had to leave. Within a half hour he had her on a speedboat to St. Martin where she took a flight to Chicago and from Chicago to Toronto. Mr. Mottron had advised her to use her own passport out of St. Martin and to ditch the other one. She had taken his advice. She was Jasmine LaPierre again.

When Justine arrived home in St. Kitts, she told the immigration officer that she had seen Jazz in St. Barts. She phoned Celine and told her and Celine phoned the police and told them. The St. Kitts police phoned the police in St. Barts, and the police in St. Barts investigated and found no one by the name of Jasmine LaPierre had entered or left that island. With a population of less than 9,000 people, it did not take long to ascertain that there was no known Jasmine LaPierre on the island. Justine insisted that she had sat and talked with her for an hour but she did not know the name of the place they were.

Holy shit! Do you know that everybody thought that Justine was wacko! So she did see you! Add her to the list of people you hurt, Jazzie. Crystal commented, awed.

You can't blame me for Justine, Jazz said. *She did promise not to tell and obviously she couldn't wait to blab. So if it backfired then, tough.*

Tough, Jazzie, Tough? Just like that. They wanted to charge her with mischief! What sort of person have you become? I can see you had a problem and you were frightened ten years ago, but some time in those years could you not have found a little time to get in touch? After you were 21 maybe. Your mother couldn't make you marry Jordan then.

Jazz thought for a moment and then said. *I had made a promise to Pim. He helped me. If I broke that promise I would have betrayed him. Right or wrong, I thought he could go to jail.*

Hmm. Debatable. So you owed Pim. Did you not owe his son? I thought you were supposed to be so madly in love with him. All you ever talked about was Jase this and Jase that. What was up with that? Did you not really care for Jason at all? That man was tormented! Now, I know why you left but you should have found a way to get to him. Damn! You propose to a woman and she runs off and disappears into thin air. Not a self esteem booster.

Fair enough. I may not have done right but I thought at the time I was. I did not know how to get in touch with Jase. He was about to leave for university when all this happened. I didn't forget you. Sometimes I sent you a sketch, Jazz said to Crystal. Jazz had always loved making sketches and caricatures and as a schoolgirl, had often done them of and for her friends.

Yes. With no return address, and always from a different state. I thought you were in America. What about Jason? Did you forget Jason, Crystal asked. Was there somebody else?

Jazz was getting a little annoyed.

'*What's with all the Jason questions? Did you and Jason get together after I left?*'

No. I got together with Jared Scott before you left and after you left and will be together with him till death us do part. I am now Crystal Scott and we have two sons. Crystal said, waving her left hand.

Jazz was embarrassed and guilty at her own insensitivity in not asking, but Crystal had come in firing on all pistons.

I apologize Crystal. Tell me about your life and your family.

I found a new best friend when you left.

Jazz felt the bitter taste of jealousy in her throat, but she would be damned if she was going to ask who. She didn't need to.

My sister, Elle. She doesn't want to be called Ellie anymore. We grew really close. Jared and the kids are coming over later. You will meet them and find out everything you want to know but until then, this is all about you.

I love you Crystal. I always loved you and I loved Jason. I even love Mommy. I don't know what I will feel when I see them but I know I will have to face them all at some time.

Tonight.

Yes. Your family, but I meant the others.

I'm asking Jason to come over this evening. Sorry honey. We are going to get this straightened out, and the sooner the better. Tomorrow we deal with your mother and Pim.

Damn Crystal. You were always pushy and you've got worse.

Jazz was relieved even though she was not exactly looking forward to facing Jason or her mother.

Do you ever see Mommy Jazz asked.

From time to time. She seems to be doing fine, but with all due respect, your mother is a snob so there isn't much to talk with her about.

Jazz was aware that this had always been the general opinion, and yet she knew that her mother could be warm. Jazz had loved and admired her mother. Celine was beautiful and elegant. A bit aloof, she was into fashion and appearances in general. Daddy used to say that in another place Mommy's aesthetic eye could have made them rich and famous in a high fashion and decorating career.

One of Jazz' most cherished moments was an afternoon she shared a special closeness with her mother. Jazz was off school and Brett was at work. Brett had always avoided talking about his family and always looked uncomfortable when she tried to bring up the subject. On the few occasions when he made any reference at all, he referred to Mommy's father as The Old Goat.

Jazz was upset because Brett had said no, and wouldn't change his mind. She couldn't go to Nevis with all her friends to see the football tournament, and Jason was playing. When Brett left, Celine had been especially kind. They had shared a pot of herbal tea and Celine sat with her. She asked Jazz not to press him. She told Jazz that when Brett was a teenager, his family had missed Christina, an overcrowded ferry which went down on its way from St. Kitts to Nevis. They had missed it because their bus had broken down and he and his father had tried to help fix the problem. That made them a little late getting to the ferry dock, and saved their lives. Three years later he had lost all his family in a boating accident anyway, and had been severely traumatized. He couldn't bear the idea of the possibility of losing her too. She had then shared the family history with Jazz.

There had been long standing animosity between her grandfathers Kenneth, Mommy's father and Jean, Daddy's father. Jean LaPierre had arrived on the island from the Haiti before Mommy was born, with his wife and daughter. Brett and two younger sisters were born on the island. They were poor but Jean was a skilled and hard worker, and could work at practically anything. Celine was not sure what caused the granddads to despise each other but she grew up hearing that the LaPierre's were low and not to be associated with. Brett and Celine had attended the same school, but as Brett was there on a scholarship and as he was three years older their paths seldom crossed. At Celine's first school dance, Brett asked her to dance and she discovered he was quite nice for a low scholarship boy. They started to meet secretly and as she got to know him she realized he was not low, just not well off.

When Brett graduated he received a full scholarship to university and they celebrated – Pamela Martin blabbed and grandfather Kenneth found out. Celine said it was awful. She disobeyed her father for the first time in her life. Grandfather Kenneth, in a rage, got out his shotgun, ordering her to stay in her room while he went to 'give the low class Haitian scaliwag his scholarship to hell' and while he was at it he said, he might send the rest of the family to keep him company. Celine said she was terrified! There was fire in her father's eyes and she truly believed he was going to kill Brett. She argued with him and when she saw he was adamant she ran to the LaPierre's house so that when grandfather Kenneth arrived, it was Celine who answered the door and told him he would have to kill her first.

Grandfather Kenneth was influential but Grandfather Jean was well liked, and soon the neighbours were all there surrounding the LaPierre home. Grandmother Celia, Celine's mother arrived just before the police and begged Grandfather Kenneth to come home. She was so humiliated by the exhibition. Grandfather Kenneth ignored her at first but Grandmother Celia was so distressed she collapsed and had to be taken away by ambulance and spent the next two weeks in hospital recovering from a stroke.

During the time grandmother Celia was in the hospital, Celine refused to speak to her father, and stayed the entire time with the LaPierre family. When Grandmother Celia came home she was a changed woman, and she begged Grandfather Kenneth to call a truce. She complained that he had forced her daughter to live in sin and now her family could not hold their heads up in their community. Celine moved back home but Grandfather Kenneth could not forgive the LaPierres. He counted their allowing her to stay with them as one more mark against them.

Brett went off to university and life on the estate went back almost to normal for a year or two, until Old Joe the gardener was found dead. Grandfather Ken claimed to have evidence and publicly accused Jean LaPierre. Old Joe was about eighty and shouldn't have been working at such a taxing job in the first place and he also drank, but despite Celine threatening to move back with the LaPierres and Old Joe's autopsy showing no signs of foul play, Grandfather would not leave it alone, and harassed the police to arrest Jean La Pierre. LaPierre, in the meantime, tired of the constant animosity and harrassment, told Celine that he had got a job and booked passage for him and his family on a small boat to Anguilla. When the police came the LaPierres had already gone. The boat sank that night. Noone was saved. Their flight convinced some people that Jean might have been guilty.

Celine said she believed that Grandfather Kenneth was convinced he had good evidence, but she had been disappointed that when he later found out that he was wrong, he never told anyone outside his family. He felt it did not matter since Jean LaPierre was already dead.

Brett and Celine got married while Brett was still in university, but was home on vacation. Celine made it clear to Grandfather Kenneth that she was not about to tolerate another distressing show, but Grandfather was at that time suffering his own distress. He told her and Grandmother Celia that he was 'done for'.

Over the years Grandfather Kenneth had been running the estate for a family trust based in England. They had shown so little interest in the actual running of it, never putting in an appearance, that everyone looked at the estate as Grandfather Kenneth's, even, to some extent, Grandfather Kenneth himself. The owners had become tired of wrangling with the government of St. Kitts and Nevis, which wanted to take over all the sugar estates, and had given in and were selling the estate to them. He would receive a small pension but he would have to give up the residence. When she heard the news Grandmother Celia suffered another stroke. She did not survive it and Grandfather Kenneth became a broken man. After Brett returned home from university, Grandfather Kenneth came to live with them. During this time Brett found out that Grandfather Kenneth had known he had been wrong about his accusation of Grandfather Jean. Brett could not live with him after this, and found a small house he and his friends renovated for him where he lived until he died shortly after Jazz was born.

Celine had always felt a little guilty about his death. She had visited him every day, with Jazz, bringing his meals and cleaning and keeping him company, but he persisted in denigrating Brett. Fed up, Celine had threatened to stop visiting if he continued, but he ignored her. To teach him a lesson, she asked Mrs. Greaux to take his lunch for two days, and when Celine went on the third day, she found him. He had died in his sleep. She always wondered whether it was caused by a possible belief that she had deserted him and that he had no one left.

Jazz suggested after Celine had related the story, that maybe her grandfather was just showing off. She couldn't believe he would have shot her father. Celine assured her that he definitely would have. She told Jazz that she had a brother, Jazz' Uncle Aaron. She did not know where Aaron was.

Aaron was twelve years older than Celine and she could remember him lifting her up in the air and twirling her around. She must have been five or six years old when Aaron and her father had a big fight. She was too young to know what it was about but it was loud and bitter. Her father had something in his hand and he was hitting Aaron and Aaron got mad and punched him in the face and her father's nose started to bleed. Aaron looked stricken and turned and walked out of the house. She had seen her father go for his gun and screamed. Aaron heard her and turned and her father's shot missed him. Late that night Aaron came to her room and kissed her, and she never saw her brother again. She had waited day after day for Aaron to come home and play with her and she had asked for him. Till the day he died, it was as if Aaron had never existed to her father. He was, however, always kind to her and her mother. Sometime ago, Brett had helped her try to find Aaron. They got an address in Germany and she had written to him. From time to time she had written and sent pictures. Her letters were never returned but they were never answered.

Jazz believed that house her father and his friends built was the house she now sat in. She had always got satisfaction from the thought of her mother defying her arrogant overbearing grandfather for her father. There was warmth in her mother. She was not a snob.

I am trying to get into your headspace, Jazzie. Crystal said. *What happened, happened, but since then, all these years, how could you not wonder, or want to get in touch. There is something missing from the story Jazzie. It doesn't add up. How could you just excise everyone from your life like we never existed? Didn't you ever wonder why Pim sent you into exile? Maybe he did not want you and Jason to be together. Did you not want to find out? Did you not look at his reference letters? Did you not wonder why the people who helped you never asked any questions? They probably think you murdered somebody. Was there somebody else?*

Eventually there was, Jazz said and started to cry again. *It blew up like a grenade. My problem, Crystal, is that I put everything I have into the people in my life at the time and when they leave, I'm no good. I was totally shattered when Daddy was killed. I couldn't cling to Mommy. Jase was there so I clung to him. I loved him. I fought Mommy for him but there was no way to win, and Jase couldn't help me even if he wanted to. Pim could and did, with a condition. I never saw I could break that trust. All I saw is that Pim would go to jail for helping me. He had given me a forged passport.*

You must have been addled. At sixteen and in a panic you could think that, but it shouldn't have taken long to figure it out, Jazzie. You used to be smart. You didn't have to even let on Pim had anything to do with it. Why would anyone think he did? I'm afraid, Jazzie, that you are totally incapable of looking after yourself. We will have to hook you up with someone reliable poste haste. Tell me about the grenade. Did you love him very much.

I was quite fond of him, and we had a comfortable relationship.

*A comfortable relationship? You mean like old people, Jazzie? You were screaming on the beach over a **comfortable** relationship! Jeez, you need to be in an institution.*

Jazz smiled for the first time. *Now that I think about it, I mixed things up, it wasn't a cataclysm. It was a catalyst. The rage and pain and everything else could have been for the years I've lost. Who knows? I'm not going to live down the screaming on the beach thing, am I?*

When Jazz arrived in Toronto she made some inquiries and found the person Pim's letter was addressed to was in a small town, a four hour bus ride from Toronto. His name was Alistair Delisle. Jazz took a room in a small hotel for a couple of nights to use the time to work things out. She was so tired and so alone. When she phoned Mr Delisle to alert him, he said he would be in Toronto for a meeting the next day and would meet with her for lunch.

She liked Mr. Delisle on sight. He was a bit older but he reminded her a lot of Brett. They had a nice lunch and she gave him Pim's letter. He didn't ask any questions. He told her to call him Alistair and that he ran a ski resort with his wife, and could let her work for him. She would have to get accustomed to the winter. In the meantime, if she wished, she could enroll in the nearby university.

She drove up with Alistair to her new home that afternoon and met his wife Millie. Millie was either very well preserved or much younger than Alistair, but she appeared to love him very much and they seemed to get along really well. Millie was nice. She had been a professional skier but her career was cut short by an injury. She gave ski lessons to groups of the resort patrons, and offered to teach Jazz. During the summer the crowds were different but the resort did a fair business offering shows, trips to the nearby lake and theatre in the town. There was enough to keep Jazz employed year round, although in the winter it was hectic.

Jazz settled into the staff quarters at the resort. She worked for the resort, in reception, equipment rental, serving tables, wherever her services were required. It was discovered she had a knack for decorating, and they paid her to decorate the place for the resort's various events. She registered in Waterloo University nearby, and earned a business degree while working for the resort. She was pleasant, efficient and well liked and got good tips and sometimes propositions. She pocketed the tips and declined the propositions. From time to time the other staff, mostly students, would invite her out and on occasion, she went with them to a movie but mostly she declined. After awhile they left her alone.

She was comfortable in her hideout. Five years had gone by and she had never seen anyone she knew from home. One day Millie asked her to dinner at their home. They asked her if she had any plans for her future. Since coming to them, she had not had much of a social life. She now had her degree, was she planning to go for a postgraduate degree or strike out on her own. Jazz read this as a gentle prod from the nest. She explained she had some thoughts of starting a small business. She was making it up as she went, but somehow managed to convince both the Delisles and herself. They offered to help as much as they could, getting her in with the bank and suppliers etc., and in a few months she had a small boutique in Punky Doodle Corners, a nearby town on a lake, selling souvenirs, maps, flowers and knickknacks, even a limited stock of retro clothing. The unusual name and the quaintness of the town attracted a continuous flow of visitors and the business thrived.

The town was picturesque, the population transient, and Jazz' boutique, near the lake attracted an assorted clientele among the weekenders, cottagers, tourists. Even though she did not stock the usual cheap, tacky stuff, she was surprised at what people on holiday were willing to pay for insubstantial objects they would most likely never look at again once they returned home. She made obscene profits but had no social life on which to spend her earnings. She lived in a very small flat back of the boutique where, once the boutique was closed she retired to read or watch TV, listen to music and sometimes sketch. She sketched scenes she remembered of her friends and family having a good time: Jason lining up for a corner kick, Jason's cousin, Gareth passing him the baton in a relay, Crystal dancing on the beach, and scenes of Brett and his friends liming, of Celine playing a piano, a rear view of Brett and Celine, his arm touching her lightly on the back, Brett playing cricket.

One day she put a handful of sketches down in the shop to do something else, and forgot to pick them up again. A customer browsing, spotted them and asked the price. They had never been intended for sale. They were a hobby. Jazz threw out a number she thought was ridiculous, and the customer paid without raising an eyebrow, and in fact bought two. Jazz put the rest on display and raised the price by ten dollars. She could not sketch them fast enough.

Jazz was fairly attractive. She was also blessed with an instinctive knowledge of what worked best for maximum enhancement of her appearance, which made people who saw her imagine she was stunning. After all, she was raised with Celine, whose mantra was that although everyone deserved to be treated with respect, it was an ideal that never would be achieved. You would always be treated based on your appearance, therefore, if you looked like a bum you could expect to be treated like a bum.

Jazz bought beautiful clothes, and with nowhere else to go, she dressed up every day in the boutique. She had always had a talent for decorating, and had laid out the small shop rather tastefully. Visitors enjoyed coming into the little shop. The tastefully arranged shop and the well dressed young proprietor made them feel they were in a far more upscale place than a mere souvenir shop.

She had run the boutique for two years when Paris Thomas walked into her life. He claimed he had been talked into coming with some friends in response to a promotion the Delisles were running to fill up the resort for summer. He was the odd man out and the others had gone on a cruise on the lake. He was from Toronto and wondered if she would like to have dinner with him that evening. Jazz accepted and they talked and talked over dinner. At least she talked. He asked questions and she talked. He came back to see her a few times on weekends, before inviting her to Toronto, and eventually talked her into moving there

Jazz realized that she had inherited her mother's aestheticism. She found a nice spot in Toronto and opened another boutique. This time she ventured into decorating, at first doing floral layouts for weddings, then she got commissions to do several banquets and other larger events, and some private events, and an occasional house staging. Her business grew and she took on an assistant. Her relationship with Paris also grew and she eased into a feeling of security. Life was pleasant and comfortable.

Jazz was overseeing the decorating of a ballroom for a political event when she met Sandy, a brash young reporter with an obvious chip on her shoulder. Jazz liked Sandy despite her attitude and they became better acquainted. Jazz tactfully toned down Sandy's attitude on occasion, and from time to time Sandy would benefit from the advice. Sandy thought all men were pigs and Jazz would point out that Paris didn't do a lot of the things that Sandy claimed all men did, qualifying them as pigs. Sandy had met Paris briefly, but was better acquainted with Jazz.

For awhile in Toronto, there had been some talk in the halls of government of selling off some real estate and closing some municipal offices to ease the financial straits in which the government had found itself. Sandy was gathering information for a piece she had been assigned. She was visiting one of the municipal offices alleged to be slated for closure when she noticed a wedding. She ordered her cameraman to take pictures, as many as possible. He couldn't figure what it had to do with what they were researching but she was adamant he not let them go unless he got really good shots, lots of close-ups of the bride and groom together. He was to flatter them, coax them, whatever was necessary. The bride was talking with a woman guest while the bridegroom was off chatting with some others. Sandy saw her chance and honed in on the bride, congratulating her and asking permission to take pictures. She said she might use them for a piece she was doing on weddings. The bride was keen and agreed and when the bridegroom came over and saw her, he couldn't change the bride's mind and had to go along.

Sandy interviewed the bride. They were going on a one week cruise for the honeymoon. They had been together for three years and had been engaged for six months. The bridegroom was wonderful, a one of a kind man. The bride was a busy entrepreneur, hence the civic wedding.

Sandy rushed back the studio and got the pictures from the camera. She left the office and went directly to Jazz' shop.

Do you have anyplace here we can watch a video? she asked as soon as she saw Jazz.

In the office in the back, Jazz said. *What's up?*

Sandy asked if she had any alcohol on the premises and when Jazz said no, she pulled a couple of airline sized bottles of cognac from her purse. You might need to have one, she said as she slipped the CD into the machine. Jazz saw Paris in a tux she thought he was giving somebody away and wondered why he hadn't told her. It took a few seconds for what the bride was saying to sink in, and then she slumped over, tears streaming down her cheek. *Where did you get this? Is it real?* was all she could gasp out.

Sandy opened one of the cognac bottles and handed it to her, and Jazz slugged it down directly from the bottle.

Sandy explained the circumstances. She looked through Jazz appointment book. At least the afternoon was free. She was sorry for her friend. Jazz was a mess. She knew that, had she not done this, this man would have walked back into Jazz' life with some glib excuse to explain why he had been missing for the duration and she would have welcomed him with open arms, never guessing that she was the other woman.

Jazz was obviously gutted. She was gasping, tears streaming down her cheeks, slumped on her desk, her nose running, makeup smudged, mascara tears running down her cheeks, shoulders and hands shaking. She was obviously incapable of supervising her business, at least for the rest of the day.

'Is your assistant capable of running the business while you take a little time off?'

Jazz nodded yes, and Sandy offered to take Jazz home.

Sandy had known Jazz would react, but she hadn't expected a total meltdown. The woman had literally fallen apart. Sandy had to ask Jazz' assistant to help her get Jazz into the car. When she got Jazz into her house, Sandy was very sure that Jazz was having a nervous breakdown.

Is there any place or any family you could go to for a few days? I'll help you pack.

Jazz picked up the phone and called Pim Coolidge's number. Jason Coolidge answered the phone.

When Jason came home with his crisp new diploma declaring him an architect, his father, imagining there was little call for an architect on the small island and that there would not be enough business to pay for office space, offered his son space in his own establishment. His office was across the hall from Pim's, and Jason had stepped into his father's office for a moment and had absent mindedly picked up his phone.

Surprisingly, Jason recognized Jazz' voice immediately. When Pim took the phone Jazz was blabbering incoherently. Finally, Pim was able to understand what she wanted and promised to have someone meet her at the airport, and assured her everything would be taken care of. Pim could hardly bear the look on poor Jason's face. He had some explaining to do.

Jazz took an early morning flight. She could barely see through her tears. When she boarded the plane and realized the seats next to hers were vacant, she wondered if the check-in clerk had set this up. She had been kind. Jazz was grateful. She didn't think she could or should share her misery with fellow travelers. Less than 24 hours ago she'd thought she had a good life, was maybe even a little happy. She would never have imagined the bottom could drop out of her world so suddenly, or that it would be so devastating. Why, she asked silently, was she so unlovable. Why did she not deserve happiness. Her world exploded whenever it appeared she might achieve happiness. How could Paris have betrayed her like this? She thought she had found her niche. So, theirs was not a torrid love but they had been happy, she thought. She'd trusted him.

Jazz misery increased as the flight progressed. It was not just about Paris now. She had forfeited ten years of her life and there was nothing she could do about it. She was so alone. She had no one. Paris was the only person who had paid her any real attention in the last ten years and he had betrayed her. It rankled not so much that he had married somebody else but she suspected he would have come back and carried on just as before without her knowing he had married. What kind of pig was he! She hated him. She hated her life. She hated that they had forced her out of her home. She hated most of all that Satan's spawn, Jordan Little. She wished her Daddy was alive. None of this would have happened if her Daddy was alive. She would have been happy with Jason now, she was sure, but she didn't want to think of Jason. He had sounded odd on the phone, like he recognized her, but he didn't call her name. He probably hated her.

Misery and self pity can be tiring. Jazz slept for the last hour or so of the flight. The stewardess awakened her when they were about to land to remind her to fasten her seat belt. She did as she was told and closed her eyes. She did not want to look out onto the island she had left in the dark so long ago. The airport was new and completely different.

Jazz did not notice, even though she had come to the old airport with her father many times.

Out of Customs and Immigration, Jazz looked for Pim, but did not see him. She thought of taking a cab but didn't know where to, then she heard her name. It was the same kind man who had driven the long way to avoid passing her father's accident site, on the way to Jason's birthday party. Why did she not remember his name? He helped her into the car with her only bag, and drove her to the little house and saw her settled in. He didn't say much as she was crying all the way. He seemed embarrassed and anxious to get away.

It was 11:45 a.m. and the sun was at its peak, the house was like an oven and Jazz was alone, abandoned, her soul churning with hurt, anger, depression, despair, all fighting for dominance. She felt she would explode. She ran out of the house, down to the beach. It was deserted at this time of day, and she screamed. Long drawn out yowls that seemed to come from deep within her very soul. She screamed and stamped her feet. She fell in the sand, got up, screamed some more, and hurled some stones into the water. She was like a banshee, and she couldn't help herself. As she was about to hurl another stone she felt someone pin her arms to her side. He turned her around. He was a rasta with a kind voice. He said laughing, "musta been real bad, but you can't take it out on the sea. I get you some coconut water. She hadn't noticed the coconuts and the machete in the sand. He chopped off the head of one of the coconuts and gave it to her to drink. She hesitated and said she had no money.

Drink the coconut water, Missy. I know you. Drink the water and don't try to go in the sea today till you cool off.

She drank it, said goodbye and thanks and walked away. He watched her walk home and gave a final wave and warning. *I mean it. Don't go in the water today.*

I'm going to call Jason and tell him some of what you have told me, Crystal said. *If he is up to it, I'll ask him to come over. You may not want to see him but it is well past time to clear the air. Hell, we can't have you losing your mind, and screaming on the beach will not help. There are noise pollution laws, you know,* she said jokingly, *although I can see now why you would have done that. I was really worried for you when I heard.* She went into the kitchen to call Jason, leaving Jazz to mull over the situation.

Jason arrived fifteen minutes later. Their meeting was predictably awkward. Jazz congratulated him on his upcoming wedding. He thanked her stiffly then made a snide remark about a disappearing fiancé, and Jazz started to cry. She apologized to Jason. He was kind. She remembered he had always been kind. They talked for awhile. Jason had come to the same conclusion as Crystal, that his father must have not wanted them to be together, for Jason could easily have come to her and everything would have been fine. Parental consent was not required in Canada after age 18.

Considering everything straightened out, and all forgiven, Jason hugged Jazz. He should not have done that. Life could be complicated. All the feelings that she used to have for him came rushing back like the evening train. Jasmine LaPierre fell in love with Jason Coolidge all over again and resolved to fight for this man. He was hers, and it was as if Paris had never existed. She was not sure what Jason felt for he quickly let her go and called his father.

Pim must have been waiting around the corner for he was there in a very short time. He corroborated everything Jazz had said, and no, he did not do it to prevent Jazz and Jason getting together. When Jazz came to him, she had not mentioned any transaction with Jason. Based on what she had said, he judged her concern to be that, against her will, Celine was marrying her off to Jordan whom Celine knew that her father disliked. He had only discovered Jason's proposal after it was known that Jazz was missing.

Jazz had omitted mention of what had started the fight in order to spare Pim's feelings. In actual fact, he had not thought he had to keep them apart. He did not mention it, but he had always assumed when they were youths that, although she spent most of her early years making eyes at Jason, she was more suited to Ian, and things would work out with her finding her way to Ian in the end. As a boy Ian had hated her with the vehemence of a young lad in love. Pim had felt that Ian's personality would tame her, while her personality would run circles all around Jason. He did have to concede, after her disappearance, that he might have been wrong because when she went missing Jason was torn to shreds but Ian, apart from the initial concern shared by everyone, did not appear to be particularly affected.

Celine might not be everybody's dream date, he told them, but Brett had adored her and Jazz, and protected them. Because they were happy, nobody noticed how totally in control Brett was. He had a great personality and was able to get people to do whatever he asked. Neither his wife nor daughter had ever challenged any decision he made. Brett had always taken charge and maybe Celine needed someone to take charge, and this was her best solution. She could leave the burden of everyday decisions to Jordan. She wouldn't to a teenaged boy like Jason. Celine did not want a husband herself, he suspected. She had always been too obsessed with Brett, but she had always been looked after and she wanted to be looked after. She had no money that Jordan could snatch, and between Payne and Pim Jazz would be protected. Jazz had been trained to obey. As far as he knew, she had never disobeyed either parent, and in the end would likely not have changed the pattern.

Brett would not have approved of what Celine had planned. He would have had a seizure at the thought of Jazz with Jordan. Pim was carrying out what he thought would be Brett's wishes the only way he could think of at the time. He did not expect that Jazz would completely give up Jason and everyone forever. When she did, he assumed she hadn't cared enough, or had met someone else and moved on. He apologized to both Jazz and Jason and before he left, he offered to meet with Jazz at her convenience to go over her affairs. She might want to take over if she planned to stay, as Payne Smith had been thinking lately of moving to the U.S. to be near his kids and grandkids.

Jason surprised everyone by offering to take Jazz to see her mother next morning. Jazz felt a glow rise and spread inside her. She thanked him and they arranged a time for him to pick her up. She did not ask about his fiancé.

Crystal phoned her family to come over and within the hour Jazz had met her sons, Jarvis and Steele, and become reacquainted with her husband. Jazz could not help remarking that had things gone differently, she would have been their godmother.

Remind me to show you their baptismal certificates, Crystal said. *You are.*

It turned out to be a wonderful evening after all.

Jason was right on time to pick Jazz up next morning. She didn't know whether it would be appropriate to greet him with a kiss, although she wanted to so very much. She couldn't help but notice last night how well he had matured. He had retained the keen athletic look. She wasn't sure if it was just due to the occasion, but his attitude combined a serious studiousness with a gentle sort of sophistication. He had always been amazing but he seemed new and improved to coin a Canadian phrase. She giggled to herself. Jason bent and kissed her at the door. The decision was taken from her. It was just a peck, but it was enough to make her day.

On to the next challenge.

Jasmine! I heard you were here, Celine LaPierre said as she held the door for her daughter and Jason to enter. Jazz was nervous. Celine had forbidden her to bring Jason to her house in their last verbal exchange. Her attitude was chilly, but it wasn't directed particularly at Jason.

Good morning Mommy. I hope you are well, Jazz said stiffly.

I am well

Mommy, I have come to apologize for everything that happened between us and to ask you to forgive me, Jazz said, as meekly as she could manage.

Celine raised an elegantly outlined eyebrow, turned to Jason and said *Mr. Coolidge, I see you are escorting my daughter but I understand you are to be married.* She sounded like someone straight out of the sixteenth century.

Jazzie is asking you to forgive her, Mrs LaPierre. Will you?

Jasmine must want something from me. She sneaked out of here in the middle of the night and I have not seen or heard from her in ten years. Why now?

Mommy, what do you have that I would want? Certainly not Jordan Little. Jazz said hotly. *I slipped out ten years ago because I didn't want him then, and I certainly do not now. How anyone could is beyond me. Are you still together?*

Jasmine, I have never been 'together' with Jordan Little. If you have come here to pick another quarrel, please go.

I am here to reconcile with my mother. If you do not want that I will leave.

Celine made a graceful little hand gesture towards the door. Jazz led Jason out. Back in the car she remarked '*That did not go well.*' Jason did not comment. He seemed preoccupied and said nothing until they arrived at her house. When he opened the door for her he said

'*Jazzie, you and I have to talk - alone.*'

I know Jase. Anytime. It's not like I have anything to do or anywhere to go.

Jason followed her into the house. He seems so solemn, Jazz thought. She turned to him to say how sorry she was about her mother but he took her in his arms. Emotions long in abeyance came rushing back as Jazz kissed Jason. She was truly home.

Coming back was the best thing she could have done. Yesterday, when she arrived, she had reached the absolute lowest point of depression, frustration and exasperation, but when Crystal entered the front door of her house, worries about Paris and her recent past life had hastily exited the back door. She could not believe she was here, with Jason, happier than she believed possible, selfishly putting any thought of his impending marriage to the nethermost regions of her mind. She had not even tried to find out who was his bride to be.

Jason was fit, not in the bulky, veined way of a body builder. He was obviously an athlete, hard, well proportioned, well shaped, very well toned. Jazz had not missed many days at the gym either. They may have been mentally urging restraint on themselves, but the tension in those two well toned bodies straining for each other was more than their combined will could hold apart.

When Jason left several hours later they still hadn't talked much, but their lives, especially his, had become considerably more complicated.

A little boy delivered a note that evening. It was from Celine. It was a short note, a sort of apology for her behavior earlier, and it asked if she could come to see Jazz. Jazz dashed off a note on the back of her mother's. 'You are my mother. I love you. You are welcome at any time.' She tipped the boy an American dollar, and gave him the note to take back to her mother.

Jason came back in the evening. He said he didn't know if there was a phone and he really wanted to talk to her. He had brought her a cell phone in case there was none at the house. There wasn't. Jazz was uncertain of what Jason would say and thought she would start the conversation, get her point in before she lost the nerve.

I suppose you want to tell me to forget what happened between us today because it meant nothing and you are getting married. Well, I'm sorry but it meant everything to me Jase. I won't cause you any trouble. I want you even more than I ever did, but I screwed up and have only myself to blame. Jason put his finger to her lips, shushing her.

You are wrong, he said. *This morning meant everything. I have to figure out how to solve this dilemma. This is not fair to anyone. I hope you are here to stay. I'm over all that stuff in the past and, if I can untangle my situation, I will ask you again to be my wife.*

Jazz was sure she had died and gone to heaven. *I've always been yours, really. I'm sure of that now.*

Jason did not stay long. He had already got himself up to the neck in hot water. He was heading into the mother of domestic storms and it gave him a distinctly uneasy feeling.

Jazz sat back to ponder the last few days now that there were no distractions. The house had minimum furnishings. There was no

TV and only a small portable radio but the surf created a beautifully peaceful soundscape. She was considering staying. She could decorate the place and live here. She didn't want to think that if Jason couldn't get out of his engagement, she would be his mistress and this could be their little love nest, but the thought kept popping up anyway.

She went over all that was said yesterday. She had never seen her father as controlling, but Pim had known him all his life. If she had been a stubborn person she would have noticed, but her parents never made unfair demands on her, and she had never got the impression that Celine resented any decision Brett had made.

Crystal had sometimes called her a wishy washy daddy's girl. Crystal and her parents sometimes had battles of will when she thought they were being unfair, but she couldn't remember Brett being unfair. She wondered if she had been brainwashed. Maybe not. Pim did not exactly say Brett was controlling. He said he was in control. Daddy just cared and paved the way to make life easy for them. She decided to go with that idea, but Pim had said he was sure she would go along, and no one could see her going into hiding for ten years as logical. Now that she was looking back it did seem pathetic. When Jase really thought about it, would he still want her? Jazz didn't like where this was going. It might be better if she used the time to work out the details of selling her business. She was staying here. She had decided. She was going to fight for Jason.

Jazz was pondering what Jason had said. She knew that he was a kind person and that getting out of such a commitment would not be easy for him. She began to wonder about her rival. She didn't even know her name. What a mess! She decided to call Crystal and get some information

Jared answered the phone. Crystal was out he said, but he could give her the cell phone number. Jazz had not had enough time to get to know Jared before she left, but he seemed a nice person and he and Crystal appeared to be happy. She pondered whether to ask him about Jason and decided against it. She hung up after some small talk without getting the cell phone number and was too embarrassed to call back. It would probably be better to ask Jason himself anyway, if she could get past wanting to jump into bed with him each time they were in the same room.

She phoned her mother to give her the cell phone number. The ensuing conversation was quite pleasant and Celine agreed to come to visit the next day.

Celine came over and spent most of the next day with Jazz. They discussed what she had been up to during her absence. Jazz carefully omitted the names of the people who helped her. Jazz told her that Brett had been right and that with her taste she could have earned a great living in Toronto. She told her mother of her discovery that she must have absorbed by osmosis, all her mother had said over the years and had put it to good use in her business.

Celine remarked on Jazz being right back in with 'those Coolidges'. *I hope you know what you are doing Jasmine. It can't be much more than two months to that young man's wedding.* Jazz asked if Celine was invited and she said no, thank God. Those Coolidges are sick from top to bottom. Take that idiot father, she said. With a name like Pim, why would you marry a woman whose name is Pam, unless you planned to start a steelband or something. Pim pam, shanananana, she sang. Jazz laughed till tears ran down her cheeks. She had never thought of that, perhaps because she always thought of Mrs. Coolidge as Pammy. This was funny. Mommy never made comments like that. Since Celine was in such a good mood Jazz was tempted to ask her who Jason's fiancé was, but again decided against it. She needed to know but didn't want to spoil the mood.

When Celine left, Jazz phoned Crystal on the pretext of giving her the new phone number. Naturally, Crystal saw through it at once and, always outspoken, said so. *If you want to talk about Jason, Jazzie, say so. You know I already have the phone number. You called here today.* They both laughed. *So what do you want to say about Jason? You have the hots for him again, don't you?*

I want him back Crys. And I want to know who he is engaged to.

Jazz' heart sank when she found out that the fiancé was Yola Ross. Yola had flirted relentlessly with Jason when they were schoolgirls but nothing had come of it. She was sure that if she had come back earlier Yola would not have got him. Crystal told her that Yola had married some pretty boy foreign salesperson, passing through the island, and had moved with him to Aruba, but it hadn't worked out. There was some talk of a possible extra wife or two he had forgotten to mention, but it might have been just a rumour. Whatever it was, she was away for a few years and came home divorced. She made a big play for Jason and at first he resisted her, but they hooked up in the end, and are to be married in less than three months.

Tears were streaming down Jazz' cheeks. Reality had hit her with the force of a two-ton truck. When she didn't say anything, Crystal asked, *Jazzie, you aren't going to go screaming down the beach again, are you?*

Jazz wished she had come home sooner. *I want him back Crystal, she said bleakly.*

Well then, Crystal said, *Stop crying and hop to it. You have about 8 weeks. If you haven't got him back by then, you will have to stop trying. And Jazzie, don't do it unless you really want him. Jason is sensitive. He has been through a lot and he doesn't deserve to be played with.*

What about Yola? How would she take it?

Who the hell cares, Jazzie? You want the man or not? Yola is a hard ass, show-off you-know-what, she can take care of herself. She went after Jason and he gave in. If she loses him she will cuss and swear and then go after somebody else. Jazz pretended to be reassured, but she wasn't at all sure she was a match for Yola.

Tell me about Jase. I don't know anything it seems.

He went to university a year late because of you. Sorry, Jazzie, I'm not trying to bust your ass, I just want you to know you cannot play with him anymore. He is a fine man, but a lot more subdued than I think he would have been if he hadn't been put through all that. Just saying. You need to get together with him in a nice public place, like a nice restaurant. That way you can have a healthy exchange before jumping them fine bones. If you try it at home, you are going to end up in bed and defeat the purpose. Bed could always come afterwards.

Thanks, my wise friend. How do you know he will want to end up in bed with me?

Please, girl. I ain't no fool. Jason neither. You go screaming and throwing a tantrum alone on the beach. Even Jason gotta know that you need some real good you-know-what to calm you down, and lady, have you looked at the man! Testosterone in overdrive. He's the man to do it. They laughed.

Jazz was pacing the room like a caged cat. What if Jason could not get out of the engagement? She would become the other woman. She had taken Crystal's advice and phoned him to ask him out to dinner. He had answered and immediately said he would call back. She was sure she heard tension in his voice and possibly quarreling in the background. Maybe she had broken in on an altercation between him and his bride to be. God, she prayed he was not having a hard time of it.

Perhaps she should go for a walk. Apart from raging on the beach and the trip to see her mother, she had not been out since her arrival. She was embarrassed, and put off facing people. Apart from everything else, as she had expected, everyone seemed to know about her scene on the beach, but she was suffocating in this house. In the end, however, she decided to stay in a little longer. She would call her assistant and find out how business was going. She had to decide what she was going to do about it.

She had just hung up when she heard a car screech to a stop in front of the house. The door slammed and quick footsteps ran up the few steps to the veranda. She had left the front door open to let the air in. Jazz started walking towards the open door and was startled to see Yola enter her living room. Jazz started to shake. She was unaccustomed to confrontation and was not sure she was up to it. She just stared.

Hello Jazz

Hi .

So you are back. Crazy, I hear.

'*Yes, back, but not crazy*'. This woman was still annoying. '*What are you doing here?*'

I came to invite you to my wedding

Really? You deliver all the invitations personally? That must be tiring. Small wedding?

No. Just the ones to the crazy people, and you are crazy if you think you can waltz in here, snap your fingers and Jason is yours. Jason is mine. My 'fee-an-say'. Put that in your pipe and smoke it.

Jazz remembered Pim saying that she had been bred to obey. They all thought she was tame. She would show them.

Dear, dear Yola, she smiled an obviously fake smile. *Thanks for the wedding invitation but there isn't going to be a wedding. You just made my crazy mind up for me, so here's a heads up. I will take Jase off you, plus, if you are still in my house in 30 seconds I will cut your ass to strips.* She looked at her watch and strode into the kitchen and pulled open the cutlery drawer. Yola took a step towards the door, but Jason was there, about to enter.

Why are you here Yola?

His voice was strained and angry. Jazz came to the kitchen door. There was nothing in her hands. There were no knives that could cut anything more solid than properly thawed butter in the kitchen, anyway. Nobody had lived in the house for a while. Even if there was, her bravado had fizzled out the minute she entered the kitchen. She just wanted to get Yola out of her house.

Crazy bitch threatened me and pulled a knife on me, Yola snarled. Jason stared at Jazz, incredulous. Jazz just shrugged, empty palms up.

Go home Yola. He escorted her out the door and watched her drive away. He locked the door and turned to Jazz. So what happened here?

Jazz started to tell him and realized her voice was trembling. Jason laughed and said it was a good thing he got there when he did. *Jazzie, if you got in a fight with Yola, she would cream you. Where is the knife?*

Jazz also laughed. *I couldn't find one.*

Do you think Yola would cause a public scene if we went out for a nice dinner so we could catch up instead of ending up in bed?

Jason looked embarrassed. *I apologize for Yola. We had a talk and it did not go well. It's hard on her so if you don't mind, perhaps we could postpone the dinner a few days? We can catch up now. I won't lay a finger on you. Promise.*

Fine, but I'm not making any such promise to you. Jazz was trying to hide her unease. Was she already falling into the role of the other woman?

Jason said he had not actually intended to come by. If he hadn't seen Yola's car parked out front he would have driven right by. He had been nervous of what he might find.

Were you expecting blood on the floor?

I was hoping for nothing unpleasant.

What do you think your parents will say?

What do you expect them to say Jazzie?

Well, they haven't seen me for a long time, they don't really know me now…

You should expect them to say nothing, Jazzie, like I do. I'm not a boy. Jazzie, he took her hands in his. *I love you and I want to be with you, but what I also want is for you to be confident and assertive. All that we talked about the other night is disturbing. It bothers me that even now, you asked my father's permission to come home. Whatever happened to make you finally want to come home, you should have just booked a flight and come on home. My father is in no position to approve, admit, or deny anyone entry onto the island. I need you to get over the compulsive obediency syndrome.*

Is there really something called that? Jazz asked.

Jason smiled. *I just made it up. I will look after you as much as I am able, but I want to know that if I am not able you can take care of yourself. Promise me Jazzie that you will work on your self confidence. It shouldn't be too hard. If you could run your own business in Toronto, you must have some self assurance. Although I must say, you did show a little bit to Yola today. Don't get me wrong, I'm not advocating your wielding knives or threats at anybody.*

Not even when they break into my home? But to set the record straight, I only threatened to cut her to strips. She just assumed I could find a knife. Jason kissed her.

Are you here to stay, Jazzie? Tell me your plans.

Jazz told him that she had just hung up from her assistant in Toronto when Yola walked in. She hadn't actually told him yet, but she was thinking of offering him first refusal on the business. She would then call her friend who had helped her and given her the idea to come home when she told her she should go away. She would get her to oversee the sale of her townhouse and her business.

Jason wanted to know what line of work this friend was in and how well she knew her. He didn't think giving that responsibility to a person who was not in real estate and barely more than an acquaintance from what Jazzie seemed to know of her, to be fair. He thought she should deal with it herself and offered to take some vacation and accompany her, for moral support and to let things blow over. He expected the next few days to be tumultuous. He would have to stay a couple of days to face the music, but they could go by the end of the week. He would give her some time to consider it. He didn't want her to feel pressured. She was free to say no.

Jazz did not need time to think about it. It shouldn't be her first thought, but it would be nice to have Jason around when that slimeball Paris came back. What a pig! She did not share that particular aspect with Jason. She was excited by the prospect of them together, away from all this for a little while, and told him so. They talked for a long time and then Jason and Jazz spent their very first night together.

As predicted, the next two days were harrowing. Jason went out in the morning to find his vehicle sitting on rims, his four tires slashed. He came back in and asked her to get dressed. He didn't want her to stay there alone. While she showered, Jason made a few calls. His cousin, Gareth showed up half an hour later to give them a ride. They dropped her off at her mother's. Jason told her that while she was in the shower he had phoned to borrow a car from his mother, so Gareth would drop him there and he would bring in one of their workers to replace the tires. After that he would go have a talk with Yola. He would call her later to let her know when he would be picking her up and, by the way, yes he had reconsidered and would make reservations for dinner out tonight. Jazz silently thanked Yola. She hoped she could handle hanging out with her mother for the while.

Celine appeared to be happy to see her, and Jazz settled down for their visit. She told her about what Pim had said about Brett being in total control, carefully omitting the context in which he made the comment. Unaware that her mother knew all, Jazz was still wary of letting on that Pim had assisted her flight from the island all those years ago. To Jazz' astonishment, Celine said Of course he was. He was a man and all men liked to be in control. Didn't he take Jazz away from her and raise her like a pet poodle? That stung, and Jazz again remembered Crystal calling her a wishy washy daddy's girl. Celine said that it was no wonder she did not have any more children.

She told Jazz that it was hurtful that she hadn't been in touch for so many years, but that she had actually admired her for having the backbone to take off rather than marry Jordan. She accepted the blame because at almost seventeen, Jazz was having her first family fight and did not know how to, which was an example of her father turning her into a pampered puppet. If she'd had a normal childhood, she would have understood that sometimes people said hurtful things when they were fighting, totally remote from anything they meant. She said she would never have actually considered marrying her off to Jordan. She just had the unfortunate habit of being nasty and making malicious threats when she was angry.

There was something else that Jazz did not know about, which might have contributed to their unusual family dynamics. She would never know, as the secret was held by only two people, one was dead and the other would never dare to tell her.

There was no question that Brett adored Jazz, but that did not completely account for his taking her along almost everywhere he went. Although he loved Celine dearly and was aware of the tendency she had just spoken of, to make malicious threats in anger, he couldn't always dismiss them. When, as a baby, Jazz' crying had kept them up, and Brett had been trying to soothe her, Celine had told him to throw her against the wall and that would shut her up. He did not believe she meant it but couldn't take the chance. He completely took over the care of the baby after that, and had carefully inserted himself between them in an effort to keep Jazz from getting on Celine's nerves. Celine, resentful that he had taken away her baby, and a little jealous of their close relationship, continued from time to time over the years, to make ludicrous and alarming threats.

She also did not mention, and never would, that to Brett's consternation, she had without consulting him, had a tubal ligation in that awful Dr. Haberlast's office. She hated the memory of how her even tempered Brett had reacted. He was livid! She, at first, had taken the attitude that it was her body and he had no right to tell her what to do. He had accused her of carrying on her father's campaign to eradicate the LaPierres. It was the only time she had ever seen him cry, and he had threatened to leave her and take Jazz and start a new family with someone less deleterious. She had learned humility then. She had begged and pleaded with him not to leave her, even threatened on her recently deceased father's grave, that she would murder anyone he became involved with.

He had indeed left her for a short time. He had moved into the little house Jazz now occupied, and had taken Jazz, then almost two years old. She had followed him and made a bed on the floor. Brett's character would not allow him to let his wife sleep on the floor. He offered her the bed and she thought he meant to share it with her. He'd slept on the sofa. When he awoke he almost stepped on her. She was sleeping on the floor next to the sofa. They went through that ritual for several nights. Wherever he slept, she would follow him. When he awoke, she would plead with him. One night he had not shown up. She thought he had followed through with his threat and found somebody else. She went home, dejected. He was there, playing with Jazz. He'd bought a daybed and installed it in their room, and made Celine work every wile she knew to get him to move back into their bed. That was a hard time for her, and she hated remembering it.

She told Jazz that Jordan was not a great man and never would be, although, to give him his due, not everything he had been accused of was accurate. She told Jazz that it was not true that the housekeeper's children were his. His wife had accused him of that to get out of the alimony claim. She knew Jordan could not have children but he was too conceited to want that to come out in public. She also told Jazz that had she not been such a twit, running off in the middle of the night, she would have found all this out the next day. There were things Jazz did not know about, but it was a long time ago and she didn't want to get into the details. She had been surprised when Jazz had stayed away so long. Given the circumstances, she had assumed Jazz would return when she was twenty-one and had prepared for her return, ready to kiss and make up. It was very hard when she had not shown.

Jazz talked about her business in Toronto, telling her mother that she planned to sell it and move back home. She was trying to lead up to telling her that she was in the process of breaking up Jason and his fiancé but her mother went straight to the point.

I expect you are hoping to reclaim Jason Coolidge. Is that fair, after you left him for so long?

Without getting into names, Jazz told her mother that she was afraid of being traced because she thought that what she had done could put people who had helped into jail.

'*You are a silly girl*' is all her mother said about that, but she asked how Jazz planned to get Jason back.

Jazz confided in her mother that she had already taken him back, so to speak, and that the ex-fiance was not taking it sitting down. She told of all that had happened since she had seen her last. Celine sat back and studied Jazz for awhile. *Damn Jasmine, she said, there's a tiger under that tame veneer. I hope you know this fight could get bitter.*

Fingers crossed, Jase has got it in hand, Jazz said. She went back to the telling of her plans for selling the business in Toronto and Celine said she wished she could see it. She thought that Jazz should offer her assistant a partnership, rather than selling outright, and that way she would have something to start with should she find that she needed to return to Toronto. Jazz thought that was an excellent idea, and confided that she and Jason were planning to go soon. She told her that her townhouse had two bedrooms and if Celine could handle being there with Jazz and Jason sleeping together in the other room, she was welcome to come along. She told her that they would likely leave in the next couple of days and if that was too short notice, she could come up in a week.

Jordan called round while they were talking. Celine didn't seem particularly pleased to see him, but she had never shown great emotion towards him in Jazz' presence. He claimed to have come by because he'd heard that Jazz was back. Jazz did not like the man and couldn't help herself asking sarcastically when she and he had become best friends. She got out of talking to him by asking if she could use Celine's phone to make some calls claiming that she did not think there was enough credit on her cell phone.

Jazz went into her old room to make the calls. She called Sandy and got her voice mail. She left her phone number but told her she was coming back in a couple of days, anyway, and would get in touch. She phoned her shop and spoke with her assistant, Brian. She threw out the ideas of purchase or partnership for him to consider and told him she would be back in a couple of days. She apologized for leaving him holding the bag and promised to make it up to him. She was getting excited. She couldn't wait to introduce Jason to the other side of her life. She couldn't wait to actually have him to herself for at least a week before her mother joined them.

When Jason came for her he seemed down. Jazz assumed his meeting with Yola had not gone well. She wondered if he was still up to their night out, but she didn't ask. She was thinking of a way to introduce the information that her mother would likely be joining them in Toronto.

When they arrived at her house Jason took a bag from the back of the vehicle. A few changes of clothes he said. He thought he would hang around to make sure she was safe. He told her that Yola had made an embarrassing scene. He had expected her to be upset but he wanted to keep it as civil and private as possible, but she had forced a nasty, public scene. He had changed the locks on his house and told her to come get anything she had there on Saturday at 1:30. His father would let her in and he was a busy man and would not wait for her. Anything still there when he got home he would donate to charity.

Why 1:30 Saturday, Jazz asked. Jason said he was just pissed off and he wanted her to understand that after that display the door was firmly closed and she could never again come and go as she liked. He hadn't even asked his father to do it. He would, though, because he would be in Toronto. However, he was fairly certain she wouldn't show up. She would never accept those constraints. She would rather let the stuff go.

Jason Coolidge. You have a mean streak after all, but speaking of Toronto …

Jazz related all that had happened in her day. He actually thought the partnership rather than sale idea was a good one, and he did not mind Celine being there with them, especially as they would have a week on their own. Jazz reminded him that she loved him dearly, as they got ready for their dinner date.

The evening was wonderful. Sandy had packed Jazz' case well. She wore a lovely red evening dress and looked and felt wonderful. Jason was pleased and proud, and he soon relaxed. He complimented her on how lovely she looked, and told her how happy he was to be together, how much he'd missed her and how much he loved her. They talked and ate and held hands and drank wine, and Jazz felt she was in a dream – a very, very good dream.

At the end of the evening, as they were walking to the car, Yola stepped out of the shadows and blocked their path. Jazz froze and Jason stepped in front of her, standing between the two women. Yola gave him a resounding slap and walked away to her car. Jason pulled Jazz close to him, took out his phone and made a couple of calls, one in which he asked someone to come and check out the car to see if she had done anything to it. Ian showed up shortly after and drove them home. Jazz' euphoria had evaporated. She was trembling. She was terrified.

Back at the house, Jason told Jazz how sorry he was that the mood had been spoilt. It was less than two days before they left and he was sure Yola would not follow them to Toronto. He promised he would stay close and protect her. Jason's phone rang at 2:30 a.m. The caller ID was blocked. He turned it off and Jazz prayed for the next day to pass quickly.

Celine phoned early next morning to warn Jazz to be careful. Yola called last night to tell her that Jason had broken off their engagement to be with Jazz. Celine had said that it was a personal matter between her and Jason so why was she calling. Yola had said she had hoped to get Jazz' phone number so she could ask her not to take Jason away, and Celine told her that as far as she knew Jazz would not need or have a phone and probably used Jason's phone if she needed to. Jazz prayed even harder to get through the day. Jason said he would take her down to Mont Yves to spend the day with his mother.

Jazz had always loved Pammy Coolidge. She was such a warm person. She greeted Jazz with a hug and said how happy she was to see her all grown up. Pammy was a little bit gossipy and she spent the day feeding Jazz tidbits of gossip and food. Yola had phoned her as well about Jason breaking the engagement and Pammy had told her she hoped Jason had been gentle. She had taught him to be kind and considerate. Jazz laughed at that, and Pammy told her not to feel too bad for Yola. She related some incidents when Yola had been downright rude to her and Pim and when she embarrassed Jason, getting drunk at some event. He had monitored her drinking since then whenever they were out. Whoever Jason married would be her daughter in law and she would treat them as such, she said, but she wasn't particularly heartbroken that it wasn't going to be Yola.

Pammy said they were welcome to spend the night to get away from the stress until it was time for their flight and Jazz said she would ask Jason.

Don't do that, Pammy advised. *Start as you mean to go on. Don't give him the right or the responsibility for every decision. Make up your own mind.*

There it was again. Everyone thought she was indecisive and dependent. She really needed to get over that. When Jason called, she told him of his mother's offer and he asked what she had said. She told him she had said she would find out what he thought. He said sure, fine, but he did not sound impressed. She wondered if he might find fighting with Yola more interesting than waiting for her to make a decision.

As the day started to fade into night, Jazz was not surprised to see Crystal's vehicle follow Jason's into the yard, but you could have knocked her over with a feather when she saw her mother on the passenger side of Jason's vehicle. Jason's face did not have that clench-toothed look he gets when someone says or does something he doesn't like, and Celine was smiling. Good Lord! A miracle! Jazz thought. Pim drove up shortly after. All we need is Daddy, Jazz thought.

Jason kissed her and said he thought that as it was her last night they should have a party. She smiled. The Coolidges thought everything deserved a party. He would be gone for 2 weeks and she was coming back as soon as her business was wound up, but hey, party on! She was thrilled her mother had thawed out and joined them. Jason would have to tell her how he'd managed that.

Pim was seeing to drinks for everyone, Jazz and Crystal were chattering, the kids were outside exploring, Jared and Jason were earnestly discussing some sports thing like it was of vital importance. Celine followed Pammy into the kitchen and they heard her say in a strange, high pitched voice.

'And Pamela Martin's rolls have turned out perfectly again. You could all take some pointers from Pamela'.

Jazz' jaw dropped. *'That's who Pamela Martin is! My God!'*

Jason had been watching her from the corner of his eyes and asked what was the matter. She said it was nothing. Pammy realized what it was and explained that she had told on Brett and Celine when they were dating in secret and of the dramatic outcome, which was why Celine had been chilly towards her ever since. She turned to Celine. *I was afraid Brett might make you pregnant. I didn't expect he would go for him with a gun, for goodness sake!* Celine waved it away.

You should have minded your own business, Pam. What? You thought Pim was sterile?

I didn't give him nuttin' more than a little kiss

So you were jealous! Celine retorted.

Everyone laughed. The cold war seemed to be over. Thank God.

When Celine announced that she was joining Jason and Jazz in Toronto, all eyes turned to them. Pammy looked concerned. She wanted to know if they had planned to get married in Toronto, but Jazz' response was resolute. They would be either married on a catamaran or have the reception on a catamaran near Daddy's stone. Daddy had to be a part of it. Nobody said anything.

Jason took her to his house the next day after they had said goodbye to his parents, and showed her around. He told her that he had been buying the lots around it. He now owned four lots. He had grown up in a large house with lots of land and felt claustrophobic in a little house in the city. In time he would build his dream house. It would be in the middle of at least five lots. He then took her to her little house to get her things. The rasta who had helped her when she was raging on the beach waved at them from across the street and said *Take care of her, Coolidge, she more dicty than the other one.*

In the car Jazz was indignant. *I'm dicty!*

Sure you are. Jason said. *He's saying you are different from Yola. She is fine but she's fiery and you are sensitive and well mannered. Dicty is another word for dainty.*

Jazz was not appeased. She was five foot ten and Yola was at most five foot five and small. How could she be the dainty one.

Chill Jazzie. It was a compliment. Dicty has more to do with aura than size. It's the thing that makes clerks serve a woman ahead of the four people ahead of her in line, or men open doors for her and seat her, run errands and generally do cartwheels for her. Your mother and you have it. Where are you from? You must have heard the term before. It's our colloquialism for elegant.

As she opened her mouth to continue her argument Jason explained that if Yola had been screaming on the beach, it wouldn't have been a concern. Even if she had gone into the water, he would have known she would swim out and come back. He wouldn't have done a thing unless he saw she was actually in trouble, with her, he called Crystal and watched out for her.

He called Crystal! How did he know I know Crystal?

Don't you recognize him Jazzie? That's Jakey Fletcher.

Jakey? My God! Turn around. She had known Jakey since they were toddlers, and she hadn't recognized him. *What happened to him?*

Jason turned the car around. *Nothing happened to him. Everybody gets to choose their own life. He's a rasta, not a drunk or dope addict. His earns enough to keep himself and then he relaxes. His needs are not great and he chose not to be part of the rat race.*

Jason pulled up the car just ahead of where they saw Jakey walking down the road and Jazz got out. She ran back towards him and hugged and thanked him. *Jakey, I'm sorry. I didn't recognize you, but as you see, I wasn't exactly at my best. Thanks for caring.* She hugged him again, and got back into the car. Jason drove off with a light toot of the horn to Jakey. Just a few more hours before their flight.

Yola did not show up at the airport, their flights had not been unaccountably cancelled, nothing unusual happened and their flight was on time. Once they were in the air Jazz commented on it to Jason and he told her that Yola had a short fuse but it spent itself quickly. She had probably had enough. He believed slapping him in front of her was her way of ending it. He told her that when he had spoken with her the first day she had given him a wicked left hook to the shoulder and tried to knee him in the groin but he had averted that. A jab in the stomach had doubled him up and she had driven away and left him there. That was how he came to drive by and arrive at her house while Yola was visiting.

My knight in shining armour! Jazz cooed and laughed. *I can't wait to show you Toronto.*

There is something I must tell you, Jason said. *I know Toronto like the back of my hand. I studied at U of T.*

Jazz was stunned. *I thought you went to England.*

Jason just said he had lost his place at the university that year. He did not mention that it was because she had gone missing that he had not gone with Gareth and Ian, as planned. In the intervening year he had applied and been accepted to U of T. He had no idea she was so close.

Why didn't you tell me this Jase?

I haven't told you anything, Jazzie. We haven't had the time, and besides, my head has been all over the place ever since I picked up the phone and you asked to talk to my father. Interestingly, I never answer my father's phone and I don't know why I did then. Jason's office was across the hall from his father's.

Do you mean you recognized my voice?

I thought I did. You have a rogue vocal chord that makes your voice unique, like two separate tracts a nanosecond out of sinc, so I said hello again and you said Jase, please let me talk to Pim. Honey, there are some people who call me Jay, but you are the only person in the world who called me Jase. Actually Crystal does sometimes, but only when you are around. I never noticed until you came back. She never called me that once while you were gone.

I didn't know that. Do you hate it when I call you Jase?

No. I love it. I always loved the way you said it, like it was sacred or something. Maybe I'm vain but I treasured it as something special between us.

I love you Jase, she said in a Greta Garbo voice and giggled. *So what happened then?*

I had a big row with my father. I went to mother to see if she was in on it too, we all rowed and then they went to see your mother. She gave them the key and they prepared the house for you. I went over to Crystal's and wept on her shoulder.

So Mommy knew I was coming? Nobody told me any of this. What's most amazing is that you got Mommy to come to the party last night. How did you do that.

I called her and told her we were all going down there, you were leaving tomorrow and I wanted her to come, I could pick her up at 4:30. She agreed. Maybe I reminded her of Brett, not offering her a choice. Jazz let the reference to her father's control pass.

I'm glad she and Pammy patched it up.

Yeah. Could you believe her! She and Brett were at it in school. If you had asked me I would have bet the other way around. I would have thought Pammy would be the one giving it up and Celine would be wearing the chastity belt, but she wasn't even put out. She said Pammy was jealous!

She didn't get into it, but she ran away from her father and moved in with Daddy when she was 16. My mother was ahead of her time! Maybe I took after her. I let you feel me up pretty good when I was only sixteen. Do you remember in the back at the movies you pulled off my panty so you could get to me and suddenly the lights came up and we had to evacuate because of a fire next door! There was no privacy to put it back on and you put it in your pocket. I could feel the air up my legs all the way home. By then I was so scared my dress would blow up, I ran inside and you took my panty home in your pocket. I still try to work out from time to time what you had in mind. There were fixed armrests between the seats, and maybe fifty people sitting in the theatre ahead of us. I think Daddy created the diversion to prevent you spoiling my reputation.

They both laughed at that, and Jason told her he had slept with it many nights after, and he kept it between his mattress and spring until Pammy found it. Jazz was appalled. What had Pammy said! Jason told her that he had found it neatly folded in his drawer with his own underwear, and she had said absolutely nothing. She would look at him strangely from time to time but she never said a word. He thought she was scared he was becoming a pervert. She didn't have to worry. She had washed out the magic.

Have I messed up your life too much, Jase?

It's been a tough week. I hated doing what I had to do. I don't like hurting people. She is a handful but really a good person once you get to know her. When I heard you were coming home, I tried to push it out of my mind but I knew what I had to do. It would be a lot better now than later, for no matter how hard I tried, and I would have tried, you and I would get together eventually. He chuckled to cover his embarrassment. *I guess had to finish what we started in the movies.*

Really though, Jazzie, this has still been the best week of my life so far, which is odd since I've been beaten up twice by a woman, spent more money on my vehicle in one day than I ever have, and have been humiliated in a nasty public scene. I'm happy you came back to me Jazzie. Jazz kissed him.

They were about an hour out of Toronto when Jason asked *What's this Paris like?*

Nosy, Jazz said

I'm not being nosy, I just want to know the competition.

No. Paris is nosy. It's his most noticeable characteristic. He asks a lot of questions. It can be annoying or embarrassing sometimes and he gets quite personal. Mostly he asks about money, people's personal finances. 'So your dear mother passed away, how much money did she leave you'. Two people have a spat and he starts calculating how much the divorce settlement will run to. He knows the allowance of every rich person. It could be a bit much.

Does he ask about your finances?

Sure. All the time, but I won't discuss it. He even tried to grill Brian. I got really angry with him when I told him how Daddy died. All he could come up with was "Wow, you guys must have got millions out of it". He didn't think it was an inappropriate comment, given the circumstances. It's just his way.

Why is he so interested in other people's money?

He hasn't any of his own, I guess, or hadn't. Apparently his new wife is loaded.

Sounds like a peach

Actually, outside his obsession with other people's finances, he is quite okay.

Quite okay. The love of your life is quite okay! You went screaming down the beach over quite okay!

Jase, Crystal already said that. I was not screaming so much for Paris as rage against all the things in my life that were shitty and unfair; loneliness, abandonment, lovelessness ….. Paris' taking advantage of me was just the last straw.

Okay, okay. You are fine now. I'm here. He hugged her. *There won't be any more of that. I love you and I will take thee Jasmine LaPierre …. We will take care of each other.*

Jase, I'm not crazy. Really. It's important to me that you understand that. I thought Mommy didn't love me. Do you know how enormous that is? We had a family of two. I am an only child. She had nobody else to love. You know the term 'a face only a mother could love'? Mothers love you unconditionally and forever. Mommy didn't take care of me after Daddy died, so I tried to take care of her and she wouldn't let me. We lived like two boarders in the same motel. When she threatened what she did, that just proved it as far as I was concerned, and I went into a desperate downward spiral. I've always adored her, by the way.

Jason loved Jazz' townhouse. He told her that he had shared a house with four other guys within walking distance of it. Of course, it hadn't been built yet when he left. She told him she had got it relatively cheap, considering, because the original owner had bought it pre built for his only son as a wedding gift. He had all the extras put in, but the son had gone somewhere in South America on his honeymoon and had been killed or committed suicide. The father didn't want to see the place again. He told Alistair and Alistair told her and they settled it in a private deal.

There were many messages on Jazz' voicemail when they arrived at her townhouse. There were two messages from Paris, one several days ago telling her he had to go out of town and would call. The second one was just last night. He was coming home. He'd missed her. Jazz wondered. Had he not recognized Sandy? She was sure he had met her. Did he not remember that Sandy and she knew each other or did he just assume that she hadn't told. His messages did not sound like 'I have some explaining to do' *or* 'this is not what it seems' messages. These were status quo messages. What a pig!

There was an excited message from Brian, her assistant. He hadn't slept since her enticing offer and he just couldn't possibly wait till Monday to see her, could he please, please come over tomorrow. Jazz called and left a message. *Sure Brian, come tomorrow. Bring food. For three.* She laughed. *He is such a drama queen*!

Brian was at her door by eleven o'clock on Sunday with enough food to feed a small nation. Brian was a mixed heritage person, born and raised in the Caribbean to Asian and Black parents, he had travelled for a year in Asia to find his other roots. According to him, he had already known everything there was to know about Caribbean cooking and since his Asian trip he knew everything there is to know about Asian cooking. Jazz didn't know about the everything part, but he certainly was a damn good cook.

Brian greeted her effusively. He was surprised when she introduced Jason as her fiancé but surprised her by keeping quiet. He said he was sure he knew Jason from somewhere but couldn't remember. They talked about how he had managed in her absence and Brian had some ideas for 'the partnership'. He couldn't afford to buy her out completely but he saw where they could expand to include antiques, particularly Asian, and home decorating, beyond her current stagings for house sales. She would require staff to expand that but she thought it a good idea and told Brian so. They played around with ideas and numbers for a while. She told Brian of her mother's imminent visit. She was sure Brian would just love her mother so much, he would want to adopt her. She also told him that she planned go home and be Jason's wife.

Since she had already met with Brian, Jazz did not go to the shop on Monday. She took the time off to get settled in, and reacquaint Jason with Toronto. They had reservations for dinner and Jason was in the shower and did not hear the doorbell. Jazz opened the door and Paris walked in with a pretty bunch of flowers. Jazz was rooted to the spot. She couldn't think of what to say now that the moment had come.

'Hi. Did you miss me?' Paris asked, not noticing anything amiss, and reaching to kiss her.

Jazz put her hand up to hold him off and called *'Jase'*. Jason was just stepping out of the shower when he heard her call. He did not know they had company, but put a towel around his waist and went out to her. Jason knew instinctively who the *fool with the flowers*, as he always thought of him afterwards, was.

Jazz was exultant! Jase in a towel, still damp from the shower just exuded testosterone and sensuousness. He should be on a calendar! The dumbass look on Paris' face begged to be preserved on film as well, she thought. Both men asked at the same time *'Who's this'*?

Jazz was ecstatic! She could barely hold it in. *This,* she said holding her hand out towards Jason, *is my fiancé, Jason. Jase, this is Paris. We used to be friends,* she added casually.

Hello, Jason said, nodding. *I guess I should get a robe. Are the flowers to congratulate us?'* he asked, as he walked away.

Your fiancé! Paris whispered fiercely. *I've only been gone a week. How did you get a fiancé in one week?*

Oh Jase? I've always had him, she answered, flippantly. Paris left, still looking dumbfounded, taking the flowers with him.

Cheapskate! Jazz thought. Bet he tries to get a refund, but she was jubilant!

Hallelujah! She wanted to scream again, this time with joy. She wanted to turn the stereo up to its loudest, to jump and dance and stamp her feet. She wanted to run up the stairs and slide down the banister, to break crockery in the fireplace! Why, oh why were there no cameras! Those few minutes made up for the last ten years of her life, by jingers! to borrow Alistair's phrase. She would never get a shot of that oafish, dumbfounded, drowned fish look on Paris' face, however it was stamped in her memory, but she would damn well get one of her darling Jase standing as he had been, wrapped in a towel, damp shoulders and all. She went to get her camera. She was exhilarated! There was only one way to calm her down.

They did not go out to dinner after all.

Jason was impressed when Jazz took him to her store on Tuesday. He had imagined a little corner shop with flowers in buckets and perhaps a few garden gnomes. She had said she sold flowers and knick knacks. The shop took up the ground floor of a small 3 storey building. It had tasteful displays of flower arrangements and houseplants and it extended outside where the outdoor plants and garden decorations were displayed, again tasteful and neat. In a section which was connected but somehow delineated as separate, was a display of a variety of party supplies.

She took him to the back where she had a small office and lunch room. There was also a consulting room with a small conference table, a chalkboard on one wall and a video display screen at the opposite end. Efficiency in use of space was evident. There was a small room into which was neatly stored an amazing amount of decorating stores, their shelves systematically coded. Jazz explained she got temporary help from an agency, as required. Jason had a hard time reconciling the person who set up and run this operation with the person who asked permission to come home, however, he was glad now that restoring her self confidence would be easier than he had expected.

When they went back out to the shop, Jason with his arm around her shoulder, Paris was there talking with Brian. He said a quick hello and beat a hasty retreat. Jazz refused to ask about him being there. She knew Brian couldn't keep it secret for long anyway.

Brian looked at Jason, patted his forehead and, open palm in the air, said '*Howard Carstairs*'.

What about him? Jason asked.

That's where I know you from. His wife is my cousin. I was at the wedding when the best man collapsed, drunk, and you caught the microphone and continued like it was choreographed.

Jason laughed. *They should have stopped drinking after the stag. They were drinking right up to the church. Howie wasn't all that sober himself. Where are they now?*

Brian said that last he'd heard they were in Atlanta. Jason explained to Jazz that Howie was one of his housemates in his university years. Jason offered to get some take out lunch for them and left.

You're dying to know what Paris and I were talking about, aren't you? Brian said to Jazz. He didn't necessarily want an answer, and launched into his narrative.

Brian said Paris had told him he had met a naked man in Jazz's place last night and that Jazz had pretended the guy was her fiancé. So far as Jazz knew, Brian was not aware of Paris' recent marriage, and she didn't tell him. Brian, prone to dramatization, had confirmed that Jason was, indeed her fiancé, he had told Paris that Jason and her had been engaged a long time ago and she had left because she wanted to earn her own money before marrying him because he was so wealthy. He had hired detectives to find her, and having found her, had turned up out of the blue. The reconciliation was something to watch. She was so happy, she was giving Brian the business. Jason was so wealthy, she didn't need the money, she just wanted to know she could earn her own. Brian said he knew how Paris liked money stories. Jazz laughed. Sonuvabitch was probably wondering why she hadn't given the business to him instead.

The telephone rang and Jazz picked it up. *The fiancé left, I see.* It was Paris.

Just for a while, Paris. What do you want?

I missed something. I want to know how I could have a loyal girlfriend one day and the next she has a naked fiancé in her house. Why did I not know anything about this, Jazz

Have you told me everything about you, Paris?

Is that what this is about, Paris is not very talkative so I'll teach him a lesson? How much do you really know about this man?

Paris, I'm marrying Jase. That's all I need to know. It's all you need to know.

I just have my girlfriend snatched from me and that's all I need to know, Jazz?

Get a grip, Paris! Jazz snapped. She'd be damned if she was going to let this snake know that she knew. *I have work to do. Goodbye.* She put the phone down.

Incredible! Damn shitface is putting this all on me! She hurled a package of preserver across the room.

'With due respect, Jazz', Brian said, 'anybody would feel a tiny bit upset if they found out they got ousted like that.'

Brian, Paris got married about ten days ago. I found out only because Sandy happened to see the wedding and had her cameraman film it. He hasn't mentioned it yet.

Oh. My. God. Is that what that was all about the other day? The beast. He will have me to deal with. I am going to fill him up with so many stories he will chew his own head off. If that's the case, though, Is Jason real?

She smiled. *Jase is real. The original, and your story wasn't all that farfetched. I did agree to marry him and then run away some time ago. He didn't find me though. I found him, and just in time. He was getting married to somebody else.*

Again. Oh. My. God. You have to tell me all. I'm going to bust. Jason walked in just then carrying their lunch.

Jazz did not get to spend a lot of time with Jason for the next few days as she had several projects that were more than Brian could handle on his own. Their nights together were precious though, and Jazz was loving the idea of living with Jason. She did not want to think he would be leaving shortly and besides with Celine coming on the weekend they would not have the pleasure of this time alone. They made the most of the intimacy and created their own little paradise.

Jason was in the shower when his cellphone rang. Jazz answered and instantly regretted it.

Who's this? Yola's voice came through loud and clear.

Who do you expect? I'll give you one guess, Jazz answered.

I expect Jason to answer his goddam phone when I call him.

He can't answer now, Yola. His mouth is busy. Bye Yola, you're disturbing us. She got a kick out of that. Jase would be shocked to know how much she enjoyed that. She heard the text alert go off and decided she had better tell him about the phone call. When Jason got out of the shower Jazz told him that Yola had called and that they had a rude exchange. She didn't go into the details but she had a struggle to keep from laughing.

The night before Celine was due to arrive, they were at home savouring their last night together alone. They were on the sofa, Jason sitting and Jazz lying, her head on his lap. She was telling Jason how wonderful it was that he was there with her, she had so much enjoyed the last two weeks. She told him that one thing had been worrying her was that she wasn't sure she knew how to cook. She had never had to. She had lived at the resort almost six years, no cooking, and on her own it wasn't viable. She had good meals when meeting with clients, on their tabs, and Brian loved cooking and brought her samples constantly. Jason informed her that he was a good cook and was quite capable of cooking for their little family. Jazz laughed and asked how little was their family and Jason told her he was thinking two kids. She could have twins if it would be easier for her, he wouldn't mind. She thanked him graciously for his consideration. He lifted her head and kissed her. *This is bliss*, she told him. Then his cellphone rang.

Jason answered. He listened then said

I'm sorry too, Yola

I know. If there was any other way that wouldn't hurt you I would have taken it. I didn't like hurting you either.

No. Yola. I'm so sorry. That is not an option. It's over. It has to be.

Jazz got up and went to her own phone to call Crystal. Bliss never lasts, she thought.

Brian insisted on coming with them to the airport to meet Celine. They decided to rent a large SUV. Jason said that if he knew anything about Celine, she wasn't travelling light so they needed something with room for the four of them plus all her luggage. Jazz jokingly suggested the company van. She could imagine Celine's face when they told her she had to ride in it. Jazz had a picture of her rushing off in her high heeled shoes trying to hail a taxi.

Jason was right. When Celine came out of Customs, elegant as ever, there was a man with her, pushing a cart laden with luggage that was so obviously not all his. She looked as pleased as the cat that swallowed the canary.

Who the hell is that with Mommy, Jazz asked, looking wide eyed at Jason. *He looks like Daddy!*

Well he can't be Brett but looks like she found a replacement. He whispered in her ear. *'She probly done give him some so don' say nuttin' fore she say you jealous too'.* Jazz laughed.

Even close up the man was almost a dead ringer for Brett, and Jazz tensed. Introductions were made all around. Mommy's friend was Jaime Bertrand, whom she had met while waiting for her plane in Miami. Mr. Bertrand lived in Toronto and told them that he would be happy to drive the delightful Celine, if their car wasn't big enough. Jazz looked over at Jason. He smirked. Celine was beaming. Hot damn! Jazz thought. She snagged one. Wait till I tell Crystal. She stared at Jason, willing him to say something.

Jason said they had got a large car especially for her but Bertrand was welcome to visit Celine once she settled in. He was sure she had given him the number. They loaded her stuff in the SUV and Celine ignored the back door Jason was holding open for her and stepped daintily round into the front seat. Jason smiled and Jazz climbed into the back with Brian.

Tell us about Mr. Bertrand, Mommy. Jazz demanded.

What's to tell, Jasmine? He is a man I met in the airport departure lounge and we travelled together.

Jasmine, Brian mouthed.

That's my actual name. Besides the church people, who called me Young Sister Jasmine when I was a kid, Mommy is the only person who ever calls me that, and she only started that since Daddy died. At first I had to look around to see who she was talking to but then I got used to it. She turned to her mother. *Is that all, Mommy? You are smiling like the Cheshire cat. You must have noticed how much he looks like Daddy. Is this going to be a hot romance?*

All Celine said was: *Jasmine dear, Just point out the sights.* The subject of Mr. Bertrand was shelved for the time being, but Jazz knew she was going to google him the minute they got home.

In the meantime, Jason wanted to know what she meant by church people calling her Sister Jasmine. They were Anglicans, and Anglican never did that. Jazz told them of the period when she was a child, if her parents were going out at night, they would get Mrs Greaux to babysit her. Mrs Greaux used to go to a 'side way' church, and would take her along. That's where she learned all the spiritual songs, and to play a mean tambourine. She got so much into it that one night she got up and gave what seemed to come over as a very moving testimony. They almost baptized her right there. Somebody told Brett about it, and he came home and told Celine. Brett thought it was funny and called her his little holy roller. Celine hit the roof!

Brett laughed and said it was time for a female televangelist and offered to let her make him walk again or heal whatever she wanted him to have. Celine fought with Mrs Greaux. Mrs Greaux said she had to go to church, she didn't have to babysit. Celine said she would stay home with her baby and never go anywhere again rather than have her turned into some religious freak. In the end, nothing changed, Mommy and Daddy went out, and Mrs Greaux took her to church, but she didn't give any more testimonies and when she got old enough to stay home alone, Daddy died and Mommy stopped going out.

Celine couldn't wait to see the shop the next morning and so Jazz took her in early enough to open up. She liked what she saw and spent a lot of time chatting with Brian, learning the ropes, according to her. They were getting on like a house on fire. In the afternoon, Jazz let her sit in on a meeting with a prospective client who was managing an upcoming convention. She introduced Celine as her partner, and Celine beamed. By the end of the day she was nattering like an excited magpie. She was enjoying 'the business world' and was quite prepared to become a part of it.

There was a message on the phone from Jaime Bertrand when they returned home that evening. He had left it in the morning, hoping to take her to lunch, or dinner. If that was not possible, he left his phone number.

This Bertrand is very keen, Mommy. What did you do to him? Are you going to call him back?

I have just been delightful. He told you that. Celine said matter-of-factly. *It would be in poor taste not to call back.*

Well if you want to go to dinner with him, we could postpone our dinner, or we could all go out together. Jase and I could be the chaperones, she laughed. Jason just smiled and raised his eyebrows.

Call from my cellphone. See if a woman answers. Both Celine and Jason stared at her.

What? Like it never happens? Jazz challenged. Nobody said a word. Celine held her hand out for the cellphone and called the number she had written down from the message. She chatted for a few seconds and then told him that Jason and Jasmine had arranged to take her to dinner but she thought it would be nice if he joined them. They wrote the name and address of the restaurant for her and she read it to him. They would meet him there.

It was a good dinner and Mr. Bertrand turned out to be quite nice. He said he was a widower. His wife had died of colon cancer two years before. He was on the Computer Sciences Faculty at Ryerson University. He resembled her father so much Jazz really wanted to ask about his origins but she wasn't sure how Celine would take it. She thought she would wait to see if Celine would bring the subject up. Maybe she didn't want him to know how closely he resembled her late husband.

After dinner, Bertrand wanted to drive Celine home and she accepted. Jazz fretted in the car with Jason. *Suppose he kidnaps her, she doesn't know her way around.*

I thought that was why you slipped her your cellphone. Jazzie, she's going to be fine. He's legit. I know you googled him when you took your phone to the bathroom. Let her have some fun. Brett has been gone for a while. She must need someone.

People always think every woman needs a man.

I hope you do, and I hope that man is me. I need you. But right now, I need you to relax.

Bertrand brought Celine home half an hour later and Jason invited him in for cocoa, despite Jazz' wild signals no. He came in and they chatted for a half hour or so. Jason could see that Jazz was uncomfortable. He wanted them to go to bed so these two people could be alone but she refused to recognize any hints.

Sweetie, he said. *What became of the nuts we bought yesterday. I couldn't find them in the kitchen.* She got up to look for them and he followed her into the kitchen, feeling quite pleased with the trick.

Honey, he turned her to face him. Forget the nuts. We have to go to bed and leave them to themselves. Jazzie. Don't stand in the way. Maybe she has found Brett again. Maybe not, but it's her decision. When Jazz opened her mouth to protest, he said *What's the risk, Jazzie. All she has to do is raise her voice and I'll be on it like white on rice. I would much prefer to be snuggled up with you than listen to stilted conversation. Besides, based on recent revelations, nobody can't stop yo mamma getting some if she want it.* He kissed her and Jazz laughed and agreed. They said goodnight and went to bed but Jazz did not sleep and could not relax until she heard Bertrand leave half an hour later. *Jason pulled her to him and said Now you can come gimme some.* He nuzzled her ear.

What if she went with him?

Then he will get some. Can you please, please come over here and give your man at least a hug. Shortly after they heard Celine go into her room. Jazz snuggled Jason.

Celine was up when Jason went into the kitchen next morning. Jazz was still asleep.

Jason. I'm glad it's you. Jasmine seems uncomfortable with me seeing Jaime. Do you know why? Jason made a gesture to say your guess is as good as mine.

People tend to favour particular features. The fact that he resembles her father means only that that's the type of physical appearance I like. I've been a widow for a long time and Jaime seems nice. I'm going to go out with him to see if he really is. Please try to get her past this. I don't want to quarrel with her over it. I'm meeting him this afternoon. I don't know what time I'll be back.

I'll take care of it, Jason said and they sat and had coffee together.

Jason joined Jazz in the bathroom. He hugged her from behind, put his chin on her shoulder and pressed his cheek to hers. *Baby, are you happy? Do I make you happy?*

Hmm. Course you do, Jase. You know that. She turned around and put her arms around his neck.

Do me a favour. Cut your mother a little slack. He kissed her, muting whatever she was going to say. *Really honey. She told me to ask you. She doesn't want you to fall out again and she seems to like this guy. Maybe he's a frog, but if he is, she will kiss him and walk away. You can't protect her from life. Trust me on this one. By the way, she has a theory that the reason she likes Brett's double is that people always go after other people with the same features. Can't say I agree with her on that though. I'd hate to think that I look like that troll that was in here the other day with the flowers.*

I don't look much like Yola either.

Hmm, but you and I look perfect together. Hmm. Hmm, hmm. Love you honey. He kissed her again and left. She smiled. *Silly man.*

When Jazz was ready to leave for the shop Celine told her that she planned to stay at the shop only in the morning because Jaime Bertrand was showing her around the city in the afternoon. He would pick her up at the shop.

Jazz' throat tightened. She counted silently to ten and then said: *How nice. What time are you coming back, I mean should we wait dinner for you or anything?*

Celine smiled. *I don't know, but don't wait dinner or anything. I will be fine, Jasmine. Maybe nothing will come of it, maybe something will. I wasn't looking for anything but this person whom I like came out of the blue. I'd think you would understand and be happy for me.*

I want to be happy for you Mommy, but you hear about so many things happening with strangers. Jazz told her mother what had brought about the bout of screaming on the beach.

Celine patted Jazz. *Treat it as just one road to bring you home. Sometimes they are rocky and hard, but if you have faith and stay the course, it will lead you home. I have to admit that the Coolidges are not too bad and Jason is a good man. I've been so mad at Pamela for so many years. We used to be best friends. All I could see was that she almost got Brett killed. Brett forgot it, but I just couldn't.*

Jazz was crying. *Thank you Mommy. Jason is a good man and I've always known it. I can't bear to think I almost lost him.*

Don't dwell on it darling. Use it as a reminder to appreciate and take care of what you have.

Jazz wiped her eyes. *I love you Mommy. Have a good time, but take the cell phone with you. Sorry. I seem to have trust issues.*

Celine spent a lot of her time with Bertrand so Jazz and Jason had lots of privacy, however, the night before Jason was to leave she decided to stay in with them. Brian and Celine had hit it off and he had practically adopted her, just as Jazz had predicted. He offered to cook a farewell dinner for the four of them. They ate and drank and bonded. Jazz teased her mother about her preoccupation with her new love and Celine told her that Jazz had been assuming, just as her father had, that she needed minding 24/7. She told them that firstly, she had no desire to rush into anything, and secondly, contrary to what everybody, including Jazz and Brett had thought, she was capable of taking care of herself. Then she told them of the nightmares she still had of the time she faced her own father down for Brett, but if she had to do it again, that is exactly what she would do.

A schoolmate had walked in on Brett and her and had blabbed. Her father was going to shoot Brett. When she realized that, she had dashed to his Rover, grabbed some wires in and pulled to disable it, and then ran the three quarter mile to Brett's house without stopping. She thought she had actually flown some of the time. She had dashed into the house and pleaded urgently with Brett not to come to the door or window, and when her father strode into the yard with his gun she went to the door and faced him down. She had told him he would have to shoot her first, and she meant it. At that moment, she said, he was lucky the LaPierres did not own a gun or she would have shot him down, father or not. She was sixteen and her father was a tyrant. On seeing him pointing a gun at her, her mother had collapsed with a stroke. Celine had refused to go back home or speak to him, and spent two weeks living with the LaPierres. Brett's parents let her share a room with his sister, who cheerfully exchanged beds with Brett once their parents were asleep. She laughingly admitted that Pammy was right, they had been going at it like rabbits. They had never been able to get enough of each other.

She didn't expect to find another Brett, but she had to live on, he had loved her and he would have wanted that.

She had never felt she could do enough to deserve Brett. Her own father's actions had caused Brett to lose his family yet, for her sake, Brett tolerated him and bought a little run down place and built it up, with the help of Jason's father and some other friends, into a nice little home so he could have a comfortable place to live out his life.

She said she wanted Jazz to really know her father. They had worked hard to build up his business. He had started an import/export business and it had thrived. One shipment had got mixed up and he got a load of garments. The company didn't want to pay for the return and pretty much told him to discard it. She told him to sell them himself and she put together pieces and made attractive combinations so instead of buying the one piece they wanted, people started buying the sets. The thing was, there wasn't much space for display, so she talked him into renting some space for the clothing, and now he had two businesses. She would go through the catalogues and magazines and tell him what to order and she would draw the model display he should put in the windows, and in the store.

The merchandise was selling fast and they kept ordering more, but the women's were selling faster than the men's. She convinced him that men did not like shopping with women so they let the women pick out their clothes. The women bought the men's things with what's left from their own shopping. With a separate men's store the men would go in and buy whatever she put there and pay whatever she asked to get out quickly. It wasn't easy to convince him because they could not really afford to rent another place yet but she coaxed him and it worked, and that is how he came to have two stores.

Jazz said, stunned. *"So, those magazines you were always thumbing through were for Daddy! I thought you didn't like business.*

Please, girl. You think your father stocked those stores on his own? For goodness sake, he was colour blind. I could never even let him out of the house in anything I didn't select or he would dress like a clown. He had no dress sense at all. I didn't get into the actual daily grind of the business because the cut and thrust was what Brett liked. I wouldn't take anything away from him.

I adored your father, Jasmine. He was the essence of my life, and when he died I wished I was in the car with him to hold him in our last moments. I can't imagine how he must have felt those last few seconds, and I don't know how I got through that bizarre funeral. He was whistling when he left that morning. He was in a really good mood and he murmured something to me on his way out, which I will not share. He has been murmuring it in my ears ever since. He was coming home to me, Jasmine. I had wine chilled, and Frances had given me a manicure and a pedicure and a massage. I had a hard time for the longest time trying to get my head around the fact that he wasn't coming back.

He was a great man that was given to me for a short time. I still mourn him, and not an hour has passed since he died that he has been absent from my mind. Nobody can replace him. Even if I spend time with someone else, I will never forget Brett. You don't have to worry. Be happy, and let me have a little happiness as well.

Jazz was in tears. She hugged her mother. *I love you Mommy.*

I love you too, darling but if you are committing yourself to Jason, turn to him. Right now, I'm going to call my friend Jaime Bertrand to see if he would take me to see a late movie or something. She said goodnight to them and went to her room. Brian left shortly after.

On their own, Jase hugged Jazz for a while. She was still a bit teary.

Wow! I can't imagine your mother standing in front of a gun for your father. I guess she knew it was all bluster.

It was real. I'll tell you the rest of the story sometime.

Well I hope you can love me like that.

I hope you can love me like he loved her.

I already do.

Me too.

He pulled her up from the sofa. *It's been a long time since I danced with my lady.*

When Celine came out of her room to answer the door the radio was playing and Jazz and Jase were wrapped in each other's arms swaying to, of all things, Under the Boardwalk.

I'm going to hate to leave you tomorrow, Jazzie. This has been the most incredible three weeks of my life. I love you. Come home soon.

I'm going to miss you too. It's probably going to take a couple of months to get things straight here, Jase and I don't know how I'm going to stand being without you now. Maybe Mommy will want to stay with Mr. Bertrand and in that case she could run the shop. She has taken to it like a duck to water. Then I could come home to you. Thing is, she won't make up her mind yet. She wants to go to Germany.

Joan Liburd

Germany. Why Germany

She thinks her brother might be there. Long story.

Well, thank God for modern day communications. He drew her closer to him.

Jase, am I going to be able to hold on to you? You won't go back to Yola when I'm not there?

Jazzie, hear this. I'm a one woman man. That woman is you. Yola was my Jaime Bertrand. Not bad, but not you. I'm sorry about that on so many levels but I won't go back. I want you to have faith in me. You can leave everything up to the lawyers and come back with me tomorrow but, as much as I want you with me, I would like to know that you trust me.

I do. I won't bring it up again. I have something for you. Jazz brought out a sketch she had done of him wrapped in a towel the way he was when he met Paris. There were beads of water on his shoulders and he was playing a saxophone. Jason laughed. It was pretty good.

What time did you have to do this?

She told him she could do them pretty quickly and joked that if things fell through she could set up a stand on a street corner or a park. She had put extra time into this one though. Every time she had a spare moment, while Brian and Mommy were yakking, she would work on it.

So this is to remind me to cover up the goods, he joked.

Jazz' heart was pumping wildly in her chest. *Jase, I will try to be with you as soon as I can. Please be careful down there. Drive carefully and* all that.

I'm guessing this is not the time to tell you about the hawg.

Hawg! What's a hawg?

Jazzie, you do remember that I liked motorcycles. I like them even more now and I have two big, powerful Harleys. Just so you know. I'm a good rider and it's okay.

Jazz was wide-eyed.

It's okay Jazzie. We wear helmets. Even my father comes out sometimes. I'll take you for a ride when you come home.

Thanks, Jase, but no thanks. Do I want to know if you've ever fallen off?

Jazzie, I used to ride all the highways of Ontario. I can take on a few curly little streets at home.

You didn't answer the question so I guess I won't want to hear the answer. Please don't get hurt.

Too soon it was morning and time for Jason to go. Jazz' eyes kept tearing up. It was just the two of them going to the airport and she decided they would take a taxi. She was in no shape to drive. At the airport, after he had checked in, he stayed with her till the last possible minute and as she walked with him to the checkpoint, Jazz' heart and feet were heavy. Jason was trying to keep conversation light to cheer her but it wasn't working. He kissed her goodbye and walked through the security check, he turned, blew her a kiss and walked away and a tear coursed down Jazz' cheek. Standing there, alone in a crowd, she felt like all the air had been let out of her party balloons. Bye Jase. See you soon.

Joan Liburd

Celine announced that since Jazz had survived a whole week après Jason, she would make reservations for her trip to Germany. She expected to be back in two weeks.

Good luck, Mommy. Tell Uncle Aaron that he should come back home at least for a visit. I would love to get to know him. He could give me away in place of Daddy. I hadn't thought of who would give me away.

I had assumed that I would, Jasmine.

You would? I'd love that. I just thought you would want to be traditional.

And wear those horrible pastel mother of the bride dresses! Do you know me at all, Jasmine?

Celine left for Germany ten days after Jason's departure. Jazz was surprised at how bereft she felt. She had lived on her own for several years and had shared her home first with Jason and then her mother for a total of three weeks, yet now they were both gone the house seemed huge and empty. She hoped she wouldn't have to live alone for much longer.

Celine texted her on arrival, and when she phoned two nights later, Jazz was excited, but Celine's voice sounded flat.

How did it go? Jazz asked, picturing a dramatic reunion.

I was writing to the wrong person, Jazz. It wasn't him.

All that time! How could that be?

Apparently he enjoyed hearing from us, but he seems to be only semi-literate.

Are you sure it's not him Mommy? Maybe he just looks different. You were very young.

I said he is semi literate, Jasmine. Try to at least pretend that you think my head has more than cotton wool in it. Besides, this man is ten to fifteen years older than my brother, and nature might change a lot about you, but never your race. This is not my brother. I'm going to England. Maybe I'll find something there.

Celine had been in England for more than a week when the phone rang at 5:30 on Sunday morning, jarring Jazz awake.

Jasmine, do you know where Helmsman Avenue is in Toronto?

No, but I could look it up. Why?

Maybe Aaron is in Toronto. He may have taken mother's maiden name and is now known as Aaron Allen. She gave Jazz the address and asked her to call her back.

Jazz got out of bed and looked the street up. It was within walking distance. God, Mommy, what's this. She decided she would check it out later and went back to bed.

Jazz always went for a morning run on Saturdays and Sundays. Today she decided, since it was fairly close, she would check out the address on her run. When she got there, she found she could not just run past. She knocked. The man who answered was her uncle. She knew it. He looks like Mommy, Jazz thought. It's got to be him.

Are you Aaron Allen?

Yes

Were you ever known as Aaron McLean

Why?

I think you are my uncle.

Come again?

Jazz told him about her mother writing to the wrong man and going to England and finding him as a possibility.

You are Celine's daughter?

I did not say my mother's name is Celine

Tell her to come home. I'm right here. Welcome niece, and he hugged her.

Jazz pulled out her phone and called her mother. *I'm at Uncle Aaron's house Mommy. Come home.* Aaron chatted with his little sister for awhile, then returned the phone to Jazz. *She's catching the next available flight. There is a lot of catching up to do. I'll arrange for your cousins to be here.* He gave her his numbers so Celine could get in touch, and he would arrange the reunion.

Thank you Uncle Aaron. Jazz hugged him and left. She couldn't wait to tell Jason.

Celine came back the next morning. She had not called to say when she was arriving. She'd taken a taxi from the airport and stepped out of the cab just as Jazz was leaving for the shop.

I will just put my things in the foyer and come along with you. They walked together the few blocks to the shop and Jazz gave her the details of the meeting, starting with the moment she left home. Jazz remarked to Celine that she was as nervous as a new bride.

Celine phoned Aaron's cell as soon as she arrived at the shop and he promised to come over to meet and take her to lunch. Jazz was expecting a client and went to make preparations. It was her second meeting with the man. Celine had sat in on the first meeting, as her partner. Their business concluded, Jazz escorted her client out, where they saw Celine and Aaron in earnest conversation.

Dad! What are you doing here?

Jazz stopped to make sure she had heard what she thought she had heard. *Uncle Aaron is your dad?*

***Uncle** Aaron!* He Looked puzzled.

Let's go over. It's a long story. God. She couldn't wait to tell Jase.

Aaron arranged for his family to meet on the weekend. He had three sons and two daughters from two marriages, several grandchildren, and he was currently between wives. It was something to look forward to. Imagine that! She had relatives. She couldn't wait to meet them all. She wished Jase could have been here to go with her. For the rest of the week Celine chatted or visited with her brother frequently. She seemed to be forgetting Jaime Bertrand. He had phoned several times, but their conversations were short. Jazz wondered if she was just excited about having found her long lost brother or had she got tired of Jaime, but she didn't dare bring it up. If Jase was still here she would have got him to do it.

There were so many things she wanted to discuss with Celine but she never seemed to be available. She wanted to discuss the German Aaron. At least Celine had found the time to tell her that Uncle Aaron had lived in Germany, not far from the German Aaron but left for Canada many years before. He told Celine he had written to their mother for a couple of years and had sent toys for her but his letters were not answered. He had tried calling once and their father would not allow him talk to their mother, and had hung up on him. Aaron hadn't called back again. It was expensive. He hadn't actually changed his name. He found out when he tried to get his birth certificate to obtain a passport, that he had been born prior to their parents' marriage and in those days the fathers of illegitimate children did not appear on the certificates. According to his birth certificate, he had no father and that was alright with him.

On Saturday Jazz was surprised to find that Jaime Bertrand was coming to the family gathering with them. She thought that was significant and called Jason. She got his voicemail. She texted him: Big day. Bertrand invited. Mean something? He responded: Chill Jazzie. Luv u. He was no use at all. She wished he was here. She was actually apprehensive. With Bertrand there she was the odd one out.

The party was a great success. A new auntie and cousin was a big surprise that everyone seemed to appreciate, and as the time passed Jazz began to feel comfortable, and a part of something. So this is what it feels like to have a family. Mark, the oldest it turned out, regaled everyone with the story of how he had done business without knowing the women he had been meeting with were his aunt and cousin. He told them that when he had seen Aaron chatting with the elegant assistant from the decorating firm, he had thought she might be a new girlfriend, even though she resembled Veronica a bit. She did. Celine could pass for Veronica's older sister.

At the end of the day, email addresses and phone numbers exchanged, promises to keep in touch made, and lots of hugs and kisses left Jazz feeling both happy and sad at the same time. Celine went off with Bertrand and she went home alone. God, she missed Jason. She started to phone him, thought maybe she was being too clingy and phoned Crystal instead.

She told Crystal how much she missed Jason and that she might chuck everything and come home. Crystal didn't think it was a good idea and Jazz became alarmed. Crystal said Jason was on top of things but Yola was still on the rampage. If she was there he would be more tense and worried for her. Crystal thought that, even if she got her affairs together before, she should wait until after the cancelled wedding date. Once it is past Yola should calm down. Jason had been getting calls from people involved with the wedding, the caterers, the church, everybody, because the news was out that it was off but Yola had not cancelled anything. Jase was feeling pretty bad but he was resolute.

Crystal sensing her friends anxiety, told her to be patient with Jason. He was solid. He had said, in the presence of Crystal and her mother and his own mother, that when he walked into the little house and saw Jazz, he had seen himself with her in the delivery room, birthdays, graduations and celebrating their anniversaries, and he had seen his parents. He said before then, his wedding was mainly a party starting with the stag, before the sacrifice of having to live with a woman. He was really sorry for what he had had to do, but he had to do it.

One thing, she joked, the stress hadn't affected his football game. She had watched a game earlier and he had played like the devil was behind him. She said Jazz was not to worry, Jason had things in hand and a lot of people were watching his back.

Jazz was not quite reassured. She wished her mother would come home. It was getting late and she was so alone. She would call Jason after all. When he answered she said: *Talk to me honey. I can't sleep.* He talked to her for about an hour. Jason's normal voice was a smooth baritone, even when he wasn't trying to sound sexy, and he was trying now. *I miss you Jase. Goodnight.*

I miss you too, Baby.

When Jazz got up in the morning the house was silent and she and went to look. Celine wasn't there. She hadn't come home. Jazz knew that she shouldn't be, but she was worried. She tried to come up with an innocuous excuse for phoning but couldn't. After an hour with no word, she phoned Bertrand's number and Celine answered.

Hi Mommy

What do you want Jasmine?

I want to be nice, Mommy. I'm going out and it hit me that you might come home and not be able to get in. I just want to be sure you have a key.

You know I have a key Jasmine. What are you, twenty six going on twelve.

Well pardon moi, maman. I promise to try to never again show the slightest hint of caring.

Getting lonelier by the minute, Jazz took out her sketch book and drew a mean caricature of Celine and Jaime. She tore it up and put it at the bottom of the recycling and drew a sketch of them sitting together on a sofa with a scowling Brett hovering like a cloud. She tore that one up as well and prowled the house for something to do. Loneliness was going to kill her. She wondered if it was too soon to call one of her cousins. She tried Sandy. She had not been able to reach her since her return. She was not available now, either.

Jazz texted Jason. 'I'm lonely. Wish you were here'. He texted back:' Turn on your computer'. She did, and he chatted with her on a video call for an hour. God, she loved that man.

When Jazz left for the shop on Monday morning Celine had not yet returned. Jazz was a tight ball of mixed feelings. She wondered if Brett minded. Celine had, after all, been alone for twelve years. He probably understood, and she would try to. She thought of how Brett always put his arm around Celine, touching lightly her shoulders, her back, her waist, like he was steering her, or saying she's mine. Marking territory. It couldn't be easy to watch her from wherever he was, going off now with someone else. It would break her darling Daddy's heart.

She thought of some of the things Pammy had told her at breakfast the day before she and Jason left. Jazz was surprised to hear that Pammy and Mommy had been as close as she and Crystal until her grandfather went for Brett with a gun. She had not meant any harm to her friend, but Celine's and Brett's intensity was peculiar, indefinable, but the closest she could come to describing it was that they gave off sparks, not literally but there seemed to be some mystical attraction like they were caught in some kind of vortex, that made everyone but them uncomfortable. There were two Celines, she said, before and after Brett. The before was extrovert and fun.

Apparently Celine had been a star netballer but after Brett she could not hold onto a ball unless he was watching. She was dazzling if he was there, but a liability to the team if he wasn't. She was so protective of him, Pammy joked, if a mosquito dared land on him, she would smash it, bring it back alive, and repeat three times. Brett got detention once, according to Pammy, and couldn't meet her and Celine tore the side mirror off the teacher's car. Pammy thought it was dangerous. She regretted it ever after. Celine had cut her out like cancer, and she and Brett grew more intense over the years, but since they seemed happy, everyone stopped worrying.

Pammy said that they had been caught in their little whirlwind to the end and that even when they socialized with other people they had an air of being their own group so that even if Brett was at one end of a room and Celine at another, the people in between always felt in the way like they had inadvertently walked between a photographer and his subject. She said that when they were together, Brett's hand was always touching her. If he brought her a drink, he would give it to her with one hand and touch her with the other. Jazz recognized this. She had noticed this without actually realizing it. It was just part of her life she took for granted, but she now recalled that in all of her sketches of them together, Brett's hands had always been touching Celine.

It was odd how, in the last few weeks she had heard more people's opinion of her family than the entire rest of her life, and they were all, including her, a little right but mostly wrong. Brett was not controlling and Celine was not weak. They adjusted their needs to suit each other. He did not control them, he was in control of his life. He compartmentalized his life, his friends on weekends and, even at home, he shared time with his wife and daughter, then he gave her his undivided attention and that out of the way, he and his wife went into their world, which happened to be their bedroom, and focused entirely on each other. Everybody felt they got what they wanted from him. Her father was not a control freak. He was a genius. She loved him so much and wished he was still with them.

She didn't like Mr. Bertrand at all, but she would keep that to herself. Mommy had insinuated she was childish. Maybe she was. Celine was still young. She was still in her forties, upper forties, but that was fairly young by today's standards. She had never thought of her parents as young before, but now she realized they were. Jazz resolved to try to hide her feelings about Mr. Bertrand, because she loved Celine so much. She would start by using his first name.

It was a fairly quiet day at the shop, and Jazz was enjoying a coffee and sketching Brian when Celine wafted in. Jazz looked at her. She was so much more relaxed and beautiful than Jazz had seen her since Brett's death. She was obviously really happy. Jazz wondered whether it was finding Uncle Aaron and a family, finding Jaime, being involved in the business, or all of the above.

Can we have a bit of a talk, Mommy?

If it is about my personal life, no.

Everything does not revolve around your personal life, Mommy. I want to go home to Jase and I thought you might have some thoughts about how to deal with the shop.

Sure. Don't sell it. Don't go home until Jason tells you to.

I should wait for his permission!

At this time yes. Jason is trying to do a decent thing. Don't go down there to gloat and make things worse for that hapless woman. She doesn't get high marks for dignified handling of the situation but you should consider this is the second man to give her the shaft. Poor thing.

Poor thing broke into my house, Mommy.

Nothing happened. Don't dwell on it. Having said that, yes, you should have things in order before you go.

They discussed the options. Celine thought she should keep at least 60% interest, and let Brian have 25%. The remaining 15% she should allow to someone she trusted. Celine told Jazz that she couldn't commit herself as she was not sure of her own plans. Jaime wanted her to stay with him and she might, at least for a while, she was considering it and if she decided to, she would be pleased to do it. Communications being what they are, Jazz could oversee the business from anyplace she wanted to be, but if for some reason she wanted to return, she would have something to return to. They should go see the lawyers pretty soon. Jazz called and was able to get a late appointment the next evening.

Celine spent most of the time with Jaime now. Jazz spent most of her spare time alone. She spoke to Crystal and Jason nightly, and she wanted to go home to Jason. Would he ever ask her to come home? It occurred to her that Jason had not said she should stay till after his almost wedding date. He had said nothing on the subject. She had told him she was staying to tie up her business. She resolved that once she had spoken with the lawyers, she would ask him if that was what he wanted.

Jazz had just returned home from her appointment with the lawyer, with dinner in a bag. She was just about to sit down to Styrofoam dinner when the phone rang. It was her cousin Bonni, Uncle Aaron's youngest daughter. Bonni was very sweet. She was calling just to say hello and maybe invite Jazz out for a drink some time. They were approximately the same age, and she thought it might be nice to be friends. Jazz told her she was about to have a boxed dinner and invited her over.

Bonni had been fascinated by the idea of discovering such close family so late in life. She apologized, but Aaron had not spoken about having a family. Jazz opened a bottle of wine and told her the story as she knew it. Bonni told her that Jeff's and her mother had deserted them when she was eight. Aaron had said she was a gypsy. She had found domestic life way too mundane, and having to deal with her own two kids as well as Mark, Veronica and Giles from Aaron's first marriage too much. She had left to deal with an alleged family emergency back home in Egypt and never returned. She had written lovely, hopeful letters but somehow, could not make it back. Bonni had asked to go visit, but her mother always made an excuse so she had given up.

Uncle Aaron had had a series of girlfriends but his large brood usually scared them off. Now they had all gone their separate ways, he still lived in the large house alone, the occasional girlfriend in and out of his life. The siblings were close and they all descended on him from time to time, and Christmas was always, always spent at 'home'. Everybody came on Christmas Eve and stayed till Boxing Day. She was the only single one and whenever she fell out with whoever her current life partner happened to be, she moved back home with him.

Bonni was a riot and they drank wine and chatted away. Jazz introduced Jason via a video call, then they drank some more wine and chatted well into the night and Jazz asked her to stay over. Bonni stayed for the rest of the week and Jazz learned much more of the family she never knew she had, including the fact that Bonni was short for Ebonique, a name Jazz adored, and that Jeff's name was actually Jafari. She resolved to name Jason's two children after them.

After she left, the oppression of loneliness which Bonni's constant and cheerful chatter had banished, returned. Celine had almost completely deserted her. Very few of her things were still at the townhouse. It occurred to Jazz that she felt so low so soon after she was on her own that maybe she really was being hard on Celine. She had stayed alone for a long, long time. She phoned Jason and woke him up.

Honey. You should be waking me up in person

Jase, can I come home then?

Jazzie, this is not Coolidge Island. Why do you keep asking the Coolidge men permission to come home?

But you wanted me to wait till after your cancelled wedding date.

Why Sweetheart? A man and his wife should be together

A man and his wife

In my mind you have been my wife ever since I bedded you the day after you came home.

She laughed. Bedded me! My swain.

Would you prefer bonked, Jason laughed

I did my full share of bonking, mister. You had better stop talking dirty to me. You are starting something you are too far away to finish.

Hmm. Come home honey.

Jazz phoned her mother. She didn't care a damn if she was waking her up or disturbing Jaime. She was happy and they were going to know it. She was going home, home to Jase.

Celine was no more thrilled Jazz had called so early than Jazz expected her to be, but Jazz was excited and didn't care. She told her mother she was going home to Jase on the coming weekend and asked her to come for lunch, along with Jaime, of course. Celine and Jaime were committed to a brunch but would drop in for a drink afterward. Jazz would have to make do with that.

When they arrived, Jazz felt guilty about disliking Jaime. He must be good for her mother because she looked positively radiant and very stylish. Jaime looked proud as punch. Show off! He had taken Celine to a faculty brunch and she had been dazzling. He didn't look too badly himself. She had already managed to get some weight off him. He looked even more than ever like Brett, and Jazz remembered driving home with Brett and sharing their secret of her overindulgence because Celine wouldn't approve. It was obvious Celine had Jaime's meals under control like she had theirs. They seemed to be good for each other and yet she resented him. That was her father's wife he was fooling with.

Celine followed Jazz into the kitchen to help prepare the drinks. She asked Jazz to try to relax around Jaime. He was an intelligent man and couldn't miss the way she looked at him. He was not a reincarnation of Brett, there was a superficial resemblance and she didn't want him to know of the resemblance to her late husband.

But Mommy, he has to find out sometime. When he does it will just wipe out his manhood and anything he feels for you and replace it with disappointment and disdain, and much, much more.

I know Jasmine. He is a completely different personality but I have to admit that I like the secret, and I enjoy looking at him. God what a mess, but I'll take care of it.

Jazz asked her mother about her plans for Jaime. She wanted to know whether she should sell the townhouse, for one, or whether, if Celine was going to stay around, and would like to live in it. Celine asked how long she could allow things to hang before she ran into financial difficulty, as she did not have an immediate answer, but didn't like the idea of selling.

They brought the drinks out and were chatting about the brunch they had been to when Celine suddenly told Jaime that she thought Jazz might have something to say to him. Poor Jazz almost swallowed her glass. Celine prompted 'it's about her father'. Jazz glared at her mother and said well she thought Jaime resembled Daddy but Mommy didn't think the resemblance was significant.

Celine lowered her eyes. 'Good girl', the gesture said. She told Jaime that outside a passing resemblance to Brett, there were no similarities between the two men. She cared for the entire Jaime, not just the packaging, as she had told Jasmine. However, since it was bothering Jasmine that much, she thought she would tell him and help get her over it. Jasmine and her father had been very close. 'Goddam! Jazz thought, wait till Jase hears this!' Add acting to Mommy's talents.

Poor indulgent Jaime actually patted Celine's hand, then asked whether Jazz had a picture of her father. She could hardly say no since her mother had just told him how close they were. Casting a glance at Celine, she got up to fetch her Daddy. When she got back, Jaime put on his glasses and pulled out his driver's licence. The look on his face would give the impression that he must have swallowed his tongue. Daddy was younger when the picture was taken, but they could be brothers, so he turned to Celine and asked *'you think it's a passing resemblance?'* And Celine crossed her legs, raised her eyebrows and with a questioning look said *'Yes',* and changed the subject.

She told Jaime that Jasmine had been wondering if they would want to come down for her wedding, and there was so much to do with settling the business and everything, she did not know what was the matter with the girl, other than antsy pants, of course, but it was her life and a mother had to know when to let go, blah, blah, blah. Jazz was nothing if not stunned. She couldn't wait for them to get out of her house so she could call Jason. He had to hear this.

The next morning Celine wafted into the shop as cool and crisp as on any other day. Jazz asked her into the office and demanded to know the outcome of the little skit the night before. Everything was fine. She had unruffled him. That hurdle had been cleared. Jazz found the term odd and asked hurdle in the path to what, but Celine had never told anyone anything unless she chose to, and she didn't choose to now.

Jazz phoned the lawyer to inquire whether she had to be present in the country to close the deal. He said there were some papers that would need her original signature but they could be FedExed. It would just add to the costs. She told him of her plans, and he said she would need to have a lawyer down there look at them and witness her signature. No problem, Jase's closer-than-brothers cousins, Gareth and Ian, were both lawyers. Gareth specialized in corporate law.

The next day she was in the office with Celine going over their plans when Paris came into the shop. He told Brian that he was sure that Jazz had planted the 'Chippendale boy' to make him jealous. He was sure she would come to her senses in time. He wanted to talk to her. Celine came out of the office just about that time and rascally Brian introduced them, adding sweetly that Paris was Jazz' date before Jason came along.

Celine turned to Paris. *Oh. You are the young man who came back from your honeymoon with flowers for my daughter?* She picked up a cardboard cylinder and bopped him over the head and kept walking. Paris' shock was amusing to witness and Brian, like a mischievous imp, feigning shock and disbelief, one hand on heart, the other over his wide open mouth. *Married! Paris. My God.*

Paris left, threatening to sue, and Celine, in typical Celine style, waved dismissively as if this was something boring she had already forgotten, said *ok. We'll subpoena your wife as a witness.*

Brian, laughing hysterically, called Jazz out on the intercom to tell her.

Mommy hit Paris! Mommy, you hit Paris?

Obviously not hard enough. He is going to sue.

Celine didn't seem to be even a little bit perturbed, and Jazz almost collapsed, laughing. She went to the office and messaged Crystal. 'You won't believe this. Mommy just hit Paris over the head with a cardboard cylinder.' Crystal winked the laughing woman, which gave Jazz an idea. She checked to see if Paris was signed in to Messenger. He was. She sent the laughing lady. Sunuvabitch had been dealt with. Don't mess with the LaPierre women. She wondered if she should tell Jason about it tonight, and decided against it.

Jazz turned into the Mews where her townhouse was, dreading another night on her own but thankful she would soon be with Jason. Bonni was sitting on her steps. She had heard Jazz was deserting her so she came to say goodbye, please take me with you. Jazz laughed. Bonni was always such amusing company. She might miss her now and then.

When they were inside and she asked how Bonni had known, and she said that Celine and Aaron chatted all the time and that's how the grapevine started. She would really love to see where her father started from and was serious. She would come along, if it was okay. Of course it was okay. They chatted about the little house and how Jazz planned to decorate it. Jazz told her she had imagined living there and being Jase's mistress if he hadn't broken his engagement. They laughed about that and Bonni said she would be happy to live there.

Her second reason for being there, Bonni told Jazz, was to invite her out the following night. Aaron's treat. Celine and Jaime were also invited, and maybe some of the others. Jazz gratefully accepted. The busier her nights were the less time she had to be anxious or lonely. She videocalled Crystal and introduced her cousin.

Dinner on Uncle Aaron was lovely. Jazz was really liking being part of a larger family. Veronica came with her partner Nigel, Giles, and of course Bonni. Mark was out of town and Jafari hadn't been in touch lately. They were sure he was fine. Jazz wished she could become friends with Veronica. She was so much like Celine. Jazz told them she hoped they would all come down to her wedding, date to be announced. Jase had lots of cousins, aunts and uncles and she had only Celine. It would be so nice to have family.

Jason called just as she walked in after the dinner to hear how it went. He told her that she looked very nice. He was counting the hours. God what a man, she thought. She loved him so.

Celine invited her and Brian over to Jaime's and as Bonni was staying
over with her she went along. Dinner was lovely, and light, Celine style.
She appeared to be genuinely sorry to see Jazz go, and ordered her to
call every day, 'of course not at ungodly hours, Jasmine.' Jazz kissed
her, told her she loved her very, very much, and she was holding her
to her offer to give her away. Celine just smiled. Jazz whispered that it
was okay if she wanted to marry Jaime, she would even give her away.
Celine smiled again, but did not comment. Just a few more hours to
Jase. She was never going to be able to sleep tonight. Thank God Bonni
would be there.

Bonni was tired when they got in, however, and went straight to bed.
Jazz phoned Jason and informed him that it was okay for him to make
her hot because he could cool her down tomorrow. He laughed. He
sounded nervous, and she asked if anything was wrong.

What could be wrong? My baby is coming home tomorrow. She told him
he sounded nervous.

*Of course I'm nervous. My baby is coming home tomorrow. When do you
want to perform the formalities? Will you take my name?*

She hadn't thought about it before but, if he asked, it must be important
to him. She said *Yes darling, I will,* and silently, she said *Sorry Daddy.*

The alarms went off for them to get up and ready themselves for the airport. Jazz was surprised at what a basket case Bonni was. It turned out that this was her first ever plane trip, and her first time out of the country. She had never even crossed the border to the U.S. in a car. Jazz assured her it would be okay. It was only a four and a half hour flight and good practice for when she went to Egypt, which she though was at least 24 hours.

Everything went well. The flight was smooth, the weather good, and Bonni relaxed. Pretty soon they were touching down at Golden Rock. Jazz tried to see the faces in the terminal waiting room as they walked across the tarmac, but she couldn't find Jason. She was sure he was there but they were at the Customs building before she could find him. Her heart was racing and thumping so loudly, she was sure everyone could hear it. The line was not exceptionally long, but it was exceptionally slow. Damn! She needed to see her man right now! Why wouldn't they hurry?

When they eventually came to the front of the line, Jazz was sure the officer would ask what the loud banging was and if she told him it was her heart, he would hold her up even longer. She wished she had some water.

Finally, officially welcomed and passports stamped, they headed down the stairs to collect their bags. More waiting. In all that time waiting in line, the bags had not been unloaded. They were coming onto the carousel in dribs and drabs. She wondered if she could leave and come back for them later. She waited. She had no choice. Eventually their bags came and she grabbed them and headed to the Customs officer, Bonni in tow. The woman must have sensed her anxiety, she waved them through, not stopping them to examine their bags.

They stepped out of Customs into the bright sunlight. Jazz saw Crystal, but she did not see Jason. Suddenly she knew where he was. That was her favourite song being played on her favourite instrument! She followed the sound and there was Jason, her Jase with a sax, playing the chorus of Leonard Cohen's Hallelujah! She could not believe it. He looked so good! It was only a few bars and when it was finished Jason opened his arms, and with the biggest, cutest grin, he embraced his woman. They embraced until one of the porters shouted *'Man Coolidge, get a room'*. Everybody laughed, some clapped. She hugged Crystal and introduced Bonni all round. She couldn't believe it. She was back home with Jase. Her universe was unfolding as it should.

Crystal said she would take Bonni so the two crazy people could have some time on their own. She would see them at the party at Jason's parents' later. Jazz hugged Bonni and reassured her that these were her people and they would take good care of her. She turned back to Jason and kissed him once more. God, Jase, you are so handsome, my heart is about to stop. Let's go home.

Jazz and Jason were getting ready for the party. She didn't know what to do with herself. She was intoxicated, yet she hadn't had a drink. She was walking on a cloud and all atremble. She had dressed carefully and knew she looked good but Jason was too fine. She whispered *Dear God. Thank you for this darling lovely man. Please let me keep him for a good long while. I promise I will take good care of him.*

When they arrived, Pammy embraced her and Pim kissed her on her cheeks. She looked for Bonni. On the way there, it crossed her mind that she did not know where Bonni had been staying. She wasn't sure if Crystal had taken her to her home or to the little house. Jason said they would work it out later. She could stay with them as she might find the little house lonely. Bonni, when found, was as comfortable as if she had been there all her life. She was outside, drink in hand, sitting on the swing and amusing Ian Hollis, one of Jason's cousins.

All Jason's family and friends were there. They were toasted and roasted. People were chatting, some were dancing, some drinking and they were at Pammy's, so they were eating. The atmosphere was charged with gaiety, and the party went well into the night.

Neither Jason nor Jazz drank much. They were already high on each other, but some might have thought he was drunk. Some of the guests were dancing and Jason and Jazz joined them. Jason was doing some kind of boogey woogey, shake your booty salsa, calypso combination. Jazz was matching him step for step, shaking her groove thang, as though it had been choreographed. Most of the others stopped dancing to watch. Bonni, noticing a computer, asked if there was a webcam and called her father. Jazz and Jason were oblivious to the fact that they were being broadcast to Uncle Aaron in Toronto. In the middle of dancing, Jason stopped and announced: Woo hoo! Gareth! Ian! Is it legal for a man to be this happy! *My People, I want you to meet my wife, Jazzie, and gave her a twirl. No. We haven't had the formalities yet but she is my wife. See how well we fit together?* He gave her a kiss, a twirl and a hip bump. *Woo Hoo!*

The party finally wound down in the wee hours, that is to say, half the guests left and the other half found their way into the kitchen for early breakfast. Bonni was anxious to know if anyone there had known her father and Jazz thought Payne might have. He did, and offered to take her to the estate where they were raised. He thought some of the people he would have known could still be there. She looked forward to this. So far, she was liking her father's birthplace very well. She might stay around longer than she had planned.

Unbelievably, Jazz and Jason woke up fairly early the next day, and Jason thought they should go to church. Jazz was a little reluctant to face the general populace at first, but Jason said they needed to go thank God for bringing them back together. She would have to face the music at some time, and she had done nothing, he had; so they went. Jazz wore a lovely sunshine yellow dress, and when Jason escorted her to the pew towards the front of the almost full church, and handed her into the pew, she was uncomfortably aware of a murmur among the congregation. When Father Cardinal welcomed the visitors to the congregation, and asked them to stand and be recognized, she convinced herself she was not a visitor. She was christened right her in St. Georges Anglican Church and had attended here throughout her childhood. Unfortunately, because of those very arguments, the priest knew her and gave her a personal welcome, drawing more attention to her than would have been the case had she stood up among the other visitors. Jason took her hands, seeing her embarrassment. She sent up a silent prayer to God to thank him again for this lovely, lovely man.

Both Jazz and Bonni fitted comfortably in the community within a few days. Payne had invited Jazz to meet with him and Pim. He had also taken Bonni to Stone Haven, where her father had grown up and introduced her to the Delaneys, the couple, who had sheltered Aaron between the time of the quarrel and the time he left for England. She liked them and spent a lot of time with them.

Jazz had been on the island a little over a week when she ran into Yola on her way to see Payne. She had stopped at a drycleaners for a pick up, and hadn't seen Yola inside until it was too late. It was the first time she had seen her since Yola had slapped Jason, spoiling the mood of their dinner date. Jazz was not sure how to handle the meeting but Yola said hello, and she had no choice but to answer. The clerk was in the back, probably looking for the cleaning, and Yola was in a talkative mood.

So you're back

I am

What do you do in Canada, anyway?

Sell flowers, do some houses

Hah. I run my own travel agency, Yola announced grandly

Must be nice.

Well it is. You see, you don't have to depend on any man to support you. Jazz did not reply

Jason is only a man. He's gonna get tired of supporting you.

He isn't only a man to me. He is everything. And he won't mind if he has to support me. Look Yola, I'm sorry about what happened. Jase is sorry too.

Are you really? Is he? She asked bitterly

We are. But you weren't meant for Jase. I was. If I had to fight for him, I wouldn't have done it your way. If you knew anything about him you would know he couldn't stand violence and public humiliation.

Yola's eyes teared up and she put on her sunglasses.

I am really sorry Yola, but I have loved him since I was a child. Jazz walked out of the store. She did feel sorry for the woman. Tired of supporting her indeed!

Jazz decided she would spend the week decorating the little house. She would start work at her father's company next week, and Payne would wind down so he could leave for America. He was so looking forward to interacting with his grandchildren. She hoped he would be happy. She was choosing paint at Thurstons, when she saw Jakey. He offered to help her take the supplies to the car. She was driving Jason's vehicle, and she offered Jakey a ride. By the time she reached the little house, she had commissioned him to paint the outside. She told him she would paint the interior, starting that very day, and then she would tackle the garden. When she was done, it would be a little haven. They chatted about old times and Jakey offered to help her do the garden as a bonus. He liked gardening.

Life was beautiful. She enjoyed being back home. She was basking in the glow of being with Jason. She smiled when she heard him telling his cousins that his wife leaves her things in his car. He had found a lipstick under the seat and hairpins and such. Poor Jase. Life with a woman is tough going. He looked at her with his big, beautiful smile and asked when she wanted to do the formalities, and if she wanted to have banns read in church. She was hoping to get a commitment from her mother to come down for the wedding. She believed that Celine might be having problems with the idea of bringing Jaime to Brett's house. If she fixed up the little house, it might ease the pressure. She wanted her mother at the wedding.

Jason was in the bathroom getting ready for work when Jazz walked in. She took out a new packet of contraceptive pills and was about to take one when Jason gently took the package away, kissed her and said *Time for babies.*

Jazz was overcome. She would never have guessed this would have been her reaction to such a situation. She went all mushy inside and then a glow spread throughout her being. She kissed Jason ardently. Jason Coolidge, you are my heart.

Jazz phoned her mother at the shop later that day and asked her directly if she was afraid to come because it would be uncomfortable to have Jaime in Daddy's house. She told her what she was doing with the little house, and that they could stay there. It was a lovely place and very cosy. At any rate, whether or not they came, she was getting married to Jase in three weeks, and she was going to have a baby.

Are you pregnant Jasmine?

No Mommy, but I'm getting pregnant tonight and I'm telling Jase the date of our wedding. Three weeks, Mommy. Make up your mind. I want you there but I'm getting married whether or not you come.

I'll come, Jasmine, but I'm not sure I'm bringing Jaime.

Is anything the matter between you?

No. We're fine. Why do you want him to come? You don't like him.

Mommy, it appears he makes you happy, and I want you to be happy. Contrary to what you seem to think, I love you very much.

Jasmine, I don't want to go through this thing you have about having your wedding near the site.

That's fine. Jase has already changed my mind. He thinks it will be too sad for me and will make the mood too somber. He'll take me by a day or two before, or we'll come up with something. I'm sure Daddy will understand. It's hard for us, or me, anyway, to let go of him because Daddy was lovely. He was hale and hearty and there wasn't a body. I prayed and prayed that Daddy was thrown out of the car before the stone hit. Jazzie was crying now. *Mommy, Daddy is gone and if you are not here, who is going to stand up for me?*

I'll come Jasmine. Celine's voice was unusually husky.

Do you still want to marry me Jase?

I'm already married to you where it counts, honey, but yes, I want the formalities, and nine months after, I want us to have a baby and if its not twins you can take a break and have another one ten months later.

Jazz laughed and Jason reminded her that his cousins, Gareth and Ian, were both born in the same year. They chatted, and Jason told her how happy he was, and that he was looking forward to the things that made a man comfortable, like her messing up his stuff, and his children messing up his stuff, and her taking up all the room in the closet and pulling off the covers. He was a little flattered that she worried when he went out on his motorcycle, although he didn't really want her to worry too much. He was looking forward to the little things that gave life texture. If they put their mind to it, most people could handle the big things on their own but the details, the little things needed a mate. She laughed and told him about her meeting with his ex and her comment about him supporting her.

She thinks I wouldn't work for you? I would work till my knuckles bleed for you.

Let's hope you won't have to, darling. Sounds a bit messy. 'Damn, she thought. That sounded like Mommy. I'm already turning into her'.

Jazz asked if he thought that three weeks was enough time to get the formalities together. He said they would go to see Father Cardinal the next day. Father Cardinal confirmed he was available to marry them in three weeks.

Jason was excited. Jazz was a little stunned by the entire thing. She had always thought that men were hesitant about getting married, but Jason had thrown himself into it so much, she was almost a spectator.

He asked if she would wear a wedding dress. He wanted her to, and she agreed to wear a simple one but wondered where she could get one in three weeks. He volunteered his mother's services and they set off for Pammy's. She would have Crystal and Bonni as the bride's attendants and he would have Gareth and Ian as groom's men. Tomorrow they would go buy the rings.

Jazz found the weeks leading up to her wedding fascinating. Jason had thrown himself into the preparations with total dedication. She was flattered and flabbergasted. Just to be with her Jase was all she wanted, and she would have been quite content to forego the big ceremony but she adored Jason and seeing him so happy infected her and she felt she was moving around in some enchanted bubble. She prayed everyday for it to last.

She had noticed in Toronto that Jason never just fell asleep in bed. He always chatted and joked with her and it reminded her of her own parents. She would hear the murmur of their voices and from time to time Brett would laugh out loud and Celine would giggle. Brett had a happy laugh. When he laughed, everybody enjoyed the joke even though they hadn't heard it. She wondered if Jason's and her children would hear them chatting and cherish the memory.

They had chatted and he was now almost asleep. She wasn't sleepy. She watched his sleepy head on the pillow next to her and felt an unusual sensation in her body. She nuzzled his ear and whispered that she thought it took, and Jason, sleepy, didn't understand and wondered who had taken what. Jazz told him that he had successfully impregnated her and she had just felt the egg fertilize. Jason was fully awake now and laughing his head off. He offered some more fertilizer so they could have their two, and jazz laughed.

True to his word, one week before the wedding Jason got his friend Cal Cannonier to take them out in his boat to the area near Brett's resting place. The guys often went deep see fishing or diving on Cal's boat. Jazz woke up nervous and edgy, and Jason said they could cancel if it was too much, but Jazz said no. She was determined. They set off and Jazz was disappointed that they could not get closer, but the area was too rocky and would damage the boat. There was nothing to see. She borrowed binoculars. The rock that crushed her father's car was conspicuous. It was many times larger, and a different type and colour than the hundreds of other rocks in the area, but if any part of Brett's car was visible, it was on the side towards the land.

Jason was alarmed when she suggested she might swim out and go check. The water was too deep to wade and too rocky to swim and the rocks were sharp and dangerous. *Jazzie, there is nothing there. They searched thoroughly that day and it was sunny. Everybody loved Brett. They were very diligent. They searched every inch of those rocks. If there was anything to find, it would have been found.* Jazz was weeping and Jase tried to calm her. *A few of Brett's friends also came out by boat after the accident, but couldn't get close enough, and didn't see anything either.*

Baby, if it makes you feel better, talk to Brett as if he was here.

He would have liked to give her some privacy, but just in case she put this notion of swimming into action, he felt he must stay to prevent it. Those rocks were sharp and would cut a person open like gutting a fish.

After awhile Jazz calmed down and started to talk. She had had the best father imaginable. She had prayed and hoped that he had been thrown clear. Things had gone wrong for a while but she was so lucky and blessed to have been guided home to her adored Jase. Daddy should have been taking her down the isle to Jase. She knew he would have been happy as she would be, one of the two men she loved most in the whole world giving her over to the other, but it would be okay because Mommy would be doing it. She talked about how lonely Mommy must have been, but steadfast, but she had found someone and Jazz hoped that Daddy would not mind too much. He wasn't too bad, and he looked a lot like Daddy, but she knew he couldn't take Daddy's place. Nobody could. She turned and buried her face in her fiance's shoulder. He held her till she was calm, and signaled Cal to take them home.

Jazz told Jason that she worried that if her mother married Jaime she would have to take his name and with Jazz giving it up in a few days, there really will be nothing left of her father. Jason reminded her that the business still had her father's name. She could use it to keep the name alive. Maybe establish a scholarship fund or something.

Celine came home two days before the wedding. Jaime was with her. She may have seemed her normal, cool self, but Jazz sensed her nervousness, and when she hugged her mother she whispered that if she was nervous about staying at home with Jaime, the little house had been fixed up nicely. Jazz had indeed done a marvelous job of it. None of her cousins had been able to come, and Bonni had adopted the Delaneys, the now old couple who had helped her father. She was seldom around. Celine thanked her. They would stay in the little house but she expected she would have to show Jaime where she lived, anyway. She was not looking forward to it. Jason was keeping Jaime occupied while Jazz and her mother chatted.

Jason said that Pammy was hoping they would come down for drinks that night and Celine said it would be a good idea. After he dropped them off at the little house, Jazz told Jason she was worried about her mother. She was sure she wanted to talk but it couldn't be easy for her. She wasn't the type of person who talked about feelings. She would try to get mommy on her own for a little chat before the wedding.

When Jason returned from his stay with Jazz in Toronto, he told his parents about Celine's Brett-look-alike so when Jazz fretted on the way to pick up Celine and Jaime, he assured her confidently that his parents were aware of the situation and would act accordingly. Jazz phoned Pammy, nevertheless, to let her know that Jaime thought that he has a very slight resemblance to Brett. Could they go along for Mommy's sake, and Pammy laughed.

It was a pleasant drive down to the Coolidges. Jaime said he liked what he had seen of the island so far. They'd had a walk on the beach. He thought the scenery was breathtaking. Jason told him they swam every morning and invited him to join them, and Celine enlightened him that by morning, Jason meant daybreak, which is earlier on the island than it is in Toronto. That was what she said to him. What Jazz heard was

'Darling, you know I'm not a morning person, and there's not a chance in hell I'm letting you out of bed at some ungodly hour, so I could be alone while you hang out with the boys getting all wet and salty.' That is what she heard because she knew her mother.

Jazz asked Jaime if, at the part of the ceremony where the bride dances with her father, he would be willing to do the honours. Jaime said he would be thrilled, and Celine just smiled a very satisfied smile.

Jason led the little group into his parents' home and made the introductions. They thought they were prepared, but they were not. Pim recovered his composure quickly, and whisked Jaime off to the bar to get him a drink. That way, his back would be turned to the others. Pammy looked like a botox victim. She got Celine into the kitchen. *Lord, God, Celine. You ever miss and call him Brett? Jazz said he thinks he resembles Brett slightly. How you going break it to him that he walking round wearing Brett face?* They were chattering away in the kitchen like there was never a break in their friendship. Maybe Celine would talk to Pammy. Maybe she needed somebody in her own age group. Jazz was happy they were friends again, anyway. After all, they would be family soon. Two days.

Pim was telling Jaime that he was looking forward to a family wedding. If he had his way, there would have been many more but, due to his wife's unfortunate calamity, they had only one child. Jazz had heard the term on and off over the years, whenever Pim was in a melancholy mood. She had no idea what exactly the unfortunate calamity was, other than a Pim Coolidge idiosyncrasy. In most people's lives, it wasn't necessary to define calamities as unfortunate. Jaime asked what the unfortunate calamity was, and for the first time, Jazz heard that when Jason was born, Dr. Haberlast severed Pammy's tubes in error. One of his patients, twenty years older than Pammy, who had already had fourteen children, had asked that he do it on delivery, and he had somehow mixed up a thirty-eight year old chronic breeder with an eighteen-year old first time mother. He had performed an unnecessary c-section on Pammy and severed her tubes, while Pim was frantically trying to hitch a ride home from a job in Nevis to be with his wife.

Jaime was aghast and, unaccustomed to small island ways, said he assumed they had sued and got adequate compensation, opening the doors for Pim's pontification.

'Sued! Compensation! What is the financial worth of future children? We could have had twelve!'

Pammy entered the conversation. *'Ignore the old man and take away his glass. We didn't sue. People don't do that down here, and he likes to pretend we were above getting money from the tragedy, but we did. My parents gave this estate to me and my brother and sister. I was twenty when I bought them out. How does he think I got the money? He didn't want any money for his future twelve children but two things: He would have had to get somebody else to bring up the numbers and I would have had to shoot whoever it was, but I hope there would have been some girls in the twelve because I'm so tired of living in a testosterone cloud. As it turned out, we had to settle for one darling son and an estate, and he got stuck with me.* She kissed Pim and took away his glass.

Pim was an easy going laid back man. He loved his boys – Jason and his two nephews, Gareth and Ian. Based on his history, he could have been, but was not a heavy drinker. He had dated Pammy in school and had expected to marry her some time, but Pammy did not like him being single and away at university in case he found somebody else, so she became pregnant and they got married before he was ready to settle down and their first couple of years had been unstable, something he regretted sorely. He had been deeply affected by his twin sister's disastrous marriage and it had somehow encouraged him to settle down. He treasured his wife and son, and virtually adopted his nephews, and kept watch over the wellbeing of his twin sister.

Pim and Cat's father, Ned, had been a charming bootlegger. He made a very fine, smooth rum and was well liked around the island. Because everyone liked him – those who frowned on what he did and those who patronized his business alike, plans for a surprise raid and his arrest were leaked to him before it could be carried out. He had no problem hiding the product and, since it was in the mountains, a sudden raid was impossible anyway, because the only way up was to hike. When the police arrived they found nothing to seize and could therefore not arrest him for anything. Shortly after, he left for England with his wife and two of his children. Pim had refused to go and Cat, his twin would not go without her brother. Ned, as a farewell gift, gave his son the recipe for his bootleg.

Pammy's parents were one of the few local owners of a sugar estate, and when, in a political action, the estates were being 'nationalized', had sold their horses, signed the estate over to their children, and fled to Connecticut to join their siblings. Pammy's mother's younger sister was married to her father's older brother, and they lived in Connecticut. Believing it was only a matter of a very short time before they lost everything anyway, Pammy's siblings were happy to sell their share to their naïve little sister.

Pammy had been able to hold on to the estate probably because her parents had not exactly been one of the 'plantocrats', so hers was one of a very few independent estates selling sugar cane to the sugar factory. Her siblings were partly right, however, because there was a quota system and the amount of sugar cane she was allowed to sell to the sugar factory would not support the estate.

Her husband was the answer to her problem. He had the recipe that could use up the sugar cane she wasn't allowed to sell to the factory, but he had to fight tooth and nail to get the required licences to start his distillery. After long, rigourous, and what he considered demeaning negotiations - he had on several occasions been made to sit outside offices for hours, and then told his appointment had been cancelled – he was eventually able to secure the required licences, but with a hard and fast stipulation that he could not sell his product locally, and his business was taxed at a rate that was much higher than other businesses. Despite the harsh terms, Pim went into debt and started his distillery. His rum was every bit as good as his father's and quickly became popular in the neighbouring islands, and, with his father's help, he was able to develop a market further abroad. His market soon grew, with vigorous sales in Europe and America, and his business succeeded.

He was never able to get the ban on local sales lifted, and it riled him to see foreign companies being given special considerations never available to him, among them tax vacations . He was very bitter towards politicians and their colleagues.

A silly quote that appeared in a newspaper, possibly reflected his frustrations and feelings towards the powers that be. When a politician approached him with his spiel, seeking his support, Pim was quoted as telling him *I don't want to hear nothing 'bout nobody who ain't doing nothing 'bout nothing.* Whatever that meant. He had taken a lot of good natured ribbing for that one, but everyone knew his normal self to be quite articulate. They knew his situation and understood his frustration.

Generally speaking though, despite everything, Pim was quite a happy man, and often said so. His family was fine, his friends were true, his business had grown in leaps and bounds and his debts were paid.

Jazz woke up feeling tense. She went to the beach with Jason as had become her habit. He was a strong swimmer and she was, at best so-so. She would run on the beach for fifteen to twenty minutes and then join him in the water for the rest of the time, that way, they would both get their exercise. Jason sensed her nervousness and remarked about it. She was worried about her mother and wouldn't get a chance to talk to her. She and Jaime would be gone by the time the young Coolidge couple got back from honeymooning in Martinique. Jason said that Jaime was coming to his stag and Celine was coming to her party, she could take the opportunity. She was spending the night at her mother's house anyway, and Celine would be bound to come over to help her dress, she might even be able to convince her to stay the night too. He hoped it wouldn't be too hard for either of them. He thought it was a silly tradition that she couldn't stay with him the night before the wedding. She slept with him every other night. He would miss her warm body.

Jazz knew she was getting married tomorrow to the best man in the world. She couldn't understand the nervousness. She was dreading the night, and she surprised Jason when she asked him if he would show up. Some men change their minds at the last minute and leave the woman at the altar she explained. Jason held her. *Sweetie, we could buck tradition and stay home together tonight. Tomorrow, we could go to the church together, if it will make you feel better. Whatever we do, I will be there. I do love you Jasmine LaPierre. At this time tomorrow you will be Jasmine Coolidge. My Jazzie. Legally bound. We will belong to each other. Do you want me to stay home?*

Jazz wished he would but didn't think it fair. She said it was okay, she was just feeling a little insecure. He offered her a security boost.

When Gareth came to pick him up, Jason kissed Jazz ardently. *See you tomorrow Jazzie LaPierre. This is the last time I'm calling you that.* There was emotion in his voice. *I love you Jazzie.*

Are you going to say I take Whatsername Here? You have to call me that one more time. I love you Jase. She kissed him. *Enjoy but don't do anything too outlandish.* Jazz completed her preparations for her own party. She cried a little. *'Daddy, I have to change my name but I won't let your memory disappear.'*

Jazz was surprised when she woke up next morning at her mother's house, to hear the front door being opened with a key. She was even more surprised to see her mother enter with Jaime in tow. Mommy up and about so early! It was just after seven o'clock. Jazz did not feel at all well. She hadn't slept. She kept wanting to call Jason. She wondered if he'd had a good time. Celine was showing Jaime around. He did not seem any the worse for wear. She remarked that if Jazz was going to keep that face she could expect Jason climb out a back window when he saw her. Jazz asked Jaime if Jase had a good time at the party, and Jaime said he thought he did. Celine made her some breakfast with strong coffee, then Pammy arrived, followed shortly by Crystal, and finally Bonni.

Pim had driven Pammy to the house and followed her in bearing boxes and bags like a porter after a shopping spree. In the midst of the greetings and bustle and offers of breakfast, Pim put an arm around Jazz' shoulder and led her outside to the back porch. He obviously wanted to talk and she thought he was going to give her the 'how to make a good marriage' speech. Instead he told her she should tell Celine he had found what Jordan was after and had dealt with it. Everything was fine. And by the way, he teased, if she wanted to marry this Jaime guy it should be okay. Hell, knowing Brett, he probably organized it. He told her he was happy she was marrying Jason and advised that they should always look out for each other and try to keep each other happy.

Jase is lovely. He is my heart, my other half, the inside half, she told Pim earnestly. Of course she would make him happy, or die trying, but what did he mean about finding what Jordan was after. He told her that he

156

had never got around to looking through the contents of Brett's desk which she brought to him all those years ago, but he did recently. She had done good bringing him the documents. There was something among them that was attracting Jordan. Her mother really was not having an affair with him.

You are not going to tell me what it's all about? Pim said it had all been dealt with and was in the past.

But, let me get this straight, would I be wrong in assuming that Jordan was intimidating my mother about something my father had or did.

Sort of.

I'm making two solemn vows today. Her voice was dead calm. One to spend the rest of my life trying to make Jason Coolidge the happiest man in the world and the second to make Jordan Little the most miserable. He dared to try to discredit my father and intimidate my mother! My father would have ground the slimy reptile under his heels, and so will I, except I wear stilettos! She made a motion with her foot like she was grinding the life out of a crawling insect.

Pim smiled and hugged her. It was all just hot air to him. She could be no match for a seasoned brigand like Jordan. He *said Don't ever get angry with my son, please, but if anybody mess with me, I want you on my side.*

They went back inside and Pim left shortly after, taking Jaime with him.

The women primped and preened and curled and tweezed, manicured, pedicured and massaged her. All she wanted was to talk to Jason. Eventually she ran to the bathroom, locked them out and phoned Jason.

Did you have a good time, darling. I missed you. I hope they did not make you sleep with anybody else or anything like that or I'm coming over to cut her throat.

Where would I find the energy to sleep with anybody baby? You left me a shattered shell. He laughed. *How is it going?*

They better make me look good for you, Jase, or there will be hell to pay. Phone me when you get to the church and then don't forget to turn off the phone.

Jazzie, there is no place I want to be more than at that church today. I will be there. I will be on time.

See you later husband. I love you.

Jazz heart was brimming over. Pammy had done a phenomenal job. Her dress was simple, elegant and really well fitted. The bridal flower arrangement which she had done herself complemented the dress perfectly. Celine made her up so well, she enhanced all her best features without her looking made up at all, and Celine herself was simply stunning. Jazz figured they would bring down the house walking together up the isle. She looked around at their little party. Damn, she hoped there would be scads of pictures. They all looked marvelous. She was really getting into this. Then the phone rang. When she picked up, it was Jason and he said *'I'm here, Baby. I'm at the church, and I'm waiting for you.'* It was time to go.

The cars were outside. Pim was driving Jazz and Celine in back. Pammy would sit with her husband in front. Ian would drive Crystal and Bonnie. Jaime was already at the church. Gareth was with Jason. Jazz wanted to tell Pim to put the pedal to the metal. Suddenly, she couldn't wait to be next to Jason. Her heart was pounding. She was sure Celine could hear it. She thought Pammy and Pim might be able to hear it as well. Eventually, they arrived. It was no more than 10 minutes, though to her it felt like an eternity.

The walk from the street to the front entrance of St. Georges could be the longest most intimidating runway imaginable. The church entrance is three hundred yards from the street and the only way to get there is on foot. The gateway in a stone fence is too small to accommodate a car and after the first hundred yards, the pathway ascends three steps and three more another hundred yards away. Any bride brave enough to be married there, must walk that path, lined by hundreds of spectators, weddings being equivalent to fashion shows for entertainment value. The dramatic build up to this wedding, the groom having dumped one fiancé for another, had brought out practically the entire population. Oddly enough, when Jazz looked out of the car and saw hundreds of people lining the pathway waiting to see her, she did not feel intimidated although she remembered the many times she had watched weddings on this same path with Crystal. Sometimes the comments from the crowd could be cruel, but Celine had made them all look well above criticism.

Ian drew up ahead of Pim and opened the door for Crystal and Bonni . They stepped out, looking as calm as professionals. Show time, Jazz declared. Pim opened the door for his wife and Pammy exited the car. He then opened the back doors, first Celine's. She stepped out elegantly. There was a murmur of appreciation from the crowd. Jazz was the last to exit. Crystal straightened Jazz' dress, then looked at Bonnie and the two ladies started moving forward. Jared materialized from somewhere and Crystal stepped back, Ian stepped to Bonni's side and the two couples moved forward. Jazz looked at her mother and smiled, and they started walking forward, Pammy and Pim behind. Jazz thought to herself: Coolidge leading her and Coolidge following her to deliver her to another Coolidge, How does that fit in with tradition? Thank God Mommy was able to come.

Before she knew it, they were entering the church. She hadn't even noticed the crowd lining the path once she started walking. As they entered the church, the rich tones of the huge pipe organ greeted them as the organist began playing The Wedding March, and she saw Jason turn and look at her with a great big smile. God, she thought. I'm marrying this handsome man. I'm going to wake up to that smile for the rest of my life. The church was fairly large and the walk to the altar seemed to take forever. Mommy was walking so slowly. Jazz thought she might just be enjoying the attention. She did look marvelous. She registered that there were cameras going off all over but her eyes were on Jason.

When they finally arrived at the altar, Celine did a little hand over gesture and stepped back and Jazz took her place next to Jason. He beamed at her and whispered *Gawd 'oman, you look good enuf fe eat*, and she whispered that he should make sure to say grace before he bit into her leg.

The service was emotional. Jason's responses and vows were clear, no trace of question or doubt in his voice *'I Jason Alexander Coolidge take you Jasmine Hyacinth La Pierre...'* She tried to match him, but could not quite suppress her awe. Soon it was over and Father Cardinal was saying 'Ladies and Gentlemen, I present to you Mr. and Mrs. Jason and Jasmine Coolidge'. She was ecstatic!

It occurred to her that everything had gone very well, especially as nobody had thought to rehearse. She had not known until Pim came, how she was getting to the church. She turned to Jason and said there might be a problem. *You didn't ask me to marry you. You said you would after you got things straightened out and you didn't.* He threatened to get down on his knees in the middle of the walkway, in front of all the spectators. She laughed, and Jason hugged his bride.

After the guests left the church, they proceeded to the reception at Mont Yves. Pim paused at the site of Brett's accident and threw a bottle of champagne over the cliff. Jazz did as well, and as Gareth's vehicle, in which Celine and Jaime were travelling, reached the spot, he paused and offered Celine the bottle to throw over. Celine was appalled. She did not think it dignified to toss drinks at Brett, but she was also aware that no one would be willing to get close enough to the edge to lower it respectfully down. Jazz had been having the same thoughts in the car ahead, and they each said a prayer and tried not to cry.

In his speech at the reception Pim joked he'd always suspected Jazz was after his son because, a visitor to his home since she was a toddler, her first question was always *Where's Jase*? She was a lovely and well mannered child, but she couldn't deal with greetings and such ordinary stuff until she found Jason. So he begged Jason to always let his wife know where he is, he was tired of answering the same question.

Jason said in his speech that yes, his wife was a frequent visitor to his home and he first knew she would be his wife when she was about ten and they were eating in the kitchen with Gareth and Ian. She reached over and took food off his plate, even though she had her own. When he looked at her she gave him a big grin and popped it into her mouth. Instead of being upset, he was bursting with pride and he couldn't understand it, but when he was really sure she would be his wife was one day he came in and there she was dressed in his clothes and she looked wonderful and he felt so proud so he decided that since he liked her messing with his things, it gotta be love. He has loved her ever since. She was still eating off his plate and wearing his clothes, and he still liked it.

The party was fun. She danced with her husband, not the wild and crazy dancing they had done at the last party. She held on to Jason. She held that man so tight she felt she wanted to absorb him. She danced in turn with Jaime and Pim, and thanked Jaime because he seemed to make her Mommy happy. He told her he was happy she approved because he wanted to marry Celine. She kissed her mother and told her what Pim had said, because she wouldn't get an opportunity to talk face to face with her for some time. She kissed her again and told her how much she loved her and that she was now on side with her and Jaime. She even agreed with Pim's theory that Daddy might have arranged it, and then she went back to her husband and kissed him and told him how much she loved him and how happy she planned to make him and how nice she thought the name Jasmine Coolidge sounded. Her husband turned to his family and friends and wished them goodnight. He was taking Jazzie home. His wife, Jazzie. Jazzie Coolidge – his wife. Everybody told him to go. They got the picture.

Jason Coolidge took his wife Jazz Coolidge, home.

The young Coolidges, returning from their honeymoon, settled into life as a legally married couple. Payne had wound up his association with LaPierre's and was finally leaving for the U.S. The senior Coolidges were throwing a big farewell party for him at Mont Yves. Jazz was settling into his chair at the office. Jason was back to his business. It appeared that none of the euphoria of the last few months had worn off. They openly demonstrated their joy in each other, and even though each of their family and friends had their own secret doubts about their suitability to each other, Jazz and Jason were perfectly confident that they would succeed, loving each other to the end.

No one would ever know if Jazz had been right believing that she had felt her body conceive, but it was soon proven that on or about the time said she did, she had indeed conceived. The prospect of a baby sent Jason into sheer ecstasy. He could not wait to be a father. Jazz was more fascinated by the way he was handling it than she was by the baby itself. He started speaking to, and caressing her belly long before it was a bump. He liked the names she had chosen. Ebonique Celine, if the baby was a girl. Jafari Jason, if a boy. He announced it to the family as soon as they knew, and when Jazz protested it was too early to tell anyone in case something happened, he said if something happened the family would have to know anyway and be there to support her. It was like that. She had married a clan.

One of the things that lent warmth to the Coolidge home was the sound of music. All the men played guitar, Jason and Ian both played a variety of horns but Jason's favourite was the sax. Gareth was a dab hand at anything with keys, and Pammy was the relief organist at St. George's Anglican Church. The Coolidge men had impressive voices, both speaking and singing. Pim sang bass on the Anglican choir for almost as long as he could remember, and Pammy was also in the choir. She sang alto. None of the young men were actually permanent members of a choir but they were asked to sing whenever there was an event that required a fuller choir. Jazz always liked their musical side. She was, herself a big surprise whenever she sang for, judging by her speaking voice, she would be expected to sing alto, but she was a very strong soprano and could sing difficult pieces, even as a schoolgirl, since she took the very high notes easily, without sounding strained or screechy. She was actually, the only one in her year capable of singing the Ave Maria satisfactorily. She had not sung with a group since those days, but her singing in the shower was still pretty impressive.

On the morning of the farewell party for Payne, Jazz was in the shower singing along with the radio. Jason heard her keeping up with Celine Dion's The Prayer and joined her. They later pleased everyone at the party, particularly Payne, with their rendition of it, with Gareth on the piano. When the song was over, even Payne had a tear in his eye. Jazz was going to miss him. He had been a part of her life for as long as she could remember.

Before she started getting too big, Jazz and Jason had quite an active social life. They would strut their stuff at parties, dances, weddings, anything that was on. Yola happened to appear at one of the parties while they were dancing. She had been at another party first where she had drunk a bit, and after watching for a while with some others, became pretty riled up and started a scene. Jason was mortified. He had managed to avoid her so far, and had hoped she had got over her anger. Yola had a glass of something in her hand and was hurling abuse at both him and Jazz. They had stopped dancing, but neither had moved. Jazz saw Jason's jaws clench and felt his body stiffen. This is bad, she thought, and we were having such a good time.

Someone came up behind Yola and tried to escort her out. She threw the contents of her glass at Jason. Some of it caught Jazz and she put her hand up to stop the person throwing Yola out, and stepped forward. Jason was totally embarrassed. He did not want his wife brawling with

Yola. He reached out to grab her, but she patted his shoulder, and started to talk clearly and calmly to Yola.

Jazz apologized to Yola, in front of the fifty or so people, for the hurt they had caused her. She said that Yola knew that Jase was a good man and would not have hurt her if he could have helped it, but that she and Jase were meant for each other. He was her other half, the inside half, the essence of her being. She couldn't and wouldn't give him up, ever, so as sorry as she was, Yola needed to understand that she was never getting him back so she should move on. Yola left on her own without saying another word, and Jason was speechless. Ian drove them home. He and Gareth had come together. Gareth would bring Jason's vehicle home later. I'm sorry Jase, Jazz said to her husband. Maybe this is the last time. She knew how much he detested public scenes.

The next morning Jazz took a walk over to Yola's agency. There were no customers so she stood in front of her and said: 'I can't give you Jase back, and I can't compensate for your hurt but here's the deal. I'll give you an edge over your competitors. That's the best I can do. Don't bother us again though. You don't want to see the worse I can do. A couple of days later, a cardboard cylinder was delivered to Yola. It contained drawings and instructions of what her agency could look like, signed by Jazz. Yola thought she would give it a try and made the changes.

Jazz was right. You had to offer something better than the competition. One of the things about a small island is that the lack of competition made companies lax. It was not important to make offices comfortable or pleasing. To book an airline ticket a customer would stand in line interminably with nothing to look at, no music, nothing but the bare walls and the clerk on the other side of the counter. Yola couldn't make airline tickets cheaper, if she made her surroundings more welcoming and customers more comfortable while they were handing over their money, they would feel more justified doing business with her. Pretty soon her business picked up considerably. They never spoke again and actually avoided running into each other. Jazz and Jason could live in peace and Jazz never remembered to mention what she had done to Jason.

As her pregnancy progressed, Jazz and Jason discovered they were expecting twins. Jazz could not believe this. It was impossible. From all she had ever heard, the tendency to twins was passed down through the woman. As far as she knew, there were no twins in her family. Jason's father was a twin, but twins were up to the woman. She talked to her mother to find out if there might have been twins in their family but Celine was dismissive. She said it had to start somewhere. Jason's point of view was: 'Who cares? A man could love his wife enough to give her twins. End of story.'

Jazz was liming with Jason and some friends at a bar Jason used to lime at with Ian and Gareth, after watching a football match. Jason was in the bathroom when Jordan Little walked in. He nodded at Jazz, and she called out that she was running her Daddy's business now and that she remembered him taking his desk from her house. She wanted him to return it. He told her to come and get it and gave her the finger. She told him she would, but he wouldn't like it. By then, Jason had returned from the bathroom and asked what it was about. Jazz told him she was just trying to get an item of her father's property from Jordan, and Jason told her not to get into anything with Jordan. Jazz did not reply but Jason did not appear to notice.

A few days later Jazz registered a carefully worded, polite letter on LaPierre's letterhead, duly signed by herself as President, requesting the return of the desk. A few days after that, Hillary, her office assistant, brought the letter to Jazz. The words 'Fuck You' written in bold letters with a magic marker extended diagonally across the letter from the bottom left corner to the top right. Jazz glanced at it and told Hillary to staple the envelope to it and leave it on her desk. Hillary heard nothing more of the incident. When she was alone, however, Jazz phoned Gareth to say that maybe this was nothing, but just in case it turned into something, she was faxing him something she wanted him to see. Long before she had come to work in her father's business, Payne had made Gareth the company lawyer.

Some alarm in Gareth went off when he received the fax. One thing was certain. This was not about a desk. He remembered the short altercation at the club recently and he knew something was brewing. Jason had not mentioned anything and he wondered if he knew. Gareth's view of Jazz was a bit different from the others'. He had no doubt that she loved Jason dearly. He believed she would be a great ally, but he was afraid she would be an equally dangerous foe, and as she was likely to be underestimated, in a tussle between her and Little, Gareth would put his money on Jazz. Gareth remembered distinctly, Jason telling Jazz not to get into anything with Jordan. So much for honour and obey.

Two days later, Jazz was at the airport on business when she ran into Jordan. She again reminded him that she wanted her father's property. His reply was loud and clear *'Fuck you, you little bitch'*.

Jazz took a step back. *Never in a million years, Jordan Little, but I will fuck you, Jordan Little, right up the arse because I'm not a little bitch. I'm a big bitch, and your worst nightmare.* She walked away a step and then turned and repeated. *Right up the arse, Little, and you know what jackass? You are going through the rest of your life with the name Brett LaPierre ringing in your ears. Might as well get accustomed to it now. Brett LaPierre. Brett. La. Pierre. I am his daughter and I will make sure you remember his name.*

When Jason came home that evening Jazz ran to greet him as she always did, but instead of his big welcoming smile, his face was like a thundercloud. He must have ground his teeth down to a stump to get his jaw so tightly clenched. Jazz stopped in her tracks and stared at him open mouthed.

Jazzie, I told you I do not want my wife involved in public brawls, especially with the likes of Jordan Little. What is the matter with you?

Jazz was stung. She hated the fact that she couldn't see Jason hurt or mad at her without crying. She didn't want to cry now but her eyes filled up. She turned away. *Thanks Jase. Anything else anybody told you that you might want to hang me for without a trial?*

Jason turned her around. *I'm sorry. You're right. I shouldn't have done that. I'm listening.*

Jazz told him that it wasn't a public brawl. Anyone who heard them had to be within a couple of feet of them. She had simply reminded Jordan that she wanted her father's desk back. She told him what Jordan had said but not exactly all that she had said. Jason asked why she couldn't let the stupid desk go and she explained that the desk was part of the reason Jordan had intimidated her mother for years. She reminded him that he had lots of family to take care of things but she was sure if anybody messed with Pammy he would be on them like locusts. Her father was dead and her mother had only her.

Jason wanted to know why Jordan had intimidated her mother and Jazz told him she only needed to know that he had done it. If he needed to know why, he had to ask Pim. Jason was mad. He wanted to know why he had to ask his father everything he needed to know about his own wife. Jazz said it was all part of the same story and he stalked out, pausing at the door to ask' *why is it that every time I turn my back, you get in a fight with Little',* and Jazz answered *'I don't fight with him because you turn your back. I fight with him because he shows his face'.* He left, saying he would be back later and he drove off. She went to his den and started sketching frantically, to calm herself.

It was midnight before she heard Jason drive into the yard. She didn't go to greet him. She wasn't about to be snubbed twice in one day. He went straight to the bedroom and when he didn't see her he came looking for her. He had spoken with Pim and understood a little better, but he wished she would drop it. Celine was fine now so could she just drop all this? Jazz did not respond and he went to bed. An hour later he came back: *Jazzie, come to bed.*

She was tired so she stood up, but she was going straight to sleep.

Pim had been chatting with Gareth when Jason arrived. Gareth was asking about the relationship between Jazz and Jordan. He mentioned the altercation in the bar but not the letter. Pim seemed glad to get it off his chest, and told Gareth all he knew. When Jason came with the same question, Pim began to feel a little uneasy, like some sort of foreboding. He told him what he knew, omitting the pledge Jazz made on their wedding day. He told Jason that he couldn't blame the woman for wanting to avenge her parents, and that Brett was probably puffing up his chest somewhere, watching his princess fight his battle. He told him that it was bound to happen, the way Jordan kept going up against Brett, had Brett not passed, he would have done to him exactly what Jazz was doing. However, he said, she was Brett's daughter and Jason's wife and therefore their responsibility. He was glad he wasn't involved. 'Poor Jason', Gareth thought. His troubles were not going to be ending anytime soon. He might as well get used to it.

Jazz had no doubts whatever about her love for Jason. She hoped his love for her would be able to withstand his disappointment in her, but she was going for this one. There would be no turning back. Jason hated what she was doing. She would have to love him enough for them both.

Jordan was also a distributor. His bread and butter was a milk product widely, almost exclusively, used around the island. Jazz secretly studied the product. She researched other similar products. She had an idea, and it had to be executed well, if her project was not to pull down her father's company. She found the product she was looking for. It was definitely a better product and she might be able to undersell Jordan enough to destabilize him, but since she also had another plan for him, she intended to give him a one-two punch, she needed to ensure that she did not overextend herself. She had worked out that if things became shaky, she could shore up the shortfall from her portfolio in Toronto. She had found in university a real grasp for the market, had even earned a few dollars tutoring a fellow student, a year ahead of her, Hans. To get him to understand the market, she had encouraged him to invest a small sum with her and study its movement. Hans passed his course, she continued to invest and reinvest in the market and had built a nice portfolio. She would wipe it out if she had to, she was literally going for broke on this one.

Jazz was seven months pregnant with twins when she slipped into Gareth's office and sat across him. Gareth was surprised to see her. Her smile was winning. She said she just wanted to pick his brain about the taking over of mortgages. The pros and cons type of thing. Gareth didn't have to ask why, but he did. Jazz said she was exploring ways she could expand her Daddy's business. Gareth knew the others thought this was one strange woman. For one thing, her father had been dead for at least 12 years, yet she always referred to the company she ran as his. He knew that Jazz was perfectly aware of whose business it was, but it was her way of dealing with it. She had inherited her mother's artistry, and wholesale distribution of goods, no matter how necessary or lucrative, would not have been her own choice of business.

Brett had built a sure-thing, honourable business, providing the local population with the necessities of life and making a fair profit doing so. After doing business in a much larger market, Jazz found the confines of local business not sufficiently challenging and had spread her wings to the region. She sometimes chatted with Gareth about her plans and had made him laugh when she told him that her daddy built the business on the principle that everyone deserves the necessities of life. All due respect to her darling daddy, she had said, he was only a man, and men knew nothing at all about people, sorry Gareth. It was her idea that ordinary people would short themselves on the necessities in order to pay for the indulgences. She was going for the indulgences as well. He supposed that when she had sole distributorship of enough indulgencies, she would claim the company as hers.

They had a long discussion of the laws, the loopholes, the pitfalls of the mortgage business. When they were done, he walked her to the door, where she turned and smiled conspiratorially at him, and kissed him goodbye. He was even more puzzled by her than ever. The only things she seemed to actually want for her own was Jason and revenge on Jordan. One thing was certain. She was definitely not a stupid woman and underestimating her or falling for the ditsy impression could be somebody's big mistake.

Gareth heard nothing from her in the next few weeks and everything seemed to have returned to normal between her and Jason, so he relaxed a bit. With the babies coming, Jason was like a kid at Christmas and Jazz was all over him, just as she always was.

The Sunday morning, a week before Jazz was due to have her babies, she and Jason decided to go to church to pray for a safe delivery as they would possibly be unable to go the next week. It was a fine, sunny day. The entire family was at church. Father Cardinal had just started his sermon when Jazz felt something. Her water had broken. She turned to Jason and said she had to go. He smiled and nodded. She went to the bathroom frequently since she was carrying the babies. Then he noticed the look on her face. They had to go!!! He stood up and held his hand out to help her up and she grabbed him in a vice grip, he thought she'd break his arm. Jazz was half standing, half sitting, one hand over her open mouth, eyes like saucers, looking up at her husband, the other hand holding his arm awkwardly but more than just firmly. He couldn't get her to stand and he could neither move forward or backward.

Pammy saw them first and realized what was happening and rose from her seat in the choir. Gareth and Ian, on opposite sides of the church, noticed and came running. Between them, they were able to get Jazz out of the pew, blowing through her fingers and sucking in air, in an effort not to scream. Jason asked Ian to go to the house to get her stuff.

Jazz went down on her knees just as they exited the church, wracked by another contraction. Pammy was saying they were coming too frequently and she had to get to the hospital immediately or she would have the babies in the vehicle. Once they got her into the vehicle, Gareth drove like he had been shot out of a cannon. Jason was so much on edge one would think he was the one giving birth. In the back, Jazz just held on to the driver's seat and tried to rip it out.

At the hospital, Jazz and Jason were taken to the delivery room. The contractions kept coming, but not the babies. Jazz was exhausted. Jason was scared. The call went out to prepare the operating theatre. Things were getting dangerous. The anesthesiologist could not be found, and Jazz seemed to be passing out. Jason was begging her frantically to try, and she said weakly she was trying. He was talking in her ear now like there was nobody else in the room, and just as the news came that the anesthesiologist had arrived, Jazz gave a mighty push and her baby girl came into the world. With hardly a break, the baby boy came scrambling out behind her. Jazz was sure she hadn't pushed. Jason was spent. He wasn't sure he had quite enjoyed giving birth. It was too tiring. He left to tell the rest of the family. Pammy took one look at him and said: 'You think you had a hard time? Think about that young woman in there and remember what she went through the next time you feel like flashing your willie about. They all looked at her open mouthed, like she was an alien. Not even Pim could believe she had said that, then Jason started laughing and everyone else joined in.

Adjusting to the babies was not easy, particularly for Jason. He seemed to have expected that Jazz would give birth and return home looking like she used to before she was pregnant. They stayed at Mont Yves the first week so Pammy could teach them how to handle babies. Jason was a good scholar. He seemed to enjoy looking after the twins. He was very good at getting up at night to comfort and feed them, but he seemed to have turned off Jazz. She felt the loss deeply, and cried a lot. He hated that. He thought she cried more than the babies, and she looked at him with pleading eyes and made him feel guilty. He didn't like those humongous breasts and he hated the smell of the milk. He hated it even more when her breasts overflowed. Jazz would try to accommodate him by expressing the milk when he went for his morning swim. She tried to keep all the paraphanalia out of his way, but she just could not seem to please him, which made her cry even more.

Jason was riding his motorcycle more and more. She didn't think he was doing anything awful. She knew he rode when he was upset, or to relieve stress, but the babies were more than six weeks old and he was still paying no attention to her at all. She had been killing herself exercising to get back her shape and was almost normal again, except for her breasts. Now that she couldn't go for a morning swim with Jason, she would feed the babies, put them into their double pram and go for a run, pushing the pram, and she would spend at least another two hours exercising during the course of the day. Jason did not appear to notice.

Jason knew that he was being a jerk, but he seemed not to be able to help himself. He spoke to his father about his predicament and Pim said *'Son, sounds to me like you gotta make up your mind to drink a little milk. She won't be doing that forever but your babies have to be fed. You are going to have to work through this aversion to the milk smell or she will pick up your kids and go back to Canada and leave your house smelling empty. Just remember, only you can give us grandchildren.'*

Jazz was convinced her children would suck her dry. The more milk she expressed, the more they wanted. The babies were almost three months old and Jason still had not come back to her. She ran out of expressed milk before she could feed the baby girl one evening, and she wouldn't stop crying. Jazz put her to her breast and while she was feeding Jason walked in. She thought he looked at her like she was doing something obscene in public. She started to apologize and explain, tears streaming down her cheeks. He put his hand on her shoulder, said it was okay, and he kissed her. He hadn't kissed her for so long, she felt she had been drowning and somebody had thrown her a rope. When she was finished, he took the baby from her, burped her and put her back into the crib with her brother. They had bought two cribs but found the babies slept longer and cried less when they were together.

While Jason was settling the babies, Jazz went into the shower. She was hopeful if she could get the baby milk smell off her Jason would want her again. When he came to bed she tried to seduce him. She climbed onto him and at first he responded, but then something happened. He was on top of her and driving her like an old mule. She tried to tell him he was hurting her, but he couldn't hear, or wouldn't stop. When the ordeal was over, Jazz crawled to the bathroom and started the shower.

Jason lay in bed listening to the shower and thinking of the enormity of what he had done. He was appalled. This was well outside his nature and he had no idea what had come over him. He felt sick. His wife was in the shower trying to wash him off and out of her. He wondered if she could still love him through this, and he wondered how he had got off track and how the hell he was going to get back. He couldn't lose Jazzie or his babies. Even he could see them changing every day. Jason was ashamed of himself. His wife had been showering for more than twenty minutes. How hard was she trying to wash him away? What a mess he was in.

More than twenty five minutes had passed before Jazz turned the shower off. Jason waited patiently for her to come out of the bathroom and when she finally did, he tried to apologize. She put her hand up to stop him as she climbed into bed, and said. *It wasn't you. I felt I was being raped. My Jase wouldn't rape me.*

She lay down on the other side and turned her head away. Her hair was still wet, and Jason wished with all his heart that she would put her head on his shoulder like she used to. If he woke up in the morning with her hair all over his face and even in his mouth, like the old days, he would be the most grateful man in the world. He knew what he had and he knew he was throwing it away and he didn't want to, but somehow, he couldn't make himself stop. He needed Jazz to stop him.

When Jazz awoke next morning Jason was gone. She was not alarmed. He went for a swim each morning, but she was a bit put out. Today was Saturday and he didn't have to go to the office so he could have waited to go to the beach. She set about looking after the babies. Two hours later, when Jason had not returned, she started to worry. Things were getting worse if he stayed away that long without calling.

The Coolidge family strolled in and out of each others homes as their own. She heard a tap on the kitchen door and when it opened, she hoped it would be Jason. It was Gareth. He asked for Jason, and was about to go to see the 'beanie babies' as he always referred to them, even though he had no idea what beanie babies were. He stopped in his tracks when Jazz said she didn't know. He turned to face her and realized she was serious. There were tears in her eyes and she said Jase *has thrown me away.*

Gareth didn't like this. He was out of his depth. He could handle her fighting with Jordan. He didn't like it but it was something he knew how to deal with, but he couldn't handle this. He stood staring at her awkwardly. *What do you mean?*

Gareth, Jase does not want me. I changed around his toys.

Poor Gareth. Dare he ask? *What toys?*

These, she said, pointing to her breasts. Damn! He shouldn't have asked, but what choice did he have.

They used to be his toys, now they are milk jugs and he seems to think it's my new hobby, making milk, and he hates it. The tears were streaming now, and Gareth took her elbow and guided her to a chair.

Maybe you shouldn't be telling me this. Do you want to go down to Mont Yves and talk to Pammy? Women know more about this type of thing.

No. I want my husband to come home. I want him to look at me and see that I am the still same person. I want him to have patience and know I won't always be a milk cow. I want him to make love to me and comfort me.

Gareth was very obviously uneasy. He took out his phone and called. *Hey bro, Where are you? I'm at your house. You need to come home now.* He started making coffee. Anything to not watch Jazz cry. He wished he hadn't heard what he just did. He was relieved when one of the babies started to cry, he was out of the kitchen in a flash to get the baby. Not long after, they heard Jason ride into the yard and he handed the baby to Jazz and got up to go. He didn't know what to do so he patted her head.

Gareth and Jason greeted each other and Gareth made a quick exit. Jason looked at his wife and child. He thought she would drown his baby with her tears. He took the baby from her and took her back to the crib. He did not know what to do. He had no idea what was going on in his life or how to deal with it. He knew he loved his wife and he couldn't bear the thought he could lose her, yet it was as if there was some force around her repelling him. He missed what they had and wished things could return to normal, but he was unable to bring it about. In fact, he kept making things worse.

Jazzie hadn't done one thing wrong. She had tried harder than most people would. She was like a whirling dervish taking care of the babies and the house and working out to get back in shape for him, and she did a bit of her office work from home. She spent time daily, communicating with her mother, and with his, and as far as he knew she had told neither of them of the trouble they were having in their marriage. He was ashamed of the way he was treating her, and particularly of the incident the previous night. That was completely foreign to his nature, and he couldn't explain what had come over him.

He had to go and face Jazz. It disturbed him the way she cried soundlessly. She would look at him, her eyes pitiful, yet somehow accusing, and they would fill up and her tears flow copiously, while she trembled and her shoulders shook. She could soak up a box of tissues in no time, and the only sound would be of her blowing her nose. God have mercy! He had to try to fix this. It was more than just disconcerting. It was downright freaky.

Jason moved a chair next to Jazz' and put an arm across her shoulder. He apologized and told her how ashamed he was, and he asked her to bear with him while he worked out whatever it was that he was going through. He promised he was trying to get things back to normal. Jazz was so happy to hear this she threw her arms around Jason and hugged him as closely as she could, sitting sideways with the chairs between them. She hugged Jason and then she tried to kiss him and realized Jason was not there. Physically he was, but he was no nearer her than he was when he was missing earlier. Something inside her rebelled. She didn't care what rails he had slipped off, he had better hop the hell back on because she was tired of this. He was her husband, and she was not letting him go. She would have to try something. She was having no more of this. Jason looked at her. Damn, he thought, another river running down her face. She let him go and shook her head. *I guess I've overstayed my welcome.*

Don't say that Jazzie

We'll get out of your way. We'll go to Toronto. I'll ask Mommy tonight

Jazzie, you can't go to Toronto. You can't take the babies to Toronto. It's winter up there

They don't banish babies in winter. Babies are allowed in Toronto all year round.

Yes. Babies born to that type of climate. You are not taking our babies to Toronto. I will not let you.

So I'm going to leave them for you to take care of and nurse them with unscented milk?

Don't go.

She got up and walked away to go look for her babies. Ding, she thought. Round one to Jazzie.

Jason hung around for a few hours then came to ask her if she minded if he went out for awhile. Operation Retrieve Jase was starting here. She wanted to hug him and beg him to stay but instead she said *Like you care what I think?*

Actually, I do.

She sniffed. *Yeah. I noticed. It's been very obvious lately.*

'Jazzie..' He started to say something, but changed his mind. He walked to the door. *Call me if you need anything. Please.*

She didn't answer. She heard him ride away, her darling Jase. He didn't know what was happening to him? Maybe if it was a mental problem, what he needed was shock treatment. Please Lord, let this work. She had no intention of giving him up, but she had no intention of continuing like this. She called a car rental agency, rented a car for 24 hours and had it delivered. She transferred the carseats from Jason's vehicle to the rental. In his enthusiasm Jason had bought a playpen when she was pregnant. It will have to do tonight, if need be. She packed it in the car with baby supplies and a few dresses she had no intention of needing. Just in case he did not come for her she grabbed Jason's shirt, the one he had been wearing earlier, and put it on. She dressed it up with a fancy belt around the hip. It might be as close as she could get to him tonight. All set to go, she drove to her little one bedroom house. Fingers crossed, Jason would come looking for her.

Jason noticed when he rode into the yard that the baby car seats were missing from his vehicle and assumed Jazz might have gone somewhere with Crystal. She would normally have called to let him know, but he guessed he deserved it. Once it began to get dark, he started to worry, and called Crystal. She hadn't seen Jazz all day. Jason felt sick. Apart from Crystal, Jazz had no close friends except his family. He drove out to her mother's house. No lights. Nobody there. He drove past her little house. There was a strange car parked outside. She wouldn't bring the babies here. There wasn't enough room and there didn't seem to be anyone there either. He'd called her cell phone several times but she did not pick up. He'd left messages. God! What had Jazzie done? He drove past her office. He wasn't surprised there was nobody there. She wouldn't bring the babies there. Lord, Jazzie, where are you? Please don't let her be on a plane. He had been a shithead, but he couldn't lose her. He couldn't lose them. He phoned again. He left another message.

Jason headed back home. Maybe his wife and babies were back. They weren't. He searched his house for a note or something to say where she went. Jazzie loved writing him letters. He was sure he had the record for the most love letters a married man received from his wife *after* they were married. There was nothing. He thought of all the things she did that he liked. They had been so happy and he had squandered it. He needed help. He called Gareth. He would have been the last person to see her. Gareth and Ian were at the bar.

After talking with Crystal again, they decided to scout the places Jason had already been. She was definitely not at her mother's house. They drove on to her little house. The same car was parked in front of the house but it could belong to anyone, it was in the street. Ian said he had to consider the possibility she was meeting someone else. That was not something Jason had considered and his stomach churned at the thought. There was a dim light on inside and Jason began to feel his muscles stiffening. If there was anybody in there with his wife, he was going to flatten him. The other two must have read his mind because they decided to escort him in.

Jazz was alone with the babies. She was comforting the baby boy. The baby girl was playing in the carseat on the sofa. *Jazzie!* Jason strode over to her. He was not angry. He was so profoundly relieved, he thought he would fall over. There was no man! Gareth took the baby from Jazz and suggested she and Jason go into the other room so they could have some privacy, and Jazz retorted

I'm so stupid, I'd go into the other room so you could take away my babies? Jase doesn't want me. He came with his two lawyers to take the babies.

Ian smiled, and chewed his lower lip.

Gareth looked at her. He always looked at her like he could see her soul. Both brothers had those penetrating eyes. *'We didn't come as his lawyers, Jazz. You know that. We came as family. Your family too. Tell me what you want,* he said gently.

I want Jase.

But if you want him why did you leave?

Ian's smile turned into a grin.

He does not want me. I want my Jase back like he was – lovely and loving and kind. I want him to be my sweetheart again.

I'm here, Jason said.

You're here for the babies. I want you to come for me.

I'm here for you and the babies. We can't leave them behind. Come home Jazzie.

Ian's shoulder's were shaking with silent laughter.

Jazz was relieved. She was going to slap that Ian, but her plan worked. She wanted to go home more than they could guess, but she told Jason that she thought she might just stay there until he came to his senses, and Jason said alright, he'd just stay there too. In the end Jazz allowed him to convince her to pack up the babies' things and come home. Success! Jazz was pleased.

Ian and Gareth were leaving. Ian was laughing openly and shaking his head. At the door, he stopped and said how nice she looked all dressed up in Jason's clothes, they made her look so resolved to leave him, and he almost tripped going out the door. She really was going to slap him when this was over.

If one was listening from another room, it would be easy to mistake Gareth's voice for Jason's or vice versa, but Ian and Pim's were a few octaves lower, Ian's with a distinct sibilance. When Jazz awoke the next morning Jason' arm was thrown across her. She wasn't sure if it was an accident, but he must have sensed that she was awake because he ran his hand down her body. She was ecstatic! Her back was turned to him and he said '*Jazzie*', his voice a few octaves lower than usual. He sounded exactly like Ian and she had a horrible thought. Jason and Ian looked enough alike to be twins, except Ian's skin tone was several shades lighter. She nervously looked down at the hand caressing her. Relief! She was not in a nightmare. It was Jason's. She turned to face him. '*Don't do that again*', he said.

He told her it was a torment finding her missing. For a few moments it occurred to him she might have carried out her threat to go to Canada. He did not love her any less and he was really trying to work out whatever was the matter with him. He had even made an appointment to see Dr. Koolman, and it wasn't an easy thing going to a shrink on this tiny island. Jazz was indeed surprised and said she would go with him. The babies started to cry just then and they had to get up, but Jazz was pleased they seemed to be on the road to getting back on the track. She knew she hadn't fooled him but that had not been the objective. She had communicated to him that the option was there if he couldn't straighten up and fly right.

Jason, for his part, recognized that the idea was there, and it terrified him. She had, after all, left without notice before and he had been devastated. He was in a constant struggle to keep secret the shrieking possessiveness he felt towards her, and exercised great efforts to suppress it. Everyone knew he had been affected by her abrupt departure, but he doubted they really understood just how deeply.

Over the next few months, Jazz managed to steer her marriage to a place close to where she had liked it best. The babies thrived and Jason was affectionate again and he was just thrilled with his 'awesome' babies, to borrow one of Jazz Canadian expressions. It was not unusual to see him around town with a baby in each arm and the baby bag over his shoulder, something that scared the daylights out of Jazz, in case they wriggled and he dropped them. He may very well have won the prize for proudest father in the universe.

Everything seemed to be coming up roses for Jazz. Her family life was near perfect. Her husband adored her again, her babies were a joy and her entire family, including Crystal and her boys, adored them. She had been awarded the regional distributorship she had been angling for and that project had exceeded her dream of success. Success primarily being to knock Jordan's feet from under him. LaPierre's made money from the deal. Jordan owned and lived in a ginormous mansion, his pride and joy, and she now held his mortgage. She had given him what would appear to be justifiable enough terms to someone reading the document without knowing the history. She knew that with his bread and butter product selling as well as tainted meat, he couldn't make the terms. It was only a matter of time now. A very short time.

Zoe Tewes, an English artist, lived on the island for several years in a huge house. She threw great open house parties. Jason and Jazz were at one of these parties. Jazz left Jason to say hello to some ladies she saw in the kitchen. A young man there threw her a come on line and Jazz laughed and told him not to waste his prize lines on her because she was happily married to the best looking guy at the party. She rejoined Jason and thought no more of it.

Hillary, Jazz' assistant was going on maternity leave. She had always found it difficult to keep up with Jazz. She was accustomed to Payne sitting at his desk and giving her instructions which she would write down. Jazz talked to her while she did other things. She walked up and down, and she threw in Canadian phrases that were sometimes unfamiliar, and Hillary thought Jazz had a bit of an accent. She had found sometime ago, that the solution to these problems was to have a tape recorder. She could play things back as many times as necessary until she understood what Jazz wanted her to do.

A few days after Zoe's party, Jazz was giving Hillary instructions when the phone rang. An unfamiliar voice said he was Ralph Jerome, just calling to say hi. She verified he was speaking to the right person but the name did not ring a bell. She turned to Hillary and asked if they knew a Ralph Jerome, but Hillary wasn't familiar with the name either. After some prying, it turned out that Ralph Jerome was the man who had tried to pick her up in Zoe's kitchen. Jazz was annoyed.

'Mr. Jerome,' she said. *We did not 'meet' at Zoe's party. You made a pick up comment to a total stranger and I told you I was married and not interested. Let me tell you again. Even if I did not have a happy marriage, and I was looking for a man, if I had to go through a list of names, four columns per page, you would be around page 35. Please do not call me again.* She hung up and continued her work.

They were at another party a week later, when Jazz found herself trapped by Mr. Jerome on her way back from the bathroom. He was blocking her path and there was no one around. He reached for her and Jazz did not stop moving towards him. He opened his arms as if he expected to hug her. Jazz walked up to him and brought her knee up viciously, at the same time yelling for Jason. When her knee made contact, the man bent forward and Jazz thought he was still trying to attack her. She pushed his head into the wall. Jason, hearing his wife's urgent calls, came at a trot to find Jerome crouched against the wall. Jazz explained what happened because he had tried to grab her. Jason laughed and told the crouching man to leave his wife alone, and they left. Jazz told him of the previous encounter and the phone call. Jason stopped laughing.

An hour had passed, the incident considered over, Jazz was off with some of the women. Jason was chatting with some of his buddies when Jerome came up to them ranting and threatening reprisal against Jazz. Jason became mad.

Did I hear this man threaten to hit my wife?' He turned to Jerome. 'Are you crazy? You stay well away from my wife, do you hear me?

Someone, seeing Jason's anger and sensing the possibility of trouble, went outside where Gareth and Ian were liming with some other friends and told them. They both strolled in and, one on either side, tried to get Jason to just walk away, and he was about to when Jerome made some graphic and obscene comments on what he intended to do with Jason's wife. Ian and Gareth moved away, allowing Jason to stride over to Jerome and punch him in the mouth. He grabbed him by the collar and dragged him outside. Jason did not get angry very often. He was very obviously very angry now and Ian and Gareth stepped in again and tried to subdue him. By now Jazz had heard and come running to Jason. She hugged her husband and kissed him and cooed in his ear to calm him. She said she would drive them home, and as she turned to walk towards the cars, she almost tripped on a garden hose. It had a trigger nozzle. She reached down, picked it up and pointed the nozzle at Jerome's bloody face and squirted him, first his face and then his groin. *That's to cool your frigging jets off. Leave us alone.* The party was over for them.

When Jazz went back to work, she hired a young woman to take care of the twins during the day. Jazz often started her day late because the babysitter showed up late. She always had an excuse and since Jazz' own start time could be flexible, she tried to be tolerant. One Friday afternoon, Jason was using the vehicle and she needed to get home for something she'd left in error and needed. She took a taxi. Her babies were toddling around the house while the sitter drank vodka in the kitchen with a man Jazz did not know. Jazz paid her and sent them packing.

Hearing of her predicament at Mont Yves the next day, Cat, Gareth and Ian's mother, offered her services. She would come daily and watch the twins until Jazz or Jason returned. Jazz was stunned. Everyone was stunned. Cat was 'unpredictable' , meaning a little cracked, in Jazz' opinion. Her husband, Gareth and Ian's father, had left when the kids were two years old. They were thirty now and she was still waiting for him. Sometimes she became upset and blamed Pim for her husband's absence. The story was that her husband was a serial cheater, and when pregnant Cat was inconsiderate enough to walk into their home while he was busy with a sexual encounter with one of his mistresses, he beat her so severely she lost the baby.

Pim had taken his twin sister to the hospital and, after seeing her settled in, went back to her house, dragged her husband out, and invited him to try to beat up a man. There was no fight. Pim gave him a mighty punch in the face and he fell down, his nose bleeding profusely. It was broken. Pim took him to the hospital where, in contrast to the solicitude he had shown earlier when he had taken his sister, he just dropped him off at Emergency and went home to his own wife. He wept, and promised faithfully that he would never raise his hand against her, and she soothed him, in her inimitably pert way: *Of course you won't darling. I would kill you.*

The subject was not mentioned in their household again. Cat sometimes believed that if her husband hadn't been afraid of Pim, he would have come back.

When Cat returned from the hospital, having lost her baby, her husband told her how sorry he was. He said he did those things because he was so frustrated. He had big plans but just couldn't get a break on this island. If he had enough money, he would go to St. Thomas and set up himself and send for her and the boys. He was sure he could make it there. Cat had worked at everything possible to get the money together, and when he left, she settled down expectantly, waiting for him to tell her to bring the boys. She never heard it. She never heard from him at all, and nobody ever saw him in St. Thomas.

After two years of waiting, Cat had a nervous breakdown. Pim and Pammy took the boys to live with them. From time to time, she had a row with Pammy, accusing her of trying to steal her sons. In their early teens, the boys suggested they change their last name to Coolidge and Cat had a fit. Their father's name was Hollis, their name should be Hollis. If they were Coolidge it would mean they were illegitimate, and she had a husband. It took weeks for her to return to normal. It really didn't matter because everyone thought of, and referred to them as Coolidge, anyway.

Gareth and Ian loved Cat, but they also loved Pammy like a mother. Cat could go for a long time without appearing to mind, then some small thing would set her off and she would start a war. Like the time she heard one of the boys call Pim Daddy, as Jason did. All hell broke loose. It was an abomination! Pim could not be their daddy; he was her brother. She reacted as though it was a personal accusation of incest, and no amount of explaining that they knew Pim was not their father, could calm her. After that, the boys called Pim Da. People on the island called their fathers Daddy, father, poppa, not usually Dad and certainly never Da. Cat didn't think Da sounded in any way fatherly, so Da was alright. They never called him anything else, even though, when Jason grew up, he called his parents whatever came to his head at the moment, from their given names through every variation of parental names that he knew.

Cat could be very possessive of her boys and it sometimes got on Pammy's nerves because, in every way that matters, she and Pim had raised the boys. She said, from time to time, that she tolerated Cat only because she was Pim's twin. Had she been just a regular sibling, she would have long been out of her life.

When their mother was in a rage, Gareth and Ian slept at her house, which actually belonged to the estate and therefore was Pammy's. When she was better they lived with Pim, Pammy and Jason in the great house.

Knowing this about Cat, Jazz was more than a little hesitant to accept her offer, but either decision could set Cat off. She tried to use tact.

Oh, Auntie Cat, what a kind idea, but you know they are entering the terrible twos and can be a bit of a handful. Perhaps it might be better to get a younger person. Cat seemed to be in a fighting mood.

How much older than Pam do you think I am? You let her look after them, she challenged.

Valid point, Auntie Cat, but the babies' grandmother has them from time to time for a few hours. You would have them all day, at least five days a week. That could be tiring, even for me. Cat's face was set for a fight so Jazz decided to pass the buck. Jase's aunt, Jase's kids, Jase's decision. She would stay out of it. She would go along with anything he said and monitor the situation, if and as required. *Let's see what Jase thinks, Auntie Cat, and then we will decide.*

Jason was giving her dirty looks and she gave him one right back. The whole family was present and they held their collective breaths and Jason said *Well, Cat. Let's try it for a few days and see how it goes. You good for Monday?'*

The crisis with Cat was over, but nobody in that room besides Cat, thought it was a good idea.

Cat showed up bright and early on Monday. Jason and Jazz had hoped she would change her mind. They bit their tongues and left their precious babies with their crazy aunt. They would drop in from time to time to make sure that everything was alright, and pray as hard as they could. After a few days of interrupting their days to drop in every so often, they relaxed. Cat was doing well with the babies and she herself had perked up and was looking fresher than anyone had seen her in years. She asked if, rather than get the bus in every morning, they could fix up the empty room for her, and she would go home only on weekends. It seemed reasonable, and that is how Auntie Cat came to live with Jason and Jazz.

Back at the office, Jazz sent a letter to Jordan, reminding him of the upcoming deadline for making good on his mortgage agreement. Failure to do so would give the company no recourse but to foreclose, blah, blah, blah. She sent a copy to Gareth. Gareth came to her office. He wanted to know if she was sure she wanted to do this. It could start a lot of trouble for her, including some inside her marriage.

You know Gareth, she told him, *sometimes, whether or not you like it, you got to choose a side. I'm all the way in now, and Jase will have to side with me or leave me. I hope he sides with me because if he leaves me I will die, but I have no recourse now, what am I going to do, carry Jordan? We've already carried him enough. He drank all of my father's good scotch. Time to pay for it.*

Jazz, he can't pay it. Maybe give him more time and end this.

That would defeat the purpose, Gareth. In my life I have loved two men, both with all my heart. You have no idea how much I loved Daddy. He was everything to me. Jordan tried to discredit him, and when he was not here to protect his beloved wife, my beloved mother, Jordan intimidated her, estranged me from my mother, the only family I had, and forced me into exile, loneliness, terror, for ten years. I almost missed the other man that I love with all my heart and all my being. Ten years is a long time to lose.

He touched her cheek and walked away.

That same night, Jakey called Jason to tell him that Jerome had broken into Jazz little house. He must have been following her movements because she went there several evenings each week before going home, but after her talk with Gareth, she didn't feel like it. Jason told Jakey to keep an eye on the house for him. He reported the break in to the police and that the person was still there. They took the report but never showed.

The day Jazz foreclosed on Jordan, she went with the bailiff and the sheriff to claim the property. They told her she did not have to be there, but she said wanted to see what the procedure was. She saw Jordan and whispered '*Brett. La. Pierre*' to him. He swore at her. She reminded him that he had invited her to come and get her father's desk, well here she was. He was so incensed, he yelled at her that he would burn the place down. She made sure the sheriff took note of this and too quietly for the others to hear, she told him that if he ever tried anything like that, she would personally see to it that he was tied up and burnt alive and that, as he well knew, she always kept her promises.

The event caused a major stir on the island. Foreclosures being the rarest business occurrence. This was actually only the second foreclosure in the island's history. Creditors would normally take debtors to court, and get a bailiff to threaten them and would make do with a small downpayment and a promise of future payment. This way they maintained a good name for leniency, decency and consideration. Jazz did not care about any of this. For most of her products, she had sole distributorship rights anyway.

Things were decidedly chilly in their household, that night. Jason was not pleased that she had pursued the project, and said she could get a reputation as a dragon. She asked him if he thought she was a dragon, because his was the only opinion that really mattered to her. He said he knew her warmth and generosity, but others might not, and call her anything.

Jase, my dearest husband, hear this. I couldn't give a damn what people call me behind my back. To my face they will call me Mrs. Coolidge, unless you no longer want me associated with your name, in which case they will call me Ms LaPierre.

Is that what you want? To be called Ms LaPierre?

It's my name, Jase. I love you and am proud to carry your name, but please do not try to make me forget my father's name. Jason walked away from her and she heard his motorcycle start up and roar away.

Jazz had not taken Jordan's home without putting a plan in place for it. She had approached the Ministry of Social Welfare and the Ministry of Education, prior to acquiring the property, with a proposal for a live-in academy for disadvantaged and abandoned children. Her assistant Hillary had been raised in an orphanage and related to her many times how spartan life had been there. She had never worn anything new until she started working. They got the bare necessities, usually donated, often used, and was not taught any social skills, so that Hillary said she was still unsure of herself in company. She had learned a lot from her husband and considered herself so lucky, but they didn't go out much because it was such a strain on her limited self confidence. Jazz was determined the children in her academy would have more.

Jazz had established the Brett LaPierre Foundation shortly after she changed her name to Coolidge. This would be its first major project. She wanted the children to learn, not just the basics, but how to become contributing members of the society, confident and equal to anyone else. She would have to put some money into it, of course, but she had formulated a fund raising plan, and some of that money would come from local government. If Jason had been willing to listen, she was sure he would not be so upset. She decided to take a walk over to Gareth's office. She laid out her plans and told him what she had already done, bearing in mind she couldn't do too much until the firm actually owned the property. Gareth had done the legal work on the setting up of the Foundation, but at the time, he had expected it would hand out small annual scholarships to one or two students. He could not help but admire this strange relative of his. Another win win lose situation, with Jordan the loser. He hoped that she would leave the poor man alone now.

At Mont Yves that weekend, Jazz told the family her plans. She said she knew they all hated her for what she had done, including her own husband, but well, it was what it was. Pammy said that she for one, did not hate her. She supported what she had done. It's what women do, they look after their families. She was glad Jazz was her family because if anybody came after her, she knew Jazz would make short shift of them. She asked how Celine had taken it and Jazz mimicked her mother. *My God Jasmine! I really wouldn't have thought you had it in you.* She wasn't sure whether that was good or bad. It had better be good because her husband was throwing her out and she would need her mother. Jason did not comment.

Daddy, you're awesome was one of the phrases Jason had become accustomed to. It was one of Jazz' Canadian terms the twins had picked up. They were such fun now that they could run around and talk. Every time he came home he'd call out *'Where are my children'* and they would come running. He would pretend he could barely recognize them because they had grown so much since he'd seen them last. They never tired of the joke. When they heard him ride into the yard they would go to hide and come running out when he asked for his children. If he didn't, they'd want to know if he didn't want to know where his children were. Celine had dubbed them Bonnie and Clyde and Jason sometimes called them that, mixing them up, calling Ebonique Clyde and Jafari Bonnie. They would go into fits of laughter correcting him, Ebonique proud to tell him Bonnie is a girls name and Jafari was a boy. Whatever his disappointment with Jazz, he thought she had given him some very special children. He couldn't stay mad at her long and their life together, despite its ups and downs, was good most of the time.

Jakey had taken it as part of his day's work to look out for Jazz. She looked out for him too, recommending him for, and throwing any job she thought he might like, his way. He had become friends with her neighbors and sort of suggested they keep and eye out for her after the break in of the little house.

Ebonique and Jaffari were spending a couple of days at Mont Yves as Cat had to get some medical tests. Jakey had seen Jerome watching the little house and then followed him to Jason and Jazz' house. He phoned Jason. The man was inside when Jason came home. Jason tiptoed into the house through the back and while Jakey and Henson, the neighbor, were looking out for him, they missed Jazz coming home. She had been given a ride to the street corner. When they saw her, she was reaching for the doorknob and Jakey yelled a warning, but the door was pulled open and Jazz dragged inside. Jakey rushed for the door. The man had a knife. It was all so sudden. Jazz saw the knife coming down at her.

So this was it. She wouldn't see Jase or her babies and extended family again. Then the man crumbled and the knife cut her but not deep enough to kill her. Jason had come from nowhere and hit the man over the head with a cricket bat. She was bleeding and Jason was lifting her. Jakey was there and Henson. Jason dragged the man outside and threw him over the terrace. It was at least a seven foot drop. He was really angry, and shouting *'Call the garbage truck and tell them to get this fucking man off my property. If he's here when I get back, he's dead.* He put a dazed Jazz in the car and drove her to the hospital, teeth clenched all the way.

The family gathered at Mont Yves that night. This stalker was getting out of hand. Jason had reported the incident to the police from the hospital. Jazz was still in a daze. She was afraid the man might be dead and they would arrest Jason. She could not handle that. She was shaking like a leaf. She had come within a split second of losing her life and her hero had saved her. Goddam! She loved this man!

The man turned out not to be dead after all, and several charges were brought against him. Jason was not charged with anything. The man was given a three year sentence, and the Coolidges relaxed. It didn't come out in court that Jason had thrown him over the terrace.

In the meantime, Jordan was having a hard time trying to adjust to his new circumstances. He had moved in with the housekeeper, but her boyfriend did not like it and that didn't work out. He had moved into his office but was forbidden to live there as it did not have shower facilities. He owed so much rent, anyway, the owners, taking a leaf out of Jazz book, had asked him to leave. Jazz couldn't leave well enough alone. She wanted her father's name on everything he used to own. She didn't know what she was going to call the school she was setting up in Jordan's house but she knew it would start with Brett LaPierre, so she had an unfinished sign put up. All it said was Brett LaPierre.

When the owners locked the place and seized his goods, Jazz rented it and again put her father's name on it. Jason asked her, calmly this time, where she saw this ending and she told him with Jordan in the Poor House. She wished she could call it the Brett LaPierre Poor House but she couldn't. He shook his head and said he didn't know her, but they didn't quarrel, and they continued to get along.

Crystal was beginning to look very sad. She eventually admitted to Jazz that she was under a lot of strain. Ed, her father had been having an overt affair with the woman to whom she reported at work, and she was having a rough time with it. Jazz had noticed, since she had returned, that Frances, Crystal's mother had been dressing and acting like an old woman but had not commented. Crystal complained that Jared had been no help at all. He had his own problems at work, and was totally uninterested. He had been given a title and a mandate and no budget, and was expected to come up with programs and procedures to make the force more effective.

Actually, Crystal had been woefully unaware of the depth of her husband's resentment and discontent. Jared had never really enjoyed living in St. Kitts. Not that there was anything wrong with the place, but the most important thing to him in his whole life was being the object of envy. He was thrilled when his father got the position of Chief of Police and the family had to move to St. Kitts, and had anticipated idol status, what with being from a larger island. He had, however, got in with the wrong crowd. They were too hard to impress. He went after, and snagged the prettiest girl in his school and nobody treated it as a big deal. His father's position didn't appear to mean much to them, and nobody appeared to wish they were him. As a matter of fact, Crystal had committed sacrilege once when he had tried to introduce his father's status in a conversation and she had said that when the working day was over, the chief of police was just a man. He had smiled through it, the others had treated it as if she had said the sun rises in the east, but inside Jared was boiling.

His father had set it up so he would get a full government scholarship to study law enforcement, and he viewed it as a fast track to the top. They would have to be impressed when he became Chief of Police, so it didn't matter that when the government gave you a scholarship you were bonded to come back and work for them for a given number of years. It fit into his plans. However, while he was away at school, his father had taken another position in another island and on his return, Jared found that on the force, they were no more impressed with him than his friends were in school. If he needed awe, he would have to look in a different demographic. He was obligated to stay and work out his bond, and besides, his wife had no interest in moving to St. Vincent or any other island.

Crystal told Jazz her younger sister, Elle had come home only once since she left for university, and that she really missed her, but Elle would not have anything to do with their father because he had always been on their cases as girls about being respectable and above criticism, and he had imposed so many rules and restrictions on them, they couldn't do anything.

Elle had seen him going into a place with a woman and had broken in on them in the middle of relations. She had called him every version of hypocrite there was, and told the woman she was just a whore, all while her father was trying to get his legs into his pants. She wouldn't look away and give him any privacy and he was so nervous he couldn't get his pants on. Elle grabbed the clothes, his and the woman's and threw them out of the window. She never said another word to him since then. Frances had felt she went a little over the top and said she had behaved like a hottentot, and Elle had left home that night.

At the time, Crystal had recently been married and didn't have to bear the brunt of the fight. When Elle got vacation, she had come to stay with Crystal, but Jared did not like getting between her and her parents and it hadn't worked out. They emailed, phoned and messaged each other all the time, but Elle never came back.

Jazz was shocked to hear about Ed, and wondered if Brett would have eventually done the same thing, had he lived. She doubted it. Celine would not stand for it, and she certainly wasn't going to let herself turn prematurely into an old woman. Jazz asked her friend why she didn't just change jobs and Crystal explained that she loved being in the field of education and that outside of being an actual teacher, the opportunities in such a small island were limited.

Shortly after, Jazz had an opportunity to have an unpleasant chat with the woman who was giving her friend such a hard time on the job. She had phoned Crystal and the woman answered and asked what she wanted. Jazz asked if she was Crystal's secretary and she said no, she was her boss. Jazz asked then why the hell was she answering her phone, wasn't that ass backwards or was it because she was so stupid she got her job on her back and didn't know her ass from her elbow. She told her she had no right to ask what she wanted Mrs. Scott for. If she wanted her, she would have rung her. They exchanged *un*pleasantries, and Jazz hung up feeling better, just before she realized she may have made life worse for her friend. She told herself anyway, that the Brett LaPierre Academy had 20 children. It was a small start but if Crystal got too much stick from her boss and decided to leave, she could run it. It was a bit shaky at the moment, but it was just starting out and she was confident that once all the kinks were ironed out, it was going to be a model for future institutes.

Jazz thought she would take the twins to the park. They could get some exercise and she could watch the football game. She was walking towards the street that divided the football and cricket sections from the tennis and netball sections when Ebonique spotted Jason watching football across the street. She suddenly tugged away from Jazz and, shouting *Daddy! Daddy!* Began running towards him, directly in the path of a golf cart heading towards the gate. Mercifully, the cart was going no more than 10 mph, but the front left of the vehicle struck the child. Jason, having heard his daughter, had turned in time to see the Jazz running, dragging Jafari, to stop Ebonique and witness the accident. He sprinted across the street to his daughter, yelling accusingly at Jazz, why was she not holding her hand and, rushing to the car, ordered her to go home, and drove off to take Ebonique to the hospital.

Jazz was frantic. She saw Gareth and Ian get into Gareth's vehicle and started running towards them, but they drove away. She knew they had seen her and yelled at them. *'Assholes! They are twins!'* How dare they leave her on the side of the road like refuse. Even if she wanted to obey Jason's order, how could she get home when he had driven away in the vehicle she'd come in. Even if she knew how to ride his motorcycle, she couldn't with Jafari. She phoned for a taxi and it didn't show for nearly twenty minutes. While waiting, she hugged and crooned to poor little Jafari, who never said a word.

Ian saw her first when she burst into the hospital carrying Jafari. He and Gareth were in the waiting area of Emergency. He attempted to rise and she looked at him, dripping disdain. She hitched Jafari up a bit and, with a circular motion of the index finger she had pointed at them said, *Don't speak to me. Do NOT speak to me* and continued moving like a tall ship in full sail. She did not need to ask where Ebonique was. She could hear her screaming for her Mommy and Jafari. She took Jafari in to see his sister and on seeing him, Ebonique cried 'Jafari' and hugged her brother with her good hand. After that, it was easy sailing. They put her hand in a cast, Jafari demanded one too, so they gave him a makeshift one and they left the hospital, showing off their casts to everyone willing to look. When they were outside Jazz said *'You three should know about twins, and as for you Jase, don't you ever treat me like that again, leaving me at the side of the road like a bag of garbage.* The other two made a quick escape, but Jason had to go home with her.

When Jason went to put the twins to bed, He decided to have a chat with Jafari. *I'm sorry about what happened today. Are you mad at me?*

No Daddy, but Mommy is. She said a bad word.

Did she? You think she still loves me?

I don't know. I'll go ask her. He was up like a shot.

Tell her I still love her. Jase said.

Jazz was cleaning up the bathroom when Jafari burst in.

Mommy, do you still love Daddy?

Of course I do, my little man. She bent down to hug him. *I will always love your daddy.*

Awesome! He started to run away then came back to say *He said he loves you too.* He returned to running back to his room. *Is okay daddy,* he shouted. *She said she loves you.'*

Both parents, in their respective places, laughed.

Three months after Jerome was sentenced, he broke out of prison. There was a fire in the prison, and he was the only prisoner who even tried to escape.

Jazz was trying to get her twins to socialize with other children. She registered them in day care, mornings only, and Cat would look after them in the afternoon. Each morning, for the past week, she would take them to the day care on the way to work and pick them up at lunchtime. Today, she had an early meeting with Mr. Melville. She drove the car to Jason's office so he might pick up the children at lunchtime, in case she was still in the meeting, and walked over to Melville's office.

When Jerome was discovered missing, the police phoned Jason to warn him of the possibility that Jerome might come looking for them. Jason called Jazz' Office. They told him where she was. He instructed them not to tell anyone else where she was. He thought he'd tell them why to make sure they took it seriously. He called Mr. Melville and begged him to keep Jazz there, and went to get his children from the daycare.

Jason called home to tell Cat to get out of the house. Cat was in a mood. He yelled at her to get the hell out now! He called his father, his mother, Gareth and Ian. While he was on the phone Cat called to complain about the way he had spoken to her. He wanted to know why she was still there. He explained the situation to her. Cat just could not hear him. She was completely focused on his disrespectful tone. Jason tried coaxing, explaining, and then he swore at her. Ten minutes later she was still there, still complaining. He had told Gareth and Ian. She was their responsibility now. He called Henson and asked if they would go over and coax her out. Henson looked out the window and told him his house was on fire. He called the Fire department and asked Henson to run over to drag Cat out.

Jason was trying to anticipate the man's next move. He was hoping to keep him away from his wife. He was cruising around looking for this man before he found Jazz. He had to feed his children and keep vigil. He ordered take out, except he wanted them to do the taking out – to his car. He promised there was a good reason he couldn't come in to get the food and his children were hungry. They complied.

In the early afternoon, Pim called to tell him that the man had gone down to Mont Yves, and Pammy had shot him. Jason felt sick. Pim assured him that his mother had not killed the man. You know your mother could shoot a pea at forty paces. He was running towards the house and Pammy shot him in the knee. He kept coming, hopping on one knee and she shot out the other knee. Jason was weak with relief. He went to get his wife.

While Jason was thanking Mr. Melville for taking care of Jazz, his phone rang and he got the news that his mother had been arrested. He was indignant, to say the least. He told Jazz. She calmly took the phone from her husband and called the local radio station's phone-in show. She identified herself and listed the various incidents when this man had invaded her space and attempted to kill her. She said she had been hiding all day because he was again trying to kill her. He had burnt her family home and had attempted to invade the home of her in-laws, and that her mother-in-law had shot him in the legs to stop him. The police had kindly warned them he was on the loose and would be looking for them but, as far as she knew, had done nothing else to help them. She was on her way to bail her mother-in-law out, as she had been arrested by the police for defending her home.

She called two more stations and gave them the same information. By the time she and Jason got to the police station, all the other Coolidges were there along with a few hundred people and they had to fight their way through the protesting crowds. Pammy was released almost immediately, to the cheers of the protesters. It had been, according to her, a bitch of a day.

The wagons had been circled. The Coolidges had prevailed. Somebody had retrieved Cat from the Hensons, where she had been complaining about Jason's disrespectful language. They decided to go to The Fisherman's Net for an early dinner to ease the tension. Jason was very quiet and tense. During the ordeal, he had considered that by the end of the day either he or his wife could have ceased to exist, and he couldn't believe how calmly she had she had engineered public support. Had she not, Pammy would be in a cell now. What had happened to the trembling naïf who asked permission to come home?

Cat's complaining was getting on his last nerve and Jason announced that Cat couldn't look after the children anymore. She was furious. He was angry, frustrated, tired. He told her she was a goddam liability. If this had happened a week earlier, his children would have been in the house with her, and he was having a nightmare thinking about that. Didn't she even smell the damn smoke? What did he have to do to get her out of the effing house? Tell her that her precious Marty was outside? Jason had always been quite sensitive regarding Cat, so his angry outburst at her, though justified, was surprising. Nobody intervened, however, and Cat vowed never to speak to him again. He couldn't imagine her not speaking to him ever, and lost some of his anger. He modified his tone and said *You could have been killed, Cat, and what would we have done then?*

Everybody drank more than they should. The mood had been tense and subdued but if a definition was required, then they supposed it was a celebration – of Pammy's freedom and the sparing of Jazz and/or Jason's life. The Fisherman's Net offered to send them home in a minibus. 'Where's home' was the big question, and Jazz said she expected they'd have to move into Celine's house. It had been too harsh a day to even try to drive past what had been their home. They'd wait till morning to go look at the damage. She would have to wash the babies' clothes so they could wear them again the next day.

The entire family slept in Celine's house that night.

The next day they took the twins to the day care and went to see the house. It was completely gutted and did not appear safe to go inside, particularly in Jazz' high heels. Her heart broke looking at her husband taking it all in. She tried to reassure him that at least now he could build the dream house he had spoken about, and Jason said he was not yet able to afford it. Jazz told him she could always borrow against her house in Toronto; it was more than paying for itself since her mother had rented it to the university for twice its worth and there was no mortgage on it. Jason said he couldn't let her do that and she asked what was the big deal, did he not intend that she live in it with him? He let her off outside her office without further comment, but as far as she was concerned, the matter was far from closed. There were things she should see to.

Sunday morning they went to church. When Father Cardinal launched into his sermon he talked about forgiving those who trespass against us and not ourselves meeting evil with evil. It sounded to Jazz that he was talking against what Pammy had done and she was a bit annoyed until he made a direct reference to the incident, and then she was enraged. Jazz got to her feet and interrupted the priest's sermon.

Excuse me! You owe my mother in law an apology. You are talking as if this man was sent from God with some test she failed. He is NOT a godsend. He is pure evil, who left her son and grandchildren, never mind me, homeless, has stalked us, invaded our home and came within a split second of killing me. He came back that day to complete the mission. He was not just merely a casual trespasser on her property. How do you dare tell the congregation that this spawn of Satan was a godsend. You owe my mother in law an apology! I will never come back to this church again.

As she took her children's hands to usher them out of the pew, she saw Jason's incredulous face. He was shocked, but he was shaking with laughter. He followed them out, then Pammy and Pim came down from the choir loft and Gareth and Ian also joined them. Crystal stood up with her two sons and followed them out, and a few other members of the congregation started to rise from their seats as well. Father Cardinal announced that he would apologize to the Mrs. Coolidges, but they seemed to have left.

Jazzie! I have never seen anyone challenge the priest in the middle of a sermon before. You sure don't give me a chance to get bored. Do you? And Jason laughed. His tension was easing away. True to his word, Father Cardinal did go to her office to apologize to her and went, as well, to Mont Yves to apologize to Pammy. Jazz continued to attend his church with her family.

Jazz told Jason, probably for the four thousand and sixtieth time, how much she loved him, he was her innermost soul, all she needed in life to make her happy was to live with him. She wanted him to have his dream house because it would make him happy. It had broken her heart to see him discover the damages to his house. Her mother had turned out to be a shrewd businesswoman, not above using her looks and personality to make lucrative contacts.

The Delightful Celine was admired by the people she was able to meet through Jaime's connection with the university, and in return she practically picked their pockets. Where Jazz was happy to offer a good service for a good price, Celine auctioned everything: A good service for as much as she could take anybody for. The business Jazz had left in her mother's care had quadrupled and Celine had barely broken stride. She wanted Jason to have the money for his dream house, and she also wanted them to have joint accounts, something they should have done years ago. It's what married people did.

Jason hadn't responded. He hated when she took the reins like that. He went for a ride and stopped at the bar where he, Gareth and Ian often limed with their friends. Neither was there, but he had a Carib anyway. Carib is the local beer. Ian walked in as he was about to leave, took one look at him and asked what was wrong. They went to Ian's house and Jason told him about the situation. Ian laughed and asked how was it that Jason was okay with Jazz getting his house burnt down but not with her helping him rebuild it, and Jason said that he'd expected to take care of Jazzie but she took care of herself. He also liked having something solely his own and it felt she was taking over his life.

Poor Jason. Ian laughed again and told him that he was the only person who did not know that Jazz had taken over his life long ago, and she had done that the day she came home screaming on the beach and he and his brother couldn't keep Jason from going to see her. He said that it was time to stop thinking of her as a pet. When they were kids she followed him around and he took care of her like a puppy. Now she was all grown up with woman parts in the right places, he still acted like she was a pet.

Ian also told him he should really count his blessings. Yola would have let him build his house on his own and if he stepped out of line, she would take every hinge and doorknob and walk away. All Jazz wanted was to stay, and he could have anything he wanted. That was most men's dream. He would get no argument that Jazz was crazy but Jason was lucky she was also crazy about him.

Jason found a note from Jazz when he went home. It said the offer was real, no strings attached except that he let her live with him. It would remain open for him to take or leave as he saw fit, but she had to insist on the joint accounts. The next day she went to the bank and opened joint savings and checking accounts. She told the staff that Jason was unable to be there but would come in a day or two to sign whatever needed to be signed. A week later the bank called. Jason had not been in. She apologized and said he had been really busy but she would remind him and that, if their checkbooks were ready when he came in, would they give them to him. She doubted she would be able to drop in soon either.

Jazz allowed Jason to go through his evening greeting ritual with the twins before she brought up the subject. She said she hoped they wouldn't have a fight about being married. The bank had called, and he hadn't gone in to sign their accounts, but Jason said he had, and gave her the checkbooks. He had gone in after they had phoned her. It was unlikely, however, that she would need to raise the money for him as he had got some big news. His designs had won the contract for a huge new resort. If he wanted to, he could probably build two houses. This called for champagne. They toasted and killed the bottle, and got frisky, and Jazz asked him if he thought there would be many foreign women involved in the project, because she didn't want too many women ogling her sexy, sexy husband. The locals already knew she was crazy. Might he consider wearing overalls? Jason said he loved it when she talked possessive. Lord, he loved this woman.

The twins were thriving and life was good. Jason and Jazz were as intimately active as they ever were, when Jason asked if she ever thought of having another baby. She was a little alarmed. She remembered their relationship had faltered after she had the twins. She asked him if that was what he wanted and he said he sometimes thought of it. They left it at that for the time being.

Jason was in their bathroom lathering up for a shave when Jazz came in and started teasing him. He was wearing a robe. She wedged herself between him and the mirror, and pretty soon he had her jacked up. In the midst of the encounter, Ebonique was tapping at her leg and asking Mommy, what you doing to Daddy. They had not heard her come into their bedroom but she had heard them in the bathroom and come to investigate the sounds. Jason froze. *'Holy shit'* Jazz said in his ear. He dare not let Jazz go or she would fall and he had to get Ebonique out without revealing much more. Luckily, you could convince a three year old of practically anything. He told Ebonique that he was helping Mommy and needed her to run get some stupid thing so she could help too. She was off and they drew apart, giggling.

Ebonique might not have been as easily fooled as they thought. She might not have understood exactly what had been happening, but she knew something different was happening and she wasn't sure she liked it. She decided that whatever it was, it was her mother's fault. Jazz noticed that after the incident, Ebonique became less affectionate and actually defiant, and whenever she hugged her, her little body became rigid. She hoped Ebonique would get over it. She was such a delightful little girl.

Pammy taught the twins to use the speed dial to phone her, probably to her own regret. The twins had been playing outside with Crystal's boys, while Crystal and Jazz chatted in the kitchen. They had not heard Ebonique come in, or leave. Miles away Pammy, in her own kitchen answered the phone to hear her granddaughter ask if her daddy was in the hospital.

What happened? Why would your daddy be in the hospital, darling? Pammy asked, alarmed.

Mommy cut off his Peepee.

What! Your Mommy wouldn't do that, would she?

She did! I heard her tell Auntie Crystal.

Pammy was trying not to laugh. What the hell was Jazz telling Crystal? *OK, darling. Hang up the phone and I will find your Daddy and call you back.*

She phoned Jason. He was in the park watching a football match. She asked him what had happened between him and Jazz and he said everything was fine, nothing had happened. She told him about the hilarious conversation she had with his daughter and he said he would look into it. He hung up and rode home.

Where are my children? They came running, and were all over him, even more than usual. He chatted to them about things that had nothing to do with peepees, and then focused on asking Jafari questions and got him to follow him into the bathroom where he peed while talking to him. Jafari was agape*! Daddy, you have a peepee,* he said in awe.

Of course I do, all men do, you know that.

Ebonique said Mommy cut it off.

Now why would she do that. Mommy wouldn't do a thing like that. Jafari was out of the room like a shot calling to his sister that Daddy's peepee was not cut off. He saw it.

Jason went into the kitchen. He wanted to know what Jazz was telling Crystal to make Ebonique think she had cut off his peepee. They thought he was crazy, so he told them of the little drama. Jazz wanted to know how he had cleared her name and he told her he peed in front of Jafari. After all, he could hardly whip it out in front of his daughter. He went back to his game. Jazz had a foreboding she was going to have some trouble with that little girl.

Jazzie! What is this? Why are you getting so bony? Are you sick? They were in bed and Jason was feeling her ribs. Jazz had been running herself ragged lately, trying to set up the Boarding school. She had lost a couple of staff at the office to maternity leave and illness, and she was trying to spend more time with the twins and especially to repair her relationship with the little madam that Ebonique was turning out to be. She had been missing meals. Jason told her to eat something to cover up 'them bones'. He didn't make love to her.

It was Saturday and Jazz went through her usual routine. When she had a break, she realized she was hungry. There was a sort of seafood salad thing in one of Pammy's dishes in the fridge. Jason usually cooked, but Pammy often sent dishes to her young men via Pim, who complained he felt like meals on wheels. Jazz figured it was something from Pammy and she had gobbled down maybe three forkfuls before she really began to taste it. She was sure she shouldn't have eaten it. She was deathly allergic to conchs and they never had it in the house but she was sure she tasted it.

It looked like it was going to rain and Jazz went outside to take some clothes off the line. She began feeling really sick. Her vision was becoming cloudy and she was weak. There was a ringing in her ears. Yes. She had eaten conchs. How had it got there? She asked Ebonique to go call her Daddy and the little girl wouldn't go. *Please Ebonique, just this once, do as you are told. Go get daddy and tell him to come quick. I'm in trouble.* The little girl left and Jazz passed out. Ebonique went to watch TV.

Jason called out to tell Jazz he was going out for a few minutes. She didn't answer. The phone rang as he was leaving, and he answered it. It was Pammy asking how Jazz liked the conch dish she sent her.

Joan Liburd

The what, Momma?

I know she said she doesn't like it but it's all in the way you cook it. I had it nicely concealed.

You did what? Jazzie can't eat conchs, mother. It's not that she doesn't like it. She is acutely allergic. I hope you didn't kill my wife. I'll call you back.

He went through the house calling Jazz. He asked Ebonique if she knew where Jazz was and she said she was laying down in the backyard and she wanted him to come. He rushed out to find Jazz unconscious on the ground. She seemed to have held on to the sheet on the line and pulled it down with her. She was all tangled up in it. Jason knew one thing. There was no time. He had to get her to the hospital now and there was no one with whom he could leave the children. He had to get the carseats out of the vehicle so Jazzie could lay in the back. He dragged them out and went back to get Jazzie and the children in the car. The children had to sit in the front. Please God, don't let anything happen to any of them.

He got Jazz to the hospital and got help for her. Toting two little children, he couldn't go into the room with her. He was praying hard. Lord, please let him have found Jazzie in time. He had the kids on his knees and Jafari asked him if he was going to cry because Mommy was sick. He asked Ebonique if Mommy had told her to call him and she said yes. He asked why she didn't call him and was shocked when she said because she didn't like her. He knew he should speak to the child but he was just not up to it at that moment.

It was a harrowing night. Gareth came and took the twins to Pammy. How does he end up in these predicaments, Jason wondered. Between his mother and his daughter, they could possibly have seriously damaged his wife, to say the least. The nurse allowed Jason to stay at Jazz' bedside

222

all night. In the morning Jazz woke him up. He could feel her fingers running along his head, which he had rested on the side of the bed. He raised his head and spoke to her but she was drifting in and out of consciousness. He needed a shave, a shower and some food, but he wanted to be there when Jazzie came to properly. The nurse who came to change the drip couldn't say how long she thought Jazz might be like that but she suggested he talk to her and it might wake her up. He did. He talked about everything and anything. He told her the things he knew she loved to hear, how special she was, how much he loved her, how happy she made him, how little his life meant without her. When she did wake up, he had just been pleading, *Jazzie, wake up. Please wake up, Jazzie.* She seemed fine. He called the nurse. They sent him away so they could tend to Jazz.

When Jason returned to the hospital, Jazz was fully awake. He had decided that he had to tell her exactly what had happened. She took the news well, and she told him not to tell her mother how it had happened. She was sure Pammy did not mean her any harm. The crisis was over. He called his mother to tell her that Jazz was awake now and what she had said. Pammy spoke to Jazz. She apologized, and explained that she had not understood that Jazz was allergic, she thought she just didn't like the taste and she wanted to show her it was all in the way you cooked it. She also said she thanked her for not having her crazy mother come after her. Jazz laughed.

Gareth always tried to come over as a curmudgeon, but he was actually quite sensitive, and quite knowledgeable about many things. He had a photographic memory and he was an avid reader. Not only did he remember everything he read, he remembered where he read it. Gareth loved the twins as though they were his own and he had noticed the change in Ebonique which Jazz had seen but not spoken about. When Jason mentioned that Jazz had asked Ebonique to call him for help and she refused, he related it back to something he had read. He would go back and study it more carefully before mentioning it to Jason.

In the meantime, he was going to have a little chat with her. Ebonique also loved Uncle Gareth, so when he asked her why she hadn't called Daddy to help Mommy, she had no problem telling him it was because she hurt Daddy and laughed. Gareth asked her how Mommy had hurt Daddy and the child described her perception of the incident when she had seen her parents having sex in the bathroom. She tilted her head back, emulating the joyful look on her mother's face, and then she imitated her father face and his painful grunts. Gareth wanted to laugh but he didn't think it was really funny.

They kept Jazz in hospital for four days to make sure there was no nerve damage or other negative effect. Jason did not quite appreciate just how close he had come to losing his wife but he was at least grateful to have her back. Everybody was happy to see her when she arrived at the office, and during the course of that first day back, she found out that Jordan had been hit by a car while crossing the road. He was pretty banged up and might need surgery, which he could not afford. She called the hospital and confirmed that this was true. She told them to go ahead with the surgery. Her firm would pay for it.

When Jordan was well enough to be discharged Jazz was contacted by the hospital. They wanted to know whether they could discharge him into her care as he had nowhere to go.

Hell, no. Jazz answered. *He has two sisters, try them, but no. He cheated them out of their inheritance. Try his wife. No. He cheated on her and tried to cheat her out of her money too. Well.. he must have some friends, but no. It looks like he hasn't met anyone he hasn't cheated. Send him to the Poor House.*

That had to be the most often repeated conversation on the island. It was embellished, corrected, told and retold, and Jason went nuts. Jazz was sure that this time it was over between them, and for the first time, she didn't care. They had a fight at Mont Yves in front of his family, and she was not likely to forget it.

Things can change very quickly. Jason had been outside showing Jafari the rudiments of football. Ian and Jazz were watching and Jazz asked him wasn't her husband cute. Ian told her that maybe he would get back to her on that if she got Jason a push up bra, some high heels, lipstick and a wig. Just about that time Pim drove up and Jafari ran off to greet him. Jason came over wanting to hear the joke that put Jazz and Ian in stitches and they told him. He sidled up to Jazz and asked '*so you think*

I'm cute? Wanna go on a date?' and Jazz said *yes, You gotta car? We could go park at Greenhill and make out in the backseat.* Ian said that even for the two of them that was just nuts and walked away warning them jokingly that if he saw their car at Greenhill he was calling the police.

Shortly after, they were all hanging out, when somebody mentioned the famous conversation, and she could see Jason getting furious. She was on her way to help herself to some of Pammy's cooking, when Jason blurted out that everyone was treating his wife's behavior like amusing antics. It was no different from Jerome's stalking her. Every morning, he said, she was like a priestess, praying for the will for them to be kind even when it is hard, and then she goes and ruins a man.

Jazz stopped and gaped at him, a torrent of tears, ready to flow. She was stunned. How could Jase say that? She hated herself for crying. She could face down Jordan or anyone else, but if Jason frowned at her, she cried, and couldn't help herself. Jason's face was like a thundercloud, and anger filled her up.

Sometimes God says no, she retorted.

You're going to hell, he tried to joke, realizing how angry and hurt she was.

Well, you don't have to wait till then to get rid of me. I'm not living with him, anymore, she announced angrily. *Ian, I want a divorce.*

'I'm not married to you, Jazz' Ian answered and smiled at his own joke. Jazz was not laughing. She called the twins, and without another word, led them outside. They sensed her mood and didn't protest, although Jafari kept looking back to catch his father's eye, but Jason's back was turned.

Jazz walked out to where the vehicles were parked. Gareth's keys were in the ignition. So were Jason's, but she was cutting all ties with him so she transferred the carseats to Gareth's. He could hitch a ride with Jason. She'd return the vehicle later.

Inside the house, Ian was saying that another hilarious episode of Jazz leaving Jason was underway, and Gareth said he didn't think it was funny. The circumstances were different, and warned Jason not to let this happen. Ian told him it was funny because it was his vehicle she was taking and Gareth trotted outside to talk with Jazz.

He told her she couldn't take his wheels and leave him stranded, her fight wasn't with him. He coaxed her to come back into the house and tell Jason exactly how she felt and why she did what she did. Whether or not he liked it, he would at least get to see her perspective. She was still a flood of tears and, her relationship with Jason aside, he did not want her crashing his vehicle, injuring the twins, or herself, for that matter. He thought she was a nut, but he liked her. He was eventually able to convince her to go back to the house, although she said she did not want to be alone with Jason.

Back in the house, the children sent off to play, Jazz announced that sometimes people had to choose a side. In any dispute involving her husband, she knew which side she would be on. Her husband had chosen the other side. She had not been lucky as he was, to be surrounded by a warm family, and the small family she had was taken from her by Jordan. She did not want to go into it because chances were they wouldn't understand what it was like to lose so much of your life. Admittedly, a lot of it was due to her naivety, but he was first and foremost, responsible, and when she was gone, he continued to intimidate her only known family.

She said that maybe Jason's perfect wife would be more like Mother Theresa, she would have forgotten the past and welcomed Jordan into their home and entertained him like royalty, but she was not Mother Theresa nor was she a Stepford wife. She had approached Jordan, politely, at first, then he turned it ugly. Having done that, the lines were drawn in the sand. If she had shown any weakness, Jordon would have come after her and tried to do to her exactly what she had done to him. As a matter of fact, she said, he had nothing with which to pull down her father's firm and therefore, knowing her husband to be her Achilles heel, he would probably have gone after him.

Her fight was only with Jordan and only Jordan was hurt. There were already twenty children already moved in to the school that the house she had taken from Jordan and his office, would be used for. She had offered the good people of this island a better product than Jordan had, and for less. The population saved money, Daddy's firm made money, and Jordan's firm was wiped out, because Jordan was a jackass. She had worried she could pull her father's company down trying to knock him off his legs but, despite cheating everybody for years, he was on spindly legs and it had taken virtually no effort to take him down. As long as he is in the poor house, she will always make donations in her father's name. The other occupants will benefit, all he had to do was live with the name Brett La Pierre like a sonorous drumming he couldn't escape for the rest of his miserable life. She was not sorry, and would not apologize for what she had done, and though she had loved and obeyed him in everything else, Jordan had won because her ex-husband Jase, had chosen his side. Since he felt that she was as hateful as the man, and he had such empathy for Jordan, all three could join together to come after her. She turned away and said she would wait in Gareth's vehicle, would he give her a ride home.

Gareth said no. Her husband was there and, as she had told him many times, she loved him with all her heart so, they have a disagreement, they can take it home, in their own vehicle, discuss it, and work it out. He'll see them soon.

Jason came home with her that night. He was aware that his remark had hurt her to the quick, and they hardly spoke for the next two weeks. He slept on the daybed while she lay in the bed not sleeping, not for more than a couple of hours each night. She missed Jason terribly and she didn't know what to do. She did not believe he really meant what he had said, and even though for a few minutes, when she'd told Ian she wanted a divorce she meant it, she had now forgiven him. When Jazz thought of all the years she had spent alone, and of the difference he had made in her life after she came back home and found Jason again, and how good it had been living with him, she could not contemplate life without her Jase.

Desolation is the most appropriate word for what Jazz felt during those two weeks, so it was not a good time for Celine to tell her that Brian wanted to sell his share in the business. He had met a man and had fallen madly in love. They needed the money for some other venture. Jazz vented a bit and ranted against Brian, but eventually realized that he had been a good friend and associate to her, and that he could sell his share to a stranger. She phoned Brian and tried to discourage him but he was immovable, so she warned him that it was not a revolving door. Once he was out, that was it. She was never going to consider letting him in again. They agreed, and she set the wheels in motion to buy Brian out. The business deal distracted her just a little bit but once everything that she could do was done, she began be enveloped in a cloud of loneliness, depression and regret again.

Late one night she phoned Mont Yves. She knew they would be up because they had been entertaining guests. Pammy answered and Jazz said *Mama, tell him to come back to me.*

Pammy laughed and asked if Jason was still sulking. She told Jazz that she and Jason were always feeling each other up when people were looking, now nobody looking, feel him up where she should be feeling and stop bothering her. She laughed and hung up.

Jazz went to the daybed and stood over Jason. He was pretending to be asleep. He had heard her call his mother. He actually did want to go back to her but he wanted to make her work at getting him back. She had got on his nerves, and he could wait. She got down on her knees and started caressing him. A man's body can betray him, and Jason realized it was no use pretending to be asleep now. He opened his eyes and she stood up and slipped off her gown, and when he'd had a good look she said *'You dumped me for Jordan? You think he was worth it? Get up from there Jase and come play with your wife.*

Jason got up. What could he say? He was cheap and easy, she was cute, and he was her slave. He would tell her some time, how much he missed her and that he loved her, but let her wait – a few minutes, at least. The Coolidges were together again.

When the twins turned four Jazz registered them in Junior Kindergarten at the Erindale School. She quickly got on the outs with their teacher, Miss Ward. Wanting to get an early start for Mont Yves on Friday, she arrived at the school early, just in time to hear Miss Ward call Jafari a very stupid little boy. Jazz blasted into the classroom like a gush of cold wind and, in front of a roomful of gaping four year olds, ordered Miss Ward to sit her arse down and, her face very close to Miss Ward's told her that if she ever heard her call Jafari, or any other child in her care stupid, she would personally see that she never went anywhere near a child ever again. She lowered her voice to tell her that if it is one of her children, she would break her arm.

The twins were left handed, like Jason. They had settled in the school but they complained from time to time that they were not allowed to sit together, and Miss Ward wanted them to write wrong. At first Jazz didn't get what writing wrong meant, but she had another, more civilized talk with Miss Ward, who explained she wanted them to spend some time apart so they could make friends with the other children. She also thought it would be better if they wrote with their right hands. Jazz told her that they were left handed. She was to leave that alone but it was okay to separate them for short periods from time to time. She wanted Miss Ward to remember that they are twins. She considered the matter closed.

The twins had been in school for about four months. Jazz went, as usual, to pick them up after school, and was most surprised to see them outside, crouched in a corner. It had rained that day, and Jafari was soaked. She hugged them to her. *Why are you out here? What happened?*

It turned out that Jafari did not want to be separated from Ebonique and Miss Ward sent him out of the class. Miss Ward had forgotten him when it started to rain but Ebonique had not, and when she started acting up about it, Miss Ward sent her to join him. Poor Jafari tried to find shelter in a corner, but the wind had driven the rain into his corner and he was soaked. Jazz was way past enraged. She took her kids into the classroom, where a few children were still waiting to be picked up. She sat them down.

You stupid bitch! Jazz yelled. She was enunciating her words as clearly as possible, each word independent, as though separated by a period. *They are four years old. Four years old! What if something happened to them out there? I'm paying big money so my children could be left out in the rain? Bitch. I'm staying over here, because if I get near enough to your throat, I will not stop squeezing until you stop breathing. You hear me? Get me the headmistress. Get me the fucking headmistress!*

She's gone home. Miss ward said. Her voice was shaking.

I don't give a damn. Get her. On. The fucking. Phone. Miss Ward dialed on her cell phone. She listened and then said '*She won't speak to you. Her work day is over.*

Give me the number. Give me the kiss me arse number! Jazz ordered and Miss Ward complied. Jazz dialed.

When the phone was picked up Miss Holness, the headmistress, did not answer in the usual way. She just said. *My work day is over Mrs. Coolidge. Talk to me during school hours tomorrow,* and she hung up.

Jazz phoned Jason and asked him to bring clothes for the children and told him what had happened. Jason couldn't get his head around what his wife was saying. It was impossible. Jazz told him to hurry because she needed his calm personality to stop her killing this woman, but just in case, get a lawyer. Miss Ward heard, and cringed. Jazz phoned the police and made a formal complaint.

By the time Jason arrived, the children had all been picked up, although they were still in the parking lot with their parents, waiting to see if there would be any further action. He took the clothes in for the children and helped them dress, careful to block the aisle accessing Miss Ward. He spoke to his wife and confirmed she had called the police. They had not shown. She had phoned the headmistress. He said they would go home and pursue it through the courts. Jazz openly acquiesced. Inside, she said *'like hell we would'*, and Jason told Miss Ward she could go home. She would hear from their lawyers. The Coolidges went home.

When they got home, Jazz kissed her babies, let Jason feed them, and went on her computer. She remembered hearing that there was to be some Child Welfare and Children's Rights conference which was to be attended by an American Senator. She was supposed to touch down on the island for a few hours some time this week. She thought: Timing is everything.

The next day, the story of the four year old twins who were expelled from an expensive private school without their parent's knowledge, and left in the rain for their parents to find, was all over the media, local, regional and international, and the island was swarmed with reporters. The headmistress, Mrs. Holness, feeling her reputation besmirched, decided to seek the help of the best law firm in the region, Hollis and Hollis. She had no idea of the connection between the firm and the children. She was astounded to be advised by the receptionist to leave as quickly and quietly as she could - not only would the firm not represent her, they were themselves considering suing her on behalf of their nephew and niece. By the next week attendance at the school was less than half of the students registered, and by the end of the term, most parents had withdrawn their children. There were no new registrants.

Jazz did not need to be told that something was wrong in Crystal's life. She was so sorry for her friend. She wished she could do something. According to Crystal, Jared was pretty much gone. She believed he was seeing someone else. Her mother was miserable, her father was a cheat, her boss was her father's mistress and her life was totally stressed. Jazz decided to help her friend win back her husband, and while she was at it, help Frances win back Ed. She told Crystal of her plan, and Crystal agreed.

While running LaPierre's, Jazz had come to know several sales representatives who frequently visited the island. One of them was Don Marcellus. He was early to mid forties, handsome, single and, according to him, loved ladies but was not looking for a wife. They had become friends, and when the Coolidges gave a party, Don was invited, if he was on the island. Don was good looking enough to make any man jealous and young enough to make Ed stand up and take notice. She would solicit his help. The annual Eagles Club gala was coming up. She decided this would be the big event.

Don had agreed. It was a simple plan. They were going to be the most stunning and charming they had been in their entire life. Don would ask Jazz to introduce him to the lovely lady at her table, or whatever term he thought would get Ed in gear, and Jazz would introduce them. If Ed became demonstratively jealous, Don would back off, if not, he would just have a good time. In the case of Crystal, she would just look fabulous. Crystal was easily the most beautiful woman of any age on the twin islands, if not in the region, and Jazz believed that many people admiring his wife would remind him of what he had, and bring Jared in line.

They chose their outfits carefully. Their hair and make-up were professionally done. Jared said he would have to meet Crystal at the event, as work would make him late. Not a problem. The ladies were so excited. Jason had the enviable task of escorting the three of them to the event, and they looked good, very, very good. He was proud.

The gala was very well attended. Heads turned when Jason arrived with the three women. They were stunning! No one could have missed Crystal's beauty. She looked more beautiful than a movie star. Don took a satisfied look at Frances, and decided the gig was worth it, and Jason, well he was always sure of Jazz.

The meal was great and the dancing had begun, but Jared had not shown up. Don did what he had to do, and everyone was dancing, except Crystal. Ed was obviously disturbed his wife, looking so beautiful, was dancing with a younger man, and apparently enjoying it. What's more, the man seemed to enjoy dancing with her. He had sought her out. Ed had heard him himself, asking Crystal's friend for an introduction. He hadn't seen his wife look so good since they were young. As for Don, he actually liked this woman and was enjoying dancing with her. He even invited her for lunch, and maybe dinner, the next day.

Crystal sat alone at their table, embarrassed, waiting for Jared. The dinner was completed, there was a short address, and the dancing had been in progress for more than an hour and he had not yet shown. Finally, she saw him at the door. He looked right at her but made no effort to join her. She saw Jason's nice cousin, Ian, standing and looking at the dancers and decided to talk to him. She walked over and whispered an order to dance with her now. Ian did not need to be asked twice. He took her onto the floor and they danced like they had been dancing together their entire life. In actual fact, they had barely spoken to each other, despite their respective relationships with Jason's family. Jared made no effort to dance with his wife, and after a half hour, he left. At the end of the evening, Jason took the party he had brought to their respective homes. The Eagles gala was over for another year.

Jason was liming in the park with some of his buddies when Jared joined them. He asked him how he could allow a woman as beautiful as his wife to sit unattended at the event the night before, and Jared said that he noticed she wasn't alone for long because Ian took up the slack. Ian said somebody had to because Jared was an ass if he thought Crystal was the type of woman anyone did that to, and Jared lunged at Ian. Jason stepped between them: *'Don't to do that, Jared'*. He advised him to go home and apologize, and try to make it up to his wife. Jared left, and they considered the matter closed.

Crystal was cleaning up after dinner, when Jared started a fight about her dancing with Ian, and Crystal said that if he had danced with his wife, she wouldn't have danced with anyone else. She pointed out that she had been waiting for hours while he was probably out with his bimbo. Jared slapped her so hard she thought she would pass out. She was wearing a track suit, but only house slippers. She didn't stop to change. She started to run and, and didn't stop till she was in Jazz kitchen. By then the entire left side of her face was swollen, and her left eye was partly shut.

Geez hombre! Jazz was aghast. How could a man do this to his wife just for looking lovely. She hugged her friend and got some ice. She wanted to at least tell the bastard off, but as she reached for the phone, Crystal stopped her. She did not want him to know where she was.

Jazz was pretty sure he could easily guess, but she believed Jared would not want to try getting past Jason to beat up his wife some more. She was surprised when Crystal said she wished Ian was there. She had enjoyed dancing with him the night before. Jazz wrote down his number and told her to call him. Ian was a very sensitive man, and would come if she called him. Crystal had never done anything like that before, but she phoned. When Ian answered she told him that her husband had beaten her up, she needed a lawyer, she had enjoyed dancing with him last night and she had felt something. He asked where she was and said he would be there shortly.

When Ian saw Crystal, he cringed inside. He had seen her many times, but he barely knew her. She was Jazz friend and he liked her a lot, but she was married, so he had never tried anything. Last night when she asked him to dance he thought it was Christmas, and had really enjoyed the experience. When she phoned, he did not know what to think, but now he thought he was going to take this woman as his own. She was too good for the likes of Jared. He sat next to her and touched her face gently, and then he kissed it, just as gently, and asked her if she wanted a divorce. She confirmed that she did, but added that what she wanted was for him to hold her a little bit. Ian was surprised, but had no intention of flying in the face of fortune. He hugged her and kissed her gently, and asked her if she needed a place to stay. He took her to his house, and did everything he possibly could to ensure that this lovely woman would want to be his for the rest of her life.

When the phone rang early next morning, Jazz assumed it was Crystal. It was Crystal's son, Jarvis. Unfortunately for the poor child, he had witnessed his father's assault on his mother, and was very much disturbed. He said it wouldn't have happened if he was big enough to take on his father. He was sure his father did this because of the woman with the ugly shoes and fake hair and ugly mini jeans skirts. Jazz was flabbergasted! Crystal had not mentioned this person. She wondered if she knew her.

Ian dropped Crystal off shortly after. She wanted to go to look for her kids, but she didn't want Ian to take her to the house. Jazz took her. At the house, Crystal's things were outside and her keys didn't work in either of the doors. Jared had changed the locks. She phoned the house.

She could hear the phone ringing. She phoned Jared's cell. She phoned his office. There was no answer at any of these phones. Poor Crystal! She started to cry. Jazz advised she call Ian again.

Before Crystal could call Ian, her phone rang. Jarvis was creating a disturbance at the airport. Jared was trying to put the kids on a plane. Thank you my darling son! She thought. Crystal told them that under no circumstances were they to let her children get on a plane. She had not authorized it, and was not aware of any such plans. Her children were being kidnapped! Then she called Ian. He met them at the airport and, once everything had been straightened out, he took them back to his home and told her that, if she wanted, he would order twin beds to be delivered for them. The boys were happy, and it was done.

Crystal went to see her mother that evening. Frances was getting dressed. While Crystal was there, her Father Ed walked in and asked where Frances was going. He wanted to talk to her. She told him she was going on a date with the handsome young man she met at the dance, and he was furious. He told her it was important he talked to her and maybe she could cancel. Crystal was sure she had entered the Twilight Zone when she heard her mother tell her father it would only be important if it was a joke about his bimbo, but he could tell her some other time. Tonight she was going to get laid. It was painful to laugh so loud with her ruined face, but he deserved that. At least one part of Jazz' plan seemed to have worked.

When Crystal told her sister Elle of her predicament, Elle told her that one of the reasons she had not been visiting, was that when she had stayed at Crystal's years ago, she awakened one afternoon to find Jared in bed with her. She had had to fight him off and he had told her that Crystal would be okay with an encounter between them.

Crystal was more than just a little disgusted with all she was discovering about her husband, but she was overwhelmed, and grateful for how wonderful Ian was being. For goodness sake! He hardly knew her!

In addition to throwing her things out, Jared had turned the garden hose on them, ruining a lot of her stuff. She went to the clothing store to get something for herself, but her credit card was denied. She went to the ATM and it ate her card. She could not believe Jared was doing this to her. She did not deserve this and besides, her paycheque had just been deposited. He could at least have left her the money she had earned. She phoned Jazz. She was too embarrassed to call Ian again. Jazz told her to go to the LaPierre stores. She would clear it. She did, and then she called Ian.

Crystal was in Sister Chic, the LaPierre Ladies store. She was dejected. It was almost Christmas. She had two boys, no money, she had lost her home, and she was living with a stranger. No disrespect to Jazz, but this must be how Jordan felt. She was wallowing in self pity when her phone rang. It was Ian. He wanted to know if she was keeping Scott's name or reverting to Vanderpool. She hadn't thought about it, she supposed she would return to her maiden name. Ian said he needed to know because he was having her issued with companion cards on his credit cards.

Good Lord in heaven! Where had this good man come from?

Ian took care of everything. Crystal was overwhelmed, and most grateful. Now she appreciated what Jazz was talking about when she said the Coolidge men swept you off your feet. She made up her mind that she was holding on to this one. She deserved to be as happy as Jazz, and Jared had just not worked out. She had tried to be a good wife. Her children were happy to be with Ian, and she delighted in it whenever she protested about some thoughtful thing he had done, and he said *'You're* **my** *wife now, I'll take care of it,* or *You are* **my** *wife now, forget about Jared.* He was gentle and caring, he was generous and understanding, he was good looking and he was fit. He had promised her a quick divorce, and when he got home at night, he loved her like the second coming. She was keeping this man. Bye-bye Jared. She hoped Jared's new love's fake hair came off in his hand every time he made love to her.

It was almost Christmas and school was out. Ian took Jarvis and Steele to Mont Yves for the school holidays, along with Ebonique and Jafari, so they had the place to themselves. Crystal wanted to make her position clear, to herself at least. She asked him if his relationship with Bonni was over. He was a bit surprised. Bonni had been gone for years. He said that he had dated Bonnie, but not long into the relationship he realized the focus of her affection was someone else. She asked if it was Gareth, because she remembered Jazz saying that Bonni was actually after Gareth, but Ian got to her first.

Ian was surprised that she thought it was Gareth. He said she was not Gareth's type. His brother, he said, tried to give the impression of being a rascal, but what he was, was an intellectual. A lot of women seemed to be attracted to him. He flirted outrageously, but only after the woman came on to him. He never initiated it because he was actually shy and afraid of being shot down, and he never took them to his home because he was concerned in case they got wrong idea and he could not get them to leave. He wouldn't want to hurt a woman and was afraid he would be stuck with someone he didn't love, if she thought there was something serious when there wasn't. Ian believed it was the result of seeing how their mother's life was spoilt by her husband's actions. He was never able to think of Hollis as his father – whenever he thought of him, it was as his mother's husband.

He told her of Gareth's photographic memory and his avid reading and that the women he liked were smart, witty, confident women, independent thinkers. The women he saw tended to do the wrong things to try to please him. He didn't like it when they pretended to be helpless belles or when they pretended to know more than they did, but none of them seemed to try being themselves. The girl he had spent most time with was Avonelle Curtiss, a girl he had dated for a while when they were in England in university. She wasn't especially pretty and she had a short leg, but she challenged him and he enjoyed her company. Her mother, seeing how well they got along, warned Avonelle not to challenge him so much and to be more 'womanly'. Avonelle took her mother's advice and began acting the dumbass southern belle, which is the surest way to turn Gareth off.

Ian told her that Bonni went out with him because of his resemblance to Jason. She was in love with Jason. Crystal was stunned. She knew that Jazz knew Gareth's characteristics. She had mentioned it, but she was sure she did not know Bonni's aims. She wondered if Jason did, but she didn't ask.

Crystal was apprehensive about spending Christmas at Mont Yves. Ian said they would all go down at Christmas Eve and those who did not have to work would stay till the New Year, and those who had to, would come back for the working days in between and return on Old Year's. She confided her anxiety to Jazz and Jazz assured her that the warmest, most welcoming place on the island was Pammy's kitchen, and that as long as Ian liked her everyone would, and it would be fine. Crystal told her friend how wonderful Ian had been and Jazz said he was standard Coolidge issue, she'd get used to it. Just be nice to him and she was set.

The 'Coolidge triplets' had a reputation as serious ass kickers. If one of them was involved in a row, somehow, the other two would materialize, and the opponent would be facing three tall, very fit men, totally changing the odds. Together, they defined Pammy's expression of 'the testosterone cloud'. There was no person, however, who could truthfully say that they had ever seen them actually involved in a fight. Their opponents probably just fell in love with them because they really were an impressive sight.

The day before Christmas Eve, Gareth was sitting in their usual bar with some friends. A few blocks away, Pim was also enjoying a drink with friends at a restaurant. Jason was at home, where his wife and her best friend Crystal were sitting chatting in the kitchen.

Ian, driving by the Circus, decided to stop to get something for Crystal's boys, and there, as he came back to his vehicle, was Jared. Jared's car blocked his in, and Jared yelled at Ian, and Ian told him he was a jackass. He had a lovely flower and the best he could do was crush it. He promised to make Jared famous by getting him the quickest divorce outside of Reno, and yes, he would be taking his wife, and his family, thank you.

Less than twenty feet away, Sean Pinney, who worked for Pim, was liming. He made a bet with his friend about how fast Coolidge reinforcements could get there. He was a watchman at Pim's distillery and knew how to get in touch with him at any time. He phoned Pim, and then he phoned Gareth. Gareth phoned Jason. Pim told his friends his boys were making a ruckus, he had to go. Gareth just told his friends he'd be back. Jason told his wife he was going out for a bit, he hoped she had money for bail as Ian and Jared were creating a disturbance in town. Ian could take Jared easily, but Jared was a member of the police force. That was a lot of dangerous back up. Jazz immediately jumped up saying she was coming, and Jason said she was not, it was man's work.

He had no doubt his wife would follow him anyway, so at the door he said it would hurt Crystal's case. That should keep her where she was for the couple of minutes it would take to get a headstart and lose her. He smiled. He had worked out the reason she convinced Father Cardinal to replace 'honour and obey' with 'honour and respect.' He was surprised she didn't insist on him adding 'as she saw fit.' She was lucky she was cute. He rode off laughing at his own joke.

They were all there within seven minutes. Jason knew Jared best so he rode his motorcycle up to where Jared was, throwing words at Ian. Jason wasn't angry. He was calm, and actually in a good mood.

Jared, man. What you doing? Leave Ian alone. You threw the woman away. Didn't we tell you to apologize to her? Smashing her face was your apology? We thought better of you, man. What kind of man does that shit, anyway?

Jared just said *Jason, I have no quarrel with you. You're ok.*

We're all okay Jared. Go home. If you let this get ugly you're not going to come out smelling of roses. Go home, man.

Jared turned away, walked to his car and drove off. The Coolidges congregated at Jason's.

Christmas at Mont Yves was everything that Jazz and Ian had promised. The children were ecstatic. The family welcomed Crystal like she had been one of them all along. In the surroundings, nestled in the mountains, spectacular views in every direction, she almost forgot that Jared existed. She found she agreed with Jazz that the sound of conversation between the Coolidge men was a comforting rumble. Pammy called it sonic boom. Like Jazz, Crystal enjoyed their rich deep voices and felt a childish pride that next to Pim's her man's was the deepest. She studied Gareth when he was relaxed. These were indeed fabulous men. She was lucky to have one, and there was only one left. A plan was formulating in her mind and she couldn't tell anyone, not even Jazz.

Crystal related to Jazz what Elle had told her. She was sorry Elle had to live all this time with that, and she missed her sister. She wished she could tell her face to face that it wasn't her fault that Crystal had married a snake. Jazz could not see what the problem was, maybe Ian's place was full, but Elle could stay at the little house. It was set, Crystal would ask Elle.

New Year's at Mont Yves was all about family, love, warmth and renewal. The Coolidges never bothered with the various events around the island scheduled for 'Old Year's Night'. They congregated at Mont Yves, so that's where Crystal found herself this year, her first as one of the family. The gathering was intimate and, as usual, very fun. They dressed up, even the children. They dined in the big dining room. The table was nicely decorated and dinner was not buffet as usual, but formally served. They were still Coolidges and they teased and tested each other, they ate, drank, joked, laughed and danced. Crystal enjoyed the embracing atmosphere and the warmth of the Coolidge fold.

Jason and Jazz were dancing, a close, slow dance. Ebonique wanted to dance with Jason and kept nagging. Jason was not in a physical condition to let go of his wife and dance with his daughter. Gareth understood, and asked Ebonique to dance with old Uncle Gareth instead since he didn't have a wife. She loved Uncle Gareth so she agreed but informed her father that she wanted to dance with him after and Gareth lifted Ebonique up and danced with her.

Jason and Jazz decided to step outside for a bit. Ebonique was watching and saw them. She wriggled out of Gareth's arms before he could do anything, demanding shrilly to know where they were going, saying that she was coming too. Jazz was annoyed and, pointing her finger in the little girl's face ordered her to stay. It did not matter now anyway, the mood had been spoiled. She went back and took Ebonique's hand and took her over to a sofa where Crystal was sitting, and sat her down next to her. Then Jazz took a seat. Ebonique was now sitting between the two adults. Jazz told her that now she was sitting among the adult ladies, her daddy would come over and ask her to dance and she could get up like a little lady and go dance with him.

Jason came over. He was smiling when he bent over and said *Hmm. Three beautiful ladies. Which one should I dance with.* Ebonique was up like a flash. *Me! Me, Daddy.* Her shrill little voice demanded. *Dance with me!*

No, Ebonique. Jazz reached to show her how it should be done but the eager determination on her little girl's face made them all burst into laughter. Jason danced with his daughter, and she beamed.

On the way home late New Years' Day, it occurred to Jazz that she had neither heard nor seen Jakey since Christmas Eve. Jason said it was probably because they were at Mont Yves much of the time. She didn't think so, he could have got in touch on Old Year's Day. She decided to stop by. Jason dropped her off and took the twins home to change into their costumes. They had found out that the men in the family were dancing with a Clown Troupe in the Carnival festivities and insisted on joining them.

At Jakey's house, she called and wasn't sure she'd heard an answer. She went in. Jakey was lying down. His leg was roughly bandaged but did not look good. He had apparently got speared somehow, fishing the day after boxing day. She called a taxi to take him to the hospital.

The nurse in the Emergency was very offhand with Jakey. She obviously didn't like the dreadlocks. Jazz was all over her like a rash. She demanded she treat her patients, *all* her patients with respect, and remember she is a nurse, which meant caring person, or get a job grooming cats or something. Jakey had not eaten or showered since his accident, and he was a little bit gamy. Jazz had demanded a private room for him and the nurse said he had to have a bath but she was busy. Jazz said she would do it and gave Jakey a sponge bath, which embarrassed the blazes out of him. When he was settled and clean smelling, she promised to bring him some pajamas. He'd have to turn up the sleeve and the legs because they were bought for Jase, and the stores were still closed.

Jakey spent two weeks in hospital and Jazz went to see him at least three times a week. One day, in the second week, when she entered the room she thought for a second that Jakey had been discharged. His locks were gone and his beard was neatly trimmed. He smiled sheepishly and told her that he had a thing for one of the nurses but she didn't like rastas so, he let her 'fix him up'. She was off duty and had gone home, but he would introduce them the next day.

Jazz liked Nurse Jeannette Lacey and told her to take good care of Jakey. She had known him since they were toddlers and, when she needed a friend, Jakey had been there for her.

The day before he was discharged, Jakey asked her if she could use her influence to get him a proper job because he was serious about Jeannette, and she wouldn't care for his lifestyle. He would fix up his house and he wondered if she could give him some decorating tips. Jazz said she would be happy to.

On the way out she met Jeannette. Jeannette told her that Jakey was a nice man and she really cared for him. She hoped he would ask her to marry him by the end of the year and if he did, would Jazz consider coming? Jazz told her she would come even if they didn't invite her, so try to stop her. She was very pleased for Jakey.

The New Year looked hopeful. Crystal and Ian were enjoying each other immensely. Jarvis and Steele had settled in like they were Ian's. Jazz and Jason were getting along well. The twins were delightful, and Jason was thinking it might be nice to have another child. He mentioned it to Jazz and she had not dismissed it, but he was sure she was afraid. They had gone out of sync after the twins' birth, and in desperation, she had faked leaving him. It had only lasted a few hours and she could have been a little less eager to come home. He had to laugh whenever he thought about it. He had known she was faking it but he had to admit that the thought she may have gone to her mother had come up and scared him from time to time. He had found the scene when he found her totally wacked. To begin with, she was wearing his clothes, for God's sake, but he had to admit, it had brought him to his senses.

He had taken a lot of ribbing about the incident. Sometimes she got on his nerves, but he wouldn't trade her for the world. Who else could love him so completely? It was the one thing he could be sure of. Jazzie loved him unconditionally.

He was riding past her office. It was a sweltering day but he had the visor down on his helmet. There were cars and an older truck parked at the curb. The driver, sitting in the truck, had his window rolled halfway down, and Jason saw a man in the backseat. Ahead, about a block and a half, his wife was walking towards him on the way to her office. She was on the opposite side of the street. Jason rode up to her, flipped his visor and told her to get on.

Jazz had seen Jason. She was amused he thought he had to flip his visor for her to know it was him. She wondered why he was riding on the wrong side of the street. She had never been on his motorcycle and she was wearing a narrow skirt and high heels. What was the matter with Jase? Jason ordered her, more urgently, to get on. Jazz was leggy and Jason didn't mind her short little shorts she wore at home, but he didn't like her to go outside in them, yet now he wanted her to get on his bike in her skirt! His voice had an edge to it so she hitched up her skirt and got on, and she put her cheek against his back and her palm against his shoulder blade. He told her to make love to him later but to hold on tight now. He was in the way of traffic. She did as she was told, although she couldn't figure out why she was on the back of Jason's motorcycle.

Jason maneuvered his way back into the traffic flow and took off like an Indy driver. He pulled up outside the police station and strode in like the God of Thunder.

How hard does a man have to work in this place to keep his wife safe?

The officer on duty obviously did not know what he was talking about, nor did he appear to care. As he was yelling at the officer, Jared walked by and asked what was happening. Jason told him that the man who had made several attempts on his wife's life was sitting in the back of a truck watching her office. If they were to send someone there, he'd bet he was armed. Jared picked up the phone and related what was happening. He was going to do his best for Jason because, despite the thing with his 'brother,' Jason had always been decent to him.

Jazz was just learning why she had been kidnapped by her husband, and began to shake. Suddenly, she needed a seat. She needed a drink of water. She needed to go to the bathroom. Would she never be safe from this man?

A police jeep was coming along the road in traffic. Nothing unusual. From the opposite direction two Tactical Unit officers jumped off a jeep and slipped up behind the truck, simultaneously with the two who jumped out of the moving jeep travelling in the opposite direction. Barely noticed by anyone, they had the driver out and was in the back seat with the man. He was indeed armed. After extensive grilling, the officers were satisfied the driver's story was true. He had given the man a ride out of pity for his situation, being unable to walk. He had believed his story about problems with his compensation cheque, and that someone in the office was going to kindly bring the forms out to him, in consideration of his condition. He was just a gullible country bumpkin.

When Ralph Jerome recovered from the gunshot wounds to his knees, it was deemed unnecessary, given his new handicap, to put him back into custody. The Coolidges were happily unaware of this. He would be kept in custody now.

Elle confirmed she would be happy to come home to meet Crystal's new love. He sounded amazing. She thought she might know who he was, sort of, but they all looked alike and she could not tell which was which. She was due some vacation and would come in a few weeks. Crystal was over the moon. She couldn't wait to see her little sister.

The day Elle was to arrive, Ian had to be in court. Crystal said she was too excited to drive and she might take a taxi. She knew Ian well enough by now and expected his answer. He would see if Gareth had a few minutes free to do it.

Gareth showed up. He said he had nothing urgent. Picking them up and dropping them off was no problem. She smiled her best smile, and thanked him.

When Gareth met Elle, he was obviously thrown off balance. He tried to be cool but he kept looking at her in the rear view mirror. He could think of nothing to say after he had delivered them, bags and all, to the little house, so he said bye and left them. He did not go back to his office. He tried to think up a good excuse to go back to the little house. Eventually he decided they would need to pick up the kids from school. That was his excuse when he came back. Of course, school would not be out for another two-and-a-half hours. He ordered lunch and sat and chatted with them in the meantime, and he liked Elle more with every word she said. This was not one of his casual chicks. This woman appeared to be everything he wanted in a woman; that she was pretty was a bonus. She was even prettier than Crystal.

When the time came to pick up the children, Gareth gave Crystal his keys. They wouldn't deliver the children to him, and if they all went, the vehicle would be crowded. Crystal smiled. All the Coolidges drove jeeps and SUVs. Mont Yves was off-road, halfway up the side of a mountain, and required 4-wheel drive or a donkey to get there. Of course there was room for two small children. Her plan was working!

Alone with Elle, Gareth became surprisingly tongue tied, so Elle spoke up. She told him that now he had managed to get her on her own he had better not waste time. She walked over and stood close to him and told him it was okay to touch her, she wasn't that fragile, and besides, she thought he was cute. Gareth invited her to dinner. He said he knew she wanted to catch up with her sister but he would take them all, the kids, his brother and Crystal and of course, her. She thought it was a good idea, so that night they all went to dinner. When it was over, she left with Gareth.

The next morning, she called Crystal to say she would pick her up and they could go visit their mother. Crystal assumed she was going to rent a car and started to give her a rundown of the rental agencies. She was awestruck when Elle told her she had a vehicle, Gareth's vehicle. She also told her to thank Jazz for the house, but she was staying with Gareth. Crystal told her that Gareth doesn't take women to his house, and Elle informed her that perhaps he didn't realize at first that she was a woman, but he sure as hell does know now. She had stayed the night with him, and he was picking up her stuff from the little house after work.

Wow! That was dazzlingly fast! She had hoped for success but this was success on steroids. When she hung up and told Ian, he almost collapsed laughing. His brother was hooked.

Elle was pleased to have heard that Gareth's bringing her back to his house was unusual. She liked him a lot, and it was time she had a man. She had had a couple of unsatisfactory relationships and was more than ready for the big one. Of course, there would be some things she would have to get straight first, but this sure appeared to have potential.

In his excitement, Gareth had forgotten his cell phone in his automobile. It rang as Elle was about to drive off, and she answered it, thinking it might be him. A woman wanted to know who she was, answering Gareth's phone. In answer, Elle asked who she was, calling him. The woman said she was calling to remind Gareth of their date, and Elle told her to consider it cancelled, and she should erase his number, and for good measure, added she would see to it he paid her whatever her normal fee was. The woman was offended, and asked her name, Elle told her to just remember her as his fiancé, and hung up. She had enjoyed that.

That night, Elle told Gareth that, if he was to be her man, and she had decided he was, he had to get rid of all the bimbos. She told him what she liked and wanted in a man, and he told her what he liked and wanted in a woman. She told him she could spend an extra week so they could get to know each other, and he told her they would have to consider which island they would live on. She would have to meet his family because they were so much a part of him, and she had to know if she could stand being part of such a crazy clan. Then she told him she had dismissed his girlfriend. Gareth looked at her with his beautiful, penetrating eyes, then hugged her. Just you and me from now, baby. Just you and me.

Elle told Gareth that she had never really felt comfortable alone, away from home. She had fallen out with her father and did not want a reconciliation. She had no tolerance for infidelity or hypocrisy, but she did miss her mother and especially her sister. It wouldn't take profound arguments to get her to come home, if she was able to set up a practice and earn a living. In the meantime, they would have to visit each other when they could, and thank God for current technology. Gareth said, .. or they could just get married and think about everything else after. She liked the way he was thinking. This man had become very precious to her in the short time they had been together. She was never going to let him go.

The next two weeks were halcyon days for Gareth and Elle. Unsurprisingly, the family gathered at Mont Yves on the weekend and welcomed Elle. She enjoyed the physical beauty of the estate as well as the family closeness, as much as Crystal and Jazz had, and Pammy said that since the two brothers had gone for two sisters, maybe they could have a double wedding. It was interesting that, on hearing this, both men's faces took on identical contemplative expressions.

Crystal's divorce came through. Gareth had got her everything. She was now the sole owner of everything that had been jointly owned by Jared and her, and she had custody of the children. Jared would be allowed supervised access. Now that it was a fait accompli, she felt stunned, disoriented. She had dreamt of driving up to the house in Ian's vehicle and throwing Jared and his low grade twat out, but now that she could, she felt differently and hadn't the nerve. She couldn't actually miss Jared. He had been beastly to her. The one decent thing he had done was acknowledge that Crystal had never had an involvement with Ian, or any other man during their marriage, before he had struck her. She had been lucky to have found Ian. She couldn't imagine what her circumstances would have been otherwise. It bothered her that she could have made such a grave error in judgment.

At first, Crystal had worried the boys might miss their father and give Ian a hard time, but, fortunately, Jared had done everything wrong. He had allowed his kids to see him interact with Ms Ghetto Fab and, although he had not been aware of it at the time, he had allowed Jarvis, at least, to see him brutally assault his wife, and while their consternation was at its peak, he tried to kidnap and export them. If that had not been enough, when their beautiful mother came to rescue them, there was no way to disguise her wrecked face. The overall result was that they became afraid of him, and their fear of him overshadowed any other emotion. Ian was kind to their mother, and to them, and they accepted him without reluctance.

Ian was supportive and Crystal clung to him. She was so thankful to have been blessed with this good man who loved her despite her baggage. He was so capable, confident, good looking and, without any apparent baggage of his own, he could easily have moved on, but he told her he was ready to marry her whenever she was comfortable, and though she thought before he couldn't get any better, she was sure he was more thoughtful, more loving, more her idol. He was the quietest of the Coolidge men, but he loved intensely and took care of their world with easy proficiency. Yes. She had done well. She had landed on her feet.

Jason was contemplating his life. Interesting how quickly emotions could go from euphoria to crap. An overheard conversation between his wife and his mother's friends had lifted him over the moon not two weeks ago, and now his balloon had been popped.

They had gone to Mont Yves. Pim had taken the kids for a drive. Pammy had some ladies over and Jazz joined them. Neither Gareth nor Ian was there, so he went to visit Cat, but she had snubbed him so he did not stay long. He had slipped back into the house, apparently unnoticed, and heard one of his mother's guest ask what were the things that made them happiest, and Jazz' answer was prompt: her husband's arms around her. They had teased her but she insisted that that made her most happy, that and wet sticky kisses and hugs from her twins. Nothing they said could change her statement and she told Pammy that maybe it was her fault for making him so good. It was not the first time he had heard that sort of statement from her but somehow, it put him on a cloud. Jazzie did love him, and she demonstrated it constantly. Sometimes he wondered if he deserved her. Two days later Ralph Jerome came back into their lives and Jazz had been a wreck since.

Jazzie had gone through so much and come out fighting, or screaming on the beach at least, but somehow that last episode had knocked her to her knees. In their years as a couple, he had always enjoyed going home. The way she greeted him, the way she treated him, he could have been a conquering hero returned. No, he didn't mind being at home with her, but now he *had* to be at home with her. She was afraid to be alone, she slept little, and when she did, she was restless, and she had started talking in her sleep, even though she claimed not to have had any dreams, and when he held her, he would detect a slight tremor in her body.

He was so sorry for her. His mind kept going back to the night at Mont Yves when his comment had so hurt her she had told him to let the man kill her. That had hurt him too. He wondered if that was why this time she had been so completely knocked down. She hadn't even seen Jerome. The police had taken him without her ever having seen him. He was trying to do his best to help her get past it, and he thought it might be time for a vacation, but Jazz wouldn't go without him and the project he had taken on was making it difficult to get away for more than a day or two.

They hadn't been to the love nest for a long time. As a matter of fact, the last time he had visited the house, was to bring her home when she had faked leaving him. The twins were babies then. That would have been four years ago. He hoped she had kept it pretty and romantic. He would make a thing of asking her out tonight.

When Jason got home, Gareth was there waiting for him. He hadn't been visiting them much lately. He and Jazz were drinking coffee and talking in the kitchen. She left them and while they were talking, Gareth mentioned a property his friend had been trying to get him to buy in Nevis. He had been to the place some time ago and it was nice, on the beach. It had five bedrooms, a lovely patio and great grounds. Each bedroom had private access. It was meant to be offered for rent to people on holiday, but he had not been successful, Gareth could not understand why. Jason told Gareth that if he bought it, Jazz could have them lining up to rent it. That sort of thing was her forte. Gareth wondered if Jason and Jazz might want to check it out for him the long Easter weekend. He couldn't do it as he would be visiting Elle. Jason saw the solution to his vacation problem, and the trip would only take 35 minutes. He was in. He was sure Jazz would like it. He would ask her on the date first, and when they were at the Love Nest, he'd bring up the vacation. It couldn't fail. It was only next door to Nevis, there were ferries going back and forth all day, it was a holiday weekend, and they wouldn't have to miss one hour of work. Many of the people he knew lived on one island and worked on the other.

Jazz was thrilled when Jason asked her out on a date. She said yes, she had maintained the décor at the little house. He told her he would ask his father to take the twins to Mont Yves for the night and bring them back to school in the morning. She was to come to him at the there at 8 o'clock.

Jazz dressed up for the date. She was still afraid to be alone, so Pim stayed, and gave her a ride to her own house to meet her own husband. Shaking his head and rolling his eyes, he watched her walk up the steps and knock on the door, and watched his son open the door and greet his wife like a new lover. He shook his head. He was proud of Jason. He was proud of himself. Despite his wife's unfortunate calamity, they had raised three worthy men, he and Pammy.

Jason put everything he had into the evening. Everything was beautiful, the flowers the food, the wine and the company. He was his most charming and loving, and Jazz reveled in his charm. When they slept, she slept well, and Jason hoped it was the beginning of recovery for her, this lovely woman, his woman, who wanted nothing more than to spend time with him. How lucky could a man get! In the morning, he told her about Gareth's suggestion, and she was all over it. Gareth had nothing to worry about, his place would only be vacant when he wanted it to be.

Crystal was sitting in Jazz kitchen. Her and Ian's wedding date was set for the beginning of June, she told Jazz. That would give them almost three months to prepare, so Jazz had better get cracking. She needed help. She hadn't done it right the first time because Jazz was not there so now she had to do it again, she joked. She was indeed very happy. Ian was wonderful. She thanked Jazz for telling her to call Ian when she was in trouble. She still couldn't believe that she had called a man and told him she wanted him, but it had worked out. She couldn't believe that with a face like she had at the time, she had the nerve, and she found it even harder believe he hadn't taken one look and backed out the door. She did wonder, briefly, if there was something wrong with these Coolidge men. Jazz had been a mess when Jason came to see her and he also seemed not to notice, and so far as she could tell, five years later, he still adored her.

Jazz told her that they were kind, all of them, from Pim to Ian, even Gareth, who liked to portray himself as a rogue. He was probably the kindest of all. Crystal smiled. She still hadn't told her secret.

Crystal told Jazz that Gareth had really touched the right place with Elle. She was determined to have him and he wasn't putting up a struggle. She wished they could have the double wedding Pammy suggested, but it was probably too soon for Gareth and Elle, especially as they didn't live on the same island, they would need more time together. Jazz told her that maybe Elle needed more time, but if Gareth took her to his house, if she wanted, he would have married her the next day. Gareth didn't take women to his house. He was very sensitive and if a woman thought there was more to an encounter than there was, if she wouldn't leave, he wouldn't be able to throw her out. Elle had a place to stay. If he just wanted a fling, he would have slept with her at the little house. He took her home because he intended that it would be her home too. He was like Jason. In his head they were already married. He was just waiting for the formalities. Crystal told her that Ian had said much the same thing.

Gareth stopped by while Crystal and Jazz were talking in the kitchen. Jazz teased him about Elle managing to make him an unrogue. Crystal said that he and Elle probably hadn't known each other long enough to commit themselves. Gareth laughed. He told her that interestingly enough, the day after he met Elle, she cancelled his dates and told them he had a fiancé. They thought he was joking, and Jazz asked whether she did have a fiancé. He said she had him, he was anything she wanted him to be. Jazz declared *'Now that's commitment.'*

Crystal would be surprised when talking to her sister that evening, to find out that Elle had indeed cancelled his date and identified herself as his fiancé, and she'd told him to get rid of any other bimbos. No more dates with anybody else. Good going, sis. Now the good men are all taken.

Crystal told Jazz there wouldn't be a double wedding. Elle had said double weddings were magazine stuff, besides she imagined Ed was going to give Crystal away and she didn't want him at her wedding. Crystal told her sister that their father was the only man she knew, unless her wedding was like Jazz': Ian led her into the church and Pim and Pammy followed her, Pammy having made her dress and supervised her dressing . She said it was like she was marrying her brother. Funny thing, at that time she was walking behind Ian, never imagining that she would one day be here, planning their wedding. Strange world.

Ian had said it wouldn't be a good idea as they would have to close the firm and put a sign on the door: Hollis & Hollis on Honeymoon. Clients would think they married each other. Jazz laughed and told her that Mr. Ian considered himself some sort of comedian and if he hadn't made Crystal so happy, she would slap him. Ian had never hidden his amusement at her shenanigans.

Now that they were adult, Jazz found she really liked Ian. He looked so much like Jason, but their smiles and their carriage were different. While Jason had a big smile that showed a lot of teeth, Ian's smile was wry, like he knew something you didn't. Jazz joked with him once and said she couldn't remember what his teeth looked like and teasingly asked him if he had any. He invited her to put her fingers into his mouth. In fact he had perfect teeth. They all had, possibly due to genes, probably due to Pammy's obsession. Sugar and liquor being the mainstay of their family, she was consumed with prevention of dental problems, alcoholism and diabetes.

Ian always seemed to be casually lounging and, no matter what he was wearing, he looked comfortable like he was wearing jogging pants low on his hips with his feet in sandals. Jason always looked like he was about to ride something, a horse, a motorcycle - Giddyap! Bring it on. A bit like a cowboy.

She was glad it was her friend who had snagged Ian. Ian did not have Gareth's dread of being rejected by women, he approached them if he liked them. He was cute and silent and women often tried to pick him up. When they did, he didn't flirt outrageously like Gareth, but you could tell when he was enjoying a woman's attention. He held his head back and halfway closed his eyes like he was letting it wash over him. He reminded Jazz of a satisfied cat. Women didn't usually try to pick up Jason when she was around so she did not know how he reacted. Since their marriage, he'd always worn his wedding band and most people had heard she was crazy and had tried to rip up a beach, so they wouldn't want to take her on. Jason was averse to public scenes and on the few occasions when some intrepid woman did try, he just looked uncomfortable and beat a hasty retreat to her. Crazy had its compensations. She did not resent her reputation for being crazy.

Crystal and Jazz looked at all sorts of dresses, drank wine, and chit-chatted. Crystal confided that she was embarrassed to go to St Georges as it was where, not all that long ago, she had first been married, but it was where both she and Ian went to church. At least he hadn't been at her wedding. She worried about the onlooker comments. Jazz told her that once she started walking she hadn't heard anything or even noticed that there were people looking on. Her main problem was that they were walking so slowly and she wanted to see Jase, and for him to see her in her dress. Crystal had to remember that it would be the first time Ian was going to be seeing her in her dress. She just needed to focus on something silly like that, or how she was going to love him when everybody had gone home. When she was walking back down the walkway, Ian would be with her so what the hell would she care? She would be walking off with one of the most handsome men on the island, and she, Jazz, would know because she had one just like him. They were giggling at that when Jason and Ian walked in.

For Jason, that was a sight for sore eyes; Jazz giggling with Crystal, like old times. He hoped it would last, and he thought that maybe if there were more interesting projects like this, which would keep her busy, she might forget to be scared of Jerome. Ian had petitioned the court to have him declared a dangerous offender or something like that, and have him incarcerated for life, and was hopeful because of his repeated attempts to harm Jazz every time he was allowed to be free. Hopefully, they could move on and he could enjoy his wife's love again, the way God intended. He bent over and kissed her. *And don't you forget it*.

She smiled. *Don't you forget it.*

The family seemed to have acquired an anthem, and Jazz was responsible. One of the biggest joys of Jason's life was his twins. They were happy and active kids and never ceased to surprise him with their energy, or acquisition of new skills. Jazz taught them all sorts of things. As soon as they could talk she taught them to count, The Lord's Prayer and Gentle Jesus children's prayer, and to sing the alphabet. He was sure he had baby geniuses. They were now under five, and they had an impressive repertoire of songs.

At home Jazz loved to wear shorty shorts and tanks, mostly cropped, and she would put her hair up in a ponytail. It was not unusual to come home to find her teaching them some song or dance, shaking her barely clad body with them. She had taught them the cultural heel and toe masquerade and clown dances, and had even made them little clown costumes to match Pim's. They were pretty good for their age, and Pim would sometimes make them dress up and dance with them.

A few months before, Ebonique's attitude to Jazz had become a little combative and one day, after a frustrating event Jazz, rather than yell at the little girl, had hugged her and told her she loved her. To bring the point home, she taught them the song 'I Love you and Don't You Forget It'. Jason had come home to find his wife and children in the kitchen singing I Love you and Don't You Forget It, Jazz putting up a finger each time they sang the line, so they would know when to sing There, that's seven times that I've said it, then she would shake her hips and, ponytail swinging, put up her thumb and they'd sing the line again and sing there, that's one more time that I've said it, I don't see how you can forget it now. They were having such a glorious time, they did not notice him watching. When they did, she asked them what they had to say to Daddy, and they sang together I love you and don't you forget it.... Since then, they greeted their parents and grandparents with it, Uncle Ian, Uncle Gareth, Auntie Cat and Auntie Crystal and her boys. The simple song was now like background music to their life.

Jazz' dislike of being alone had not started with Jerome's attack, just her fear. She always disliked being alone. He'd first noticed when he'd visited her in Toronto, that she would turn the music on in every room. The sound seemed to comfort her, and if Jason was ever out at night, when he returned, their home looked like a lighthouse, ablaze with lights on in every room, and Jazz would most likely be in bed with the children. Sometimes when he worked at home at night, after she put the children to bed, she would come into the den and sit quietly in the room with him, reading a book or some other quiet pursuit, and she would stay until he was finished and ready for bed.

Jason was never sure what he would come home to, but it was usually pleasant relief from any tensions during the day. The day before Jerome skewed their world, he'd come home to find his wife, her usual mode of home dress accessorized with rubber gloves – she had been washing dishes – teaching the children a dance that involved finger snapping and hip shaking. Ebonique was getting into it. She couldn't snap her fingers but she was managing pretty well in the hip shaking department. He wondered whose sons he would have to be chasing away from his door, and how soon.

Jafari was not always comfortable these days with how much he could participate in his mother's activities. At four years old, even he appeared to notice just how totally feminine she was, and seemed not to be sure whether following her might cross a line. He would always look questioningly at his father or one of his uncles before throwing himself into whatever the activity was. He found his comfort zone with his father and uncles showing him how to kick a football, or play cricket or basketball. Gareth had bought him a portable basketball hoop suitable for a small child. He looked at Jason now, and Jason gave him the nod and joined them for a few moments.

Those were the little moments he thought a lot about nowadays, because they didn't happen anymore. His new house was ready to be moved into, and it was more than twice the size of Celine's. If Jazz was afraid to be alone in Celine's house, she would never be able to move into theirs. Pre Jerome, they had gone to look at it so she could choose the colours and plan the décor. She had been excited, and had sketched models of the rooms, decorated. She had made no reference to it since Jerome. She seemed to have been robbed of her soul and he wanted to get it back for her. Seeing her laughing in the kitchen with Crystal was wonderful, and gave him hope.

In the end, Celine may have accelerated Jazz recovery, or at least contributed to it. She finally decided to marry Bertrand and wanted Jazz to return the favour and give her away. Her wedding date, it turned out, was one week after Crystal and Ian's. In the excitement of the preparation, Jazz began to forget to be scared.

Jazz came up with an idea no one could shake her of. On the day after Crystal and Ian's wedding, when they would be heading off to their honeymoon, she and her family would also be headed out to Toronto, only she would also be taking Jarvis and Steele with her. She argued that Crystal wouldn't enjoy her honeymoon with the thought hovering in her mind that the kids were back home, open to abduction by Jared. While Crystal and Ian were enjoying each other in Rio, Jazz would be giving their children the time of their lives in Toronto, foiling the plans she was sure Jared had, to abduct them. It would be good for the children, and Ian and Crystal could relax.

Jason did not think she could manage four excited kids in Toronto but his big problem was that his wife, currently fragile, was expecting him to go with her to Toronto for two weeks, and he could not. After all this time, why had Celine chosen now! He was caught between a rock and a hard place. Jazzie was just emerging from her dispiritedness, and he wasn't sure if saying no would not set her back. This was not an event she could miss. If he didn't go it would be good for him but it would ruin it for her, and the ripple effect could touch Celine, Crystal, her boys, and shake their marriage a little bit. He believed Jazzie would always come back to him, but he liked her best when she was happy. She wouldn't be happy about this. He would have to go. He wondered if he could talk her down to one week.

Jason was lying in bed when Jazz came in and kissed him playfully. He liked that. It had been a while since she had been so playful. He pulled her down on top of him.

Jazzie. It's not a good time for me to go to Toronto. He saw her eyes fill up. He hated that. She rolled off him and went to sleep. She hadn't responded. She had said nothing, and yet he felt she had slapped him. The next morning when he tried to bring the subject up she said she had heard him the first time. God! She was giving him the silent treatment. That was right up there with her tears for things he hated. Leaving for work, he told her *I love you and don't you forget it* and she said *uh-huh.* A kick in the stomach would have hurt less. He had grown accustomed to being adored, not ignored, and he did not like this one bit.

Having an office across the hall from his father's was sometimes an asset and kept Jason's relationship with Pim close. When he saw Jason that morning, Pim remarked that he looked like he had been kicked by a mule. Jason told his father his predicament, and Pim asked if he thought Jazz was glamourous. He didn't see the relevance but said he did, actually. Pim asked what her hobbies were, and Jason told him, even though he knew his father knew all this about her. Pim said that from where he was standing, the question was *when* he was going to Toronto: to escort his wife and take part in her mother's, her only family's wedding, or later: to try to talk her into coming back home. She was glamourous and artistic. She and her mother owned a business in Toronto, the nature of which was artistic and glamourous and she was here selling toothpaste, toilet paper and diapers, wholesale no less, to be with him. To quote Jazz, Go figure. He walked away whistling I love you and don't you forget it.

Ian and Crystal's wedding day dawned clear, bright and cloudless. Crystal had selected a gold dress. She looked marvelous. The colour suited her own skin tones perfectly, but she was having second thoughts. She had never seen a bride wear gold before. Jazz was trying to calm her. It was too late now, she couldn't even wear Jazz' dress. It had been destroyed in the fire. Jazz was cooing to her about how great she was going to feel when Ian saw her and those beautiful eyes lit up.

Pim and Pammy would not be walking into the church with them at this wedding. They would already be in the church when the bride arrived, as would Frances and Cat. Ed would be walking down the aisle with her, being ignored by his other daughter, walking ahead of them. Poor Ed. He was one miserable man. He had completely destroyed his status in his family. He felt lucky and grateful that Crystal was including him in her wedding. Frances had changed dramatically, and his little Ellie pretended he did not exist. He had to go over and make his own introductions to her fiancé the night before, at the pre wedding dinner. It had been awkward. Elle had turned away while the embarrassed young man tried to make stilted conversation. He was pretty sure he wouldn't get the honour of walking her down the aisle. If she had her way, he doubted he'd even be invited. He had made a thorough mess of his family life.

The wedding party was led by the Coolidge twins, beaming away, obviously very well aware of their importance. They were followed by Jarvis and Steele, also very obviously aware of their importance. They were honorary givers of the bride, and had a special part in the ceremony. Jason and Jazz followed, then the bride and her father, Elle bringing up the rear. The children carried out their parts beautifully, and the video caught Ian as he turned, moistened his lips and smiled, looking at his bride as if he could eat her. She did look marvelous! When her father delivered her to him, he whispered *Don't you forget it* and she smiled. That clip would be played in his family a hundred times at least.

That and the part where Father Cardinal asked *Who gives this woman...* and Jarvis and Steele stepped smartly to each side of their grandfather, and all three responded *"We do"*.

The reception was a great big bash, and the excitement could light the night. Even after the guests were gone the family stayed up. Even the children could not sleep. They were going away by plane in the morning, and were far too excited. Jazz warned them that they would miss everything because they would fall asleep in the plane. It didn't help.

In the morning there was a big bustle, a big breakfast, and lots of suitcases. Ian and his bride were taking an eleven o'clock flight to Miami, where they would transfer to a flight to Rio. One hour later, Jason, Jazz, the twins, Jarvis and Steele would take a flight to Toronto. As they were saying goodbye, Crystal hugged her lifelong friend and whispered *Be careful of Bonni, she wasn't after Gareth. It was Jason.*

Jazz felt weak and ready tears came to her eyes. *Does he know?* but Crystal couldn't tell. Jazz went to the bathroom and threw up. Jason heard her and came in. That never happened. He wondered if she could be pregnant.

Poor Jazz. The thought of Jason with someone else was not something she was prepared for, and she didn't know whether she should confront him. Maybe he didn't even know. She sure hadn't known, or even suspected. She went outside to get some air and saw Gareth sitting on a fence. She and Gareth understood each other. She wondered if he would tell her if he knew. She doubted it, but she had to ask.

Gareth, do you think Jase and I are suited to each other?

Sometimes

Do you know anybody else he might be suited to?

Jazz. This is Gareth. Get to the point.

Right. She took a deep breath. *'Has Jase had an affair since we've been together?'*

Jaazz! What's this? Why aren't you asking him?

Because if he hasn't, it would spoil things, and if I don't know, I'll go crazy.

Relax and enjoy your holiday. I have never got that impression.

Do you remember my cousin Bonni? Did she ever come on to you?

The girl that hung out with Ian? Why would she do that? Besides, she's not my type.

She told me it was you she wanted. I think she lied. In Toronto, she came over for dinner one night, and stayed four days. I barely saw her here where she didn't know anyone. I was so happy with Jase, I didn't notice. If she was normal, she would have grabbed Ian and never let go. Ian is a catch, unless what you want is the other version of Ian. It's okay if she loves my husband, as long as she stays well the hell away. If he was involved with her, Gareth, I'll die. I'll just die.

Jason joined them then. It was time to leave. *Gareth, why you making my wife cry?*

Gareth got off the fence. *Have a good holiday, man. I got to go look for my wife and make sure she don't cry. He gave them two thumbs up. 'Don't you forget it'.*

Don't you forget it, they both responded.

The kids fell asleep on the plane for most of the flight. Jazz pretended to be asleep, tormenting herself over whether to ask Jason. Pretty soon, they were landing in Toronto. The kids were fascinated by the high towers, and all the cars. They couldn't wait to experience 'the sun shining in the night'. Jazz had explained that in the summer, the sun did not set till well after nine and they couldn't understand the concept. Jarvis kept looking at his watch. It was after five and it looked like lunchtime, so maybe it was true.

Once Jazz showed the papers that proved she wasn't kidnapping Jarvis and Steele, they were ushered through Customs pretty quickly, and soon Ebonique and Jafari met Gran Celine in person for the very first time. They knew her, they spoke to her and saw her on their mother's computer nightly, but they had never been hugged by her. Celine seemed delighted to hold them, especially as Jafari placed his tiny pinky fingers on each cheek in her smiling dimples, something Brett used to do. Jazz was also delighted to see her mother. She couldn't believe just how happy she was to see her. She was weak with joy. She was babbling to Jarvis and Steele that this was her Mommy and they had met her before but they had been too young to remember. She hugged Jaime and congratulated him. Jason had done that already, and they were all packed into a minivan Jaime hired for her, and off they went to a three-bedroom furnished house Celine had rented for them. Their very first night in TO.

Jarvis and Steele both had cameras and were snapping at everything they saw. Jazz told them that Toronto knew they were coming some day so they named some streets for them. She would take them and show them later. Unfortunately, Ebonique and Jafari did not have streets yet because their names were unique and Torontonians did not know how to spell them.

If Celine had other ideas for her wedding, her grandchildren changed them. They wanted to be part of the wedding party, just like at Uncle Ian and Auntie Crystal's. Jazz listened, amused, as her mother explained to her daughter that, if she was going to chase after either Jarvis or Steele for the rest of her life, like her mother did her father, she couldn't let him see her at two weddings in the same dress. Celine had already chosen clothes for them for her wedding. Ebonique was willing to concede that point but she was adamant they were taking part in the wedding. She explained how she and Jafari had walked ahead of the bride and how impressed everyone was. She assured her grandmother that they knew how. In the end, Celine had four junior attendants at her wedding, her daughter by her side, and her son-in-law as her husband's best man.

Uncle Aaron threw a party for them. Jason got to meet the new branch of Jazz' family, and they all liked each other. Bonni was absent. She had finally gone to Egypt to see her mother, so Jazz was never to make a judgment based on the way Jason interacted with her. She became better acquainted with Veronica, something she wanted from the time they met, and Veronica promised to come down to St. Kitts with her partner and their son. Jafari, her cousin, and Jafari, her son, became bosom buddies. He also promised to visit them.

Prior to the wedding, Jazz visited the shop. She hardly recognized it. Celine did not have time to sell flowers one bouquet at a time, she was brokering them now, and she had a staff, not a large staff, but a permanent staff. Celine said she still used the agency but the business needed permanent staff. Jazz felt it was unfair that her mother had done such a great job and only owned twenty-five per cent of the business. She told her mother she was willing to let her have the greater share but Celine said that she and Brett had worked their wills that, should either pass, Jazz would benefit solely, if the survivor was to remarry. Jaime had no children, but just to be sure that there were no distant relatives lurking out there, ready to pounce and grab what should be her only offspring's, she would like to leave things the way they were. She was confident that Jazz wouldn't cheat her, anymore than she would cheat Jazz. It was settled.

As would have been expected, the wedding was an elegant affair, the little hall stunningly decorated. Jazz took several copies of the university newspaper home to show her family and friends the article and pictures of her mother and stepfather's beautiful wedding, and the picture of the decorated hall. Jason remembered his father's warning and wondered whether he would have been able to pull his wife back from this.

Jason came out with something from the trip as well. He'd liked Jaime from the beginning and they became close. Jaime hooked him up with some programming that would make it much easier for him to keep on top of things with his business in such events as this, when he needed to be away. He and Jazz had also done some shopping and shipping for their new home.

Just for the record, Celine told Jazz, Pammy had told her about Jazz' dealing with Jordan without questioning why Jordan was intimidating her. She wanted Jazz to know that Brett had not done anything horrible. He had helped a friend outsmart Jordan, losing Jordan quite a bit of money. With Brett gone, and unable to defend himself, he could get the decision reversed, but Brett could come out looking like a crook. He knew Brett had the incriminating papers, but when he found only her school work in the desk, the only explanation was that either she was onto him and switched papers, or Brett had known he was going to be killed and moved them, which was impossible. Anyway, Jazz had come down really hard on him and could ease up now. People were becoming afraid of her. Jazz told her she had not done it just for her parents, but also for herself. The man was outright rude. He needed to be slapped.

Jazz went to the office for a few hours two or three times after Celine left on her honeymoon. Celine's assistant did not appear to appreciate her presence, but Jazz was in a holiday mood and let it go the first day. The second time, she asked her why she thought the company was called Jazz, and the woman responded that she supposed Celine named it after her daughter.

Nah ah said Jazz, wiggling her index finger. *Ask Mommy when she gets back. You'll be surprised and even consider yourself a very silly woman.* She enjoyed the puzzled look on the woman's face, and assured her that it was okay because she was in a great holiday mood, no harm done. She was here with her darling husband, her perfect twins and her most delightful nephews, and was having a wonderful time. However, she didn't think it was a good idea to disrespect her mother by trying to veto her decisions, because Jazz adored her Mommy and was very sensitive where she was concerned. *In future*, she told her, *If Mommy says a homeless man could come in and sit at her desk, your response is to be 'so it is written, so let it be done'. Comprendez?* She smiled and sashayed out the door.

In a while, when Celine returned to work, she would mention that her assistant thought Jazz didn't like her, and Jazz would innocently ask *'Why? Because I didn't kiss her?'* and Celine would know something had happened, but that it had been dealt with, and would not pursue it. After all, she had given birth to the woman, and Jazz had no idea just how much like her mother she had become.

By the time they boarded the plane to come home and the children's cameras had taken all the pictures they could, they were exhausted, but happy and ready to tell about all their experiences. They had visited several malls, the sizes of which were astounding to them. 'Almost *the same size as the whole of Basseterre*, according to Jarvis. They sat at the base of the fountain in the Eaton Centre which shot jets of water several stories into the air, that fell straight down without getting them wet. Most importantly, as far as they were concerned, they had driven up Jarvis Street and across Steeles Avenue. Steele was sure the extra 's' was because it was named to be his avenue. They had been to, and had pictures of, Niagara Falls where they had been on the Maid of the Mist and visited the Wax Museum, African Lion Safari and the Toronto Zoo, (wait till they showed their friends at school the lions and tigers and bears they had seen!) they had rides on Toronto Island and Jazz and Jason had rented bicycle rickshaws that they had to pedal while the kids sat in the back. Even Jason had enjoyed this immensely.

They had their faces painted, and laughed at Jason's concerned expression when he said that somebody had taken his kids and left a lion and a cat in their place. They had seen a performance of the RCMP Musical Ride after which they had been able to touch the horses and speak to the riders. Steele was over the moon because the horse ridden by the officer Jason had been talking to was also called Steele, and Jason lifted him so he could pat his namesake. They went to the CN Tower and stood on the glass floor hundreds of feet above ground, they saw fireworks from Ontario Place and a demonstration by the fireboat, and were surprised that Toronto actually had beaches, and the size of them. They went to the movies, and chidren's theatre.

Jazz had driven them past her house and explained that was where she lived until she came home and met her prince. Jafari was fascinated that his mother had met a prince and wanted to know what he was like. Jazz told him his daddy and, round eyed, he asked Jason if he was really a prince. *Yes. Your mommy's prince, Jafari, her Prince Charming, and she is my Queen.*

That was an awesome holiday, Auntie Jazz, Jarvis told her, and Jafari repeated, *that was an awesome holiday Mommy,* which brought on a round of I Love you and don't you forget it in the airport. They would be chatting like magpies for days.

Jason was pleased. He had actually enjoyed the holiday. His wife had handled the four children easily and everybody had a good time. In a few hours they would be handing over Crystal's children to her and he would be taking his wife and kids home. She was lovely and relaxed, and she had proven she was able to handle more than two children. She was always so good with their children, she was patient and answered all their 'whys' without ever becoming frustrated, never shouted at them, and somehow, always managed to turn events, good or bad, into learning opportunities for them. She praised and encouraged them. They were never shy, and he believed their confidence was the direct result of the way she interacted with them.

It was a good time to count his blessings. He'd had five wonderful years of marriage to her. She had made his life interesting and mostly truly enjoyable. There had only been the one subject that they had clashed on, and he could try to see it differently. After all, everything else she did was positive, and there were many people who would not hear a bad word against her.

During Jerome's trial, when it was suggested Jazz might have led him on, Hillary had come back to the office from maternity leave and listened to hours of tape to find one she hoped she had not had time to erase before leaving, which would prove Jazz had not encouraged Jerome. She didn't have to do that. Jazz was not even aware the tape existed.

Twenty children, now living in Brett LaPierre Academy loved her. She had called it that because she did not want it labeled any kind of institution that would single out the students. To all intents and purposes, according to her, it was a boarding school, just that the boarders didn't go home for holidays. He especially admired her for enrolling their own children in the school. She knew it would require a paying component, and hoped others would follow her lead. She even dared to hope they would get paying boarders, possibly from other islands to help keep the school afloat and increase the chances of the children it was actually established for, accepting themselves and assimilating as part of a normal environment.

There was nothing Jakey wouldn't do for her, and as far as he was concerned, she was the kindest and second most important person on the island, next to his fiancé, and Nurse Jeannette also thought very highly of Jazz.

Renata, the albino cashier at Django's thought she was the greatest. Jazz had intervened when an obnoxious customer was harassing her and when the manager tried to give Renata a hard time Jazz had told him he ought to be ashamed. The customer was always right only when they had a valid beef. It was his responsibility to ensure that his staff was protected from harassment and discrimination. She started putting her groceries back into the cart then ordered him to do it himself since she would not be shopping in his establishment again unless he changed his policy, and she told Renata that she would get her a job with a more worthy employer, if she felt she wanted to be rid of this ass. Mr. Django apologized to Renata, to Jazz and to the customers who had witnessed the debacle, and subsequently put up an anti discrimination-anti harassment sign in the store. Renata didn't have to leave and she always reminded Jason to take good care of Jazz.

He had no doubt Gareth and Ian would have got his mother out when she was arrested for shooting the intruder, but Jazz had made it a national cause, forcing the police to release her quickly to avoid a riot, rather than wait behind on the slow turning of the legal wheel. Besides that, she had stopped Father Cardinal in his tracks when he got on his high moral horse, preaching against Pammy. He still couldn't help chuckling about that one.

His wife was a fine lady and she loved him. This was not news. Everybody knew that, but he was awed by it sometimes. He had assumed her enthusiasm would wane with time but she had loved him constantly, whether or not he deserved it, and he knew sometimes he did not deserve it. She loved being with him. She would not let him buy a second vehicle. She could afford to buy one herself, she gave generously to various charities, she'd blow gasp inducing amounts on clothes and shoes, even for the children who'd outgrow them in months, but she said families with separate vehicles went separate ways. It might have something to do with all the time she had been alone when she was away, but he wasn't going to analyze it. He just thanked his lucky stars.

Sometimes he did think about it though, the time she was away. If Celine said she hadn't meant her comments that sent Jazz running off into the night, but that it was just her way to say mean and malicious things in anger, what was it like in their home that Jazz did not know this? And yet, she loved her mother almost as much as she loved him, and did everything she could to please her, just as she did him. He would probably never understand it, but she was good to him and to their children, so he would put it to rest. Nobody else had expected it but, of all his married friends and acquaintances, he had the best, happiest and most stable marriage.

He was going to have a chat with her, assure her they were solid. He couldn't wait to go to work on giving her two more babies. With the new house, there was room enough. They would move in as soon as possible and they would throw a big house warming party. He would dance with his wife and they would be close, as close as they were at the beginning, and happy. God, he loved his woman! He leaned forward and sang in her ear 'I love you and don't you forget it' and Jazz turned and kissed him full on the lips.

By the time the Coolidges moved into their new home three weeks after they returned from holiday in Toronto, Jazz believed she was pregnant. She prayed earnestly that this pregnancy would go well and that her husband would not go 'all squirly' on her after the birth. She prayed and she crossed her fingers so often it was a wonder they did not grow crooked.

Jason was also praying. He resolved to be as close to the perfect husband and father as was humanly possible and he was praying for help in this. He was praying that his wife was indeed pregnant and that, if she was, he wouldn't go 'all squirly' after the birth like he had after the birth of the twins. He was praying also that, if God didn't mind, could they please have another pair of twins. He did not communicate this with his wife.

Pim had told them as young men growing up that they should marry women they love and having done so, commit themselves to making them happy. He said women gave back tenfold, they could make a man's life bliss or total crap, and it all depends on the man. Jason was on the road to bliss and he liked it, and was determined to stay the course.

Jason had been adorable and he and Jazz were getting along really well. They were having a house warming party and Jazz was looking forward to it, since her social life might be curtailed over the next few months if she was indeed pregnant. Jason had bought her a pregnancy kit but she considered it too early and refused to use it. He was very excited about becoming a father again. Jazz thought he was cute. He had been a very good father so far.

Thank you, dear Lord for this good man.

Jazz was walking past a corner shop and she was dying of thirst. She went inside to buy a drink and the owner had a problem making change for the note she gave him. To solve the problem, she bought a lottery ticket. The draw was that night. The next day she discovered the ticket had won five thousand dollars. She decided to do something nice for Jason with the winnings but couldn't come up with anything in particular; the only thing Jason wanted from her that he didn't already have was that she leave Jordan alone. She wrote a note and took a walk over to Gareth's office.

Gareth always welcomed her. She had the impression that Gareth and Pammy understood her far better than the others, including Jason. After sitting herself down and greeting him, she told him that Jason was being so lovely, she wanted to do something really nice to make him want to stay sweet. What did Gareth think Jason would want? Gareth told her that the only beef he was aware that Jason ever had with her was her pursuit of Jordan. She showed him the note. It read: "You could discard this or use it to buy your way out of purgatory, but you must leave us alone. Compliments of Brett LaPierre." The winning ticket was attached. Before Gareth could ask she said '*five thousand dollars*'.

This is not a trick Jazz? You would do this?

It was a ten dollar investment. Ten dollars to make my husband perfectly happy is well spent. Besides, I think I have taught him not to mess with us. What do you think?

Gareth told her that, if she would let him, he would deliver it himself. He would be so happy to see the feud over, and so would Jason. She kissed her 'brother-in-law' and walked back to her office to continue her day.

Elle was visiting Gareth the weekend of the housewarming. She had found a job and would be moving home to be with him. They would be married in three months' time. Gareth, the former rogue, was over the moon! Jazz was happy for him. She always liked Gareth. He was discerning and kind. He got what she was feeling when even Jason didn't, and he spoke to her kindly. She teased him that in typical rogue fashion, he had got the young one. She did not know Elle very well. She had grown up in Jazz' absence. Jazz remembered her as Crystal's little nonentity sister, Ellie. Their parents had named her Ellen and called her Ellie until they discovered when she was in her early teens, that by an error on her birth certificate, her name was Elle. They would have tried to correct it but she preferred the name and informed them that she would no longer respond to the childish Ellie. Jazz wondered if she would get to know her better.

Jazz was feeling a bit left out. Crystal had picked a fight with her shortly after they returned from holiday, because Jazz had threatened to slap Ian. Jazz was stunned. She had been threatening to slap Ian practically all her life. He was always the one to tease and make fun of her. He had no fear she would slap him and she never would. She had apologized for offending her friend, but now felt strained in Ian's presence. She believed Crystal was discarding her to make room in her life for her sister, and though she didn't blame her, she was very hurt. Jazz had lots of acquaintances, people whom she liked, and who liked her, but she had never developed or sought to develop a closer relationship with anyone. She wished she, too, had a sister. She had hoped she and Bonnie would have become close but that had not turned out right either. Well, she should cheer up. She had her darling Jase and who needed girlie friends, anyway?

Jazz had not told Jason of the upset with Crystal, so when he announced he was going over to Ian's and the twins got excited to see Jarvis and

Steele, she couldn't find an excuse for declining his invitation to go with them. Crystal was out when they arrived, and while Jason and Ian talked about the expansion Jason was to design for Ian's house, Jazz chatted with Jarvis and Steele.

Elle was with Crystal when she returned. Elle said hello and a few words to Jazz. Crystal kissed the twins and greeted her family and Jason, and she and her sister went off to another room. Jazz sat stunned, the sting of the snub as harsh as that of a wasp. At loose ends, she asked who wanted ice cream, and of course, all the kids did, so she packed them into Jason's vehicle and drove off to an ice cream parlor at Port Zante. The kids were enjoying their ice cream when Jazz saw Jared walking towards them. She quickly called Ian and told him what was happening.

Jared came to their table and Jazz asked him not to put her in an awkward position. He said he had just seen them and wanted to say hello to his kids. He was not rude or even a little impolite, but Jazz was uncomfortable, and she told him that she had been on the phone when she saw him walking in and had told Ian that he was there, so he had better go. It would avoid an embarrassing scene. He said it was okay, he said goodbye to the kids and left. By the time Ian got there, Jared was gone and Jazz was getting the children into the vehicle. They all drove back to Ian's place

Crystal was enraged when Jazz brought the children back and asked how she dared take her kids out without her permission, and Jazz told her that Ian knew where she was taking them. It wasn't unusual for her to take the children out, and she had handled Jared. She said his behavior had not been aggressive, and mentioned that he had said he was moving back to St. Vincent. Crystal's face drained. She quickly regained her composure but Jazz had seen it and she believed, so had Ian. Jazz hugged the boys and told them she was sorry, she couldn't take them out anymore because their mommy did not like it.

Jason and Ian were surprised at Crystal's outburst and Jason told Crystal she wasn't being fair, so Jazz explained that Crystal had been offended when, several days ago, Jazz had threatened to slap Ian, and that she had already apologized. Jason laughed and said Ian could take Jazz in a fight any day. Not to worry.

It should have been the end of the dispute, but Crystal, not yet appeased, said that Celine had hit Paris on the head so one could never tell what Jazz would do.

This was the first time Jason was hearing about the altercation between Celine and Paris, so startled, he asked about it but Jazz was now furious that Crystal had brought it up. Hand on hip, she glared at Crystal '*Why are you bringing Paris up? What the hell does he have to do with this?*'

Jason was still trying to get an answer about the incident, but Jazz was not listening. *Let's go outside,* she said to Crystal, and put her arm around her shoulder, urging her forward. Jason tried to stop her, fearing the worst, and Jazz let go of Crystal and faced him. *What is the matter with everybody? When did any of you ever see me hit anyone? We are going to talk this out between women. Elle can come and if I get out of line they can beat me up together.* She hugged Crystal again and pretty much dragged her outside. Elle followed them.

You're not impressing Ian with this shit, whatever it is, Crystal. Like it or not, you married a clan. Coolidges fight together, not each other. It's a culture. Crystal interrupted her.

I'm tired of you and this Coolidges this and Coolidges that. Ian's name is Hollis. My name is Hollis.

You really should get to know your husband. I wouldn't take that attitude with him or with Gareth, either. How often do you hear him mention his father? What does he call Pim? They are Coolidges. You're not going to change that. Ian wouldn't know Hollis from Jimmy's backside if he stepped on his foot in a crowd, but if Pim was within a mile of him he would know that the only father and role model he has ever known was in the neighbourhood, and Pim's name is Coolidge. Ian and Gareth are not strays Pim picked up. Pim is their mother's twin. He's a Coolidge, she's a Coolidge. They're all Coolidges. She chuckled. *Have I conjugated it clearly enough? You went to the trouble of arranging things so Elle and Gareth could get together, and now you want to start an identity war before they are even married?*

Elle looked from one to the other and Crystal opened, then closed her mouth. Silly Crystal had thought the obvious was a secret. Jazz continued. *I can step back if you want to bond with your sister, that's cool. I have a live-in best friend anyway, but for better or worse, we're all part of the same family now, so if you have a grievance against me, other than I threatened to slap Ian, because nobody believes that, come out with it so we can resolve it and get on with being family, which we became, whether you like it or not, when you said I do to Ian.*

Ian has a high speed brain. He can come up with a perfectly amazing retort to any comment the same second the words are out of your mouth, as if he already knew what you were going to say. I can come up with the same thing but ten seconds later. It doesn't have the same impact so I threaten to slap him. That's all there is to it. Words to cover up my inaptitude. Get over it. I love you, Crystal, and don't you forget it.

I'm tired of that shit. Crystal said. *Come Elle, let's get inside.* Jazz assumed she was not invited in. Ian and Jason were at the door and Jazz walked up to them and hugged Ian and kissed him on the cheek: *Goodbye darling Ian, my dearest brother in law*, she said loud enough for everyone to hear. *It appears I'm no longer welcome in your home so I'll, hopefully, see you around.*

Ian answered: *Don't be silly, Jazz.*

Jazz called the twins and told Jason to get a ride home with Ian, if Ian was allowed to, otherwise she would come and get him. If Crystal wanted to fight she should know the enemy, Jazz thought. She had no intention of staying away from Ian's or any of the other's houses. She and Jason and their kids would be in and out of Ian's house exactly as they had before. She knew that Mrs. Hollis-not-Coolidge was going to be read the riot act the minute she and Ian were alone. Stupid Crystal believed because Ian was nice, kind and quiet, he must be weak. She was about to discover otherwise.

Elle had listened attentively. She was much smarter than Crystal and Jazz was sure she would be discussing the subject with Gareth shortly. Crystal should know her own sister. She was not going to be onside with this Hollis not Coolidge thing once she knew what Hollis did to their mother. Hell, she wouldn't cross the street to spit on her own father if he was on fire, because of his infidelity to their mother. Maybe she could become Jazz new best friend. Wouldn't that be a kick in the ass for Crystal. It would serve her right.

When Jason came home he wanted to know what that was all about, but first he wanted to hear about Celine hitting Paris and why he had not heard of it before. Jazz pointed out that she had never told him anything about Paris that he hadn't asked because the minute Crystal had walked into the little house that day she came home screaming, it had somehow reoriented her world and she had forgotten Paris. She told him that Celine had not brought a blunt instrument crashing down on Paris head but had bopped him with a cardboard cylinder. Paris had blustered about suing, and Celine had dismissed him in her own inimitable style. The story was over in maybe seconds.

The story about Crystal was a different matter, however. As expected, Jason did not think it had anything to do with her threatening to slap Ian, nor did Ian.

The next day Ian dropped Jarvis and Steele off at Jason and Jazz'. He didn't say much, but that was not necessarily out of the ordinary. When he and Crystal arrived at the party later that evening, everyone else was already there and, hand about her waist, Ian led Crystal over to Jazz and started a conversation, forcing Crystal to participate, then he walked away, pointedly leaving the two of them together. Jazz virtually dragged Crystal into one of the rooms and locked the door.

OK Crystal. Spill. It's Jared, isn't it? I saw the look on your face when I said he was moving home. I'm sure Ian saw it too. You can't be for real! Are you one of those women who get addicted to abuse? The words kept spilling from Jazz' mouth and she wasn't waiting for answers. *You can't hurt Ian. You can't hurt darling Ian. He's lovely. What's the matter with you? I will not let you hurt Ian. Ian is forty times the man Jared is. 'My God!'* She paused finally, and her tone changed. *We were wrong all along weren't we? Jared's hitting you had nothing to do with how you looked, or dancing with Ian! Jared was already mad at you when he came. You let us believe that but it wasn't true. You just wanted Ian for the night, but Jared locked you out, and Ian gave so much! Why did you let it get as far as marriage? I'm sure Ian has figured all this out, but how do I fit in? Why are you mad at me? Anyway, Ian is lovely, please don't hurt him. I'm not just concerned for him, but for you too. You really need to get to know your husband. Ian seems quiet because he doesn't chat a lot but he hates to lose and he can be ornery and downright intolerant.*

Crystal sighed. *You are right about everything as usual, and I won't hurt Ian.*

You do remember I told you Ian has a high speed brain. If I'm working this out now, go figure. I guess you know that he knows. He probably found more bruises all over you, because I don't believe that was the first time Jared hit you. In the face, maybe, but abusers don't usually start that big. Poor Ian must have been so sorry for you, he wanted to protect you and take care of you, and compensate for all your misery, and you wanted to go back for more all along. You had better go see Dr. Koolman. This is intensely abnormal.

Jazz' dazzling party lost some of its dazzle for her. Thank God Jared was leaving. He had messed up his own credibility and jeopardized his position on the force with his handling of his domestic affairs. Even on a ragtag police force, certain standards are expected to be maintained by senior officers. She hoped Jared wouldn't change his mind, and he would leave soon. She didn't know if she should share her fears with Jason. It would break his heart. It was likely their hearts were all about to be broken soon. Jazz loved everything about this family. She loved the way they moved in tandem, the way they loved and supported each other and still let each other do their own thing, and came together as one in a crisis. She hoped a crisis could be averted now. She went back to her guests, searching specifically for Elle. If Elle loved and wanted Gareth as his lovable, unperturbed self, she had to help Ian.

On the way to look for Elle, she was stopped by Vanessa Cannonier, Jason's friend Cal's wife. She wanted Jazz and Jason together so Cal could do a tribute. Jazz was flattered. She liked Van and wished she had become close to her. She had avoided her after inadvertently walking in on a fight between her and Cal at their home. It was loud and ugly, and she was sure they would be divorced by morning. That was probably between three and four years before, and they still seemed fine. She guessed everybody fought differently. She and Jason never swore at each other or called each other names. She promised herself she would get over it and work on being more friendly towards Van.

When she and Jason were together, Cal sang a beautiful song she had never heard before for them, and then he played You're My Lady and Jazz danced with her husband. Afterwards, she missed Elle as she and Gareth were dancing, so she had to wait to talk to her. In the meantime, the kids were looking on and Jazz asked if they wanted to join the dancing. Only Jafari wanted to dance, but he wanted to do a clown dance. She got Cal to play some string band music and she danced a clown dance with her son. For goodness sake! The boy was good! Everybody stopped to watch and Jafari, realizing he was the centre of attention, turned it up a notch and did his thing. Somebody called out to Pim that this was truly his grandson and Pim quipped that he was a chip of the old, old block. He ended up joining the dance and Ebonique, not one to miss out on attention getting opportunities, joined them.

Gareth and Elle slipped out while Jazz was caught up with dancing with her son.

The party was a success despite Jazz' preoccupation. When the guests were all gone, Jason hugged her and asked if she and Crystal had settled their differences. She told him that she still hadn't worked out why Crystal was so upset with her; she had a suspicion something was going on in Crystal's life but couldn't see what it had to do with her. He assured her that Ian was a very capable man - she knew that – and he was sure he had it in hand and would handle the matter appropriately. Jazz was sure he knew more than he was telling. No-one, not even their parents, was ever able to penetrate the closeness of those three. When she tried to get around him, Jason told her to stop worrying. Ian had got Crystal a quick divorce once. If necessary, he could do it again. Jazz shivered. She asked him if she and he were solid. *Of course, baby. You're my life.* She must be oversensitive. It didn't sound right. She had better tell him she had ended the feud with Jordan.

Jason seemed satisfied when she told him of the end of the Jordan feud. He asked when the event happened and why she had told Gareth instead of him. She reminded him that Gareth was their company lawyer and that she needed to consult him to be sure that it could be done without implications to the company. She had thought she would let the party go by first and then tell him. He accepted the explanation. The matter was closed.

The months passed, and it was confirmed that Jazz was indeed pregnant. Her relationship with Crystal was not repaired and Jazz missed her intensely. There was no obvious deterioration in the relationship between Ian and Crystal, but Ian did not tease Jazz much anymore and they did not spend as much time at Mont Yves as before.

Gareth and Elle got married in November. It was a beautiful affair, not too large and very tasteful. Ed was not invited but sat at the back of the church, and came to the reception after all the formalities and the dinner were over. Jazz found him on the patio outside the kitchen crying like a baby, and sat and chatted with him to cheer him up. She had no significant part in the wedding so she had the time. Poor Ed was a broken and most rueful man. She prayed such a fate would never befall Jason. So far, her darling man had conducted himself admirably. They had been married for six years and she was as much in love with him as she was on their wedding day. She recommended that Ed write a letter to Elle, telling her all he felt inside and asking again for her to forgive him, and to be a nice as he could be to Frances so they could see he meant it, and to give up philandering completely. Then she got Frances to come and socialize with him.

This Christmas at Mont Yves was different. Only Jason and his family came on Christmas Eve, and for most of Christmas day. Not a word was said about the difference. Jazz missed the usual banter and general gaiety, and she was sure that Pim and Pammy and Cat were disconsolate. Gareth and Ian had gone to the Vanderpools. Jazz did not voice her thoughts but she did wonder since, last year, when Crystal's face was still bruised, it wasn't necessary to go to her mother's. They all showed up in the early evening, and the atmosphere became more festive, but a little bit of Jazz' heart was broken as, she was sure, were those of her in-laws.

They braced themselves, or Jazz did, for a repeat on Old Year's Night, but everyone showed and the party was, as usual, fantastic. Jazz was so happy and relieved, after dinner she proposed a toast which turned into an impassioned speech about how wonderful their family was and how much she loved her Jase. She forgot it was a toast and left her seat to kiss her husband and ask him to dance with her. Jason got up with a big grin and a shrug and said *she loves me, what can I say? I'm her prince,* and Jafari piped up *and she's your queen. You told me so.* Everybody laughed and Jason and his wife danced.

On New Years' Day, all the men went to dance in the Clown troupe and they took the children along. Elle and Crystal left to go to town to watch the festivities, leaving Jazz and Pammy alone. They chatted and bonded all over again, and Jazz told Pammy how much she missed the relationship with Crystal and in fact Ian and Gareth, as her relationship with them had also changed. Pammy told her that changes can always be expected in life but even if circumstances caused them to redirect their focus, they were all aware of what she had done for Jason, and loved her for it.

Jazz was not aware that she had done anything for Jason and told Pammy so. Pammy told her that Jason had become difficult when she went away. It had come to a head when he got aggravated at her oft heard moan about living in a testosterone cloud. He had been obnoxious and she and he had fallen out and he moved into the sugar mill house. She was so irritated herself that she advertised it for rent and made him move out so the new renter, the American man who still rented it, could move in. When he left for university in Toronto, he was still cold and sullen. On his return, his attitude had improved but he was quiet and reserved and gave the impression of being lonely, even when he was engaged. Jazz had come home and restored him to the lovable son she had known and delighted in, and for that she would always be grateful.

Jazz went into labour on March 3rd. Nothing dramatic, no church or anywhere public. She was at home, and she woke Jason to take her to the hospital. Pim had been taking the children to Mont Yves each night, in case she went into labour in the night. As Jason drove erratically to the hospital, Jazz could not help thinking that in a different time, Ian or Gareth would have been driving and both would have been there in any case.

At 11:30 on March 4th she gave birth to young Ian Brett Coolidge, seven pounds six ounces, with a pair of lungs they were sure would qualify him for town crier. She was most delighted to see, when she was taken back to her room, Ian and Gareth were indeed there. She asked Ian's permission to give his name to her baby and he was so pleased, he could have walked on the ceiling. Jazz was so thrilled to experience the closeness to them she had missed, she almost cried.

Celine said she and Jaime would come down for the March break and see the new baby. Jazz was over the moon. Let those stuck up Vanderpools see if she missed them when she had her beautiful Mommy.

Now that Celine and Jaime were married, she seemed to have got over her hesitation to stay in her and Brett's marital home. They stayed there for the week, and appeared to be comfortable, although they spent a lot of time either at Jazz and Jason's or at Mont Yves. Celine was, as usual, spectacularly chic, and Jazz was as proud as punch to parade her and Jaime around. The only thing to distract her from her joy was the news Celine brought that Brian had been deceived by his new love and had lost the money he made from selling his share. He was asking to be allowed back into the business. Jazz said *'Hell, no! I know you love Brian, and I do too, but we can't touch him with a ten foot pole. Our business stays totally family. Sorry, but it would be a mistake even to employ him.'*

Ian fell in love with his little namesake, and began again to spend a lot of time at Jazz and Jason's, and Crystal slowly began to thaw and come around with him and the kids. Gareth, still a newlywed, considered he'd been there and done that with the beany babies.

Jason did not go off the track after the birth. Perhaps he was a little overzealous in his determination not to, for Jazz found herself pregnant again before her body had a chance to recover. Jason was ecstatic. Jazz was embarrassed. Baby Ian thrived.

Veronica came to stay for two weeks in September. Jazz was still lonely for a girlfriend and was again thrilled to stick it to the Vanderpools, as she secretly thought of it, when she showed off her elegant and beautiful cousin. Veronica loved Mont Yves and Pammy, and her partner, Nigel and Pim liked each other and he and Pim and Gareth had some obviously interesting and animated discourse.

Crystal must have been feeling a little overshadowed because at lunch on Sunday, she inquired about Bonni, and informed Veronica that Bonni had dated her husband, but had been in love with Jason. Jason almost swallowed his spoon. Ian said nothing. He just put his elbow on the table, his cheek on his hand, and stared at his wife like she was a foreign object he was seeing for the first time. Jazz said nothing. If Crystal wanted to make a fool of herself, that was her own business, but this was obviously news to Jason, and that made her happy and secure in her world. Gareth broke the awkward silence at the table with an anecdote that had everybody laughing again.

When the meal was over, Pim took Veronica and Nigel off to show them Stone Haven, where her father grew up. Ian went off to see his mother, and Gareth used the opportunity to deal with whatever was going on. He told Crystal to snap out of whatever it was that she was caught up in, that they didn't hurt each other in this family and certainly did not embarrass their guests. She had better apologize to both Jazz and Jason for her stupid and unnecessary remark, and to try never to embarrass his brother like that again. Jazz walked over to Crystal and hugged her *Don't you forget it Crystal. I'm here if you ever want to talk. If you don't want to talk to me, talk to Elle, to Pammy, to Ian, but you need to talk to somebody about whatever it is that is eating you up. You were never a malicious and detestable person before.*

She went over to Jason and hugged him, and Jason said *Honey, it's not true,* and she said *I know.* She left and went over to visit Auntie Cat.

Over at Cat's, she found Ian sitting in front of the television. She stood behind him and started rubbing his shoulders and she kissed his cheek. *'I'm sorry Ian.'* He didn't say anything. She continued rubbing his shoulders. His muscles were tense. *Love her through it, whatever it is, and it will, hopefully, pass. You're lovely, she isn't going to let herself lose you.*

Jazz

Hmm

I'm a man. I'm not lovely. Jason isn't lovely either, he just doesn't want to tell you. He looked up at her and laughed, and she laughed too.

Jase is awesome, and so are you.

Just then Crystal walked in. *You want to take your hands off my husband?*

Jazz stopped rubbing Ian's shoulders. She touched his cheek with the back of her pinkie and middle fingers and said *Don't you forget it* and walked out. She heard Ian say tersely, *Into the car. Let's go. Now, Crystal.*

She quickened her pace and went back up to the great house. At the end of the visit, Jarvis and Steel rode home with Gareth and Elle.

A few days later Ian cornered Jazz in her kitchen and said he owed her an apology. He told her he had told Crystal the story about Bonni and Jason. It had been entirely made up and he hadn't expected her to blurt it out, or ever mention it. She had been asking him questions about events previous to their relationship, which he hated, but under the circumstances, instead of shutting her up, as he normally would have, he gave her a story, and regretted it.

Life ran smoothly over the next few months. Ian visited frequently. Baby Ian, now dubbed Chip because of his resemblance to the old block, his grandfather Brett, and to distinguish him from his uncle, grew rapidly, as did Jazz. The twins were precocious, and Jazz was enjoying her life. Christmas at Mont Yves returned to normal except Ed and Frances joined them, Frances looking like she had a new lease on life and Ed was as attentive as a new lover.

On Old Years' everyone gathered at Mont Yves, as usual. Jazz had a cough she couldn't get rid of and was a bit tired, so she went to Jason's room to rest. She was eight months pregnant. She had hardly been down for most of the day but, considering her condition, the family had left her alone. Early in the evening, she came hurrying down the stairs, calling for Jason, missed the last two steps, and fell, and Jason came running, alarmed. She told him she was fine and that he was going to get his wish. He wasn't sure what she meant. *I'm in labour. You got to take me to the hospital.* Jason said it was probably a false alarm, but she was adamant. She was in labour, and it was time to go to the hospital. Pim drove them.

When they finally got to the main road, the traffic was extremely slow, almost at a standstill, and Jazz' pains were coming more and more frequently. She kept babbling to keep her mind off it – she asked Pim to tell Jason not to give her any more babies; she told him that her babies weren't stray babies, that she got pregnant when Jason told her to, and that he told her to get twins and she did, and he told her to get two babies in one year and it looks like she would; that Jason was trying to make up to Pim for his wife's unfortunate calamity. Then she told Pim to turn around at the next possible opportunity, because there was no way this baby was waiting for them to get to the hospital. She begged Jason to say nice things to her, while taking short breaths through her mouth.

Pim realized the next possibility of a turn off, given the blocked traffic, would be another twenty minutes or so. The road was narrow, atop a cliff, one lane in each direction. There was not enough room to make a u-turn. Mercifully, whatever was blocking the traffic, was blocking the oncoming lane too. He pulled out into oncoming lane and backed up at least a half mile to the last turn off, telling Jazz he would probably never be able to get his face all the way forward again, and it would be her fault. Jason called to alert Pammy of the situation and they drove back with Jazz babbling and blowing and Jason cooing all the way.

There is no possible way to drive fast to Mont Yves once you exit the main road, and the tortuous trip felt like it took the better part of a week. When they arrived, everybody was outside waiting for them. Pammy would have to do the delivery as they couldn't find anyone. The traffic had been stopped because there was a major accident and nothing was getting through, and everybody nearby had gone into town to celebrate. Pammy had seen animals give birth, but had never participated in a human birth. Gareth was going to talk her through it from what he was reading on the internet. Ian, Crystal and Elle wanted to know if they could witness it and Jazz said everybody could, that birthing mothers had no dignity. Pim opted to mind the children. Cat had a headache and had gone home earlier.

Jason's bed had been prepared, and everybody took their places. An old hand at this, Jason coached, Jazz pushed, and Pammy waited. It was harrowing, and Jazz tried not to scream. Downstairs, Pim was entertaining the children, but Ebonique, being the only girl, was becoming bored. She knew something major was happening to her mother upstairs and she wanted to help. Pim saw her sneak away but, in order to stop her he might lose the other children, so he let her go.

Upstairs in the bedroom, Jazz was pushing but having a tough time getting the baby out, and the pain was unbearable. Just as Ebonique got to the first landing of the stairs, a scream escaped Jazz, making Ebonique sprint the rest of the stairs and dash into the room. *'Mommy!'* In that instant, she saw he father holding her mother and talking into her ear, her auntie Crystal wiping her mother's forehead, her grandmother sitting at the edge of the bed looking between her mothers legs. He mother's face was contorted. When Ebonique's cry startled Jazz, she gave a mighty push, and Ebonique saw the baby emerge from her mother. She stood agape, taking it all in. The baby started to cry, and she saw her grandmother take a pair of scissors and cut the baby from her mother.

When Pammy said 'It's a Girl', it was five minutes to eleven p.m. Jason had got his wish: Two babies in one year, this one born early enough so there could be no question as to whether she was born in this year or the next.

She's my baby, said Ebonique, awed. Ian lost his balance. He sat on the floor. Gareth was sitting, but he dropped the laptop. Elle was calm. She'd seen it before. There was silence for a few seconds, except for the baby's cries. Pammy and Jason dealt with Jazz while Crystal cleaned up the baby and Elle revived Ian and Gareth. They would never acknowledge that they needed to be revived. Ebonique refused to leave. She was staying with *'my mommy and my baby'.* Using bathroom scales, they estimated the baby was about five and a half pounds. Pammy called the hospital and reported what had happened. After she answered a few questions, it was determined that there were no particular concerns so they said a doctor would come out the next day to check the mother and baby.

By the time Jazz was cleaned up and all the evidence removed, it was almost midnight, so the party was brought to her room, and she and the baby were toasted as the New Year was rung in. Ebonique was in bed with her mother. She informed the crowded room that this was her baby and her name was Leigh. Jason, always tired after Jazz gave birth, grinned. *Leigh it is. Ebonique's baby's name is Leigh.* He must have been the happiest man on earth. He had everything he wanted.

After they raised their glasses, Jazz said *Darling Jase, I'd give you thirty babies if there was an easier way to have them. Please. No more babies.*

Jason smiled. *No more.*

What else was there to do? Give her quadruplets? He phoned Celine's cell. It was turned off. He phoned Jaime's. *Happy New Year Jaime. You have a new granddaughter!*

Celine took the phone. *Jason, my dear, don't you think that is enough?*

It's enough for me. A beautiful wife, twins, plus two babies born in the same year, and the prettiest mother in law in the whole of North America. Woo hoo! Happy New Year! I gotta go kiss my wife, but Jazz missed it. She had fallen asleep.

Jazz was awakened on New Year's Day by Ebonique's voice. She was seated on the bed next to her mother and Jason was holding the baby. She would be christened Pamela Leigh. Ebonique was telling him she was ready. Jason had promised she could hold the baby, provided she was properly on the bed and very careful not to drop her. Ebonique was very determined. This was her baby. She had named her and claimed her. Jason let her hold Leigh for a little bit before Jazz fed her, and he offered to bring breakfast on a tray for Jazz. He was surprised when she said she could walk and wanted to come downstairs, but when it was time, he helped her down.

Everyone was surprised Jazz had come down but she said she couldn't resist the excitement. Jarvis, Steele and Jafari were already dressed in their costumes and practicing their dancing, the jingle bells of their costumes a nice background to the chatter and clinking of cutlery. Ebonique had decided she would be staying behind to look after her baby. They indulged the little girl but, over the years they would find that Ebonique never wavered in her maternal devotion to Leigh.

Jason was telling Gareth that he might need to be flying back and forth to St. Vincent because of a project he had designed for The Grenadines. Crystal heard him and, loud enough for everyone to hear, said she guessed that was why he had lumbered his wife with a houseful of children, so he could gad off and do whoever he wanted. Jazz was shocked. Jason was livid.

Jazz exclaimed: *I'm lumbered with a houseful of children. Poor darling Ian is lumbered with you!*

Darling Ian! Gareth is such a sweetheart! How many darling men you want? Darling Jase not enough for you?

Jazz' ready tears filled her eyes. She dashed her wrist across her eyes to wipe away the tears and said as coldly as she could muster. *Newsflash!! I belong to Jase,* and before Crystal could comment on the political correctness of her statement, she said *Of my own free will, I have given myself solely to him, heart, body and soul, and by the way, you forgot Pim, Jarvis and Steele.*

I let the people I love know that I love them, so sue me. Because I do, my darling daddy died knowing it. No matter how many times I tell him now, and I do, Daddy will never hear me, but it is the last thing I ever said to him. I will never stop letting the people I love know that I love them, so if it bothers you, Crystal, Bite Me! Nobody has ever lost self esteem because they were loved.

She got up and walked out. Pammy rose to help her up the stairs. Jason and Crystal were staring each other down. He asked what was the matter with her. He said Jazzie loved her and missed her, and they had been friends. He hoped she wasn't as vile to his brother as she was to his wife.

Not your brother! Your cousin. You have no brothers.

I do not need you to explain my family tree to me.

Jason walked away to go after his wife. Everything except the music had stopped during the short altercation. The children were no longer dancing. Ian was sitting calmly as though he had missed the entire thing. He said nothing. Gareth led Elle outside and Pim headed for his den, followed by the children. Ian rose and walked over to Cat's. Crystal was angry and left standing alone. It had taken her a minute or so to clear the room. She walked out to the patio. She was sorry, but all this closeness that was so attractive to Jazz got on her nerves.

In their room, Jason was trying to calm Jazz. He promised her that when he was away it would be only for work. He loved her and their houseful of children and would always think of them and come back to them as soon as he could. She had to accept that things were changing. Mont Yves was not the Shangri la to the others it was to her, because the wives had their own families nearby, while she related Mont Yves to her childhood visits and good times with her father. It was her personal experience they could not share.

Jason told her that she was right about love boosting self esteem. He said they were an ordinary family and had never seen themselves the way she saw them, but her expressions of admiration and love had made them feel good and likely made them try to be the way she saw them because it was a good way to be. As long as it meant so much to her, his family would always come frequently. The others had come often because they were single and had the time, and her joie de vivre was infectious had made it a delight. They all still loved her and each other, and she always had him. Crystal was dealing with her own demons, whatever they were, and she should step back and allow her to handle it her own way. He added that, if Celine was there, they would probably have gone to her for Christmas too, and Jazz told him that Celine would have fed them tiny portions of braised chicken and a salad with vinegar dressing, definitely no oil. They both laughed and their world reoriented itself.

In a little while Pim, Gareth, Ian and the boys were off to take part in the New Year's Day Carnival festivities. Elle was a little annoyed. She had intended to announce that she was pregnant at the party last night but Jazz had gone into labour so she had postponed it for today, but Crystal had started her room clearing battle just as she was preparing to make her big announcement. Now only Jason and his flaky wife and Pammy were here to tell. She'd had enough of this group thing for a while. They would have to find out individually. She and Crystal were about to leave. Crystal's behavior was actually inappropriate, in her opinion. Something was up with her and she would try to find out what on the way back.

Driving down the mountain road, Elle asked Crystal what the performance was about. Crystal told her sister that Jazz got on her nerves. Jared had never cared for her, and resented their relationship since Jazz' return, and they had fought a bit over it. Ever since their divorce became final she couldn't stop thinking of Jared, and she regretted how the divorce turned out for him. Elle stopped the vehicle. She could not believe what she was hearing. She adored Gareth. He was wonderful, and she was sure his brother was too, and she believed that somehow, if Crystal hurt Ian, she would feel the shockwaves in her own marriage.

Say that again! You have a prince and you want that fucking toad? She was livid! *Did I not tell you that Jared almost raped me? Count me out of your life if you ever go back with that animal.* She slapped her sister. *That's because you like being beaten up. Get the fuck out of my husband's car.* She opened the door, shoved Crystal out, and drove off. A few minutes later, one of the estate workers driving by gave Crystal a ride to the bus stop. He wondered why Ian's wife was walking, but said nothing.

Jazz did not go back to the office right away. With two babies, she was busy, plus, when Ebonique was home, she was always underfoot. It had not turned out that Leigh was an eight day wonder to her, as everyone had thought. She persisted in trying to be a surrogate mother to Leigh. She helped bathe her. She wanted to do it alone, but Jazz would not allow it, she fed her, she learned to change her. Leigh was her last concern before she left for school, and her first when she returned home. She wanted to carry her around, but Leigh was getting heavy and Ebonique was, after all, just six, so Jazz would only allow her to push the baby in her pram, providing she or Jason was present.

Jazz still missed Crystal, but had given up all hope of salvaging the relationship. Sometimes, she would reach for a bottle of wine and remember sitting in the kitchen drinking wine with Crystal, and realize that on her own, it was no fun. Jason would share a glass with her if he was available, but he couldn't share girlie talk, and she knew he didn't really like wine, he would prefer a Carib, so she tried to foster a relationship with Hillary, from her office. They communicated daily, with regard to business but sometimes, if there was something she could justify as urgent and needing her signature, she would get Hillary to take a taxi to her home. Once there, Jazz would find every possible reason to detain her, and as Hillary had always liked Jazz, she did not mind. Jazz found, however, that she couldn't bare her soul to Hillary as she had to Crystal. She found it easier to do so with Van Cannonier, but Van was often harried. She also had a baby as well as a toddler. Her parents minded the children while she worked, but she had to get the children to them. They lived a few miles away in one direction and she worked a few miles away in the opposite direction. Cal's work schedule did not permit him to help her with that particular task.

Ian came over often and was telling Chip one day that when he grew old enough, Ian would establish a pee wee football team and coach them. Jazz confirmed that he had her support in this as long as Ebonique and Leigh were allowed to join. She had already had this conversation with Jason. Ian's response was the same as Jason's or any other Kittitian man's would be. Football was for men. Jazz pointed out that she had been a member of a mixed league in Toronto. Jason walked in at that point and prompted Ian to ask how that had turned out. She admitted that she had not liked it and did not continue, but Ebonique might enjoy it. She wanted her children to know that discrimination is wrong, and aim towards making opportunities open to everyone.

Ian asked if the fact that she couldn't play in high heels and sunglasses had turned her off the game and she told him that he and Jason probably shared brain cells and it was his turn to use them today because Jason had said pretty much the same thing.

Jason had actually said that her mother was a girlie girl, she was a girlie girl and chances are her daughters would be girlie girls. Not to worry, he probably wouldn't have fallen for her if she was a tomboy. Stupid male chauvinist pigs! She conceded that now that Ebonique had a baby, she probably wouldn't be interested, anyway, but even is she wasn't, Leigh might be, and her children were never going to be shut out of anything. Ian had better not challenge her on this because, clever as he might be, men were not equipped for challenges with women and he would not win.

Jason smiled but was silent. He avoided arguments with her much because he always ended up feeling like a heel. He was convinced that women did not fight fair. When all the principles of logic would suggest he was winning an argument she would come up with something like

You're wrong but I forgive you, or *Jase, my heart belongs to you, break it if you feel like it.* What would be an appropriate response to this? Your heart doesn't matter here? Sure, bring it on over. Do you want it just broken or shattered? He suspected that had he been sappy enough to come up with that line had the tables been turned, she would have had a good response. Women were like that.

The busy child raising months flew by, and Jazz soon hired Venetta, a nanny, and went back to work. Ian continued to drop by to visit his namesake, now talking a bit, and Jazz resumed her habit of dropping in on Gareth in his office now and then. It was the best she could do to keep in contact with her family. She never asked about Crystal, and tried not to notice Venetta's come-on attitude whenever Ian was around.

It was raining one afternoon when Jazz drove in from work. Ian was sitting chatting with Chip, sitting on his lap. They chatted for a few minutes and Venetta, ready to leave, walked in and asked since it was raining, would Ian mind giving her a ride home, when he was leaving. A reasonable request, but Jazz was sure the woman had stuck out her ample chest and, even if she had been mistaken about that, the excessive smiling and eye fluttering was definitely not necessary. This woman was coming on to Ian big time. So long as she didn't try that crap with Jason, she thought. If Ian buried his face in those huge hooters, it would serve that stupid Crystal right.

Ian walked into Gareth's office and told him to start working on his divorce, to check his mail, he'd forwarded a file. Gareth did not comment, he just turned to his computer, and Ian walked away. He went about his business, outwardly as composed as ever, and no one, by looking at him, or at Gareth either, could guess at the enormous outrage they were experiencing.

Crystal had been communicating with Jared since their divorce and throughout her and Ian's marriage. He hadn't read it all, but even if they may not have qualified entirely as steamy love letters, the general trend of what he did read, was of deep affection and regret at losing him. A bitter Jared had forwarded them to Ian with a gloating note saying 'pretty outside isn't always pretty inside. How lovely is your flower now?'

That evening, Ian told Crystal he was divorcing her. He didn't mention the notes. Crystal, stunned at first, decided he was joking and began telling him what she wanted. *Don't make demands, Crystal. I've given you all I'm going to give.* He picked up his pillow, pulled off the covers, and went to sleep on the sofa.

Crystal was alarmed now. She had learned that he could give a cold and harsh tongue lashing, particularly when she upset his precious family, but he had never slept on the sofa. The next morning he was as sweet as pie with her sons, as he always was. He did not acknowledge her presence.

Jazz was surprised to see Crystal walk through the door of her office. Before she could say anything, Crystal demanded *OK. What did you tell him?*

You have to give me more than that to work with, Mrs. Hollis-not-Coolidge, Jazz responded. She really did not know what Crystal was talking about.

Crystal sat down. *Ian is divorcing me.*

Jazz did not know what to say. *Is that good or bad for you?*

Have you ever heard of a good divorce?

Yes. Yours and Jared's. Look. Ian is a decisive expediter. If he has told you this, you have no time. Start begging now. I know if Jason told me that, I'd be on my hands and knees begging and pleading, and to hell with dignity.

Crystal stood up, and Jazz walked her to the door. *I love you, you know Crystal. We could still make up.* Crystal said nothing and Jazz wished her good luck.

Ian picked Crystal's kids up from school. He was very fond of them. He took them to his office and showed them around. He drove them back, and made sure they knew the route and the address of his office. Then he told them that he and their mother were divorcing. She preferred to be with their father. (He refused to take the blame for this). The boys began to cry and told him how much they loved him, and he told them that if they ever needed him, they knew where to find him. He'd be home, at the office, or at Mont Yves. He made sure they had all the phone numbers. He promised them they would still have their weekly allowance, told them to be good boys and to take care of their mother, she would probably need them. Then they drove home.

Crystal did not get a chance to beg or plead, even if she wanted to. Ian told her when he got home that she should go to her parents'. She could leave the boys, if she wanted. He would take good care of them. He knew she couldn't go to her old house. She had just given tenants a two-year lease. Crystal said her boys would go where she did, and they moved out, over the tearful protests of Jarvis and Steele. Ian made her give up her keys and credit cards. Deja-vu? At least he hadn't just cancelled them without telling her, she had her own account, and she was not battered, bruised or in physical pain.

Jarvis and Steele kept in touch with Ian, with Jazz and Jason, and with Pim and Pammy. They memorized the phone numbers, and when they couldn't remember one, they'd ask the other. Crystal was never able to break those bonds. She must have assumed that when Ian divorced her she would go back to Jared. Unfortunately, Jared had sent her letters to Ian on the eve of his wedding, so he was no longer available, and Crystal found herself alone with two sons who preferred her ex-husband to her, an estranged sister – Elle had taken Ian's side – and no friends. She was living with her parents who loved her and tried to be polite, but she was obviously in the way.

She had been rescued from an abusive situation and been given an amazing second chance and, misjudging both Ian and Jared, had squandered it. She didn't think she could hold it together. She would ask Jared to take the kids. He wanted them enough to have tried to kidnap them. She didn't think he could refuse, but he did. His new wife was expecting a baby of her own, he had started over in his career, their sons had grown accustomed to the kind of life Ian could afford, which he could not, particularly at this time. She was screwed.

Jarvis and Steele kept turning up at Ian's office. He bought them cell phones so they could call him when they were sad or needed him, but they would have to top up the phones from their allowance. It broke his heart to see the boys so dejected, but, as Jazz sometimes said: it is what it is. One night, a couple of weeks after they had moved, when he returned home after liming at a bar, Jarvis and Steele were sitting on his front porch. They wanted to live with him. Ian told them that, according to the law, they couldn't without their mother's permission, or he could go to jail for kidnapping them. He took them home. The next night they returned with a document written in Jarvis' hand, saying it was okay for them to stay with their stepfather, and signed by Crystal. Crystal had written 'ex' in front of stepfather. He let them in and they never went home.

Crystal was desperate. She had lost her sons to a man they had known just two years. Her sister, Elle had been hard and cold and had told her she was Ed's true daughter, and that the 'disgusting piece of dog defecation' that she had given up a prince for had, as a wedding present to himself, sent a copy of every communication he had from her, pointing out that she was pretty outside but rotten inside although Ian thought he had a flower. She had screwed herself, and Elle was not about to let her mess up her marriage to the wonderful man she had. When Crystal pointed out that, but for her, she wouldn't even know Gareth, she had rebutted that she, at least, had the good sense to hold on to her prince. She had lost her sister to Ian too.

There was nobody left for her except maybe Jazz. She had appeared happy to see her when Crystal went to her office. Ian frequented Jazz home so she couldn't go there. She would go see her again at her office. She wasn't entirely hopeful because Jazz had never made any bones about it. She was a Coolidge. There would be no question of whose side she would be on in a scrap with the Coolidges. However, she might be willing to help her, not fight Ian, but reconcile. Jazz thought the world of Ian. She had begged her not to hurt him, and she hadn't intended to, but she had hurt him, deeply enough for him just to cut her off like gangrene.

She went to Jazz' office and Jazz welcomed her. She didn't know anything. Ian had not mentioned it but, in Jazz' opinion, if she hadn't started begging yet, she was well out of time. Jazz promised to approach Ian but, if he wanted her to back off, she would. It was more than Crystal could hope for. She promised to phone, and left.

Later, when Jason drove Jazz home from work, Ian was there playing with his namesake, Jafari hanging with Jarvis and Steele. After greeting him, Jazz told him that she'd had a visit from his wife. He didn't comment. She hadn't expected him to. She poured them some wine and went to sit with him. *She wants you back.* He looked at her but still didn't comment. *'What are her chances, Ian? She didn't tell me what happened.*

Ian stood up, took a sip of wine. *I don't want her back, Jazz. The papers should be ready shortly.*

Aww. I'm so sorry, and you are such a darling.

Not lovely? He smiled.

You're a lovely darling, and you're awesome. They raised their glasses. Look at this gorgeous man with the beautiful eyes. Poor Crystal. It could have been so good.

Crystal's heart was pounding and her hands were shaking when she phoned Jazz, and when Jazz told her that Ian had said no, she felt like she had been slapped harder than Jared had slapped her. She had been handed the good life on a plate and she had knocked it away. She had hurt Ian, and she had to admit, he was a prince. She had known he was from the beginning, but she didn't know how to treat princes. She was accustomed to frogs. She asked Jazz if she could come over sometimes, and Jazz said nobody had ever stopped her.

In the early evening of the next day, Crystal decided to walk to Jazz' house. She needed the walk to clear her head. When she arrived, Jazz had asked if terrible was the new look these days, and had made a pot of herbal tea. Three minutes later, she was sitting at the table in a corner made awkward by some boxes Jazz had piled there, with her hands covering her face, breathing in the aroma of the steam through her fingers, when Ian and Jason walked in. They must have been surprised to see her but she did not give them a chance to comment. She said *Ian, Jazz once told me that if Jason wanted to leave her she would go down on her hands and knees and beg him. I'm begging.*

Jazz stared aghast, as Crystal struggled with the chair. She was going to get on her knees!

Ian pulled Jazz' hair as he walked by her, and kept walking, straight through the kitchen and out the living room door. It was odd, as though he had neither seen nor heard Crystal. The silence which followed, apart from deafening, was entirely embarrassing. *Drink your tea, it could get cold.* It was the only thing Jazz could think of to say.

*Ian, please don't think I set that up. She appeared five minutes before you
did and I made her a cup of tea, she hadn't even started drinking it. What
she said, I told her ages ago.* Jazz had called Ian the moment Jason left
to drive Crystal home. She was babbling. Ian said it was fine. She felt
horrible. She loved Ian and hated to see him embarrassed or hurt, and
told him so. He told her he knew that, and it was fine. She was still on
edge after she hung up, and when Jason came back he found her pacing
like an agitated panther. She told him the same thing she had told Ian
and he said she was not to worry. Ian would do what's best. He wouldn't
dump Crystal on a whim and he knew that people have disagreements.
Hell, he'd seen the two of them have enough. Ian loved Crystal. If he
dumped her, the reason was serious and irreparable. Let her go down on
her knees if she wanted to, but let her do it at Ian's house. He wanted
them out of it.

Poor Crystal. She phoned Jazz the next day and Jazz said she couldn't
help her. Crystal knew she was first and foremost, a Coolidge. Crystal
hadn't liked being one of them. In Jazz opinion, of all the men in the
world, Ian least deserved to be hurt, and she had begged Crystal not
to hurt him. Crystal would have to find her own way to get him back,
and good luck.

*Dammit Crystal, you didn't just land on your feet, you cleaned up! Why
did you blow it? When I say I can't help you, I mean I don't know how. I
can read Jason and Gareth and people who talk. Ian is deep, intense, and
silent. The only people who have been close enough for long enough, are you
and his brothers and they are furious at you, so the only person who can
possibly help you now, is you. Good luck.*

Crystal was on her own.

Ian divorced Crystal. It was just a divorce. No settlement, no nothing. He just divorced her. There was only the pesky question of how to handle her children, who still lived with him. He loved them but he had no legal claim and he wanted to never see or speak to Crystal again. He didn't see how he could manage both. He had at the beginning of the dispute, instructed their receptionist to reroute any calls from her to Gareth, and threatened to fire anybody who let a call from her through to him. Gareth would have to handle this as well.

Gareth didn't have to handle it. He and Elle were christening their son, Andre, and at the party, a very attractive woman appeared to be intent on seducing Ian, and Ian was enjoying the attention when Crystal came over to say she wanted her children. He ignored her at first and she repeated the request, a bit louder. Ian told her to go look in all the children's faces and see if she recognized the ones she wanted, and went back to talking with the woman. Crystal was annoyed and started yelling. Jason materialized and, arm around her shoulder, told her she wasn't going to be doing that here, and started leading her away. Jarvis and Steele heard her and came to see what was going on. She told them they were coming home with her, and that if they ever went back to Ian's house again, she would see to it he was jailed for kidnapping. Jason escorted them to the car, telling the kids to remember to keep in touch, and Crystal drove off. The next day she sent her father to collect their things.

Not even Gareth ever knew if, or how deeply Ian was wounded by the experience, or if, or how much he missed Jarvis and Steele. He continued to talk to them on the phone. He continued to give them a weekly allowance. He continued to not see Crystal, or speak to her or hear anything she said, even if she was two feet away from him. Apart from that, he continued to be exactly as he always had been before, Lovely, Darling Ian.

Ian's ignoring Crystal appeared to have affected her more than anything else and she did everything she could to make him acknowledge her existence. Ian made no effort to change his habits, even slightly, and as Crystal's sister was still married to his brother, they found themselves at the same place or events from time to time. Ian never appeared to notice her presence or to know her and she, determined to make him acknowledge her, often created embarrassing scenes, sometimes telling anyone she could corner, that he was freak because it wasn't possible he could have loved and cherished her the way he had, and now not acknowledge her. She insisted he couldn't possibly love anyone else as much as he had loved her, but Ian never appeared visibly embarrassed or even aware of her tantrums.

Shedding friends and former admirers in every direction, Crystal decided to reestablish her friendship with Jazz. She knew Jazz was loyal, however, exactly because of the loyalty she counted on, the effort was unsuccessful. Jazz believed in Ian, and would not hear him maligned, so when Crystal, full of recriminations against Ian, expected sympathy, what she got was a flea in her ear. In Jazz opinion, she had cheated on Ian, and with somebody she, more than anyone else, knew to be miles below Ian in character, and when she could have tried to use what small window of opportunity she had to try to make it up to Ian, she had just let him go, hoping, Jazz was sure, to pick up again with Jared.

Jazz told her friend that she knew that there was an odd phenomenon where some women might become addicted to abuse, like she believed Crystal had, and that as his wife, Ian would have got help for her if she hadn't tried to have a relationship with the malicious pig of a Jared. Did she not remember how Jared tried to humiliate her and force her into destitution? And he had done it again. He got her to the point he was sure she wanted him back and when he was sure it was too late, he took Ian away from her too. What could any woman do to a man to deserve that? Ian had saved her and made her and her children comfortable, and made her his wife. In return he got that horrible man sneering at him.

Crystal felt it was unfair that Ian did not give her an opportunity to tell him her side. She did not accept she had cheated because she had no physical relations with Jared while with Ian, and Jazz said that was a mere technicality of distance, and wondered what her side could possibly be, other than she liked what Ian offered except he did not, and would never slap her around. She asked whether Crystal had asked Ian about his reason. That would be Jazz', or anybody else's, first question.

Crystal told Jazz that she didn't intend to have a physical relationship with Jared but that she had lived with him for several years and understood his weaknesses. She was just trying to console him because he had lost everything and, to Jared, things were important. They were what made people respect and look up to you, he believed, and having people respect and look up to him was the most important goal of his life.

That aside, Jazz told her, nobody had denied her right to a lawyer. They were necessary in a divorce, especially when you were divorcing a good lawyer. Ian and Gareth were extremely good lawyers and in the legal world, everyone was in awe of them, so just by ignoring that, she proved that she took Ian for granted and had no respect for him. Did she expect he would represent her against himself?

As much as she adored the ground Jason walked on, Jazz told her, if he was to decide to divorce her, first she would want to know why, then she would beg and plead and promise to do better, she would sleep on his doorstep and pester him incessantly, but while she was doing this, she would get four lawyers to counter Gareth and Ian. Crystal had made no effort to contest the divorce because she saw it as an opportunity to get back with the brute, but she was fretting only because the brute was now unavailable and she was stuck. Why else would she just accept Ian saying I'm divorcing you go away, and just walk away like she was in a trance? She, Jazz, was just so sorry Ian had been hurt.

Crystal became very upset. She felt betrayed as she had been first to support Jazz when she had come home distressed and screaming on the beach, and Jazz curtly thanked her for what she had done for her until Jason had taken over. She was, however, not going to join any campaign whatsoever against Ian. Ian was a darling, and the injured party in this particular case. She asked Crystal what exactly had gone wrong. Ian was a doll, was he impotent? And Crystal said *Don't be stupid, Jazz. Why would a young man like Ian be impotent?*

Why would a woman he loved and gave everything cheat on him with Doggie Doo? I'm just trying to figure out. Ian is lovely. He's handsome and masculine and cute and impish, if he wasn't too tall you'd want to tousle his hair. Why did you cheat?

Crystal asked sarcastically, how often Jazz felt she wanted to tousle Ian's hair and what else she wanted to do with him.

I told you before, I belong to Jase, Jazz answered. *Ja-a-ayson. The man you said looks like testosterone in overdrive? Well, he is, Crystal, don't mess with me. This is not the first time you have made that allusion. Make this the last, because if you ever drop stupid hints like that again, you goin' be falling in love wid me nex cause you are a masochist and when I done wid you, what Jared did to you would look like kidsplay. You can't tell me to take my hands off Ian no more. He ain't married to you, and I can tousle his hair any flipping time I want because he is part of my family and we sit down together. Kapiche?*

Crystal considered Jazz position traitorous and scratched her from her ever shortening list of friends. She could find no one who would support her claim that Ian had wronged her, and she could find nothing to do or say that would make Ian notice that she was around. It annoyed her so much that she started to shout at him whenever their paths crossed that she was not invisible and that she existed, and Ian never indicated he either saw or heard her. In exasperation, she scratched on his vehicle 'I am alive. I am not invisible. I exist.'

Ian took the vehicle to the body shop and had it dealt with and she did it again. While at the shop to get it dealt with a second time, a man admired the vehicle and asked if he would consider selling it. He did. There was no reason to report this to Crystal and, the next time she saw the vehicle, she started scratching it again. The new owner saw her, slammed her down on the hood, brought her arm up behind her back, and flagged a police car. She was charged but luckily, not detained, and after the court case, began to date the man. His name was Bingo Bluemartin, and he was an officer on the police force in Saba, in St Kitts on some sort of police exchange incentive. Jazz wondered if Crystal might have wanted to be close to Ian's car or was just turned on by the brute force used to stop her from vandalizing it.

Poor Jarvis and Steele. Jazz loved those kids but what could she do, their mother appeared to be on a downward spiral and it was unfortunately, her right to pull them with her. She loved Crystal and was sorry for her but had to accept that, at least for now, it was over, but she would be there for them if Crystal or her sons ever needed her.

She had done what she could, and everybody seemed to dismiss it as a crazy notion, but she thought that Jared had been abusing Crystal for a long time and she had become addicted to abuse. She had tried to talk to Frances and got nowhere. Frances said she was one to talk since she had introduced her to Don, with whom she had an affair. She seemed more concerned with her own situation than Crystal's, and Jazz had backed off. She had not intended Frances and Don to have an affair. She intended that Don would make Ed notice what he had, and he did, but in light of this news, that venture was not a resounding success either. Lesson learned. She should mind her own business in future.

She wondered if Celine would sit back and see her spiraling downward and do nothing. Jason had told her to leave it alone, and this time she would listen to him. He had made it clear that he was firmly in Ian's corner, and that he could forgive anything but infidelity. Crystal had destroyed her own marriage, and she wasn't going to pull theirs out of shape, but before she put it to rest, she had waylaid Jarvis and Steele coming from school, and reminded them that she was always there for them and they were to call her if they ever needed anything, even just to talk, and If their mother would allow it, they knew they were always welcome at her home.

Not long after talking to Jarvis and Steele, Jason came home and asked what the altercation between her and Ian was about. She told him that as he grew up with Ian that should sound to him like an oxymoron. Ian was the calmest person she ever met and he and altercation did not belong in the same sentence, so Jason needed to tell her more of what he was talking about. Jason said he had run into Crystal, and somewhere in her tiresome rant she had suggested there was something big, and told him to ask Jazz about the altercation between herself and Jazz and Ian. Jazz could only think of, and reminded Jason of the time Crystal embarrassed them all, including her cousin Veronica. Ian had walked over to his mother's and she had gone there, interestingly to plead Crystal's case. She was rubbing Ian's shoulders when Crystal walked in and ordered her to take her hands off her husband, but there was no altercation, she had stopped immediately, and left. Every moment of the entire encounter had been witnessed by Auntie Cat.

She told him that she sometimes dropped in on Gareth in his office for five or ten minutes chat, and said if he preferred she kept her distance from them she would have to. Jason told her he was not worried about her and Ian or anybody in his family. He might not like it much if she was to get too close to a stranger, but he was not particularly concerned. He just wondered what Crystal was talking about since she and Ian had never appeared to have a falling out. He suggested that maybe she might want to take Crystal out for dinner or something and have a good chat with her, before she went beyond help.

Crystal had been her lifelong friend and it pained Jazz see her so lost and confused. She was glad Jason wanted her to help her because she knew he was really annoyed at the situation between her and Ian. A plan had been forming in her mind ever since she had spoken to Jarvis and Steele, but probably for the first time in her life she would not make a move on it without Jason's direct approval. She would also want Ian's input. She wanted to help her friend without the risk of messing up her own life.

The Brett LaPierre Academy needed a live-in administrator. At the moment, the teachers, dedicated persons who wanted to see the academy succeed, were taking turns staying over, but that was a temporary measure. She had her arguments all lined up for Jason.

If Crystal could take the job, she'd move into the academy and Jarvis and Steele could move in with her and Jason's family. Crystal might get settled, the children would feel comfortable and secure, Ed and Frances would have their home to themselves again, and most importantly, Jason might stop looking at her in that baby mamma way. She didn't want to have any more babies and Jarvis and Steele would take up the vacant room. The boys would get to see Ian, whom they still loved, and they could visit their mother, and possibly attend there themselves, and if she agreed, visit Ian at his home. There would be no need for Crystal and Ian to meet, and life could go on much as it always had, and Crystal could get a chance to find her feet. All that was required was to get Jason and Ian in a receptive mood.

It was surprisingly easy to sell the plan to Jason and he told her to let him tell Ian about it.

Ian came over with Jason, and she told him she didn't want to lose him from her life and that she missed Gareth coming in and out, and wouldn't be able to stand it if Ian dropped them too. He assured her that he had no intention of allowing his relationship with them to change, regardless of who her friends were. Jazz kissed him and as she was about to speak he said *yeah, yeah, I'm lovely.* They all laughed.

He asked what brought her to a domestic violence seminar that gave her this theory Jason had mentioned. She told him the situation used to exist where abused women kept dropping charges against their abusers, and of the legislation that took away the dubious privilege, and provided for abusers to be automatically charged. She had ended up in the first seminar because of a mix-up in dates. The intention was to attend a totally different seminar, but she'd become fascinated, and attended a couple more sessions. She told him of some of the abused women she met there, and that one woman in particular, acted much the same as Crystal had been acting.

Jazz called Crystal at work the next morning and asked her to lunch. Crystal was hesitant but Jazz insisted. She would pick up lunch on the way, if Crystal was worried about the time it would take and in the end she grudgingly agreed. They were eating lunch in the garden of her office building when Jazz put her proposal to Crystal. Crystal was overwhelmed! *Jazzie, you'd do that for me?* Her parents had been gently suggesting that she get a place of her own. Jazz gave her a rundown of what the job would entail and as much information as she could on the academy, and the Brett LaPierre Foundation she had formed, under which the school operated, and they arranged that she would come visit Jazz the next day, Saturday, to discuss it further if she was interested.

Jazz called Ian Saturday to tell him that she meant it when she said he wasn't to drop out of her life, but Crystal was coming over so she wanted to give him a heads up. Ian reminded her he had no intention of changing his habits.

Ian walked in while Crystal and Jazz were discussing the proposal in the kitchen. He said hello to Jazz. He did not speak to Crystal, but he nodded at her, and continued on to look for Jason. Jazz could not believe her eyes. Crystal seemed about to cry. She hugged Jazz. *'He saw me!'* she said in an awed whisper, *He saw me, and he nodded.*

Of course he had seen her, Jazz thought, but she did not say anything. Did Crystal think that Ian never saw her, just because he ignored her? He wasn't blind. He didn't even need glasses.

Crystal said she could do the job, and accepted the package as presented. She called Jarvis and Steele and told them that she was accepting a job that required she live somewhere else and they would live with Jazz and Jason. They looked so happy and relieved, it tore at Jazz' heart. What they must have been going through! Jason and Ian came into the kitchen and the boys, seeing Ian started to rush towards him and then halted uncertainly, just in case their mother might disapprove. She said it was okay and they hugged Ian, then Jarvis went over to Jason. *Uncle Jason, you know how at Mont Yves you sometimes ride a horse? Can you teach me to ride?*

Jason promised he'd borrow a pony from one of the other estates because Orion and Sheba were too big for a little boy. Ian did not speak to Crystal although she looked at him hopefully, but he didn't walk out of the room.

Jazz turned over and nuzzled Jason. It was early Sunday morning and she had just come awake. *God*! she murmured, *it wasn't a dream!* Jason asked what wasn't, and she said she was actually married to him and got to sleep in his bed with him every night. He laughed and hugged her back.

Jase. If I had an old boyfriend.

You did

If I kept in communication with an old boyfriend, would you just cut me out like that? She snapped her fingers.

No. I love you. I would hunt him down and dismember him. The most important member first. Did you keep in touch with your old boyfriend?

What old boyfriend? You know how some people are colour blind? I'm sex blind. I can't see male, unless it's family.

You mean you're not checking out the hot bods behind your dark glasses?

Don't need to, I come home everyday to a very hot bod. The hottest.

I check you out. I check out your hot bod. Nobody would guess you have four children.

Don't even go there, Jase. I can hear another baby in your voice. Four is enough. Besides, Mommy would definitely bop you on the head. Twin grandchildren she loved, it's cute and exotic, and she might be able to pass off Chip and Leigh as a second set of twins just for extra je ne sais quoi, but she sure wouldn't want to go boast that she has a whole lot more of them back at home. I bet the twins are still four to her. He laughed at that and told her that Celine believed he was trying to compensate to Pim for

Pammy's unfortunate catastrophe, and she informed him that was the general opinion of practically everybody who knew them.

Jazz joked that, although she went through all that trouble to have four children, she got nothing out of the deal. She had hoped that Jafari would be her little man but he had snubbed her for Pim, Ebonique was solely Jason's, if they hadn't called Ian Chip, they would soon have to call him Junior, because Ian had adopted him and Leigh belonged to Ebonique. She thinks she's her dolly. She, Jazz, has to ask permission to have a turn with her own baby. She wondered if there were any awards for giving birth to your own grandchild. Jason said he would help her out with another one just for her, but she had already warned him.

We should have a toast to our anniversary later. Eight years since I ran screaming down the beach. Tomorrow we drink to eight years since we first did the coochi-coochi. Good Lord in heaven you were smokin' when you walked through that door.

Can't say the same about you. You were a mess! You kept trying surreptitiously to pat your hair in place. What a waste of time honey, but I loved you with your puffy red eyes and face all messed up with tears and smudged makeup, and lipstick on your chin, for God's sake, and your hair like you had stuck your finger in an electrical socket. I saw your messy face and I thought: Hello, my babies' mamma has come home! Even a mess you were fine.

It was an exciting and scary and wonderful week. I'm so glad I came home when I did. I've enjoyed our life together so far. I love you Jason Coolidge. I hope I have made you happy because you have made me deliriously happy.

I'm the happiest man on Earth, and it's all due to you. I have no regrets. I keep counting my blessings. I have a beautiful wife who tells me I'm lovely and, thankfully, doesn't try dress me up in a tutu to prove it, I have great kids, the ones who can talk tell me I'm awesome, one pair of twins, two children born in the same year. How much more can a man ask for? I love you Jasmine Coolidge. Wanna get married?

It's about time you asked me. You just waltzed me off to the church without a by your leave. We're so happy Jase, thank God. I wish Crystal and Ian had made it. He would have been almost as nice as you.

No Jazzie. Don't bring them in here. This is our bed. In here it's just you and me baby. Just you and me. The door opened and Jafari and Chip came in. Jafari helped Chip up onto the bed and climbed in himself. They were followed shortly by Ebonique, helping Leigh, who had just learned to walk.

Hayzoos, Jase! She knows how to get her out of the crib! As Jason helped the baby up, Jazz said *So much for just you and me.*

Just you and me and our houseful of children, baby. Just us. Another beautiful Kodak moment.